I0682210

Passions Ignite

Passions Ignite

Clayton Corley
&
Lisa Sullivan

Copyright © 2017 Clayton Corley
Published by Clayton Corley

All rights reserved. No part of this publication may be reproduced, stored in a retrieval system or transmitted, in any form, or by any means, electronic, mechanical, recorded, photocopied, or otherwise, without the prior written permission of both the copyright owner and the above publisher of this book, except by a reviewer who may quote brief passages in a review.

The scanning, uploading, and distribution of this book via the Internet or via any other means without the permission of the publisher is illegal and punishable by law. Please purchase only authorized electronic editions and do not participate in or encourage electronic piracy of copyrightable materials. Your support of the author's rights is appreciated.

Designed by Vince Pannullo
Printed in the United States of America by RJ Communications.

ISBN: 978-0-578-19276-5

Chapter 1

I should have known it wasn't going to be anything good when I saw my parents' number on the caller ID. They never called me during the day for idle chitchat.

"Hello, Mommy. What's going on?" I said, answering the phone.

"I'm afraid I have some bad news for you, baby. Your Uncle Billy died an hour ago. He had a massive heart attack, and went very quickly," my mother said, crying. After a minute, my mother said, "Michelle, are you there?" because all she heard was dead air.

Crying softly, I said, "Yeah, I'm here. Mommy, please tell me you didn't just say Uncle Billy is dead? He can't be dead…he just can't be! I just spoke to him last night. Where's Daddy? Oh dear God not Uncle Billy" I cried loudly.

"Daddy is right here. I'll put him on the phone."

After speaking to my father, and making arrangement to fly to Atlanta from New York, I stared out my favorite window, and let the memories of my favorite uncle wash over me. It was almost like watching a movie.

The next day was almost a blur. I arrived on the first flight into Atlanta, and was met at baggage claim by my best friend, Jasmine. She explained that she had begged my parents to let her come, as they had barely gotten any rest.

My parents' house was a buzz of activity over the next few days…with people in and out. Uncle Billy had been a member of the Mason's fraternal organization for thirty years. They came out to talk to the family, to see if we wanted to have a Masonic ceremony, before the official home going service. Since we knew how dedicated he was to the organization, we agreed.

As part of the Masonic service, we had his Masonic apron draped around his waist, which was customary. The brothers showed up in large numbers. All of them were dressed in black suits, white gloves, and the same type of apron we had draped around my uncle's waist. My uncle's lodge brothers were very helpful to the family. They even prepared the food for the repast. My dad told me a Masonic funeral service was a sight to behold, but this one was extraordinary, and made us all very proud.

The main speaker of the service, wearing a black top hat, read St. John 14,

1-3: *Let not your heart be troubled; ye believe in God, believe also in me. In my Father's house are many mansions; if it were not so, I would have told you. I go to prepare a place for you. And if I go to prepare a place for you, I will come again, and receive you unto myself; that where I am, there ye may be also.*

That Bible verse always brought tears to my eyes. But the delivery of the verse by him, made me feel good inside. The Masonic service ended beautifully with all of the brothers, and the rest of the congregation singing, *Walk In The Light*.

As I sat listening to people share their favorite memories of my uncle, I could tell he was well loved. His staff talked about how he treated them like family. His secretary, Yvonne, spoke of how he always brought gifts for her children, and attended their graduations. That was so like Uncle Billy. It made me remember all the time I spent with him. He always treated me more like a daughter than a niece, as he had no children of his own.

When I finally got up to speak, I noticed that every pew was filled to over-flowing…in spite of the fact our family church was very large. I didn't ever remember it being this full, except on Easter Sunday and Mother's Day.

I walked up to Uncle Billy's coffin, said a silent prayer for strength, then leaned over and kissed him gently before walking to the podium. I glanced out and saw so many tear-filled eyes upon me. I took a deep breath and began.

"Thank you for coming out to Uncle Billy's farewell party." Everyone laughed. "Those of you who knew him, know he would've said…miss me if you must, but keep the party going. All my life I've admired Uncle Billy's ability to make everyone feel welcome. His love for jazz, books and people is well known, as he always surrounded himself with all three. That's one of the reasons he started a publishing business. He wanted to be the one to provide the personal touch to all of his writers…as he called them…and the first to read their books.

"As far back as I can remember, he shared his love of reading with me, and I've never been without a book in my hand. People would often ask me -- Michelle, what are you reading, or who is your favorite author? I would tell them I'm reading an author that Uncle Billy discovered, and that I don't have any favorites, because there are just too many to choose from. Thank you, Uncle Billy, for sharing your world with me…with all of us. I will remember you each time I pick up a new book, and wonder if you'd love it as much as I do. Uncle Billy, may you rest in peace, surrounded by good music, books and the rain."

Everyone laughed at his or her own memory of Uncle Billy's love for the rain.

As I took my seat, Mommy reached over, hugged me and said, "You did fine, Michelle."

Someone else stepped forward and started playing the saxophone. As the haunting notes flowed through the church, I began to cry. The reality of what was happening set in, and I realized that my uncle was no longer here with us.

Daddy switched places with Mommy, pulled me into his arms, and whispered into my hair, "Michelle its okay. Billy hasn't left us, he's in our hearts, our thoughts, and if you listen closely to the wind, you'll hear him laughing."

Daddy then got up and spoke on how great a brother Uncle Billy was to him. He told a couple of stories of them growing up together. I was never more proud of my father as I was at that moment. I knew his heart must have been breaking at the thought of burying his only brother.

At the conclusion of the service, we stepped outside, and saw the most beautiful sight possible…my uncle's entire motorcycle club. The Black Angels, as far as I could see, were lined up in front of and beside the hearse. Uncle Billy's childhood friend, Maceo, was in the lead on a white Harley, which they only brought out on special occasions. As Uncle Billy's coffin was loaded into the hearse, they all fired up their engines, and soon a cloud of white smoke was shooting up into the air. What a beautiful tribute!

The ride to the cemetery for the interment, which wasn't far from the church, was brief. I was very proud of how daddy was holding up, even though he almost lost control when they lowered Uncle Billy's coffin into the grave.

The repast was held back at the church, and it was more like a celebration of sorts. Everyone told their own personal story of how Uncle Billy had influenced or touched their lives in some way. I even got a chance to meet some of the writers my uncle had published. One person that I remembered in particular introduced himself as Michael Ramsey. He was about 6'2, with dark chocolate smooth skin like a Hershey's kiss, a baldhead, a neatly trimmed mustache and goatee, beautiful slanted brown eyes, and long fingers. He offered his condolences rather teary eyed.

"Hello, Michelle. I'm Michael Ramsey, one of your uncle's writers. You did a wonderful job when you spoke about him at the church. I'm sure your uncle would've been very proud of you."

"Thank you, Mr. Ramsey. I appreciate you telling me that," I said with a smile, as he handed me a card and left.

* * *

The following week, the family met with Uncle Billy's lawyers to discuss his estate, and to complete the reading of the will.

I couldn't believe that Uncle Billy had decided to leave me his publishing company, Rivers, Inc., and his house. I know we had talked about it before, and he always said I had a good eye for publishing, but I didn't think he would trust me with his company.

Looking up towards the heavens, I said to myself, "Thank you, Uncle Billy. I will make you proud of me."

"Michelle, it looks like you'll be moving back to Atlanta now. Would you like me to come up to New York and help you move your stuff down here? What do you plan to do about your condo -- sell it or rent it out?" my father said all in one breath, happy to know that his baby girl would be moving back to Atlanta.

"Whoa, Daddy, everything is moving much too fast. Let me think about it for a while. Maybe I'll look into sub-leasing my condo, and decide whether to sell it later. I have a couple of articles I need to complete for Ambience Magazine. But as you know, as long as I have my laptop, I can write anywhere," I said. "Right now, the first thing we need to do is set up a meeting with the employees of Rivers, Inc., to reassure them we're still open for business," I said.

"I'll call Billy's secretary, Yvonne, and have her set up a meeting with the staff for later in the week," my father said.

"Thank you, Daddy."

* * *

The afternoon of the meeting, my father and I arrived at Rivers, Inc., to go through the mail and meet with Yvonne.

"Yvonne, I want to thank you for all you've done. We couldn't have gotten through any of this without you. I appreciate you notifying the writers and associates of his death. I'd like for you to set up meetings with the Editor-in-Chief and the editors separately over the next few days, so I can be brought up to speed. I need to keep things flowing, the same as Uncle Billy would have, and your help would be greatly appreciated. And I'd love it if you would stay on as my secretary," I said.

"I'd be honored to work for you, Ms. Rivers. I'll get to work on that schedule right away. The conference room is already set up for you, and I've placed all open files on your desk. If there's anything else you need, please let me know," Yvonne said.

We were the first to arrive in the conference room. Yvonne had set up coffee and bottled water on the sideboard. Soon, everyone started arriving, and took their seats around the table. After everyone was seated, I opened up the meeting.

"Good afternoon, ladies and gentlemen. For those of you who may not know me, I'm Michelle Rivers, your new CEO. I'd like to thank you all for making it here on such short notice. I've called this meeting to inform everyone that Rivers, Inc. will still be in business, and that there will be no changes made at this time, except that I will be running the company," I said. "Does anyone have any questions for me?" I asked.

Everyone shook their heads, indicating no.

"Okay, then I want to thank you all again for coming to this meeting on such short notice," I said.

As everyone got up to leave, they extended their condolences once again to my father and me. It was evident they were still in shock over the loss of their fearless leader.

"How do you think the meeting went, Daddy?"

"I believe everything went well, considering," he said.

Dad and I returned to Uncle Billy's office, where we began to go over the papers and files that were left on his desk.

"Michelle, do you think you can get through the rest of this on your own?" my father asked. "I need to get to a meeting with the rest of the Board of Directors. I'll come pick you up after the meeting."

"I'll be fine, Daddy. And you don't have to come back, I can take a cab," I said, giving him a hug.

Once he left, I walked over to the window and started daydreaming back to all the times I had been in this office when Uncle Billy was alive. I had always admired how he made it look so comfortable and businesslike. I remember when he had those bookcases made with the special lighting, and requested they be encased in glass, to showcase his writers' books.

"Oh well, enough daydreaming," I said to myself. I buzzed Yvonne on the intercom. "Yvonne, could you please call downstairs and have someone from the mailroom bring me some boxes, so I can pack up Billy's personal belongings?"

"Yes, right away, Ms. Rivers. I also have the schedule ready for you to go over. I'll bring it right in," she said.

"Thank you," Five minutes later, Yvonne knocked on my office door. "Come in and have a seat, Yvonne," I said.

"I've set up your meetings with the editorial staff in half hour blocks, with fifteen minute breaks in between…starting at ten o'clock Monday morning. I scheduled John Masters first. He's the Executive Editor…the one who assigns the editors to the authors," she informed me.

"Thank you, Yvonne. I believe that will be fine. Do we have a catalog for office supplies? I'd like to order a couple of things."

"Yes, there should be one in your desk drawer on the right hand side."

"Yes, here it is," I said, as I pulled the catalog out of the drawer. "I believe we've covered everything we can for today."

"Ms. Rivers, if there is nothing else…good night and you try to have a good weekend," Yvonne said.

"Good night, Yvonne. Have a wonderful weekend. I'll see you on Monday," I said.

✳ ✳ ✳

The weekend went by quickly. On Saturday, I flew to New York to make arrangements for my condo, and to bring back as many of my belongings as I could carry. Then on Sunday, I went into the office to pack up some of my uncle's belongings.

My first order of business on Monday morning was meeting with the editorial staff individually, to examine what their goals were for Rivers, Inc., and to let them know what direction I wanted to go in.

When I arrived promptly at nine o'clock, Yvonne was headed my way.

"Good morning, Ms. Rivers," she said smiling. "Would you like a cup of coffee or tea?"

"Good morning, Yvonne. I'll have some tea, thank you. How was your weekend?" I asked.

"It was wonderful, thanks for asking. How was your weekend?"

"Mine was a little busy…trying to get myself together mentally for this new venture. I must admit I'm a little nervous right now," I said.

"Don't be nervous, Ms. Rivers, you'll be just fine. I'll be here for you. I worked with your uncle for fifteen years, so I know the ins and outs of the company, and I know the staff pretty well. I'll bring your tea in shortly. I also left the file of John Masters, the first staff member you're meeting with on your desk."

"I appreciate your efforts in making me feel comfortable," I said, somewhat relieved to know she had my back.

When I walked into my office, a bouquet of fresh flowers and a sign that said, *Welcome Ms. Rivers,* greeted me. That certainly was an icebreaker and very thoughtful. Yvonne came in and handed me a cup of tea. The cup was personalized with my first name, which really made me feel at home.

"Yvonne, this is beautiful! Who did all of this?" I asked.

"I did," Yvonne answered, with a smile. "The cream, lemon, sugar and Equal are on the table, Ms. Rivers."

"Thank you for everything. And please call me Michelle, Ms. Rivers is my mother." I said, with a warm smile on my face.

"Yes, Ms…I mean Michelle," she said.

We both laughed, and she walked back to her office. I still had ten minutes before my meeting with John Masters. From his file, I saw that he'd been with the company the longest, and was also a member of the motorcycle club my uncle had belonged to. He was in charge of matching editors with writers, and from a side note that Uncle Billy had written on his file, he has a love of mystery novels.

"Michelle, John Masters is here to see you," Yvonne said, through the intercom.

"Send him right in, Yvonne," I said. "Hello, Mr. Masters," I said, extending my hand when he walked into my office.

"Hello, Ms. Rivers. Thank you for meeting with me," he said smiling.

"First things first Mr. Masters, I want to keep this very informal, so please call me Michelle."

"Okay, Michelle, and likewise, call me John. Is it okay to drink this in here?" he asked, holding up a steaming cup of coffee.

John was in his early sixties, and a very handsome and distinguished looking gentleman. His salt and pepper hair and moustache, reminded me a little of my uncle. He had a little scar over his left eyebrow.

"That's no problem. I've heard that Yvonne's coffee is legendary. John, I remember seeing you briefly when I interned here one summer," I said.

"I think I remember that. You have a good memory, young lady," he said smiling.

"I'd just like to ask you how you feel about working for a woman, and what direction you'd like to see Rivers, Inc. go."

He had a huge smile on his face. He took a sip of his coffee, before offering his view. "First, I'd like to say that I'm going to miss Bill…he was like a brother to me. We used to do a lot together. I see you still have the picture of us heading out to Myrtle Beach for the bikers festival," he said, noticing the framed picture sitting on my desk.

"Yes, I love that picture. Is that you on the Harley next to him?"

"Yes it is. That's when my hair was all black," he said laughing. "Michelle, I'll have no problem at all working for you. You seem to be very businesslike, just as Bill was. I'll do what I can to assist you in keeping his legacy going, while establishing your own legacy. I'd like to see the number of editors on board, and the authors we publish, increase. The family atmosphere is one that I cherish, and I pray it continues. It helps to keep the staff energized, and also keeps the writers focused on handing in quality work, instead of rushed manuscripts."

"My goodness, John, you've summed it up pretty well, to say the least." We both laughed.

"Was I rambling?" he asked, with a huge grin on his face.

"Not at all, this is what I need to hear, especially from the Executive Editor. I know that I can learn a lot from you. Uncle Billy always told me you were one of his most trusted employees and closest friends, so I'll be depending on you for your help."

"I'm with you, Michelle. Whatever I can do, just let me know. One more thing that you can be proud of, is that your uncle is the reason we've had five authors, with a total of eight books, make the Times bestseller list. All eight are displayed in your bookcase."

"I remember my uncle telling me that. I'll eventually have to read them if I haven't done so already."

With that said, I stood, shook hands with him, and bid him a wonderful day. Yvonne came in and handed me the file of David Hale. He was the latest editor that came on board. He handled the authors specializing in children's literature.

"Would you like another cup of tea, Michelle?" she asked.

"Yes I would, and girl, you sure make a mean cup of tea!" I said, as we both smiled at one another.

When Yvonne left out, I took a few minutes to check off a few items I wanted her to order from the office furnishings catalog. I wasn't going to change much, as far as the office went; I just wanted to add a few of my own personal touches.

When Yvonne returned with my tea, I asked her to come to my office after lunch to take some dictation. I wanted to send a letter to all the authors that we've published, assuring them that Rivers, Inc. would continue to be committed to bringing their work to reality, while also sharing the closeness and family atmosphere my uncle was proud of.

"That's a wonderful idea, Michelle. How does one o'clock sound?" she asked.

"That's good timing," I said.

As Yvonne was leaving, David Hale was waiting outside. He seemed anxious to meet with me.

"Good morning, Mr. Hale. Come in and have a seat," I said.

"Good morning to you, Ms. Rivers," he said, with a boyish grin on his face. "I'm so glad to finally get a chance to meet you. I still can't believe Mr. Rivers passed away. I'm going to miss him so much. He gave me the chance to follow my dream," he said, as his eyes became watery. "He was like a father to me. When I graduated from Clark Atlanta University, with a degree in children's literature, I came here to look for a job. After talking with Mr. Rivers, he hired me right on the spot, and the rest is history," he said.

"Tell me what your goals are, and where you would like to see the company in the future?" I said.

"I plan on becoming an award winning author one day...that's my ultimate goal. Dad, I mean Mr. Rivers, always told me to strive to be the best. That's why I like working with the authors that send in children's literature. The children are our future, and I'm dedicated to making sure the books they read are tools to educate them. As far as Rivers, Inc. is concerned, I'd like to see it become the greatest publishing company in the business."

"That was very well said, David. I have no doubt you'll achieve everything that you set out to do. If there's anything I can do to help, let me know. Trust me, I've been there. Remember, my door is always open if you need to meet with me," I said.

"Thank you, Michelle. Have a wonderful day," he said, with his dimples showing, and extending his hand to shake mine.

I heard David's reference to my uncle as Dad. That certainly made things clear to me how close knit this company really was. I just hoped that I could keep the family atmosphere intact.

My next appointment was with Pamela Bryant. Uncle Billy had an asterisk by her name, which identified the editors that have worked with some of the company's best selling authors. She handled the romance novelists, and she had also written a book of poetry.

Fifteen minutes later, Yvonne's voice blazed through the intercom. "Michelle, Pamela Bryant is here to see you."

"Send her in, Yvonne." The door slowly opened, and a woman with a smile that spread across her face like the sun walked in.

"Good morning, Ms. Bryant. Come in and have a seat," I said.

"Good morning, Ms. Rivers," Pamela said, walking into my office.

"You can call me Michelle. There's no need to be all formal around here."

"And you can call me Pam," she said, as she sat down. She was a beautiful young lady. She had neatly trimmed dreads and hazel colored eyes.

"I just have a few things I'd like to go over with you, Pam. First, I'd like to know how you keep your hair so beautiful."

Pam's cheeks flushed a deeper shade, as I had totally caught her off guard with that question. I had thought about locking my own hair once or twice in the past.

"Thanks for the compliment, Michelle. It took a couple of months, patience and Parris, my hairstylist, to get it looking this way." We both started laughing.

"You'll have to give me Parris' number," I said.

"No problem."

"I see that you worked with Michael Ramsey on his novel, *Promise of Love*. How did you like working with him?"

A broad smile lit up her face like a spotlight. "He's a fantastic writer. Editing his work was extremely difficult, because he's sort of a perfectionist, and didn't want many changes made. But we ended up working well together on that endeavor," she said, pointing to his novel in the bookcase. "I'm waiting on him to send me his latest manuscript now."

"How do you feel about working for a woman, after having worked for my uncle?"

"I'm thrilled. As a matter of fact, Mr. Rivers spoke of you quite often. He told me that he had a niece I reminded him of, and that one day I'd get a chance to meet you. I didn't know it would be in this capacity, but I'm behind you all the way…in whatever direction you decide to take us. I plan on being a part of Rivers, Inc. for as long as you'll have me. If I may, I'd like to say I'm going to miss Mr. Rivers so much. When I heard that he had passed away, it was as if a piece of my soul had also passed away. He taught me so much about this business and people. He was like a father to me, especially since my own father passed away a few years ago. He helped me get through a very difficult time," she expressed, with her teary eyes fixed directly on mine.

"I understand, Pam. I'll miss him as well…you just can't imagine how much. If it helps any, I'll say this, my uncle and the lessons he taught all of us will continue to live through us. I made a promise to myself that I would keep his legacy alive, and by hook or crook, I plan on doing just that. I must admit it does my heart good to know that he touched so many lives here," I said sincerely. "One of these days we'll have to do lunch or dinner, so you can show me around Atlanta. A lot has changed since I moved away."

"It would be my pleasure to show you around. Michelle thanks for listening to my thoughts," Pam said, wiping away her tears.

"Thank you for sharing those thoughts with me, and we'll touch base real soon," I said, as we stood and hugged each other.

After meeting with the rest of the editors, I came away feeling a great sense of accomplishment. So far, everyone warmed at the idea of me taking over, and said they would be there to help me.

I glanced at the clock, and it was almost noon. I asked Yvonne what she was doing for lunch. She told me she was ordering a salad from a restaurant not too far from us. I asked her to order me a spinach salad with grilled chicken breast, Italian dressing, and a cranberry juice.

In the meantime, I began formulating in my mind the letter I was going to dictate to Yvonne. After lunch, she came into the office with pen and pad in hand, and sat across from me.

"Yvonne, with this letter, I want to let the authors know that we're still committed to quality service and a personal touch. It should read as follows:"

Dear Rivers, Inc. Family,

This letter is to inform, and to also assure you, that the recent changes in management will not interfere with the type of relationship this company has shared with you over the years. We are as committed as ever in assisting you in bringing your work to life. Our staff of editors will continue to work closely with you, and the company in general welcomes your business. If you need to contact or meet with me, my door is always open.

Thank you for your attention and assistance.

Sincerely,

Michelle Rivers

"Michelle, this letter is a nice touch. I believe everyone will appreciate the fact that you're keeping his or her interest and feelings a top priority. You remind me so much of your uncle. If the situation were reversed, he would've put it the same way," Yvonne said, sounding proud to be a part of it all.

"I sure hope so. I'd like to get this letter out as soon as possible," I said.

"Is there anything else before I get on this?" Yvonne asked.

"Well, I do have one question for you. Can we order lunch from that place again tomorrow?" We both fell out laughing.

Chapter 2

WHEN Yvonne returned to her desk, she buzzed, to let me know a package had arrived for me by courier. When she brought the package in, along with the letter to the authors for me to sign, I recognized the writing on the package as my father's.

"Oh great, Daddy must've sent me the financial papers I requested from the board meeting," I said to Yvonne. I signed the letter and handed it back to her.

"I'll get this letter out to the authors right away. Do you need anything else?" she asked.

"No, I can't think of anything right now."

After she left, I sat back to review the financial papers my father had sent over. The company was doing quite well, actually better than I could have imagined. He included a breakdown of everyone's salary, and the dates of payroll. *I need to set up an appointment with our financial officer and lawyer, to really get a feel for how that part of the business is handled*, I thought.

While looking through the papers on my desk, I noticed the announcement, showing that one of our children's books would be coming out in time for Halloween. I liked the title…*All Hallo's Eve*, by T. Carrion. The cover design was beautiful.

I grabbed an ice-cold bottle of water from the small fridge, and sat on the sofa to read Carrion's book. A few moments later, Yvonne buzzed me on the intercom.

"Yes, Yvonne?" I asked.

"David's on line one," she said.

"Thank you, Yvonne," I said. "Hello, David, how are you doing this afternoon?" I said, picking up the phone.

"Hi Michelle, I just wanted to know if you've had a chance to read T. Carrion's book?"

"As a matter of fact, I was getting ready to read it right now. It looks like a very good read, plus the illustrations are beautiful. The children will really love this book."

"I think this is one of her best books yet. This will be her fourth with our company," he explained.

"Wow, I'm impressed. I'll have to find time to read her other books. Why don't you come to my office and tell me about her?"

"Okay, I'll be right there," David, said.

About ten minutes later, Yvonne buzzed me and said, "Michelle, David Hale is here to see you."

"Thanks, send him right in." I was admiring the illustrations when he walked into my office. "David, come in and have a seat."

"Hi, Michelle," he said, sitting down on the sofa.

"Now, please tell me about your wonderful writer."

"She's fantastic! All she has ever wanted to do was write children's books. We're lucky she submitted her work with us first, 'because I'm sure some other publishing company would've picked her up right away. She requests that all her book signings be in the children's corner of bookstores, because they love her. Terry had a tough childhood, and she writes about the things she wished she had done while growing up. Her first book is about a father who spends time with his son, teaching him to play baseball, their special Saturdays at the park, how they eat lunch at the local pizza shop, and then play video games together afterwards," he explained.

"It sounds wonderful. I remember my special outings with my dad. It was one of the highlights of my childhood. I had all his attention for the day. I'm still a daddy's girl!" I offered. We both laughed at that. "Tell me about yourself, David," I said.

"I grew up here in Decatur, and I live in Stone Mountain. I've never wanted to live anywhere else. As you know, I attended Clark Atlanta University, and have always wanted to write my own children's books. I'm the youngest of three; I have two older sisters, and my mom. My dad died when I was little, so I never really knew him. Billy was the first father figure I've ever had. He was really great to me," David said.

"I can imagine. My uncle would've made a great father, but after my Aunt Linda died, he never remarried. I think she was the one true love of his life. Have you started writing anything yourself?" I questioned.

"I'm working on something now," David said grinning.

"Oh great, will you let me read it when you're finished?"

"Of course…I'd love for you to read my manuscript. Well, I've taken up enough of your time, Michelle," he said, rising from the sofa.

"It was my pleasure. I enjoyed talking with you, and remember my door is always open. Have a wonderful evening," I told him, as I shook his hand.

"You have a good evening, also."

"Thanks, and David, please ask Yvonne to come in on your way out."

"I will," he replied.

"Michelle, you wanted to see me?" Yvonne asked, walking into the office.

"Yes, come in and have a seat," I said smiling. "I wanted to thank you again for all your help. I couldn't have gotten through the day without you. Your presence makes everything go smoother," I told her.

"It was no problem. You would've done great, whether I was with you or not. I placed the order for the things you requested. They'll be delivered on Friday, and the letter to the authors went out by Federal Express. Do you need me to do anything else before we wrap things up for the day?" Yvonne asked.

"I need you to set up a meeting with the Board of Directors, our financial officer and lawyer for later this week."

"I'll take care of those appointments first thing tomorrow morning."

"Okay. Have a wonderful evening."

"You have a wonderful evening also. Good night," Yvonne said, before leaving my office.

While cleaning up my desk for the night, I glanced over at the bookcase, and noticed Michael Ramsey's book, *Promise to Love*. I decided to take it home with me to read.

"Good night, Ms. Rivers," Curtis, the security guard said, as I was leaving the building. He had been with the company for quite a few years.

"Good night, Curtis. Have a wonderful evening."

On the drive home, I couldn't help but notice the changes that were going on in Atlanta since I last lived there. Had it really been ten years since I moved to New York? *Time really does fly*, I thought to myself.

"I think I'll stop and get some Chinese take out. I hope the *Silver Dragon* is still on Riverdale Road," I said to myself.

The music in the *Silver Dragon* was truly authentic, and the decor put you in the mind of being in Mainland China. There was a nice crowd of people eating inside, and a few waiting for their takeout orders.

"Good evening, Lee. How's my favorite Chinese chef doing?" I asked. Mr. Yuen Lee had owned the *Silver Dragon* for as long as I could remember, and he never seemed to age.

"Michelle, is that you?" he asked, rather surprised. "Oh, my God, how long has it been since you've been in here? Are you visiting your parents?" he asked, as we hugged each other.

"No, I just moved back home," I told Mr. Lee.

"That's great news. Now we'll see much more of you. What would you like to order?"

"I'd love some of your wonton soup, shrimp lo mien, and I can't forget your sweet iced tea."

"Right away Michelle, It take ten minutes, okay, ten minutes. Please have a seat," Mr. Lee instructed.

"Thank you, Mr. Lee. It's so good seeing you again," I said.

"It's good seeing you too."

My order was ready in ten minutes, which was a good thing, because I was famished.

"You take care of yourself, Mr. Lee. And say hello to your wife," I said, as I walked out the restaurant.

"Bye, Michelle. I will tell her," he said, smiling and waving.

As I turned on to my uncle's street, I got a little sad, realizing that he wasn't going to be there to greet me. *It's still hard to believe this house belongs to me now*, I thought. I closed the garage door, and turned off the alarm after entering the house.

I removed my shoes, and placed my food on the counter. I listened to the messages on the answering machine, and heard one from my mother. "I'll return her call a little later, but first I want to take a nice hot bath and eat something," I said to myself. "I'll also want to start on Mr. Ramsey's book."

I turned on the surround sound stereo, and was greeted by the sweet sounds of Kim Waters playing the saxophone. His song, *Someone to Love Me*, reminded me of how nice it would be to have someone special in my life right about now.

After a much needed and relaxing bath, I made sure the door was locked and the alarm turned on. I grabbed my takeout and went upstairs to my bedroom. I curled up in the chaise lounge with my dinner and Mr. Ramsey's book. But before eating, I decided to return my mom's call before she started to get worried.

"Hi Mommy, I got your message. How are you doing?" I asked, once she picked up the phone.

"I'm doing good, baby. I was just worried about you. Are you settling in okay over there?" my mom asked.

"I'm doing okay. It takes a little getting used to, after living in the city for so long. It's very quiet here."

"Maybe you should've stayed here with Daddy and me," she said.

"No, Mommy! Two women living in the same house would never work." We both laughed, knowing I was right. "Give Daddy my love, and tell him I'll call him tomorrow from the office. I need to set up a meeting with him and the Board of Directors. Let's get together on Saturday and go shopping. I need some clothes badly, because most of my stuff is still in New York. I'm going to have to go back up there soon, make arrangements to send the rest of my things down here, and tie up some other loose ends," I said.

"That sounds like a good idea. Maybe we can go to Lenox Mall, and have lunch at *Copeland's* afterwards," my mom said.

"That sounds like a plan. Good night, Mommy. I love you," I said, before hanging up.

"Good night, baby. I love you too," my mom said.

After hanging up, I picked up my food and started eating. *Mr. Lee sure hasn't lost his touch…this food tastes as good as I remembered*, I thought. Soon I became engrossed in Michael Ramsey's book, which I soon discovered was rather erotic.

✳ ✳ ✳

I leaned forward, taking the face of the beauty before me into my warm hands and slowly, passionately kissed her. Gently, I took her by the hand, and lead her to the comfort of the thickly carpeted floor, which embraced us closely. It was there that I smothered her face and neck with kisses…nibbling here, sucking there, and licking my way to the precious breasts on her beautiful body. I rhythmically danced circles around the peaks of her nipples with my teasing tongue.

Slowly I lingered, taking one peak, and then the other, ever so gently between my teeth, before letting go to soothe them with wet kisses. Soon I made a path with my lips, as I took the journey to the center of her essence. My tongue led me to that magical treasure. It was her warm ecstasy, with their petals so soft and luscious that awaited me. I longed for the sweet nectar of her flower. Thirst filled my mouth, which was soon to be quenched. The movements of her hips tempted me to massage the erotic petals of desire.

I could hear her subtle whispers. This beauty before me moaned in sweet surrender. The sounds were like a sweet love song to my ears.

I whispered in her ear, "You want me to go on?"

I could feel the moisture slowly filling my wanting mouth, as her warm nectar began to flow freely. She began to rock to the passion slowly, deliberately. The insertion of my warm member brought slow, rhythmic withdrawals. Her gasps turned to moans. The scent of lust and sensuality filled our senses, and captured the moment, until the last gasp exploded with the thrust of our passion.

✳ ✳ ✳

"Wow, it's getting hot in here," I said to myself. "Oh my, I need to find a man soon…or I need to invest in a vibrator," I said, gently massaging my clit. "I can't believe how wet I am from simply reading his words. No wonder his book made it to the Times bestseller list." I noticed that he had a website. "I have to check out his website tomorrow, to see what the other readers have to say about the book," I said.

I dimmed the lights and drifted off into a deep sleep.

✳ ✳ ✳

It was a star filled fall night, and I was walking along the beach in Jamaica with him, hand in hand. You could hear the water lapping on the beach, and the music playing in the background.

He suddenly stops and twirls me around, kissing me with passionate, deep hungry kisses.

He draws me closer to him and whispers, "Make love to me right here, right now on the beach. It's secluded, and no one will see us. But if they do, so what let them watch!"

I say, "Okay, I've never had sex on the beach before."

He removes his shirt, and lays it out, so I can lie on it. He starts to undress me slowly, while trailing kisses down my body. He pays special attention to my beautiful breasts…kissing my stomach, and pulling my thong to the side, so he can taste my sweet honey pot.

"Hmmm, you're wearing a coconut scent today," he says to me.

With one of my legs positioned over his shoulder, he runs his tongue around my outer lips, and nibbles ever so gently on my pearl. He uses the tip of his tongue to explore me. He holds me up by my ample ass, pulling me closer to his tongue. He begins to tongue fuck me, just the way I like it. My first orgasm is intense. My well floods him with my juices so fast that it's dripping down his chin. He takes my trembling body into his arms, and kisses me deeply until the tremors pass. I sigh deeply, and then we switch positions.

I get on my knees and trace kisses down his chest, encircling his nipples with my tongue. I begin to gently suck on them, as I caress his manhood. I work my way downward, kissing his belly button, as I make my way towards my throbbing prize. I work my way to the base of his hardened dick, and then back up again, tracing the head of his dick with the tip of my tongue, tasting his pre-cum.

"Hmmm, he tastes so good," I say to myself, as I take him into my mouth slowly Just his head at first, while gently squeezing his balls, rolling them around with my fingertips… touching that space right above his asshole. I feel him jerk from my touch, as I apply more pressure to his head. I fully engulf him, and begin sucking him a little harder and deeper. His hands guide my head, pulling me closer. I take him out of my mouth, and lick up and down his shaft again. Finally, I deep throat his manhood again, until he explodes in ecstasy.

I swallow every drop of his warm nectar. Realizing that his manhood is still hard, I quickly straddle him and say, and "Don't you dare move."

Then I ride him with a gentle fury, until we explode together. I didn't notice, until now, that a couple had been watching us from the balcony of the hotel behind us.

✳ ✳ ✳

I suddenly woke up in a cold sweat. "Oh my, it was only a dream," I said, shaking my head. I glanced at the clock, and saw that it was four o'clock in the morning. *I have two more hours before I need to get up and start my day*, I thought. "Ramsey's book really has me hot and bothered. I can't remember the last time I've woke up this horny," I said smiling. *I'll never get back to sleep now*, I thought. I had to get up and change my sheets…they were soaking wet!

"I might as well get up and do some writing," I said to myself. I finished writing the two articles I had to submit to Ambience Magazine. Then I lay there reflecting on all that had happened over the past two weeks.

"Oh, Uncle Billy, how could you die and not say goodbye to me? I'm so mad at you right now!" I said out loud, as my eyes watered. "I know they said you went quickly and didn't suffer, but I wish you were still here with me," I cried. I threw back the covers, got down on her knees, and began to pray. "Thank you God for your many blessings. Thank you for allowing me to see another day. Amen."

* * *

Around six o'clock, I got up, took a shower, and got dressed. I stopped at Krispy Kreme to pick up some donuts, before going into the office. When I got to the office, I took care of a few things before the rest of the staff arrived.

When Yvonne arrived at work, she was surprised to see me already in the office.

"Good morning, Yvonne." I said to her, smiling.

"Good morning, Michelle. You're here early, aren't you?" she said.

"I decided to tie up some loose ends, and get an early start to the day. There are donuts for the staff in the lounge. But I didn't make any coffee, because I didn't want to poison anyone with the awful stuff I make," I said, walking towards Yvonne's desk. We both shared a laugh at that statement. "Last night I read Michael Ramsey's book, and it was hot. I'd like to read the manuscript for his next book. Could you check to see if it's come in yet?" I asked.

"I'll make the coffee. Would you like a cup, or would you prefer tea?" Yvonne asked. "I'll also see if Mr. Ramsey's manuscript has arrived."

"I'd love some coffee. Thank you, Yvonne."

When Yvonne came back with the cup of coffee, I said, "It smells wonderful, and tastes like heaven. We need to sell your coffee."

"Aw, thanks. Is there anything else I can get you?"

"No, thank you. I'll buzz you if I need anything else," I said.

"I'll get started on setting up your appointments with the Board of Directors, the financial officer, and the company lawyer," Yvonne said.

"Okay," I said.

After Yvonne left, I went over my articles for Ambience Magazine again, before submitting them. Once I was satisfied there were no mistakes, I hit sent them via e-mail. Then I called to let my editor know they were completed and sent.

"Good morning, Ambience Magazine. Tina speaking, how may I help you?"

"Good morning, Tina. This is Michelle Rivers calling for Veronica Winters."

"One moment Ms. Rivers, I'll see if she's available to take your call," Tina said, putting me on hold.

"Hello, Michelle. How are you doing?" Veronica asked, picking up the phone.

"I'm doing well, Veronica. I'm calling to let you know I've finished my last two articles, and submitted them to you via email. I'll send you a hard copy by Federal Express today."

"You're ahead of schedule as usual. Now, tell me how everything is going with you?" she asked. "I was sorry to hear of your uncle's death."

"Everything is busy right now. I inherited my uncle's publishing company, and I'm hitting the ground running…making sure everything runs smoothly."

"I can only imagine. We did an article on him and his company a few years ago. He had some of the top authors under his wing."

"Rivers, Inc. does have some of the best authors," I said laughing.

"I'll read your articles, and let you know if any changes are needed, which I'm sure there won't be, Ms Perfectionist. Will you be available to take on any new assignments?" Veronica asked.

"I'll have to think about that. I'd love to keep writing, but I don't know how much time I'll have right now."

"Alright Michelle, I'll talk to you again soon. Good luck with Rivers, Inc."

"Thank you, Veronica. Have a good day."

"I'll be in touch. Good-bye."

After concluding my conversation with Veronica, I glanced up and noticed Pam standing in the door with this angry look, which changed as soon as she noticed I had seen her.

"Good morning, Pam. Come in and have a seat. Is there something wrong?" I said.

"Good morning, Michelle. Yvonne wasn't at her desk, so I decided to come right in. I understand you wanted to see Michael Ramsey's latest manuscript. But I haven't finished editing it yet," Pam said.

"Is there only one copy of the manuscript?" I asked, puzzled by her reaction.

"There's only one working copy, but John and I have the original unedited copy on disk."

"Okay, then there shouldn't be a problem. Just bring me the disk, and you can continue working on your copy," I said to her.

"Michelle, can you tell me what your interest is in Michael's book?" Pam asked.

"I read *Promise to Love* last night, and I wanted to see his new manuscript… to get a feel for the direction he's going in." I was clearly puzzled by her reaction. "Is there any reason why I shouldn't be looking at this manuscript?" I asked.

"Oh no Michelle, I didn't mean to imply there was a reason why you shouldn't read it. I'm just not used to anyone looking over my shoulder when I'm doing my work," Pam replied.

"I'm not trying to micro manage you, that would be John's job. I only want to read the manuscript," I assured Pam.

"Okay. I'll bring the disk to you right away. I guess I'm just a little sensitive about people seeing my work before it's finished."

"Pam, let's get something straight right now. As publisher of this company, I will from time to time, want to read the writers' manuscripts…edited and unedited. I believe that's my right as the publisher," I responded, in a heated tone.

"I understand, Michelle. I apologize for my reaction. I'll be right back with the disk," Pam said.

As soon as Pam left my office, I sat back in my chair and took a deep breath. "I wonder what that was about." I said to myself, as I grabbed the phone and dialed John's number. "Good morning, John. How are you doing?" I said, when he answered his phone.

"Good morning, Michelle. I'm doing well. How are you settling in?" he asked.

"I think I'm getting the hang of things, but I was wondering if you could come see me this morning."

"No problem. I'll be there right after my meeting with the staff at nine-thirty, okay?" he said.

"That'll be fine. Thank you."

* * *

Yvonne buzzed me to let me know Pam was here to see me. I told her to send her in.

"Here's the disk you requested, Michelle. I'm really sorry about the way I reacted earlier," Pam said, entering my office.

"Thank you, Pam. I won't keep you. I know it's almost time for your staff meeting. I'll call if I have any questions. Enjoy the rest of your day," I said hastily.

"You have a good day also," Pam replied, as she walked out the door.

Yvonne buzzed the intercom. "Michelle, I've scheduled your meetings with the Board of Directors, lawyer and financial officer."

"That's great, Yvonne. Would you come in please?" I asked.

"I'll be right there." She walked into the office, and said, "I tried to get all the meetings set up for the same day, but unfortunately, wasn't able to work that out. Your first meeting is with the Board of Directors this evening at six at your father's office," she said. "Your meetings with the lawyer and financial officer are scheduled for tomorrow morning. Mr. Howard will be here at ten, and Ms. Williams will be here at one. Is that okay with you?" Yvonne asked.

"I don't see any problems with how you've set everything up. Thank you for getting it done so quickly," I said smiling.

Yvonne smiled back, feeling proud that I liked her work.

"I'm expecting John around ten. When he arrives, please send him right in," I said.

"Okay. Is there anything else I can do for you?" Yvonne asked.

"Yes, could you print out a copy of Mr. Ramsey's manuscript from this disk?"

"Sure. I'll have it for you shortly."

Promptly at ten o'clock, John came bouncing into my office, with his ever-present cup of coffee. "Hello, Michelle. Yvonne said it was okay to come right in," John said, walking into my office.

"Hello, John. Please have a seat. I asked you to come see me because I'm a little puzzled by a conversation I had with Pam this morning. I asked Yvonne to see if a copy of Michael Ramsey's latest manuscript had come in yet, and Pam seemed to be personally offended that I would want to review it. Is there something going on that I should be made aware of?" I asked him directly.

"I don't know what Pam's problem could be with you reading Mr. Ramsey's manuscript. Bill always read every manuscript that came through our doors, and I'd expect nothing less from you," he said, obviously perturbed. "I'll have a talk with her, and find out what's going on."

"It's really not that big a deal, but I did want to know if something else was going on that I should be aware of. As I told Pam earlier, I have no intention of micro managing the staff, but I also don't want there to be a problem every time I ask to see a writer's manuscript either," I explained.

"I assure you it won't happen again, Michelle. I'll make sure you have access to every manuscript that crosses our threshold. Let me go talk with Pam right now," he said, as he started to head for the door.

"Thank you, John. I'd appreciate that."

* * *

John walked back to his office, kind of puzzled over what kind of problem Pam could possibly have with Michelle. It hadn't even been a month since she took over, and there was a problem already. He dialed Pam's number.

"Pam, this is John. I need to see you in my office as soon as possible," he said, in a stern voice.

"Is there anything wrong, John?" she asked, fearing the worse.

"As soon as possible Pam" John hung up the phone, and within minutes, there was a knock on the door.

"It's open. Come on in and have a seat, Pam," he said, gesturing to a chair. "I spoke with Michelle this morning, and she told me you had some sort of issue with her reading a manuscript you're working on. What seems to be the problem?" he asked.

"Well, I thought it was kind of strange that she..." He interrupted her at that point.

"Bill did the same exact thing with all the manuscripts passing through these doors. Don't tell me you've forgotten the routine so quickly. Tell me what the real problem is," he said, making direct eye contact.

Pam became teary eyed, as she tried to explain. "John, why did he have to die, why? I miss Billy so much, I don't know if I can make it without him. He was like my father," she blurted out through her tears. John went to her side and consoled her.

"Pam, you know Bill would've wanted us to be strong at this moment. His legacy will continue on through his niece, who's now in charge. It's what Bill wanted, and it's how it shall be," John said, in a calming voice. "She has every right to see anything that comes through these doors. She's a wonderful person, just like her uncle, and we have to be here for her as well," he said. "She was very close to Bill, so try to imagine what she's going through. We need to bear with her, and help her as much as we possibly can."

"I know, but it's just so hard for me to realize that he's no longer here with us in the flesh," she said, gathering her emotions.

"Well, try not to let your emotions surface in that manner again, okay?" he said softly, while rubbing her hand, to reassure her that it was okay.

"Okay John and thank you for talking to me. I'll apologize to Michelle the first chance that I get," she sniffled.

"Pam, I think she understands, and all will be forgiven. She knows emotions are still on edge, with Bill's death fresh on everyone's minds. It will pass in time, but we must cling to each other for support," he said. "After all, we're a big family, and families go through things sometimes."

"Thanks again, John. You know all the right things to say," Pam said, as she smiled and wiped her eyes before leaving his office.

John decided to get a memo out to all the editors, reminding them of the policy on manuscripts. He walked to Gayle's office, to ask her to type the memo up.

"Gayle, I need you to send out a memo to the editorial staff," he said.

"Okay," she said.

"I want this memo to be brief and to the point," he said. He dictated the following memo to Gayle:

Staff,

We're all going through a difficult time of sorrow, with the passing of our fearless leader. We must continue to do everything in our power to keep Rivers, Inc. on the top of the publishing game.

In keeping with company policy, all manuscripts will be reviewed by both our publisher, Michelle Rivers and myself, whether they are edited or unedited.

Thank you,

John Master
Chief Editor

"That should do it, Gayle. Please make sure this goes out to all the editors by this afternoon," John said.

"I'll get on it right now," Gayle said.

"I'll be in my office if anyone needs me," he said.

Chapter 3

AFTER John left my office, I decided to call my best friend, Jasmine.
"Hello," Jasmine said, answering her phone.

"Hello, Jas. It's Michelle."

"It's about time you called me, heffa! How you doing, and what took your ass so long to call me?"

I'm sorry, girl. It's been mad busy since Uncle Billy's funeral. I want to thank you again for being there for me…for all of us. I, for one, couldn't have gotten through half of it without your support," I said.

"Michelle, we've been friends for over twenty years. We're like sisters, so you can keep that shit," she said.

"Alright, Jas, I'm sorry. You can stop cussing me out now," I said.

"Okay. Now, tell me how you're really doing, and don't tell me the same shit you tell everyone else."

"I'm okay, girl. I'm still not sleeping well. I can't believe that Uncle Billy is dead. I'm still a little angry, and I miss him more than I can say," I said sighing. "My life has been turned upside down. I know we had talked about me moving back to Atlanta before, but I didn't expect it to happen this soon."

"I know what you mean, but you have to remember the good times you shared with him, and take care of business," Jasmine said, in an upbeat manner. "So, what else have you been up to?"

"I read this book by Michael Ramsey called, *Promise to Love*, and girl, it was hot."

"I remember reading that book when it came out, and you're right, it was very hot indeed. Now, tell me, how are you settling into the house, and when are you going back to New York to get the rest of your things?" Jasmine asked. "You do remember I offered to go back with you to help pack?" she reminded me.

"I haven't really done anything with the house yet, I haven't really had time. I'm sleeping in the guest room I used when I stayed with Uncle Billy. I know eventually I'll have to start going through his things," I said. "To answer your other question, I was thinking of going to New York sometime next week. You know I'd enjoy having your company, Jas. I've decided to use a moving company for the bulk of my things, so we really won't have much packing to do."

"Okay, that sounds like a plan. Just let me know which day you want to leave, and I'll clear my calendar," Jasmine said. "What are you doing for clothes now?"

"I bought enough stuff to last me for two weeks. I told Mommy last night that I needed to go shopping before I run out of clothes," I said laughing.

"Let me guess, your mom wants to go to Lenox Mall," Jasmine said.

"You guessed it. Why don't you come with us? We can do people watching like we used to do."

"No, thank you! If you were going anywhere else but Lenox Mall, I'd be there. I always feel insecure when I go up in that place. Them 'Gay Men' look better than I do, and I don't feel like dressing up on the weekend to go shopping," she exclaimed.

"Okay. Then meet us for lunch at *Copeland's*, and we can go shoe shopping," I pleaded.

"You just said the magic word. Let's meet at two o'clock. That should give you enough time to complete your shopping, because we both know your mom will be picking you up by nine in the morning." We both groaned at the thought.

"Why did you have to remind me, Jas? There'll be no sleeping in for me. I need to get back to work. I'll call you on Friday to confirm, and thanks for making me laugh. I really needed that."

"I love you, Michelle. And you don't have to thank me…you're my sister! I'll talk to you later. Bye."

"Bye, Jas. I love you too," I told her.

I had to laugh at what Jasmine said about Lenox Mall, because it was too true. People dress up to go shopping there, and the 'Gay Brothers' did look better than we did. It seemed it was their spot for shopping, but I had to admit they did have some good stores.

While I was in my office, going through the mail, I came across a manuscript from an author named, C.E. Campbell. It seemed everyone was using initials, instead of their whole names lately. Putting aside the rest of the mail until later, I started browsing through the manuscript, and realized it was erotic novel. *Oh wow, uncle, we're truly moving in a different direction in publishing,* I thought, as I began to read the manuscript.

* * *

She parted her mouth even more, as Paul licked the lips of her pussy, and then nibbled gently on her clit. She shuddered and moaned even louder.

"Oh, Paul, yes baby, lick my pussy," she moaned.

He placed his hands under her firm ass, giving him even more access to her sweet vagina. He attacked her prize.

"You like that, Debbie?" Paul asked, in a muffled tone. "Move your ass, baby," he encouraged.

Suddenly she screamed out, "I'm cumming!" She panted and moaned and screamed again. "Paul oh shit hell yeah!" A gush of her juices came pouring out of her, as he continued to lick and suck…lapping it up like a puppy. "I want you inside of me, give it to me, baby," Debbie urged.

Slowly Paul moved up to her mouth, kissing her stomach and breasts along the way. With his soft lips, he forced his tongue into her hot mouth, as far as he could get it. Paul placed his throbbing manhood at the opening of Debbie's pussy, as she grabbed his ass, trying to push him inside of her. He held back a little and continued to kiss her wildly.

"Don't tease me, baby, give it to me. Please give it to me," Debbie pleaded.

Paul entered her slowly, just the head at first, and she moaned in pleasure. Then he pushed in, and backs out again.

Damn, she feels good, Paul thought to himself. He couldn't hold back any more…her pussy felt too good. He plunged deep inside Debbie with all that he had, and her fingernails dug into his ass, sending a sharp pain up Paul's back.

"Yes, give me this dick," she ordered, and he was more than willing.

Slowly, Paul plunged in and out, as they both picked up the pace. Debbie was meeting his every down stroke with an upward push. Her tight pussy and his throbbing member were making gushing sounds together, that seemed to radiate through the room.

"Do you like this dick?" Paul asked. "Do you?"

"Yes, oh fuck, yeah!" she squealed. "I love this dick. Don't stop, baby!" Debbie said.

Paul withdrew from her hot pussy, turned her over, and pulled her up on her knees. He entered her from the back, wasting no time at all. He was inside of her, while she was slamming her ass back towards him.

"Come and get this dick, Debbie. Bring that ass back here," he groaned. "Am I hitting this pussy right, am I?" Paul asked.

"You know it, baby! Give it to me!" she said loudly.

Paul was knee deep in Debbie's pussy, reaching under her from time to time, fingering her hardened clit, while he was stroking. Paul withdrew from her and lay down on his back.

"Ride this dick baby. Come on!" he commanded.

She straddled him, looking deep into his eyes with a sultry sexy look, and slowly eased down on his awaiting rod, still moist and glistening from the juices of her dripping valley.

"Oh yes, baby, fuck me," Paul moaned, as her pussy tightened around him.

Debbie placed her hands on his chest and rode him. She rode him like she was a jockey in the Kentucky Derby. Faster and faster, she wiggled and plunged herself down onto Paul's hard dick.

"Kiss me, baby, kiss me," Paul beckoned, as she leaned over and their lips met.

Not missing a beat, Debbie cried out, "I'm cumming again, baby!"

Her body shook, and her pussy tightened on his rod. This time Paul was joining her in the realm of no return.

"Ahhhhhh shit, Debbie!" Paul screamed out.

They exploded in one another, and she collapsed on his chest. Paul put his arms around her, and they kissed and grinded until they came to a complete stop. Sweat poured from their exhausted bodies.

"Damn, Paul," Debbie said, totally exhausted. They both began to laugh.

He was still throbbing inside of her. Juices from their session ran down his shaft and onto his thighs.

"Did you like what I had for you, baby?" Debbie asked, with a big smile on her lips.

Without a word, Paul pulled Debbie's face to his and kissed her softly. "Yes I did," he whispered, before drifting off to sleep.

Oh, my God! This is hot. If the rest of this book reads this good, I think we'll have another bestseller on our hands, I thought to myself.

I buzzed Yvonne on the intercom.

"Yes, Michelle, I was just about to ring you. I have Mr. Ramsey's manuscript back from printing," Yvonne said.

"Okay, bring it in. And I need to ask you about another writer," I said.

"I'll be right there," Yvonne replied.

While I was waiting on her, I picked up the manuscript and glanced through it again. I glanced up just as Yvonne knocked on the door.

"Come in," I said. "I was just reading this manuscript that came in the mail, and I wanted to know if the writer has submitted prior work to us. The author's name is C.E. Campbell."

"If I can look at your computer screen for a minute, I'll be able to tell you," she said.

"Of course I should've thought of that myself," I said, getting up to trade places with Yvonne.

"Let me show you this. You have the same program on your computer as I do. John also has the same program, plus a complete listing of writers who have previously submitted their work. You also have a listing of new writers who've submitted their work to us, and whether we have accepted or rejected their work. I don't see a C.E. Campbell, so he or she must be a new writer."

"Hmmm, this is quite interesting. I need to spend some time going through these computer programs. But in the meantime, I'd like for you to get this manuscript to John. I really liked what I've read so far, but don't tell anyone else. I want to see what the editor assigned to it thinks," I said, handing Yvonne the manuscript.

"I'll make sure he receives it. Is there anything else I can do for you before lunch? By the way, would you like me to order for you again today?"

"Could you order me that salad and cranberry juice again? I'm going to finish going through the mail on my desk, and then start reading Mr. Ramsey's manuscript."

"I'll go place this order now. I also ordered cranberry juice to be stocked in your refrigerator…it should arrive tomorrow."

"One more thing Yvonne, Hold all my calls, please," I said, as she left my office.

I realized every day was going to be a learning experience. I prayed I'd be able to live up to Uncle Billy's confidence in me, and that the staff would continue to be patient with me, as I went through the process of learning the publishing company from this end, instead of as a writer.

Suddenly, I looked at the clock. "I better call Daddy before he thinks I've forgotten about him," I said to myself. "Hello, Sherry. This is Michelle Rivers. Is my Dad available?"

"Hello, Ms. Rivers. Let me check and see," she said, putting me on hold.

"Hello, baby how's it going over there?" Daddy said when he got on the phone.

"Hi Daddy, everything seems to be going okay. I still have a lot to learn, but I'm glad I spent time working with Uncle Billy during my years in college. The internship I did gave me some insight into publishing, so I'm not totally lost. Did I catch you at a bad time?"

"No, you actually caught me at a good time. Your mother said you called last night, and that she tried to get you to come home."

"Now, Daddy, you know we don't need to be living in the same house," I said laughing.

"I know you're all grown up, but you know to us you'll always be our baby," he said.

"See, that's why y'all should've had more children." I laughed again, because I knew he was joking. "Daddy, is there anything I should be prepared for when I come to the meeting tonight?"

"No, this will be a get to know you meeting. What I suggest you do is go over Bill's vision plan for the company, and express that you plan to continue his legacy of making Rivers, Inc. the best family oriented publishing company in the southeast."

"That sounds easy enough. Now tell me, how you are doing? And don't say you're doing fine, because we both know that's not true," I said.

"I'm hanging in there, Michelle. I picked up the phone to call Bill last night during the basketball game, before realizing he wasn't going to be on the other end of the phone," my dad said.

"Daddy, I know how hard that must be. It still seems unreal that he's gone. I was wondering if you could come over to the house on Sunday to help me go through his things, or do you think it's too soon?"

"Baby, there will never be a good time for either of us to go through his things, but we have to do it sooner or later. I'll be there on Sunday, and you need to buy some beer, because we're watching the game."

"What kind of beer are you drinking these days?" I asked laughing.

"Excuse me, but who am I talking too? This can't be my daughter, because she would know I always drink Heineken."

"I was just kidding. I'll have your beer ready and waiting for you. I'll even fix you some wings!"

"That sounds good, baby. Could you make your lemon pepper and sesame wings?"

"I'll make any kind of wings you want," I said, smiling to myself. "Well, I better get back to work. I'll see you this evening."

"Do you need me to pick you up for the meeting?"

"No, I'm driving Uncle Billy's truck," I said.

"Okay, baby. I love you."

"I love you too, Daddy. Bye."

After hanging up, I decided to write up some notes for the meeting this evening. Afterwards, I mulled over the writers' roster. It was divided into several categories, which made it easier for me to read.

Yvonne buzzed me on the intercom.

"Yes, Yvonne?" I said.

"I have Mr. Ramsey on the line. He'd like to know if he can meet with you on Friday at eleven o'clock."

"Do I have anything scheduled for that day?" I asked.

"No," Yvonne said.

"Okay, then tell him I'll see him on Friday."

I picked up Mr. Ramsey's manuscript, and walked over to the sitting area in my office. I wanted to be familiar with it before I met with him on Friday. It had an interesting title, *Determined Love.*

* * *

I was determined. I sat on the edge of the bed, taking in all the pleasures that had just happened. Sweat streaming down our foreheads, and the crisp aroma, part incense mixed with hot sex, filled the air. I wasn't tired, and wanted more, much more. I truly adored her. My precious angel was more than a dream…she was a reality. Her mind, her spirit, and her body were truly heavenly. I wasn't a Neanderthal, and wasn't about to lie down and crash. I wanted to hold and caress her naked body in my arms. I wanted to talk to her, and find out what was going on in her pretty little head.

"You know I love you precious and I never want to leave your side."

She nodded her head and laid her body between my legs.

"I want a future with you. I want you in my life always." I massaged her back, while I talked gently and rather sensually. "This is a love thing, not lust. Although I crave your body like it was caffeine, I really love you with all my heart."

Precious turned around to face me, and wiped the sweat from my forehead. "I know, baby, I know. I love you too, and we shall spend an eternity together." We both smiled.

A deep sensuous kiss ensued. She opened her eyes, because she felt me growing. "Oh, I know what to do with that," she softly whispered.

She gripped my manhood with her left hand, rubbed and stroked it. It continued to grow even more. With my legs stretched out in front of me, she climbed aboard, easing her sweet pussy onto my shaft ever so gently. Once my manhood was fully engulfed, she wiggled, gyrated and began to bounce on it.

"Oh, yes!" she sighed.

I enjoyed the view of her voluptuous body slowly, rhythmically moving up and down. Her hair was all over her face. I moved it away, so I could see her expressions. She loved the way my hands touched her. It was like magic. I was like a magician casting a spell over her mind and body, and she was performing magic of her own.

When my fingers reached her face, when they touched her lips, she was starving and wanted to gently nibble each finger in hunger. I satisfied her appetite. She bit her lip as I maneuvered her body, and put her in a position that made her squeal. I knew I would have full access with her lying on her back, and her legs almost touching her shoulders. As she held them, I lowered myself between her.

She shed tears of joy and pleasure…we felt just that good. I kissed the tears from her face, and planted a kiss on her lips. I moaned, she hissed. I was hitting that spot, and she loved it.

Precious wasn't afraid to touch her body, so she helped herself out, and placed her fingers in position. She flickered back and forth on her clit, while I pumped in and out. I could tell by the look in her eyes that it felt damn good. I felt her hands move from her secret place to my ass. She pulled me towards her with purpose.

She moaned, "Fuck me Jay fuck me." I obliged and rocked her into the wee hours of the night.

✳ ✳ ✳

As I sat, reflecting on what I'd just read, I thought back to his book I read last night. He was a good writer, and I wondered if this was all fantasy, or if he was writing from experience. I made a mental note to ask him on Friday.

"Michelle, lunch has arrived. Would you like me to bring it in?" Yvonne said, as she rang me on the intercom.

"That's alright. I'll come get it. I'm going to have lunch on the patio out back," I told her.

"Okay, enjoy," Yvonne called out.

Chapter 4

"**E**XCUSE me, Michelle. May I join you?" Pam asked, as she walked onto the patio, where I was having lunch.

"Of course you may," I said, turning around.

"Michelle, I'd like to apologize again for my behavior this morning and explain."

"Okay, go ahead," I said.

"I didn't realize how possessive I sounded, until John spoke with me this morning. I've been so used to only dealing with him and Billy, that I was totally caught off guard when you requested the manuscript this morning. My emotions are still kind of raw since your uncle's death, and I haven't quite gotten used to you yet. I promise it won't happen again," Pam said.

I paused briefly, looking at her before responding. I didn't miss the fact that she called my uncle Billy, but decided I wasn't going to address that right now.

"Pam, I understand everyone is still grieving, but you have to understand this is a business, and as the CEO of Rivers, Inc., I have to make sure everything is up and running, the same as when my uncle was alive," I said. "Trust me; it's not easy stepping into his shoes. I'd give it all up for him to still be alive."

"I understand that, and again I'm sorry," Pam told me once again.

"I accept your apology. Now, tell me about Mr. Ramsey," I said.

"Well, there's not much else I can add to what I told you earlier. Mr. Ramsey is an excellent writer, and his work rarely needs a lot of editing, because he's such a perfectionist. We did bump heads a little on his last book. But we were able to work things out, and his book did make the best sellers list," Pam said proudly.

"Yes, indeed it did, and I can see why. I read it last night, and it was a very fast read…quite sensual and erotic," I said sighing.

"I'm enjoying what I've read so far of his newest manuscript," Pam said, as she held up the manuscript. "I'm almost finished with my editing, and I think this one is better than his last book!" she said excitedly.

"I have to agree with you, Pam. From what I've read thus far, this is going to be another bestseller. I better get back to my office before Yvonne sends a search party looking for me," I said.

"Thank you for allowing me to intrude on your lunch," Pam said.

"No problem. It was good talking with you," I said, as I left her on the patio to finish her lunch.

"I'm back from lunch, Yvonne. Do I have any messages?" I said, walking up to her desk.

"There are no messages. How was your lunch?" Yvonne asked.

"Lunch was excellent. The weather is beautiful, and it felt good to sit outside," I said. "By the way, I got this wonderful idea, and I hope it's not too late to plan it," I said, as I took a seat by her desk. "How would you like to help me plan a Christmas Party for the company?" I asked. "I know it's October, and it may be a little late for planning a party, but I want to do something very elegant, with 70's and 80's music. A sit down meal, and perhaps tie it in with a book signing for one of our writers. I want to include all the staff and their spouses or significant others, our writers and the board of directors. Perhaps we can call my uncle's lodge to see if we can rent space there, or see if the Embassy Suites has a ballroom available. Maybe even reserve a block of rooms for that night," I rambled on.

"Slow down. That sounds like a wonderful idea, Michelle," Yvonne said. "We haven't had one in two years, but I don't see why we couldn't pull it off." She laughed. "I'll make some phone calls, and see if we can rent space first. Then we'll make a guest list; find a DJ and a caterer. Give me a few days, and I'll let you know what I've come up with," she said efficiently.

"Thanks Yvonne. You sound just as excited as I do about getting this party together."

"I love planning parties," she said.

"Okay. I'm going to finish up the report I need to take to the Board meeting tonight, and then I'll be leaving the office," I said.

"Is there anything I can do to help with the report?" Yvonne asked.

"I think I have everything under control, but if not, I'll let you know," I said, as I entered my office.

It took me about an hour to complete my report. I had numerous items I wanted to convey to the Board of Directors. I wanted to assure them, that while the company would be run much the same as when Billy was alive, I also had a vision on how to move forward in the future of publishing.

After making sure I had enough copies for everyone, I placed everything in my briefcase. I went into the bathroom to touch up my make-up and hair. *I'm glad I wore my brown suit and heels today*, I thought to myself.

"Good night, Yvonne. I'll see you in the morning. If you need me before then, you can reach me on my cell phone," I said to her, as I was leaving the office.

"Good night, Michelle. Have a good meeting with the Board," she said.

* * *

About a half hour later, I was pulling into the parking garage of my daddy's building. I parked and took the elevator up to his suite.

"Good evening, Sherry," I said, as I walked into my dad's suite. "I should've known you would be here, in spite of the late hour," I said, embracing her.

"Hey, baby. Let me get a good look at you. You're just as beautiful as always," Sherry said.

"Sherry, you said the same thing when you saw me at the repast," I said, as we both laughed.

"Your father and the rest of the board members are in the conference room waiting on you."

"Thank you. I won't keep them waiting. It's good seeing you again. Give your husband a hug for me," I said.

"I will do that," she said, turning her attention back to her solitaire game on the computer.

I took a few moments to compose myself, and then walked into the conference room.

"Good evening, everyone," I said, as I walked through the door.

"Good evening, Michelle," Daddy said, as the men stood to greet me, while he gave me a kiss on the cheek.

"Come give your Uncle Maceo a hug," he said, from across the room.

After everyone took a few minutes to hug and greet me, Daddy officially opened the meeting. I took my seat and glanced around the table, realizing I was surrounded by the faces of loved ones, whom I'd known for most of my life.

The board consisted of Maceo Cunningham, who was an educator at one of the local high schools in Riverdale. He wasn't really my blood uncle, but I called him that because he grew up with my dad and uncle, and they were all very close. He was also a member of their Masonic Lodge and motorcycle club.

Zakiyyah Muhammad was the only other woman in the group. She was an accountant and local activist in the community. I'd known her since I was a little girl.

There was also Daniel Simuel, who was a writer for the local newspaper, and another childhood friend of my father and uncle, as well as a member of their Masonic Lodge.

And, last but not least, my father, Robert Rivers, who was a sports agent and lawyer.

"Good evening, ladies and gentlemen. As we know, Michelle inherited the company from my brother, William Rivers, and is now the CEO and publisher. I will now turn the meeting over to her," Daddy said.

I stood and passed around the vision plan I had written.

"Thank you, Daddy. Good evening. I'll try to keep this as brief as possible. Everyone knows how important Rivers, Inc. was to Uncle Billy. While he wanted it to be one of the most well known companies in publishing, he also wanted to keep it a relatively small family run organization. I will do everything within my power to continue his legacy. For this to happen, I will need all of your help.

"Uncle Billy's vision was to give his writers the best representation possible…with a personal touch. He wanted them to feel as if they were a part of his family, and could pick up the phone at anytime and reach him or one of his editors. He didn't want them to submit their work by mail or e-mail, and then have to wait for an impersonal letter to say whether it was accepted or rejected. I plan to continue that vision." Everyone around the table nodded their pleasure with what I was saying.

"While I was gathering my thoughts on exactly what I wanted to say to all of you, I had a vision for the future for Rivers, Inc. That vision is to put together a catalog of all our writers' books, and to make it available on our new website and in bookstores. This way, people will know Rivers, Inc., and all our writers personally. We currently have ten books that have made the Times bestseller list. From the manuscripts I've read in the past few days, I believe we'll have two more in the upcoming year." Again everyone smiled. "In closing, I'd just like to say I pray Uncle Billy's legacy will continue, and that I have your support in these future endeavors. Thank you," I said, before sitting down.

"Thank you, Michelle. At this time, does anyone have any questions or comments they'd like to make?" Daddy asked, glancing around the table.

"I make a motion that the mission statement presented by the CEO of

Rivers, Inc. be received, placed on file, and the recommendations be complied with, and that we give her a standing ovation," Zakiyyah said.

"I second that motion," Maceo added.

"It's been properly moved and second, that the mission statement presented by the CEO of Rivers, Inc. be received, placed on file, and the recommendations be complied with, and that we give her a standing ovation," Daddy said. "Having heard the motion, are you ready for the question? All those in favor, signify by the usual signs made amongst board members." Everyone at the table raised their right hands. "Motion carried," Daddy said.

Everyone stood and gave me a very warm ovation.

"Michelle, we have all the confidence that you will do a great job running Rivers, Inc. the way Billy would've wanted it to be done. In accordance with his last will and testament, we have the option of having each of our ten percent shares of the company bought out by you in the next year if we're not satisfied. I'm putting my faith behind you to keep us moving forward. As the company Chief Financial Officer, I know we stand on solid financial ground," Zakiyyah said, while everyone nodded in agreement.

"Welcome aboard, Michelle," Maceo said.

"We look forward to working with you, Michelle. And we hope that you will continue to write," Daniel said, from his end of the table.

"Well, I guess this meeting is adjourned," Daddy said, looking around.

After the meeting ended, and everyone said their goodbyes and gave me more hugs, Daddy insisted on following me home.

"Daddy, it's not that late and I'm driving. I can make it home okay, without you following me," I said.

"Baby, humor your old man, and let me follow you home. So I'm not worrying with visions of you pulled over on the side of the road with a flat."

"Now, Daddy, you taught me how to change a tire, and how to do basic car maintenance," I said, laughing at him.

"I did, but you're not driving a car, you're driving a truck," he said, in a huff.

"Alright, I give up! You can follow me home, and I'll even let you check under my bed for boys when we get there," I said, laughing so hard I had tears running down my cheeks.

"Good. I thought you would see it my way! Let's blow this popcorn stand," Daddy said, winking at me.

"Can we stop and get something to eat at *Justin's*? It's your treat, since you're following me home."

"Yes, baby, we can. I'll call your mom to let her know I'm taking my other woman out to dinner, so she doesn't worry and wait up for me."

"Daddy, she's going to kill us dead one day…if she catches us out together," I said laughing.

"She'll have to catch us first," he said winking.

* * *

The rest of the week went by very quickly, and before I knew it, it was Friday. I had finally finished reading Mr. Ramsey's manuscript, and was sure even without seeing Pam's edits yet, that it was destined to be on the bestsellers list.

After having met with the company lawyer and financial officer, it was clear the company was doing well, and that we'd have no problems implementing any of the ideas I presented to the Board. But I was going to wait till after the first of the year to make any changes.

"Good morning, Ms. Rivers," the security guard said.

"Good morning, Curtis."

I took the elevator up to my office, and saw that Yvonne, as usual, had arrived early and started the coffee. When I entered my office, she was placing a cup in the middle of my desk.

"Good morning, Yvonne. How are you doing today?" I said.

"Good morning, Michelle. I'm doing quite well, and you?" she said.

"I'm doing good…looking forward to meeting Mr. Ramsey today."

"I put his folder on your desk for your review."

'Thanks. Could you have John come see me when he arrives? I need to bring him up to date, because I'm going to be out of town next week for three days, and he'll be in charge."

"No problem. Do you need me to make any arrangements for you?"

"I believe you took care of everything yesterday, when you were able to get an early flight out for Jasmine and myself for Monday. I appreciate all your help as usual."

"You're welcome. I know how important it is for you to tie up all your loose ends in New York. I'll send John in as soon as he arrives," Yvonne said, as she left my office.

I grabbed my coffee and the folder, and took them over to sit on the couch by the window. It looked as if it was going to be another beautiful fall day.

* * *

Michael Ramsey arrived at Rivers, Inc. with minutes to spare. He ran into Pam in the lobby on his way to the elevators.

"Hello, Michael. I didn't know you were coming in today," Pam said, as she reached up to kiss him on the cheek.

"Hey Pam, I have an appointment with the new CEO in ten minutes. How are you doing today?" Michael said.

"Why are you meeting with Michelle?" she asked, sounding slightly annoyed.

"Walk with me to the elevators," he said. "I received a letter from her, asking for a meeting as soon as I was available. I believe she's meeting with all the writers. I met her briefly at Mr. Rivers' funeral. What kind of person is she?" he asked.

"I don't know that much about her yet, but she seems to be okay," she said, as the elevator doors opened. "Well, when you're finished meeting with her, stop by my office, and maybe we can do lunch."

"No problem. I'll see you a little later," Michael said, as the doors closed behind him.

"Hello, Yvonne," Michael said, as he entered the office.

"Hello, Mr. Ramsey. You're on time as usual. How was your flight?" Yvonne said.

"It wasn't bad. You're looking well as always," he told her.

"Keep talking like that, and we'll have to keep you here in Atlanta. Let me ring Ms. Rivers, and let her know you're here," Yvonne said smiling.

"I'd appreciate that, but first let me ask you something."

"Yes?"

"What type of person is she I mean what can I expect?" he asked.

"I think I'll let you meet her and see for yourself. I'm sure you'll be pleasantly surprised at what you find," Yvonne said.

"I thought you would say that," Michael said.

"Michelle, Mr. Ramsey is here to see you," Yvonne said, buzzing me.

"Thanks, Yvonne. Show him right in," I said.

I stood up to greet Mr. Ramsey, and was surprised at how handsome, but understated he was. I hadn't really paid a lot of attention to his looks when we met at the repast, but now I saw what Pam was talking about.

"Good morning, Mr. Ramsey. It's a pleasure to see you again. May I offer you something to drink...coffee or tea perhaps?" I said, as I extended my hand in greeting.

"Good morning, Ms. Rivers. It's also nice to see you again. I wouldn't mind some tea, thanks."

"I'll bring it right in. Would you like another coffee, Michelle?" Yvonne asked, standing in the doorway.

"Yes, please," I said. "Mr. Ramsey, please have a seat."

"Thank you."

"How was your flight in?"

"It wasn't bad," Michael said.

"I'm glad to hear that. The weather has been quite beautiful these last few days. You picked a good time to visit us. Where are you staying?" I asked him.

"I'm staying at the Westin Hotel by the airport. It was ironic I received your letter. I actually wanted to meet you even before I read your letter," Michael said. "I wanted to know what was going to happen with the company after Mr. Rivers passed."

"Although we're in transition, you'll find that Rivers, Inc. will still run pretty much the same way it was when my uncle was alive. I want to keep the family atmosphere he was always proud of, and we'll maintain an open door policy for all our writers."

"Well, that's music to my ears. Mr. Rivers gave my work a chance, even when other publishing companies turned me down. I'll always be indebted to Rivers, Inc. for the chance to follow my dreams," he told me.

"I've had the time to read your book, *Promises*, and I have to say I was quite impressed! Can I ask you a personal question?"

"Sure, I don't mind at all."

"Are your stories based on reality or imagination?"

"Hmmmm, for the most part, they're based on reality. At times, I add some fantasy. I love romance, and hope I'm not overstepping my boundaries. I love all aspects of the coming together of men and women...physically and mentally," he explained.

"Interesting, is there a reason why you haven't allowed your picture to be placed on any of your books? I'm sure if it were, they'd sell even faster. You're a very handsome man, Mr. Ramsey," I said.

"Thank you, Ms. Rivers. Actually, I don't mind having my picture on my books, but my editor thought it would be nice to get a following based on my writing in the beginning."

"Please call me, Michelle, and may I call you Michael?" I asked.

"I would be offended if you didn't," he said.

"Michael, I'd like to use your picture on the new book. I know an artist I'd like you to meet…in hopes that he'll do the cover. After reading the manuscript, I have an idea for something quite sensual and erotic," I told him.

"So, I take it you like what you've read of my new book?"

"I loved it!" I exclaimed. "*Determined* is destined to be on the Times bestseller list. Mark my words."

"Thanks. I'm open for any ideas that you have concerning the book. You actually have me pretty excited about it."

"Michael, look at the time. How about I take you to lunch, and we can finish our discussion?"

"That sounds good. The gourmet peanuts on the plane didn't do my stomach any justice at all," he complained.

"It's settled then. I'll take you to one of my favorite places in Little Five Points called *Front Page News*."

"Okay, lead the way," he said.

"Yvonne, Mr. Ramsey and I are going to lunch. You can reach me by cell phone if it's important. Otherwise, take a message or forward it to John," I said, as we walked out my office.

"No problem, Michelle. Have a good lunch," Yvonne said, smiling at us.

"Michael, I know you've probably been to Atlanta many times, but have you ever been to Little Five Points?"

"I don't recall the name. Is it a tourist attraction or something?"

"It's not a regular tourist spot. It's very eclectic, with a lot of great little shops, restaurants and interesting people. I think you'll enjoy it!" I said, getting excited.

We continued to chitchat on the short walk to the garage. When we got to my truck, I searched for my keys.

"This is nice, Michelle. You don't put me in the mind of a truck driver though," Michael said

"This was Billy's truck. I have his Benz as well, but I prefer to drive the truck."

"Now, that's more like it…a Benz woman. But as long as you're comfortable, that's all that matters. I drive a Subaru myself," Michael said.

"I didn't drive at all while living in New York, there's really not much of a need for it. I love Subarus. I test-drove a turbocharged wagon, with a manual and automatic transmission, and I'd be in trouble driving that around here."

"Wow, a woman that has knowledge of cars. Can I ask you something personal?"

"Yes, you may."

"Are you involved with anyone currently? Before you answer that, let me explain," he said nervously. "I was wondering how a woman in your position, that looks as fine as you do, and even has knowledge of cars, hasn't been snatched off the market by now. That is, if you're single."

"I'm single. And I got my knowledge of cars from my father, and would you believe that I can even ride a motorcycle," I said laughing. "I'm a free-lance writer, and I travel a great deal, so I haven't had a steady relationship in over a year. Damn, I hadn't realized it had been that long, until you asked," I said, shaking my head.

"You're something else, Ms. Rivers…I mean Michelle," he said laughing.

"I'm just me," I said smiling. "Please tell me about yourself, Michael. What do you do when you're not writing?"

"Well, I work with the City Planning Department in Philly, and I'm a Big Brother to a very nice young boy. He lost his dad when he was four years old, and I've been his Big Brother for about six years now. We go to football and basketball games, arcades, and I help him with his schoolwork. Sometimes, I like to go to the park and fly kites with him. I also like to go bowling. As far as relationships go, I don't have a steady girlfriend, but I am seeing someone."

"That's great, Michael. Tell me more about your little brother. I always wanted to do something like that, and now that I won't be traveling all the time, I may be able to."

"His name's Kevin. He's very smart, does well in school, and loves to play any kind of ball. He just has trouble dealing with the fact his father isn't with him. He's starting to come around. He asked me recently if I'd be his brother forever."

"And what did you tell him? I can't imagine my life with out my daddy. I often wonder how he felt about sharing me with Uncle Billy all these years. It was as if I had two fathers," I said.

"I told him he would always be able to contact me, and that I'd always be here for him if he needed me. His mom does a lot with him, but it takes a father or a big brother to help raise a man, so I do what I can."

"I agree with that. It took my mom to teach me about being a woman, but I still spent most of my time with my dad and uncle."

"So, you're a daddy's girl," Michael said smiling.

"Yes, very much so, and proud of it. My dad and I used to go out on dates together. We still do as a matter of fact. I'm his other woman, but don't tell my mom, it's a secret." I giggled.

"You have a great sense of humor. By the way, I'm going to take a bite out of you, if we don't get to this place soon," Michael said, rubbing his stomach.

"We're almost there. There's the sign on your right," I said, looking at him sideways and laughing, as I pulled into a parking space.

"This area does look a little familiar, but I can't figure out why."

"Hmmmm, perhaps you've been around here with your friend? I'm sure it will come back to you. I'll show you around after we eat."

"I'm sure it will. And I'd love to have a look around," Michael said.

"They have a Sunday Jazz Brunch that's very good. Perhaps the next time you're in town, you can check it out. That someone you're seeing might enjoy it," I said. "Let's get you fed, before you start eating my arm. I saw you looking at it," I said laughing, as we got out the car.

After being seated and placing our orders, we continued with our conversation. We found out that we both had a passion for jazz.

Yvonne was back at Rivers, Inc., trying to secure dates for the Christmas party. Pam walked up with a funny look on her face, looking at her watch.

"Hello, Yvonne. Is Mr. Ramsey still in the meeting with Michelle?" she asked.

"No, Pam. Mr. Ramsey went to lunch with Michelle about a half hour ago," Yvonne replied.

"If he comes back, can you ask him to stop by and see me before he leaves?" she asked.

"I'll be sure to give him your message," Yvonne said.

"Thank you, Yvonne," Pam said, with a half smile on her face.

Chapter 5

"**M**ICHELLE, this spot is very nice, and lunch was fantastic. I'll have to remember the name," Michael said.

"I'm glad you liked it. I've been trying to work my way through the menu for a while. A group of friends and I used to come here all the time before I moved to New York," I said.

"It'll take you a while to get through this menu. Let me pick up the check," he said.

"No, this is a business lunch," I said, smiling at him.

"Well, thank you for a nice lunch," he said.

"I want to stop by the natural food market while we're down here. Are you up to walking?" I asked.

"I don't mind. I need to walk that meal off anyway."

"The exercise will do us both good. Let me pay the check, and we can be on our way. I think we've held up this table long enough."

"Do you miss the high stress of New York?" he asked, as we left the restaurant.

"I was never stressed. It may be because I traveled a lot for my work, and when I was home, I was always busy. There's so much to see and do in New York," I told him. "I'll be going back on Monday to complete my move here. I still have my condo, and I'm thinking of sub-leasing it for awhile, and then perhaps selling it."

"I see. So, how's the business going so far?"

"It's challenging. I did an internship while in college with Uncle Billy, but it's a different story when you're the one in charge. I'm used to writing and turning my pieces in, and then moving on to the next assignment. I'm a little scared that I'll mess up," I said.

"It's hard to believe you're scared. If it helps, I don't think I'll ever look elsewhere for my publishing needs. I had hoped that after Mr. Rivers passed, the mission of Rivers, Inc. would remain the same. Since meeting you and talking, I've been reassured. I know you'll do just fine, I can feel it," Michael said.

"Thank you, Michael. Your confidence that we'll continue to meet your needs means a lot," I said to him. "Here's the store. After we leave here, I want to take you over to Damon's studio, the artist I want to hire to do your cover, so I can go introduce you to him. His studio isn't too far from here."

"I can't wait to see your idea about the cover first hand."

"I'm sure you'll love Damon's work as much as I do."

"What kind of art does he specialize in?" he asked.

"He does quite a few different styles, but his best are the sensual and erotic pieces. I own quite a few, and he's done CD covers for various recording artists."

After finishing my shopping, we finally made our way over to Damon's studio.

"Good afternoon. I'll be right with you," Damon said, without looking up in response to the door chime. "Oh, my God, Michelle, is that you? How are you doing, beautiful? I heard through the grapevine you were back in Atlanta," he said, once he looked up. "I'm sorry to hear about the passing of your uncle," he said, coming over to hug me.

"Hi Damon thank you for your condolences I'm back for good this time. I inherited my uncle's publishing company, and that's part of what brought me by today. I'd like you to meet a special friend of mine. Michael, this is my Picasso of a friend, Damon Jennings."

"It's nice to meet you, Damon," Michael said, as they shook hands.

"The pleasure is mine, Michael. Any special friend of Michelle's is a friend of mine."

"You have some very nice artwork here, brother. Did you create all of them?" Michael asked.

"Yes, my man, they're all me. Take a look around, you may see something you like," Damon said, as he put the finishing touches on a piece.

"Damon, while Michael's looking around, I want to get some input from you about an idea I have. We're about to publish his third book, and I think it would be a great idea if you could design the cover for it. After all, you're one of the best in the business, and it would surely compliment the contents of his book," I said.

"That's so nice of you to say. Sounds like a workable idea, Michelle. Michael, could you tell me about your book?" Damon said.

"My latest book is about a couple that's having their ups and downs. One minute they're madly in love, the next minute, they're breaking up. But they know deep down inside they were meant for each other. The couple is determined to work through all the difficulties to make the relationship work. Hence the title, *Determined*," Michael explained.

"Do you have a vision for what you'd like to see on the cover?" Damon asked.

"Not particularly. I'd like for you to maybe design three different covers I could choose from. From what I see around your studio, you have a great eye," Michael said.

"That's easy enough. I'll design a few covers, and then we can set up a meeting to see if you like them. Do you live here in Atlanta?" Damon asked.

"No, I live in Philadelphia. But I have no problem flying down, as long as I get a week's notice."

"No problem. I assume we'll coordinate everything through Michelle, right?" Damon asked, looking in my direction.

"That's fine. When you have the covers ready, I'll set up a meeting with you, Michael and his editor for final approval," I said.

"Michael, let me give you my card, which has all my contact information and website on it," Damon said, handing Michael his card.

"Great. I'll be using this soon, because I see a piece I'd like to get. Do you ship?" Michael asked.

"Yes, I do ship via UPS. Just pick out what you like. I appreciate the business."

"Fantastic!" Michael exclaimed.

"Damon thanks for agreeing to do the cover for us. I'll be in contact so we can work out your fee. It was great seeing you again. Please give your family my love," I said, as we prepared to leave.

"It was good seeing you also, Michelle. Michael, it was great meeting you. I look forward to working with you," Damon said, walking us to the door.

"He's a dynamite artist, Michelle. I hope it rubs off on this book," Michael said, as we walked back to my truck.

"Michael, the book is a done deal as far as I'm concerned. The cover will just be the icing on the cake, so to speak!" I said smiling.

"Thank you for your confidence. Once Pam finishes the editing, I'll feel better."

While driving back, I couldn't help but think how wonderful our meeting went. Michael was so talented, and also very handsome. A smile broke out across my face.

"Excuse me, Michelle…Michelle?" Michael said.

"Oh, I'm sorry, Michael. Did you say something?" I asked, snapping back from my thoughts.

"Yes, I did. I was asking what you're smiling about over there."

"I was just going over in my mind something my dad told me the other day." I lied.

* * *

An hour after leaving Damon's studio, we arrived back at Rivers, Inc.

"Michelle, I'd like to thank you for a wonderful lunch. I'm also thankful I wore some comfortable shoes, because you tried to walk a brother to death," Michael said, cracking a big, pearly white smile. "As I said earlier, I'm with your company from here on out. I like where you're headed," he told me.

"Thank you, Michael. I'm grateful you're giving us your support. I'm also glad you enjoyed lunch, and that I don't have to buy you another pair of shoes for your sore feet." We both laughed hysterically, gazing into each other's eyes between the tears. "Hi Yvonne I'm back from lunch," I said, walking into her office.

"Mr. Ramsey, Pam stopped by, and asked if you'd come see her before you left," Yvonne said.

"Okay. Thanks, Yvonne," he said, as he gave her the thumbs up sign. "Michelle thanks again, and I'll be in touch," he said, preparing to make his exit.

"It was my pleasure, Michael. We'll talk soon," I said.

Michael made his way to Pam's office. He knocked on her partially opened door, and noticed that she was on the phone. She waved him inside.

"Yes, I was going over it now, and I want to tell you that it confused me just a little. The storyline is good, but it seems a little rushed in a few places," she said, while rolling her eyes. "I'll mark them all and send it back to you, so you can see what my concerns are. You know I'll work with you on it. Okay, Jackie, I look forward to hearing from you soon," she said, hanging up the phone.

"Hey Pam, I apologize for disturbing you while you were on the phone."

"Hello, Michael. That's okay, no harm done. Thanks for stopping by," she said sarcastically, as she walked over to close the door. "How did your lunch meeting with the boss lady go?"

"It went very well. Miss Rivers is a very likable woman, and very professional. She reminds me a lot of Mr. Rivers. You should enjoy working for her." Michael might as well have slapped her, from the way she was looking at him.

"I'm so glad you enjoyed yourself. Where did you go for lunch?" she asked.

"We went to a restaurant called *Front Page News*, in some section of town called Little Five Points or something like that. I told Ms. Rivers it seemed like I had been in that part of town before."

"You have. I took you to Little Five Points before to a restaurant called *The Vortex*. Remember the one with all the crazy pictures on the wall?" she asked, with an attitude.

"That's where I remembered it from. I couldn't pinpoint it exactly. The food at *Front Page* was very good. Maybe we can go there one day and grab a bite to eat," he said.

"Yeah, maybe we can one day."

"What's wrong, baby? Are you having a bad day today or something?" he asked, as he gently rubbed her hand.

"Well, I had planned on taking you to lunch myself, Michael," Pam pouted.

"Wait a minute, Pam. I'm sorry; it completely slipped my mind that you invited me to lunch. But you have to remember my primary reason for coming to Atlanta today was to meet with Ms. Rivers. So, don't feel like I left you out of anything intentionally."

"I apologize, Michael. I've been having a rather trying day. Are you going right back home, or are you staying for the weekend?" she cooed.

"I'm going to leave early Sunday morning. So, we have some time to hang out while I'm in town…if you want to," he told her.

"Of course I want to. Are you trying to be funny?" she said, finally breaking into a smile. "Where are you staying?"

"I'm at the Westin, right near the airport. What are you doing this evening? Do you feel like going to grab some dinner?" Michael asked.

"That sounds good, baby. I have to make a run somewhere with my sister, but afterwards I should be straight."

"How are your sister and mother doing anyway?"

"They're okay," she said.

"Here's a key to my room. Just come over whenever you're done."

"Okay, I'll see you later," Pam said, giving Michael a hug.

As Michael left Pam's office, he was starting to wonder if she had a little animosity growing towards Michelle. It's not like him and Pam was a serious item. Overall though, the meeting with Michelle went well, and he was excited about the release of his new book. He could see that Michelle was serious about keeping Rivers, Inc. on the same positive path. Michael could definitely live with that.

Michael got off the elevator and ran into Curtis, who was all up in this fine lady's face. He was holding her hand, and must have been shooting his best lines at her, because she was grinning from ear to ear. He walked by them; winked and headed to the hotel to get some much needed sleep.

Once he got back to his hotel room, he grabbed a quick shower, turned the television to ESPN, and finished reading the Philadelphia Daily News. It was then that Michael noticed the red light blinking on the phone, letting him know he had a message. He hit the button, and a smile broke out across my face.

Hello, Michael. Thank you again for coming to Atlanta to meet with me. I hope you enjoyed the meeting as much as I did, and I look forward to continuing the creative relationship between yourself and Rivers, Inc. Please don't hesitate to contact me if you have any questions or concerns. Have a great day.

That was nice of Michelle to call, Michael thought. She is really on top of things. I like strong, independent women, and having her looks doesn't hurt either. She stands every bit of five feet six inches. Her medium build, brown hair, sultry hazel colored eyes, with a little mole on her cheek, and medium brown complexion, was easy on the eyes. She was so sexy, that it was kind of hard to keep your mind on business. Michael felt himself starting to get aroused at just the thought of her, and wondered what it would be like to make sweet love to her. He lay across the bed to finally get some shuteye.

Michael couldn't believe he finally had Michelle lying in bed next to him. Ever since the first time he'd laid eyes on her at her uncle's funeral, he'd wanted to get next to her fine ass. She moved a little closer to snuggle up, and began to gently kiss and suck his right nipple, which made it get hard. He felt her hand moving down his stomach, towards his slowly hardening manhood. Finally, he was fully erect from her fondling, and she slowly moved on top of him. She leaned down to kiss him with her warm moist lips, as he gently positioned his rock hard tool at the opening of her wet valley. Michelle quietly whispered that he felt hot, as she gently descended on his hardened wood.

"Oh, yes, baby," he said, as she began to ride him slowly.

He tried to get in sync with her motions, but it was almost impossible, as she kept changing from slow grinds to fast quick jerks. *Damn, she feels good.* He grabbed one of her ample breasts, and began to suck and nibble on the nipple, until it became as hard as a pebble. Michelle moaned loudly, as he hit the right spot with each upward plunge that he made. He felt the sweat running from her back, down to the crack of her ass. He grabbed it, and began to guide her round ass down onto his throbbing rod. The pace quickened, and they were finally in sync with one another. He met every one of her downward thrusts with upward plunges of his own.

Before long, he felt the muscles of her valley tighten around his missile, and then she screamed out, "I'm cumming!"

His thighs and groin were drenched in her juices. He gently turned her over on her back, and placed her legs on his shoulders for the ultimate attack. He thrust his dick into her wet box, plunging deeper and deeper, as if he was trying to tattoo his name on her vaginal walls. Finally, he reached the point of no return, pulled out of her and shot loads of hot creamy white cum all over her stomach. He moaned in shear pleasure, pulled her close to him, and collapsed. He wrapped his arms around her warm body, as they slowly drifted off to sleep. She was truly insatiable.

* * *

Before long, Michael felt her kissing him on her forehead and neck again.

"Not right now, baby," Michael said, talking in his sleep.

"Hey, Michael, Michael, wake up, baby," a soft voice said to him.

"Huh? Hey Pam, I didn't hear you come in. What time is it?" Michael said, surprised to see Pam and not Michelle standing by his hotel bed.

"It's six-thirty in the evening. You must be glad to see me, as hard as your thing is. Looks like you had one hell of a dream," she said, laughing hysterically.

"Get the heck out of here." Michael jumped up, and sure enough, his stomach was all sticky. He had to laugh at himself.

"So, are you hungry after all that fucking? By the way, who was she?" she asked, with a sly grin on her face.

"You know me, if you're not near me, Halle Berry will have to do," he said, with a chuckle. "Let me go and grab a quick shower. Where are we going?"

"I heard about this restaurant called, *Ray's in the City*, that's supposed to have some decent seafood. I have a taste for some crab legs. How does that sound to you?"

"That sounds good. Give me a few minutes and I'll be ready to go. There's something to drink in the mini fridge if you want it, help yourself." Michael said, walking into the bathroom.

"No, thank you."

"Pam, come here for a minute," Michael called out to her.

"What do you want, Mr. Sticky?" she said, laughing and walking into the bathroom.

"I see you got jokes. So, how was the rest of your day at work?" he said, changing the subject.

"It wasn't bad, and I got a lot done with your manuscript. I'm halfway through it. I think this one will do better. You're getting better and better with each submission," she told him.

"Thanks, baby. I just let it flow naturally."

"After I left work, I drove with my sister to pick up something for her fiancé's birthday. And yes, I told her you asked about her before you ask."

"Damn, you're an editor, a comedienne and a mind reader. You should be able to retire early," Michael said, laughing and stepping out the shower.

"Will you come on, I made a seven-thirty reservation before I left the office," she said.

"Now you tell me," Michael said, moving a little faster.

Within fifteen minutes, they were on their way downtown.

"Good evening, and welcome to *Ray's in the City*. Do you have a reservation?" the maitre`d asked, when they walked into the restaurant.

"Yes, we do," Pam, said, giving him her last name.

"Yes, Bryant party of two. Right this way, please."

"Good evening, my name is Winston, and I'll be your waiter this evening. Would you like to order something from the bar?" he said, walking over to their table after they were seated.

"I'll have an apple martini, please," Pam said.

"I'll have a rusty nail with Dewar's, please," Michael said.

"Very good, I'll be right back to take your order," Winston said, before going to get their drinks.

"Michael, this is a very nice spot. And wait until you taste the food. It's excellent. By the way, what in the heck is a rusty nail?" she asked, with a curious look on her face.

"It's a mixed drink…one half of a sweet liqueur called Drambuie and one half Scotch," he said laughing. "This looks like a nice place," he agreed. "I already know what I want."

Before long, Winston was back with their drinks. "Are you ready to order, or do you need more time?" he asked, with pen poised.

"I'll have the seafood gumbo and the blackened catfish," Pam said.

"I'll have a dozen oysters on the half shell, with the broiled seafood combination," Michael said.

"Excellent choices, it should be ready shortly," Winston said.

"Thank you. Pam, do you want to take a sip of my drink to see if you like it?" Michael asked, knowing it would be too strong for her taste buds. She took a sip, and then frowned up her face.

"How can you drink that?" she asked.

"It's kind of sweet, once you get the hang of it. The scotch probably got to you," he said.

"I'll stick with the martinis. Let me ask you something, Michael. With all that cum on your stomach this evening, did you save me some?"

He almost choked on his drink. "Girl, you need to cut that out." We both were cracking up at her bold question. "You know I got some left for you, baby," he said, as she smiled at him.

"Michael, what else do you have planned until you leave on Sunday?" she asked.

"My boy, Alex, who moved down here over the summer, is going to stop by and pick me up tomorrow, so I can do a little shopping for my man, Kevin. Then we're going back to his house to kick it."

"Kevin is your little brother, right?" Pam asked.

"Yeah, He told me he wanted a Michael Vick football jersey."

Before long their dinner arrived, and Pam wasn't kidding, the meal was fantastic. *This was definitely a place to put in my Rolodex for future reference*, Michael thought.

After dinner, Michael paid the check, and then they were on their way. They stopped and grabbed a bottle of Martini & Rossi Asti Spumante, strawberries, chocolate syrup, and some whipped cream to take back to the hotel.

"What do you plan to do with all that stuff you just bought?" Pam asked Michael, as they drove back to the hotel.

"Let's just say, I have a taste for a human sundae, and you're the human," he said.

"Damn, you make that sound so good, baby. Maybe I'll use some of that whipped cream on Mr. Curvy down there," she quipped, as she grabbed Michael's crotch area.

"I'm sure he won't mind that at all," he said, winking at her as she continued to rub his hardening manhood.

Michael started thinking, *if this car doesn't hurry up and get us to the hotel, I'm going to explode.* It had been a while since he'd had a chance to make love to Pam.

"Hey, slow up, you're going to miss the exit," Pam said.

"I'm glad you said something," he said.

* * *

Once they were up in the room, Michael found an oldies station that was playing all the nice jams...like the Whispers, O'Jays, and the Dells. He grabbed two glasses from the cabinet, while Pam washed the strawberries, and lit a couple of scented candles that she brought with her. They lay across the bed fully clothed and talked about his book. When the wine started to kick in, so did their raging hormones.

Slowly Pam leaned in closer and they kissed, gently in the beginning, and then harder and more passionate. Michael unzipped her dress, and she began to unzip his pants. Soon they were completely naked and very serious.

"Lie on your back, baby, so I can do something for you," Pam said, as she reached for the tray with the makings of the sundae on it.

She grabbed the syrup, and poured it over both of his nipples, kissing his chest as she did. She then sprayed on whipped cream, and topped that off with the sliced strawberries. Slowly she began to eat the treats off him, licking his nipples until they were both hard and sensitive to the touch. She used one hand to gently massage his dick as he moaned. The feeling of ecstasy had taken over his body, and his tool was so hard, it was aching.

Pam kissed and licked her way down to his throbbing member, and sprayed whipped cream on the head, which was shiny from the blood that had rushed to the tip. She licked the tip of his dick, down the sides, and back to the tip, where she lapped it greedily. Moans from Michael accompanied her licks and sucks.

"Yes, baby, suck it." Finally words escaped his mouth, as he could barely take it any more. Michael motioned for Pam to turn over, so that he could make his own sundae, before he exploded inside her mouth.

When Pam lay on her back, Michael grabbed two of the widest sliced strawberries and poked holes in them, big enough to fit over her protruding nipples. Then he grabbed the chocolate and encircled the berries, and topped them off with the whipped cream. He made a trail down to her cleanly shaven valley with the chocolate. Her body was writhing as he gently kissed her stomach. He put one whole strawberry right at the opening of her sweet pussy, for the fruity surprise at the end of this voyage that his tongue and mouth were about to start.

"Damn, baby, you feel so good," Michael, said hoarsely.

Pam whimpered, as he slowly began to enjoy his human sundae. He started at her firm breasts, and licked each one like a child at an ice cream parlor. When he got down to each strawberry, he put it in his mouth, and squeezed the juice into her mouth and kissed her. This was driving Pam wild. He licked his way down her smooth stomach, lapping up every bit of the chocolate trail that he'd made. Finally, he reached his prize.

"Oh, Michael, eat me, baby!" she moaned loudly, as he nibbled her clit and licked all around the strawberry.

He grabbed the sweet fruit with his teeth, and gently consumed it. He could taste her juices on the strawberry. Michael reached over on the nightstand, and quickly covered his throbbing dick with a Magnum. With one swift motion, he was advancing his rod inside her warm moist pussy. Inch by inch, he entered her hot box, as her legs wrapped around his waist to keep him from escaping.

"Do you like this pussy, baby?" Pam asked, as Michael began to quicken his pace.

They kissed each other feverishly, as Michael penetrated the depths of her well, trying to leave a lasting memory of his presence inside of her. He began to pound her pussy like never before, and she loved it.

"Fuck me, Michael! That's right do it!" Pam yelled out.

Suddenly he felt her valley tighten around his throbbing member, as she began to explode into oblivion. Michael went a little longer, and then withdrew his wet pulsating wood, pulled the magnum off, and shot his hot load all over her stomach and breasts.

"I see you did save some for me," she said, as they laughed and collapsed on each other. "I'll be glad when I get the chance to feel that inside of me," she said, referring to the fact they always used a condom when they made love.

"You and I aren't in a position to bring any babies into this world," Michael said, gazing directly into her eyes.

They kissed and talked a little bit more, before finally drifting off to sleep. Morning came rather quickly. Pam was putting her clothes on when Michael finally woke up. She must have called room service, because there was a tray of fruit, bagels, cream cheese and coffee on the table.

"What time is Alex supposed to come by and get you?" she asked, as she was preparing a bagel to eat.

"He told me to call him after I got up this morning. Thanks for ordering breakfast, baby," he said, heading to the bathroom.

"No problem. I figured you'd need a pick me up as much as I did, after the way you acted last night. You were in rare form." She sighed, as she began thinking back to last night.

"You mean *we*, don't you?" Michael chuckled, with a mouthful of toothpaste. "You were good, baby."

"You bring the freak out in me," she laughed. "Listen, I'm going to get out of here. I have a hair appointment in about thirty minutes. If you get a chance before you leave tomorrow morning, give me a call."

"If I don't talk to you later, I'll give you a call before I get on the plane, I promise," he said, walking her to the door. "Thank you for a wonderful dinner, and a fantastic dessert." They smiled, hugged and kissed. Then Michael gently smacked Pam on her ass as she walked out the door.

After Pam left, Michael hopped in the shower. He then sat down and read a little of the newspaper that came with the tray. The mixed fruit and bagel hit the spot. He couldn't believe how hungry he was. He picked up the phone to call Alex.

"Good morning, Alex," Michael said.

"Yo Michael" Alex said.

"What time you coming by?"

"I was waiting on you to call me. It's nine o'clock now; I should be at the hotel no later than ten."

"That's good time. Can you take me to the Lenox Mall? I need to get a few things for my little brother," Michael said.

"Man, I bet that boy is getting big now, isn't he? I'll take you wherever you want to go. Talk to you soon."

"Alright, I'll talk to you in a few."

Chapter 6

ALEX and Michael had known each other since the third grade. Cut up isn't the word to describe how much trouble they used to get into. Michael couldn't wait to see Alex. Ten o'clock rolled around, and there was a knock on the door. Sure enough, it was Alex.

"Man, you're a sight for sore eyes. How ya doing" Michael said, opening the door. They grabbed each other tightly and hugged.

"It's good to see you, man," Alex said, while they exchanged high fives.

"Let's walk and talk. I'm ready to get some air," Michael said.

"What brought you to Atlanta this time?" Alex asked, as they walked out of the hotel.

"I had to meet with my publisher, to find out what was happening with the company since the owner passed away."

"Oh wow, you mean Mr. Rivers… the man you introduced me to when I moved down here? He passed away?" Alex asked surprised.

"Yeah, he passed away a few weeks ago, and his niece is the owner now. She wanted to meet with all the authors to touch base with us, and let us know which way the company was headed."

"Man, I'm sorry to hear about the brother. So, what was she like?"

"Man, she's gorgeous, and she doesn't have a man either. On the business side, she's very professional. I think I'm going to continue to stay on with them for my publishing needs."

"If one more woman comes to me, talking about you and how hot your shit is, I think I'm going to go crazy. You're taking these women out, man. I was with this sister, and she ran into some girls that she knew, and one of them had a copy of your book. Damn, they got to talking, giggling and fanning themselves. I started to tell them I knew you personally, but then all hell would've broken loose."

"Somebody has got to get them riled up, so they can go and take care of their men." We both cracked up. "It's a good thing they're reading my work. A brother has got to eat." Alex slapped him a high five. "But, in reality, you know I do really love writing."

"I know, brother. Ever since junior high school, you've been writing all kinds of stories and poems. You always had the girls wanting to be your girl-friend, and all the boys hating on you," he said laughing.

"I know. It's just something about telling a good story, keeping people captivated, that I've always enjoyed over the years."

"You said you wanted to go to the mall, right?" Alex asked.

"Yeah, I need to pick up a Michael Vick throwback jersey for Kevin, and a few things for myself. And I wanted to get you something for your place, since I missed your house warming party. Have you hooked up with any ladies since you've been down here?"

"Just one and it's not anything serious. Damn, if there aren't some badass southern women down here. I'm going to get me one of these southern belles sooner or later. I'm not rushing though," Alex said, shaking his head.

Alex and Michael arrived at the mall and started walking through. Women were everywhere, doing their most favorite activity…spending money. Michael smiled when he walked by Waldenbooks and saw his last book in the window.

"There you go, homey." Michael pointed out his book to Alex.

"You want to go in and check out how many women are buying your book?" Alex asked then laughed.

"I see you got jokes. Let's keep it moving," Michael said smiling.

"We can go into Sports Avenue and grab that jersey you were talking about," Alex said. "Then I want to stop in Kenneth Cole and pick up a couple pairs of shoes."

"I see women aren't the only people who love shopping," Michael said, teasingly to Alex.

"You know it. I work everyday, and I believe in treating myself to something every time I get paid," Alex said proudly.

They grabbed Kevin's jersey from Sports Avenue, and then walked into Cole's to pick up Alex's shoes. Michael picked himself a pair up too. He thought to himself, *why should Alex have all the fun?*

"Where can we get something to eat? I'll spring for lunch," Michael said.

"I usually stop in *Mick's*. You can get a decent salad or some spaghetti in there," Alex said.

"That's good, because I've worked up an appetite walking this mall with you."

Just as they were about to step inside the restaurant, Michael heard a familiar voice calling out to him.

"Michael, Michael Ramsey!" He turned to see Michelle with another woman.

"Alex, that's her. That's my publisher, Michelle Rivers. Come on, let me introduce you," Michael said.

"Damn, she's fine," Alex, said in awe, as they walked towards us.

"Hello, Michael," I said, as a broad smile came across my face.

"Hello, Michelle," Michael said.

"Mom, this is the writer I was telling you about. Michael, this is my mother, Mrs. Rivers. Mom, this is Michael Ramsey," I said, introducing Michael to my mother.

"I'm very pleased to meet you, Mrs. Rivers. Ladies, this is my best friend, Alex Black," Michael said.

"Hello, Alex. I hear you're new to Atlanta. How do you like it so far?" I asked.

"I'm still getting used to the traffic, but I'm enjoying it," Alex said.

"Good. I see you and Michael haven't wasted anytime hitting the stores," I said, looking at all the bags they were carrying and laughed.

"You have the nerve to talk, Michelle. Judging by the bags you ladies have, y'all were buying out the stores yourselves," Michael said laughing.

"It's my mother's fault," I said.

"Don't make me beat you in front of these gentlemen, Michelle," my mother said, with a smile.

"Michelle, Alex and I were about to go grab something to eat at *Mick's*. Would you ladies like to join us?" Michael asked.

"I'm sorry, but we're meeting my best friend, Jasmine, for lunch at *Copeland's*, and then going shoe shopping. Perhaps another time," I said.

"I'll take a rain check then. It was nice meeting you, Mrs. Rivers," Michael said.

"It was my pleasure. Michael and Alex have a nice day," my mother said.

"Bye, Michael. Have a safe trip back to Philly. Alex, it was good meeting you," I said, before we parted and went our separate way.

We arrived at *Copeland's*, and were just about to get settled at our table when Jasmine arrived. Heads start turning in her direction. Jasmine had an air about her. She was graceful without even trying. Her walk has stopped traffic on more than one occasion, and the best part about it is that she's totally oblivious to the affect she has on other people.

People have often mistaken us for sisters because of our hazel eyes, but that's where the similarity ends. Jasmine is 5'9", with brown shoulder length locks. She's busty, with a trim body. When she smiles, she lights up the room. She has a medium brown complexion, just a shade darker than I am, and a very outgoing personality, where I'm more reserved.

"Good afternoon, ladies. I'm here!" Jasmine said, as she slid into the booth next to me.

"Hey girl, we can see you're here, and so did everyone else when you glided in the door," I said laughing.

"Hi Jasmine, you look beautiful as usual," my mom said, with a smile.

"Hi Mom, Thank you, I just threw something on," Jasmine said.

"Stop lying, you never throw on anything, heffa," I said, smiling at my best friend.

"Did y'all buy out the mall, or did you leave something for someone else?" Jasmine asked.

"Well, we left a few things, but your friend tried to buy everything," my mom said.

"Oh no, Mommy, you didn't just tell that lie on me," I said laughing, as the waiter walked up and asked if we were ready to order.

"Yes, we're ready," my mom, told him.

After we placed our orders, and the waiter brought over our drinks, my mom began to tell Jasmine about meeting Michael.

"We ran into one of Michelle's writers while we were at the mall."

"Oh really, which one was it?" Jasmine asked.

"Michael Ramsey, right?" my mom asked me.

"Yes, Mom, it was Michael Ramsey," I said blushing.

"Michelle, you didn't say he was coming to town. Tell me, what he was like," Jasmine said, turning to look directly at me.

"I was quite impressed. He's very intelligent and funny. I took him to lunch yesterday, and then took him to meet Damon at his studio."

"She's leaving out that he's quite handsome also," my mom said. "And you should've seen how her face lit up when she spotted him and his friend, Alex, who's quite handsome too."

"Oh, Michelle, what else are you leaving out?" Jasmine asked.

"There's nothing else to tell. I just met the man yesterday, and Mom, you can get that grin off your face," I said. "I'm going to tell Daddy you're looking at other men."

"Oh, please girl. Your daddy knows I look at other men. The same way I know he looks at other women. We're not that old...we can still look," she said, laughing at Jasmine and I as we picked our faces up off the table.

I had to remember my mother was still quite beautiful at sixty, and my daddy was quite handsome too.

* * *

Meanwhile, Michael and Alex were preparing to have lunch at *Mick's*.

"Man, Michelle is fine, and her mom looks just as good. They actually look more like sisters than mother and daughter," Alex said, as they prepared to order.

"Oh, so now you like older women?" Michael asked, shaking his head and laughing.

"If they look as good as she does, hell yeah! You didn't crack on Michelle yet?" Alex quizzed.

"My brother, number one, I just met the woman yesterday. Number two, my dealings with her will be strictly business."

"Get the heck out of here, man. You saw how she looked at you, and how bright her eyes got. You could hit her in the shorts anytime you want to. If I didn't know any better, I'd think you already got in them panties." We both had to laugh at his *hit her in the shorts* comment. "After you get to know her better, you're going to have to put me down with one of her girlfriends. I know she has a few, and they probably all look like her. Birds of a feather flock together. I know you've heard that one," Alex said.

"You act like you know me so well. I'm not thinking about getting with her," Michael said, even though last night he'd the hottest, wettest dream, with her as the star.

"Hello in there. Remember me? I grew up with your ass. I've seen you in action, pulling girls even when you weren't trying. Don't even try that shit, man," he said, shaking his head.

"Okay. The next time I talk to her, or I'm in town, I'll ask her if she has any girlfriends for you to meet, since you're still pretty new to Atlanta. Is that a deal?"

"That's more like it, brother," he said, giving Michael a pound. "Now, let's eat and get the heck out of here. I have a few more things to pick up. Then I want to show you around before we go to my spot, and before we go to the Hawks game."

"What! You have tickets to the Hawks game?" Michael asked excitedly.

"Yes, sir, my brother, I know a guy who has a hook up," he said, grinning like he was the man.

"Who are they playing tonight?"

"That new team, what's their name, the Charlotte Bobcats?"

"That may be a good one. Thanks, Alex."

"I didn't say you were going." He fell out laughing.

"I see you still got jokes, but you're not going anywhere without me, so just forget that," Michael told him smiling.

"You're my best friend, man. You know I wouldn't go without you," Alex said, as he passed the waitress his credit card to pay for lunch. Michael left the waitress a tip, and they left *Mick's*.

After they left the mall, Alex took Michael on a mini tour of downtown Atlanta. Then they went to his house, which was on the outskirts of the city. He lived in a place called Powder Springs. The development was nice, and he said for the money, it was well worth it. His home had a two-car garage, swimming pool, four bedrooms, two and a half bathrooms, and a huge family room, where he could show off his big plasma television.

"You need to be on that show, *Lifestyles of the Rich and Famous*." We laughed. "This house is nice, man," Michael said, looking around.

"Thanks. I just couldn't pass on the deal, and when I sold my house in Philly, I had plenty to put down on this one. My mortgage is very reasonable. Hey, what time is your flight leaving in the morning?" he asked, as they got ready to go to the basketball game.

"It's scheduled for nine o'clock. Just make sure you drop me off in time to at least get a few hours of sleep." Michael chuckled, knowing they were going to probably make a stop after the game.

* * *

Morning rolled around quickly, and Michael was ready to get back to Philly. He couldn't seem to stop thinking about Michelle, and his thoughts weren't strictly on business. He gave Pam a call as promised, but got no response. He left a message on her machine.

Chapter 7

MICHAEL'S flight back to Philly was uneventful. Seeing Alex, and what he was up to down in the ATL was great. Getting a chance to be with Pam again was also nice. But the highlight of his weekend was meeting Michelle Rivers. Now that was an event to remember. He found himself being occupied by thoughts of her. He could see where working with her was going to be just fine. She reminded him so much of her uncle, that it boggled the mind. The part he couldn't believe was that he had a wet dream about her, even though they'd only had lunch together. He figured he had to be losing his mind, if that was all it took to get him excited, especially in the subconscious. He had to admit though, being with her felt so damn right. And not just from a professional aspect, but on a personal level.

When Michael got to his car in the airport parking lot, he could see that his baby needed a bath. He drove down to the White Glove near his house, and got the Shimmy Shammy Special. *I can't be driving around the city in a dirty Subaru*, he laughed to himself.

"Hello, Michael," this sexy voice called out to him, while he was waiting on his car. He turned around, and it was Wanda Murphy, one of his college classmates.

"Hey Wanda, How are you doing? It's been a while," Michael said.

"I'm doing well, and I finally read *Promise of Love* last week. It was hot," she said, while gently touching his arm.

"I'm glad you enjoyed it. My next one will be out in a couple of months," Michael said proudly.

"Here's my card," she said, reaching into her purse. "Call me when it's out, so we can do lunch or each other one day." They both laughed. "If you're anything like you write, then you just might hook me."

"That sounds good to me. Well, that's me over there," he said, as he pointed towards his car. "It was nice seeing you again, Wanda," Michael said.

"Nice seeing you again, Michael. Don't leave me hanging," she purred.

"I won't lose your number," he said waving, while handing the carwash attendant a two-dollar tip.

I'm not one to toot my own horn, but I must admit I have a list of women I could get with on my writing merit alone. But once I get into my writing, nothing else seems to phase me. It's almost like I withdraw from society for the moment, he thought to himself.

Michael pulled into his apartment complex around twelve that afternoon. He made his way inside, and just sat for a moment, collecting himself. The thought of Michelle once again crossed his mind. He laughed, because it was so odd for him to have thoughts so overwhelming like this. Usually he was so in control of his mind.

After unpacking, he grabbed a cold beer from the fridge, and turned the Eagles game on. Just as he started to get real comfortable, the phone rang.

"Hello," he said.

"What's up, Michael? It's Bob. How was your trip to the ATL?"

"Hey, Bob. The trip was okay, man," Michael said.

Bob had been a friend of Michael's since high school. He also worked with him down at City Hall, and lived across the street from him as well.

"Are you watching the game?" Bob asked.

"Yeah, why don't you stop through, and I'll tell you about my trip."

"Okay, give me a minute to grab a six," Bob said.

"Alright, talk to you later."

After Michael got off the phone, he started listening to his answering machine. He had quite a few messages, and one of them was from Pam.

Hello, Michael. I'm sorry I missed you this morning before you left Atlanta. I'm almost finished with your manuscript, and I have to say this one tops your last effort. I also want to thank you for a wonderful evening on Friday. Every chance I get to spend with you is so special. I hope in the future, we'll get a chance to turn those hours into years. Take care, and I'll talk to you soon.

Michael sat there for a moment, shaking his head at her message. She was starting to take things a little too serious. He felt mixing business with pleasure might become a problem. He needed to have a talk with her, to let her know she was moving a bit too fast for him. He hoped it didn't affect their working relationship. There was also a message from his mom.

Michael, this is Mom. Give me a call when you get back from Atlanta. I need you to come and take me to the eye doctor on Wednesday, after you get off from work. I'm having an eye procedure done, and they say I shouldn't drive home afterwards. Let me know if you can take me. I made a sweet potato pie for you too. You need to come get it before your father eats it. I love you.

About thirty minutes later, Bob showed up to watch the game. He was a big

Browns fan, since he was originally from Cleveland. The Browns were playing the Eagles.

"Y'all better be careful today, man. I can see your team getting knocked off," Bob said, as he sat down.

"No way brother the Eagles are the team to beat in the east, trust me," Michael said, with confidence.

"So, tell me, how your trip was? Did you get with that honey you were telling me about?"

"Well, I went down with the intention of only meeting with my publishing company's new owner. But you know I got my freak on with my editor while I was there." They both laughed. "Alex told me to tell you hello, and to give you his phone number and address," Michael said. "Man, he has a house down there that's bad! He mentioned having all his boys come down to a barbecue next summer," he continued.

"If that jumps off, I'm there. I miss knucklehead. I never thought he'd relocate when the soda manufacturer he works for moved to Atlanta." Bob sighed. "But he's single, with no kids, so it was a good move. And you better watch yourself with your editor. What's her name again?"

"Her name's Pam and you got that right. She hinted to me she wants to take our relationship to the next level and become exclusive. You know that's not me, right?"

"Yeah, I know. But it seems like you better let her know that."

"Trust me, I will. I got a chance to talk with the new owner over lunch. Man, not only did she inherit her uncle's publishing company, the woman is gorgeous," Michael said.

"Oh, boy, there you go," Bob, said.

"What you talking about?" Michael asked, laughing slyly.

"Every time you start talking that gorgeous shit, what that actually means is you're gonna try to get in those panties."

"Damn, does it show that badly?" We fell out laughing, because he was right. "Man, I had a wet dream about her right before Pam came to my hotel room," Michael said.

Bob shook his head, as he walked towards the kitchen to put the beer in the fridge.

"Hey, you know that sister, Eve? She's been asking about you," he shouted, from the kitchen.

"You ran into her? How is she doing?" Michael asked.

"She's doing well. I saw her at the movies on Friday night. Man, you got these women going crazy over your writing," he said, coming back into the living room.

"Man, I just write what I feel, that's all. I'm glad they like it though. The more they like them, the better I feel, and the fatter my bank account gets."

"I know that's right," Bob said, giving Michael a pound. "Touchdown! Your boys are in trouble, Mike," he said, turning his attention to the game.

"Don't you believe the hype; the Eagles have them right where they want them."

"Man, they've never been behind in a game this year. I'm telling you, they're going to choke," Bob said.

"Put your money where your mouth is," Michael shot back at him.

"Twenty says the Eagles get knocked off today," Bob said.

"You're on," Michael quickly said, before Bob changed his mind.

They finished watching the game, and just as Michael had predicted, the Eagles came back and won.

"Your team played a good game, brother. I'll catch you at the job tomorrow," Bob said, paying his debt.

"Okay, I'll check you tomorrow."

After Bob left, Michael gave his mom a call, and told her he would pick her up from the eye doctor on Wednesday. After fixing a little something to eat, he read the rest of his mail and crashed early for a change.

* * *

On Monday morning, Michael felt refreshed. He didn't know if it was the fact that he had gotten a good night's sleep, or his getting a chance to talk with his new beautiful publisher, that energized him.

"Good morning, Sara," Michael said, when he arrived at work.

"Good morning, Michael. Did you have a good weekend in Atlanta?" Sara asked.

"Yes indeed. The meeting I had with my publisher went better than expected."

"I told you it would be okay," she said smiling.

"Yes, you did. Thank you, my little sister," he said jokingly.

Sara was the secretary for the Urban Design Division of the City Planning Commission. Her brother and Michael had graduated high school together.

"Do we have any meetings scheduled today?" Michael asked.

"Not any departmental meetings, but you do have one with a couple of block captains from West Philadelphia," she said.

"That's right. We have to discuss the plans for a couple of murals that are to be done. What time are they coming?"

"They're supposed to be here at one-thirty."

"Okay. Let me go get some work done," he said, heading to his office.

"Oh, no you don't. Tell me about this Ms. Rivers," Sara said, anxiously awaiting his response.

"Well, there's not much to tell. She's very businesslike, just like her uncle. And she has a nice personality...friendly and a good sense of humor."

"Um...excuse me, Mister Romance writer, did you feel any positive vibes from her?"

"She has a good vision, as far as my next book goes, if that's what you mean. She introduced me to an artist that's going to design the cover."

"Man, you know that's not what I meant. Every time you meet a woman, and describe her as being friendly, or having a great sense of humor, you wind up getting close to her. Don't let me start pulling out examples. But I'm not going to press you," she laughed, and gave Michael that unbelieving look.

"Good, because I have to keep everything very professional with her," he said smiling. "One thing I can say is that you're always looking out for me."

"Somebody has to, with all these women running around, trying to push up on you. I have to scope them out, just like Debra would. She'll be home soon enough. Then you'll have two sisters screening these hot-assed women," Sara coolly said. Michael laughed, but knew she was dead serious.

"I just can't wait," he said sarcastically. "Now let me go and get some work done."

Debra was Michael's little sister. She attended the University of Arizona on a basketball scholarship. She was one of the best shooting guards coming out of Philadelphia. She was very protective of Michael, especially since he became an established writer. She had all the young ladies from her chapter reading his work, and then when they wondered out loud if he was anything like what he wrote about, she gave them the evil eye.

Michael was going over a few neighborhood improvement files he'd been working on, when an e-mail alert popped up. It was from the Mayor's office, and when he opened it, his jaw dropped to the floor.

Dear Staff,

Due to the current economy and the city's fiscal health, the city will be forced to layoff six hundred employees, which will include all departments. The fire department and the police departments will also be affected. These layoffs will go into effect starting December 1, 2004. If the situation improves, the laid off employees will be called back to work. Details will be forthcoming.

Sincerely,

Vincent Hale, Mayor

By the time Michael left his office, to see if anyone else had heard the news, the department was already buzzing. *If I get a pink slip,* he thought to himself, *it wouldn't be too bad, because I was thinking of cutting down to a part-time consulting type of a role anyway.* But it was getting really close to Christmas, and this kind of news was devastating. He could imagine what was going through folk's minds with this news.

"So, I guess you heard about the layoffs," Michael said to Bob, as they stood in the employee lounge.

Yeah, man. This shit is fucking unbelievable," he said, clearly upset at the news.

"Brother, we just have to pray that it won't hit us. That's all we can do," Michael told him.

"Man, you'll be cool, because you have other means to make a living. Some of us will be hit hard if our number is plucked," Bob said.

"Let's just wait and see. I still need my job too. And we've both been here for a long time, so we may not be affected."

"I just bought a new car and a new plasma television, so I definitely need my gig," Bob complained.

Well, hang in there, brother, and think positive about this situation," Michael said, before heading back to his office.

"Michael, you have a call on line four from a Carol Washington," Sara buzzed.

"That's my little brother, Kevin's, mom. I hope everything is alright. Thanks, Sara," Michael said, picking up line four. "Hey, Carol. What's up?" Michael said.

"Hello, Michael. Don't be alarmed. Kevin got into a fight today at school, and he didn't do too well. He has a nice shiner on his eye, and he's upset because he doesn't know how to protect himself all that well," she said.

"As long as he fought back, that's half the battle. I bought him something back from Atlanta, and I was planning on stopping by after I got off from work. If that's okay with you," Michael said.

"That'll be fine, we're not going anywhere. I'll let him know you're coming by."

"It looks like I'm going to have to get him some boxing gloves," he said, as they both laughed. "I should be there around six."

"That's good. You can eat dinner with us if you want," Carol said.

"Now that sounds good to me. I'll talk to you later."

"Okay," Carol said, hanging up.

"That's my brother. Not because he got into a fight, but because he at least defended himself. I'm going to teach him how to hold his hands a little better, even though he still may get his butt whipped," Michael said to himself proudly.

The meeting with the block committees went very well. The plans for the murals on the sides of two abandoned buildings were in place. All that was needed was the approval of the Planning Commission.

Michael was very proud of the Urban Blight Program the city had in place, especially since that particular project was taking place in the neighborhood where he grew up. It was in desperate need of a facelift.

The rest of the day went by rather swiftly, and before Michael knew it, he was headed over to Kevin's house with his gift.

When he arrived, Kevin was already standing in the doorway, ready to see what was in the bag.

"Hey, little man, how you doing?" Michael asked.

"I'm okay, Michael. What's in the bag? Do you see my shiner?" Michael laughed as Kevin bombarded him with questions.

"Can I at least get all the way in the door first?" Michael said, smiling and giving him a big hug.

Kevin grabbed Michael by the hand, and pulled him inside the house. Carol was in the kitchen.

"Hello, Carol," Michael called from the living room.

"How are you, Michael? I'll be with you in a second. I'm just finishing the steaks," she called out.

"What's in the bag, Michael?" Kevin asked again anxiously.

"Look inside and see for yourself," he said.

"Oh, wow! Thank you, Michael! Mommy, come look at my Michael Vick throwback jersey!" he said, jumping up and down, and then hugging Michael.

"Wow, that's so nice, Kevin. Did you say thank you?" she asked, with a big smile on her face.

"Yes, he did," Michael, said.

"That's so nice of you, Michael," she said, looking at him admirably.

"Are you kidding? Kevin's my main man," Michael said.

"I hope everyone is ready to eat," she said, heading back towards the kitchen. "Kevin, go wash your hands."

"Okay, Mommy." Michael went with him to wash his also.

"What are we having for dinner, Mommy?" Kevin asked, as they walked into the kitchen.

"We're having steak, baked potatoes, broccoli, and salad. For dessert, I made a cheesecake."

"Wow, Carol, this all looks so good. You picked the perfect night to invite me over," Michael said laughing.

"You're always welcome over for dinner. You know that," Carol said.

"What happened at school today, Kevin?" Michael asked, once they were seated at the table.

"This boy in my class kept talking about me being a momma's boy. Last week he hit me in gym class. I told on him to my teacher like mommy said. Then today at recess, he told me I was a tattletale and he hit me again. This time I hit him back, and we started fighting. Mommy told me the first time somebody hits me to tell the teacher. Then if they hit me again, try to tear their head off," he said, in a rush.

"I would've done the same thing, Kevin. So, did you get some good licks in?" Michael asked.

"I did, but he gave me a black eye," he said, pointing to his right eye. "Can you teach me how to fight, Michael?"

"I'll show you, don't worry about that. I'm going to get some boxing gloves and teach you. But you know it's best to try to settle things by talking it out, instead of fighting."

"I know, but he just kept picking on me, and I couldn't take it any more."

"They sent a note home saying that Kevin was suspended for three days, but I can't be taking off from my job like that. I'm going to take him back tomorrow and talk to the principal. I don't think it's fair, since he didn't start it. He was just defending himself," Carol said, in a huff.

"I agree with you. I think the principal should've talked to you first anyway. Just tell him straight up that if he doesn't reinstate him, you'll take it to the next level. He'll be back in school, mark my words," Michael said.

Carol worked in the business office for a hospital downtown. She was forty-three, about 5'7, with medium brown skin and a nice body. Michael kept stealing glances at her whenever she got up from the table. She caught him looking a couple of times, and smiled at him.

"Carol, this meal is fantastic, you sure can burn," Michael said, shaking his head.

"I told you my mommy could cook," Kevin said proudly, with his shiner glistening on his face.

"Yes, you did. Kevin, I have tickets for the Sixers game against the Heat on Friday. Would you like to go?"

"Can I go, Mommy, please?" he said, as his eyes lit up at the news.

"It's okay with me," she said.

"Oh, boy, I can't wait. Thank you, Michael," he said, getting up to give Michael a hug.

"As long as you keep your grades up to par, I'll take you anywhere you want to go," Michael said.

I'm going to do my best, Michael. Thank you," Kevin said smiling.

"The Big Brothers program is a blessing, and I'm happy Kevin has been paired with you. His grades have improved, and he seems to be more confident since you've been around him," Carol said, looking Michael directly in the eye. "I'm going to put some water on for some tea. Would you care for some?" Carol asked.

"Sure, I'll join you. But you know he's helped me too, Carol. I never had a little brother of my own, and if I did, I would hope he was just like Kevin."

"Who's ready for dessert?" she asked.

"I don't know if I have any room for dessert," Michael said, rubbing his stomach.

"Remember its cheesecake," Carol said invitingly.

"I just made room," he shot back, laughing.

"Mommy, I don't want any. May I be excused to go play video games for a while?" Kevin asked.

"Yes, go ahead. Just remember you have to hit the shower in a little while," she said.

"Okay, Mommy," Kevin said, getting up from the table, and heading to his room.

After Kevin went to play his game, Carol and Michael sat talking until the whistling sound of the teakettle interrupted them.

"How's your new book coming along?" she asked, as she passed him a slice of cheesecake and a cup of tea.

"It's finished and at the publisher's being edited. Hopefully, it'll be ready soon," he told her.

"I can't wait to read it. Your last one was pretty nice…let me stop. It was hot! Can I ask you a personal question?"

"Go ahead, I think I can handle it," he said, with a smile.

"Do you write from experience, or is it all just fantasy?" He almost choked on his cheesecake when she asked that question.

"I write a little from experience, but most of what I write is about visions I have that I would love to come true. I'm a dreamer, so I guess you could say a lot of it is fantasy."

"You're such a sensuous writer. You probably have women falling on top of each other…trying to get with you."

"I'm not involved with anyone currently. I don't have time for a steady relationship right now, if that's what you mean."

"Hopefully you'll meet someone that makes your fantasies come true," she said smiling.

"Perhaps I will. Thanks again for dinner, it was wonderful. Can I give you a hand with the dishes?"

"No, I got it. Thanks for asking."

"I'm going to head on home then. I hope everything works out at the school tomorrow," Michael said, preparing to leave.

"I'm sure it will," she said, as they walked out the kitchen. "Kevin, Michael's getting ready to leave. Come and say so long," Carol shouted upstairs, as she walked Michael to the door.

"See you later, Michael. Thanks for my cool jersey," Kevin said, coming downstairs. He gave Michael a pound.

"You're welcome, little man. This weekend, I'll start teaching you how to hold your hands better, okay?"

"Okay."

"Take it easy you two. I'll talk to y'all soon," Michael said.

"Thanks again, Michael," Carol said.

As Michael was driving home, he thought back to Carol's question. He wondered if she was throwing subtle hints at him, by asking him about his writing.

When he arrived home, he hit the shower, then relaxed and watched the Monday night football game, while listening to his messages.

Hello, Mr. Ramsey. This is Yvonne from Rivers, Inc. Ms. Rivers asked me to call, to remind you about getting a few pictures of yourself taken for your new book. She requested you get both headshots and full body shots. Ms. Rivers will be out of town for a few days, but if you have any questions, feel free to give me a call. Thank you.

Man, she's on top of things! He decided to make an appointment with a photographer tomorrow. He had a feeling this book was going to be off the chain. With a custom cover, and a picture of him on it, this one was a sure shot bestseller. At least he prayed that it would be.

Chapter 8

JASMINE and I had an eight o'clock flight to New York on Monday morning. Since I had a closet full of clothes there, I just threw a couple of things in a backpack, grabbed my laptop, and was out the door by six. We had decided to meet at the airport, because Jasmine lived downtown in the Lofts, and it would be easier.

"Michelle!" Jasmine shouted, as she walked up behind me.

"Good morning, Jas. I can't believe you're on time," I said, with a smile.

"I was too excited to sleep…I've been up since four o'clock."

"Let's get our tickets and go through security. You know how long it takes since 9/11," I said.

Before long, we had our tickets, cleared security, and took the train to the other side of the terminal. Hartsfield-Jackson was a huge airport. As soon as we got settled in our seats in the waiting area, Jasmine started the Michael interrogation.

"Okay, Michelle. Your mother isn't here, so tell me what you really thought of Michael Ramsey, and you better not leave anything out," Jasmine said smiling.

"Dang, aren't you nosey this morning! Did you drink your coffee?" I asked.

"Quit stalling and start talking, heffa."

"Alright where shall I begin? Hmmm, Michael is quite handsome, but there's something else about him I can't really describe. You'd have to meet him to understand," I purred. "He has this presence about him, confident but not conceited, and he's a perfect gentleman. He opens your doors, pulls out your chair, and stands when you leave the table. When I was reading his book, *Promise to Love*, I was impressed. But I was sure he'd be this arrogant playboy, but he wasn't, or at least I don't think so," I finished.

"Sounds like he made quite an impression on you Michelle, I haven't seen you talk about anyone like this since Tony died."

"I haven't met anyone who made me take a second look since Tony. You know how much I loved him. I thought I'd never get over losing him. After his accident, I just buried myself in work. Girl, I took as many assignments as I could and traveled, because I always remembered when I came home he wouldn't be there. Eventually, I had to face the reality he was never coming back. I've finally started concentrating on the good times Tony and I shared."

"I know, baby. We were all so worried about you. It was as if you lost a part of yourself when he died," Jasmine said sincerely.

"I did, Jas. Tony was very important to me. We had been together since our junior year of college, and we were going to get married and have a house full of children. He was getting established in the law firm, and my career was taking off. Then everything changed when he was killed in that car accident," I said, taking a deep breath.

As I was in deep thought about Tony, the gate announcer stated, "Good morning everyone. Delta flight 274 to New York will start boarding in ten minutes. We'll start with Medallion Members first, and anyone traveling with small children, or needing assistance. Thank you."

Jasmine and I gathered our things and headed for the gate.

"Good morning, ladies. Can I get you anything to drink?" the attendant asked, after we were seated in first class.

"I'd like a cranberry juice, if you have it," I said.

"I'll have an orange juice, please," Jasmine said.

"What, no coffee?" I asked her surprised.

"Not until we get to New York," Jasmine said laughing. "I'm glad you got first class tickets, because now I can stretch my legs."

"I knew you'd appreciate it. I hate sitting in coach myself. I usually ask for an emergency exit seat, if I don't travel first class, since they have more leg room," I said.

"Okay. Now tell me how we're going to handle things when we get to New York?" Jasmine asked me.

"I've decided to sell my condo back to the corporation instead of subleasing, since I'll be in Atlanta permanently. It doesn't make sense for me to hold on to it. The moving company is coming tomorrow. I'm sending my Lladros collection by Fed Ex. I don't want to take any chances with them getting broken, so I want to pack them myself. After that, I thought we'd do dinner at *BBQ's* and catch that play, *Meet the Browns.*"

"Will we have time to do some shopping? I want to go down to the garment district," Jasmine said.

"Yes, Jas. We don't fly back to Atlanta until Wednesday evening, and I've reserved a car service, since we'll be staying at the hotel Tuesday evening."

"It seems like you thought of everything Ms. Rivers. Why did I think otherwise?" Jasmine said laughing.

"I don't know, Ms. Washington. You've known me since knee-highs and bubblegum," I said, laughing with her.

Before long, we arrived in New York and hit the ground running. We caught a cab into the city, and arrived at my condo, where we were greeted by building security.

"Good morning, Ms. Rivers," the security guard said.

"As Salaam Alaikum, Raheem," I said.

"Wa Laikum as Salaam," Raheem replied.

Jasmine held her tongue until we were in the elevator. "When did you start speaking Arabic, heffa?"

"I don't really speak Arabic, I just know a couple words of greeting," I said.

"If you say so, but you could've fooled me back there."

As soon as I unlocked the door, Jasmine walked over to the window and looked out. I had a nice view of the park from the 10th floor.

"I know you'll miss living here, Michelle. This view takes my breath away every time I see it," Jasmine said.

"It's quite beautiful, isn't it? It was the first thing I noticed when I found this apartment. I opened the door, saw the view, and fell in love instantly before I saw the rest of the apartment. I spent many nights, just sitting on the couch gazing out the window. I'll miss living here. I thought about keeping it, but I can't justify paying a mortgage on a place that would remain empty most of the time," I said. "Jas, why don't you take your things to the guest room and get settled? Then we can go get breakfast before getting started."

"Sounds good to me, where we going for breakfast?" Jasmine asked.

"There's a small coffee shop around the corner, or we can go up to Harlem to *IHOP*, but it's usually crowded this time of morning."

"The coffee shop is fine. That way, I can hear more about your meeting with Michael."

"Dang, Jas. Why don't we just go to Philly, so you can meet the man yourself," I said jokingly.

"Do we have time for that?" Jasmine asked, winking at me, before continuing down the hall to the guest room.

I had to laugh at my best friend. I bet if we had time, she would actually be game for going to Philly and meeting Michael. I decided to check in at the office, and call my mom, to let her know we had arrived safely. I dialed the office first.

"Good morning, Rivers, Inc.," Yvonne said, answering the phone.

"Good morning, Yvonne. This is Michelle. I just wanted to let you know we arrived safely. So how's everything going?" I asked.

"Hi, Michelle. Everything is going fine, and before you ask, I left a message for Mr. Ramsey on Friday, reminding him to get the pictures done."

"Great. I'd like you to do something else for me. Ms. Carrion's book comes out this weekend, and I want you to order some flowers and balloons to be sent to her, with a card that reads: *To the success of your new book. May it fly off the shelves*, and sign it from the Rivers, Inc. Publishing Family. And another thing, please check with David to find out the time of her book signing at Camp Creek on Saturday. I plan on attending."

"No problem. When would you like for them to deliver the flowers and balloons?"

"Tomorrow or Wednesday should be soon enough. I'm also going to have some packages delivered to the office. When they arrive, just put them in my office."

"Okay," she said.

"I'll see you on Thursday. Have a good day," I said.

"Bye, Michelle," Yvonne said, hanging up.

Next, I called my mother, so she and daddy wouldn't start worrying.

"Hello, Mom. We made it," I said, when she picked up the phone.

"Hi Michelle, I was waiting on you to call me before I went out," she said. "So, what are you two girls up to?"

"We're about to go out to breakfast, and then come back to pack up my figurine collection and send it off. Then pack the clothes I'm going to bring back with me. The movers will take care of everything else tomorrow."

"Sounds like you have everything under control," Mom said.

"Yes Mommy, Jasmine just walked back into the room, so we're out of here. Give Daddy my love and I'll call y'all when we get back Wednesday night."

"Hi Mom" Jasmine yelled out.

"Tell Jas I said hello, and y'all be careful up there," she said.

"Yes Mommy. We love you, bye."

"Bye, baby," Mom said, as she hung up.

"Are you ready to go get our eat on Jas?" I asked.

"Yes ma'am, Lead the way, I'm in need of coffee," she said.

We grabbed our coats and headed out the door. *I won't miss this cold weather when I leave New York, that's for sure. Old Man Winter was nothing to play with up here, and it was quite windy outside*, I thought, shivering.

As soon as we were seated, and Jasmine had her coffee and I had my tea, Jasmine started with the questions again.

"Okay, heffa. I've waited long enough. Start talking about the writer, because the suspense is killing me!"

"Damn, Jas, you're an impatient woman," I said laughing. "There's not a lot more to tell you. I just met the man. He lives in Philly, and works for the city in the Planning Department. He said he's mentor to a little boy with the Big Brothers of America program. He's close to his parents, and very close to his little sister, who's away at college and plays basketball."

"Keep going. Is he involved with anyone?"

"Boy, are you nosey," I said. "Yes, he's involved with someone, but he said it wasn't serious."

"Hmmm, okay. So, he's available…good," Jasmine, said, with a huge smile on her face.

"Jasmine, get that look off your face. The man writes for my company."

"And your point would be? It's not a conflict of interest, Michelle. The man doesn't work for you directly."

"Jasmine, I repeat, I just met the man. Give me a chance to find out whether he has any bad habits before you have me married to him," I said, laughing again. "Oh, thank God, here comes our food," I said, as the waiter approached our table.

"Michelle Rivers, you're not off the hook yet," Jasmine said, laughing and shaking her fork at me.

We are almost finished eating, before she started asking me questions again.

"That was good, I can't eat another bite. Now I remember you saying that Michael has a friend who lives in Atlanta. Do you know anything about him?"

"Jasmine, you're a mess, girl. Okay, let me see. His friend's name is Alex, and he's very good looking. About 6'3, piercing brown eyes, black hair closely cut, dark complexion, and I couldn't help but notice he had a dimple when he smiled."

"What's his status? Does he have a job, and is he single?"

"Dang, woman, I don't know all that. We only talked for a minute, but I'm sure we'll find out soon enough. I'm planning a Christmas party for the staff, their families and our writers in December. I'll extend an invitation to Alex if Michael comes. As a matter of fact, I'm pushing for Michael's book to be released at the same time, if it's ready. We can make this a book release celebration also."

"Michelle, that sounds like a great idea. What can I do to help?"

"I'll let you know, Yvonne is working on finding a location now, and setting up a DJ and caterer. We're either going to have it at the Masonic lodge or the Embassy Suites Hotel. I'm hoping the hotel has space, so that I can rent a block of rooms also."

"Well, if Yvonne isn't able to get the hotel, perhaps I can pull some strings and get it. You know I have connections through my travel agency. Do you have an idea of which location you want to use…by the airport or Buckhead?"

"I was thinking near the airport, but either one would be find with me. Thanks for offering your help, girl. I'll have Yvonne call you when we get back to Atlanta."

"That's what friends are. And instead of you having Yvonne call me, I'll contact her when I get back, and we'll put our heads together and do the damn thing."

"Okay. Let's get out of here and get this packing out the way, so we can have a night on the town," I said, signaling the waitress for our check.

"Sounds like a plan. Lead the way, lady," Jasmine said.

After paying the check, we headed back to my condo, and started packing my figurines. I'm glad I had kept the original boxes, because it made things easier. I put on a pot of coffee for Jasmine…so she could feed her addiction. We called Fed Ex to pick up the boxes, and then moved on to the den and my bedroom.

"Michelle, I see you removed the picture of Tony from the nightstand," Jasmine said, looking at me.

"It was time, Jasmine. I put it on the bookshelf in the den…with all my other pictures," I said smiling. Jasmine walked over and hugged me.

"I'm happy to see you're moving on with your life, sweetie, Tony wouldn't have wanted you to stop living because he died," she said.

"Moving forward with my life hasn't been easy, but I'm doing it. Now, let's finish packing the clothes that I'm taking back to Atlanta with us. We'll leave the rest for the moving company, because we have a play to attend tonight!"

By early evening, we had finished packing my suitcases with clothes, and sealed the final boxes in the den. I went through the kitchen, and threw out all the opened packages. Then I took a final look around to see if we had missed anything. I was really going to miss my condo. I had a lot of pleasant memories of this place, but it was time to move on to bigger and better things. I just wish my uncle didn't have to die for me to realize it. Life was indeed short.

* * *

Jasmine and I shared a wonderful dinner at *BBQ's*. We arrived at the theater just as the curtains went up at eight o'clock. When they said the play would start on time…they weren't kidding.

After the play, we decided to call it a night since we had to get up early in the morning for the moving company. I had enjoyed spending time with my best friend. It had been too long since we'd a chance to hang out with each other.

Neither of us could sleep, and ended up in the kitchen for some sister-talk.

"I see I'm not the only one who couldn't sleep," I said to Jasmine, as she entered the kitchen.

"I guess it has to do with sleeping in a strange bed, no matter how comfortable it may be. Then I thought I heard you moving around and decided to join you," Jasmine said.

"Can I interest you in some hot chocolate?"

"Yes, I'd love some. Do you remember when we had sleepovers, and your mom would make us hot chocolate and popcorn?" Jasmine asked.

"How could I forget? I think you spent more time at my house than your own," I said.

"That's because there was peace and quiet at your house. Between my parents fighting, and my brothers arguing, I would much rather be at your house than mine."

"I was happy to have you, Jas. Before I met you, I spent many lonely days. My parents were wonderful, but I needed someone my own age to talk to and share things with. I'm happy it was you," I said smiling.

"I'm happy it was me too," Jas said laughing, as I reached over and playfully hit her on the arm.

"Let's rinse out these cups and go talk in my bedroom. Go grab the pillows off your bed," I said.

Soon we were settled in my bed, propped up against the headboard.

"Daddy came over to help me pack away Uncle Billy clothes and other personal things. We've decided to donate his clothes to the men's shelter they both volunteered for, and sell the furniture I'm not keeping," I said.

"That sounds like a good idea. How's your dad holding up?"

"You know my dad, he's putting up a good front, but I know he's really hurting. Uncle Billy and he were more than brothers…they were best friends. He's going to keep most of the jewelry, and give a few pieces to special friends. We still have to decide what to do about the Harley; it's too big for me to be riding."

"I forgot you could ride a motorcycle. Your mom would have a fit if she knew you were thinking of keeping that thing," Jas said laughing. "I remember when your dad taught you to ride; she was fit to be tied."

"Oh my God that was the first time I ever remember them arguing. She was off the hook mad. She read Daddy the riot act, but he didn't back down. He told her that he'd teach her to ride too, if she wasn't so afraid of messing up her hair," I said, as we laughed together. "Mommy took off upstairs and slammed the door. I think Daddy slept in the guest room that night. But he still taught me to ride, and she never said another word about it, except, to remind me to be careful and to wear my helmet at all times."

"That's what I loved about being around you and your parents Michelle, The way y'all show love. I wish my family was more like yours," she said, with a sigh.

"Well, you know we love you too, Jasmine. Our family wouldn't have been complete without you in it."

"I'm grateful you've always shared them with me. More than you know," she said seriously.

"Okay, enough of the mushy stuff. Let me tell you about these pictures I found when I was going through the desk in my uncle's den. Remember I told you I was getting strange vibes from one of my editors, Pam?"

"Yeah, I remember you mentioning her. What's up?" Jasmine asked curiously.

"Well, I found some pictures of her and my uncle, and they looked pretty close. In some of the pictures, she wasn't wearing much, if you know what I mean. I should've brought them with me. Remind me to show them to you when we get back home, okay?" I told her.

"Uh oh, sounds like Uncle Billy was getting his freak on. I'm not mad at him!" Jas said laughing so hard she almost fell off the bed.

"Heffa, that's my uncle you're talking about!" I said, before joining her in laughter. "Damn, now I can't get that picture out my head. The thought of Uncle Billy and Pam doing the nasty…yuck," I said.

"Well, your uncle was a good looking man. You can't really blame her for sleeping with him."

"I don't blame her, but I wonder if there was more to it than that. She does act a little strange around me at times. Like she resents that I'm in charge," I explained.

"Well, if she does, then it's too bad for her. You're in charge, and she better get used to it, or find somewhere else to work," she said seriously. "I'm so glad you're moving back to Atlanta. Now I'll get a chance to see you more than every few months."

"You'll probably see so much of me, you'll wish I was back in New York," I said, laughing and reaching over to give her a hug.

"Seriously, Michelle, I've missed having you near. It wasn't fun going shopping by myself. I stopped doing clubs all together." Jasmine sighed.

"You sound like you don't have any other friends," I said sadly. "And I know that's not true. What gives, lady?"

"Yes, I have other friends, but it isn't the same, and you know it."

"I do know what you're talking about. You and I have a special connection, and no one can touch that," I said.

"Exactly now do you really think Michael's friend was cute or what?"

"Oh no, we're not back on that, are we?" I said laughing. "Heffa, take your butt to sleep."

"Nope, I want to talk about Michael and his friend. Why don't you call him up, and ask him if his friend is single, available or gay, please?"

"Oh hell no, I'm not calling to ask him that." I glanced over at clock, and saw the time. "It's three o'clock in the morning. Jasmine, don't make me beat you. I know I can still take you."

"You know there are a lot of men running around Atlanta who aren't into women, or on the down low, so you have to ask," she said.

"Jasmine, I'm not calling Michael at three o'clock in the morning, and asking if his friend is straight," I said, laughing and coughing. "Good night, I love you," I said, pulling the covers over my head and laughing some more.

"Good night, Michelle. I love you too. But this conversation isn't over!" she said, as she turned over on her side and settled down.

"I didn't think it was," I said, groaning and closing my eyes to get a few hours sleep.

Chapter 9

"HEY Michael, How's your day going?" Sara asked. "I haven't seen you all day."

"It's going pretty well, Sara. I was in the field most of today, going over a proposed playground site with some neighborhood task force members," Michael said, entering the office.

"You had a call today from the *Forever Yours Photography*. They left a message that you have a six o'clock photo shoot this evening."

"That's great. I'm going to take some shots for my book," he said excitedly. "I need your opinion on something, Sara. Do you think I should take the pictures with this blue suit or with this outfit?" he asked, showing her a burgundy long sleeved silk shirt and black pants.

"It really doesn't matter, Michael. Most books that I've read only have head shots of the author, so whichever outfit you pick will be okay," she said.

"Thanks. I think I'm going to wear the silk shirt and pants for the shoot," Michael said.

"Good choice. I think you'll look sexy with that hook up on," she said laughing.

The rest of Michael's day seemed to go by rather quickly. The anticipation of his first real photo shoot was getting to him. He thought the idea of putting a picture of him on the book was a good one. He had seen many authors' picture on the back cover, with their bio below it.

He arrived at the photography studio about fifteen minutes early. The receptionist greeted him in the lobby.

"Good evening, and welcome to *Forever Yours Photography*. Can I help you?" she asked smiling.

"Yes, you may. My name is Michael Ramsey, and I have a six o'clock appointment with a Mr. Chris Johnson for a photo shoot." She laughed when he said that, and then abruptly stopped.

"Please forgive me for laughing, but Chris Johnson is a woman." Michael joined her in laughter. He felt so embarrassed.

"I'm glad she wasn't standing here to hear me say that. I would've just curled up in a ball if she was," Michael said.

""Wait a minute," she said in a serious tone. "Are you Michael Ramsey, the writer The Michael Ramsey that wrote *Promise of Love?*"

"Yes, I'm one and the same," Michael, said.

She let out a muffled scream, and then reached into her desk drawer and pulled out a copy of his book.

"Can I please have your autograph, Mr. Ramsey?" she asked, barely able to contain herself.

"No problem. What's your name?" he asked, reaching into his suit jacket for a pen.

"Belinda Coles," she said, as she came and stood by his side. "I can't believe this," she kept saying over and over to herself.

Michael wrote, *To Belinda with all my love, Michael Ramsey.*

"So, I take it you liked the book," Michael said smiling.

"You don't even want me to start telling you for real," she said. "Would you like some cappuccino or a glass of white wine while you're waiting?"

"I'll have some wine, if it's no problem," he said politely.

"It's no problem. Have a seat, and I'll be right back."

As he was waiting for Belinda to come back, he overheard her talking.

"Girl, you'll never guess who's sitting here in the studio. Michael Ramsey. Yeah, the one that wrote that hot ass book. He signed my copy, and he is so cute too! Chile, let me get off this phone so I can go and look at him some more. I'll talk to you later, and stop hating." She quickly went to the break room for the wine.

"Here you are, Mr. Ramsey," she said, handing him a glass of white zinfandel.

"Thank you, and you can call me Michael, okay?"

"Okay, and you can call me hot...I mean Belinda," she said, as they both smiled. "I'll let Chris know you're here," she said. "Chris, your six o'clock appointment has arrived," she said over the intercom, still looking at Michael.

"I'm finishing up. I'll be out in a moment," Chris told her.

Moments later, the door to the photography room swung open, and two children came bustling through, with a man and woman walking slowly behind them. Michael was guessing it was a family portrait she had just completed.

"I'll see you on Friday, so you can view your proofs," Chris told them. "You children be good now."

"Okay, Chris, and thanks again," the gentleman said.

"You must be Michael Ramsey. I'm Christina Johnson," she said, extending her hand to Michael. "I've been expecting you. Won't you come into my office, and you can bring your glass with you."

Chris was gorgeous. She was about five feet tall, with an almond complexion, green eyes, and shoulder length, light brown hair. She wore tight black jeans and a close fitting sweater.

"Please have a seat, Mr. Ramsey. What can I do for you this evening?" she asked.

Michael's mind had a few thoughts about what she could do for him. "I need to take some head shots and a few full body shots, for the cover of a book that I've written. I need all eight by tens."

"I don't know if I've ever read anything by you. Is this your first book?" she asked, while sipping from her glass.

"I've written two books actually. My second book, *Promise of Love*, made the Times bestsellers list."

"I'm impressed. I'll have to look for it the next time I'm in the bookstore. Any particular type of poses you're interested in?" She had to smile at her own statement after she said it.

"I have a couple I can think of right off the top of my head," Michael said, smiling at her. "But you're the pro, so you lead the way. One thing though, I want to change into this outfit I brought with me."

"Let me see the color scheme, and I'll figure out a nice background for you." Michael showed her the outfit. "Okay burgundy and black. I have a few ideas. Why don't you change in the room over there, and I'll start setting up. Would you care for another glass of wine?" she asked.

"Yes, please" he said, as he walked towards the dressing room.

She had an elaborate studio. It was filled with different backgrounds, flood and strobe lights, umbrellas, booms, cocoons, and so many cameras and monitors; it would make your head spin. Michael could tell this was a real pro he was dealing with.

When he stepped out of the dressing room, the entire studio seemed to have transformed. Cameras of all different sizes, with many different sized lenses, were set up from quite a few angles. He could also see himself in a monitor across the room.

"Michael, I need you to stand over here for the moment. When I tell you, I want you to take half steps around slowly, and turn your head in whatever direction you feel comfortable. Do you think you can do that?" she asked, as she directed him in front of a light gray textured looking canvas. "I have a video running also, but it's more or less a tool to help me improve my photo taking technique. If you have a problem with it running, I'll turn it off."

"It's not a problem, Chris," Michael said, as he did exactly what she asked.

"Oh yes, very nice. Wait until you see the way the background enhances the colors you're wearing, along with your complexion. I want you to keep as serious a face as possible. As I'm moving around you, try not to look directly at me," she said, snapping pictures from every angle. "Now smile for me very, very slowly, and gradually work towards a big one. I know you're not a professional model, but you look like one. You're doing very well," she said, while the cameras never stopped flashing. This was a true photo session. She was the artist, and Michael was the canvas.

"Okay, step this way, please," she said, as she led Michael onto a taupe colored canvas, and again snapped away. The difference this time was he sat on a padded stool and remained as motionless as possible, while she zoomed, faded, and angled all around him. All told, Michael was at her studio for an hour and a half.

"Michael, thank you so much for choosing *Forever Yours* for your photography needs. I'll have your proofs ready by Friday for you to review," she said, as they shook hands.

"Thank you, Chris. I'm looking forward to seeing them," Michael said, as he walked out the studio.

On his way home, he stopped by the *Hideaway Lounge* to get a nightcap before he called it a night. He liked the spot, because you could get a quick meal, and it was close to his place. He used to go to school with the cook, who was the bomb.

"Hey Tim how you doing brother" Michael asked when he saw Tim coming out the kitchen area.

"Hey, Writer Mike. What's going on, man?" He had called Michael that ever since they were in high school. That's when Michael first started writing. Back then it was just a lot of poetry.

"I've been trying to keep a low profile, Tim," Michael said. "Let me get some wings, potato salad and greens," he told Tim, as his stomach growled in agreement.

"I'll bring it to you when it's done."

"Okay, thanks. I'm going to be sitting at the bar."

Michael eased over to the bar, and ordered a scotch on the rocks and a cold beer. This was a nice adult spot to have a drink and socialize. He knew most of the people that frequented there.

"Hey Michael nice to see you again," a sexy voice called to him.

He turned toward the voice, and saw that it was Wanda. "Hey, Wanda. You're looking well. How are you?"

"I'm doing fine, handsome. You're looking good yourself. I just stopped by to grab a drink before I head in. What brings you by?" she asked.

"I wanted to get some grub before I went home myself. Are you here with someone?" he asked.

"I came with my girlfriend, Stacy. That's her sitting over at the table with the green blouse. So tell me Michael, when are we going to find time to hang out?" she asked, while looking him directly in the eyes.

"Hopefully we'll be able to hook up soon. I've just been busy," he told her.

"Well, that's a relief. I was hoping you weren't avoiding me. I won't bite you too hard." She laughed and gently touched him on his earlobe.

"If you keep that up, it'll be very soon, baby." Her touch felt really amazing.

"Well, it was nice seeing you again. I don't want Stacy to be by herself too long. Michael, use my card, that's why I gave it to you," she said, reminding him that she had given him a card with her number on it.

"You'll be hearing from me soon, I promise," Michael said smiling.

"Well, I hope so. You take it easy," she said, kissing him on the cheek.

She turned and walked back to her table. Michael sat watching, admiring her curves. *I don't know why it's taken me so long to get with her. She's built like a brick house*, he thought to himself.

Tim walked over to Michael, carrying his platter.

"This looks good, brother," Michael said.

"You know how I roll, Mike," Tim said. Michael gave him a ten spot for his troubles. "I hope you enjoy it," he said.

Michael grabbed the barmaid's attention, and asked her to send Wanda and her friend whatever they were drinking. After Michael ate and grabbed another cold one for the road, he headed home. He felt like a stuffed turkey. Tim had outdone himself this time. When he got home, he checked his messages.

Michael, this is Mom. I need to get to the eye doctor's by four tomorrow, so I'll see you then. Bye, bye.

"Okay, Mom," he said to the phone.

How are you, Michael? This is Carol. I just wanted to call to tell you that the meeting went well with Kevin's principal. He agreed with what I said, and the suspension was rescinded and wiped off his record. I'll talk to you soon, and thanks.

That was a relief, but Michael had known she was going to make out well. Kevin was one hundred percent right by defending himself, and should have never been suspended.

The meal was catching up with Michael like a sleeping pill. He took a quick shower, and then crashed for the night.

* * *

Seven o'clock Wednesday morning seemed to come quickly. But the sunrise wasn't helping Michael's body rise out of his warm bed. He decided to call out from work and sleep in. He wasn't one to miss work, but this morning would be an exception.

Hello, Sara, I'm not feeling so hot this morning. Let them know I won't be in today, will you?" he said, when she answered the phone.

"Okay, Michael. Take care of yourself, and I hope you feel better," she said.

"Thank you, Sara," Michael said, as he went back to sleep. He finally got up around ten, and went to the *Wawa* to grab the Daily News.

"Do you come here often?" a familiar voice said behind him.

"Hey, Carol," Michael said, turning around and shaking his head. "Yes, I do. As a matter of fact, I live right around the corner."

"I usually stop here to grab a coffee on my way to work," she said, filling her cup up at the coffee bar. "I took off today, just in case Kevin had to stay home. I guess you're doing the same thing," she said smiling.

"You got that right. I decided to take a mental health day today."

"Did you get my message?" she asked.

"Yeah, I got it. I was going to call you later, so you could give me the details of your meeting."

"Well, here I am," she said softly. "You said you live around the corner, right? Why don't you show me your place? I'll treat you to coffee and a Danish, while I tell you what happened with my meeting at his school."

"That sounds good. But you're not allowed to laugh at my bachelor pad when you see it," Michael said jokingly.

"Don't worry, your secret will be safe with me," she promised.

Since Michael had walked the two blocks to the store, he rode back with Carol. After they arrived at his house, Michael took her jacket and hung it in the closet, as well as his own. He put some jazz on the stereo, and the nervousness he felt having her over was slowly subsiding.

"Michael, you have a nice house. Why would I laugh at your place? You keep it very clean," she said, in admiration. "I've seen some bachelor pads, as you call them, and this one isn't typical."

"My mother is a stickler for neatness. I remember when I was growing up, I couldn't leave the house unless my bed was made up, and everything put away. Once, I had a sock on the floor after I cleaned my room, and she made me clean it all over again. It's stuck with me since that time," he told her.

"This is a nice piece you've got here. Who's the artist?" she asked, taking a walking tour around his house.

"I got that piece on a trip to Chicago, while on a book signing tour. The artist name is Roxie Johnson. All the art I have was done by African-American artists," Michael said proudly.

"You have good taste. I'd like to get some art of my own. My walls are bare, and some nice art would bring my rooms to life."

"Well, last Friday I met a brother in Atlanta named Damon Jennings, and he has some art that will knock your thong off," Michael said smiling.

"How do you know I have on a thong?" Carol asked smiling.

"It was just a figure of speech, Carol." They both laughed. "I'm expecting a piece I ordered from him any day now. When I get it, I'll show it to you."

"Thank you. Now let me tell you about my meeting with Kevin's principal," Carol said.

They sat down on the sofa, along with their coffee and Danish. Michael couldn't keep his eyes off her. He was feeling something that maybe he shouldn't. He'd hate to ruin anything that would have an impact on him and Kevin.

"His principal was very cordial, but I was ready to read him the riot act. I had to back off, because he was so nice and attentive. Kevin explained to him what happened, and how he did at first try to avoid any confrontation with the other boy. I told him how I taught Kevin to respond to bullying by telling the teacher the first time, and then knocking his head off if it happened again. His principal laughed, and said not to worry about the suspension, because another witness had stepped forward and told him the same thing that Kevin said. He did, however, explain to Kevin that he could come to his office if anything happened again. Kevin's teacher explained to him his grades were very good, and fighting, or generally being disruptive, wasn't in Kevin's character. That worked in his favor."

"I'm so glad that everything worked out. I know from my dealings with him, Kevin's a good kid. But push him in a corner, and you're in trouble," Michael said knowingly.

"You're exactly right. After you left our house the other night, and you told him you would teach him how to defend himself, he told me that he loved you. I was surprised, because he's never told me that about any man. Not even his uncles. When his father died, I thought I'd get more support from his uncles. But they never visit him, call or anything. So I don't press the issue," Carol said sadly.

Michael could see the tears starting to well up in her eyes. He grabbed a tissue, and told her everything happens for a reason, and that everything would be fine. She leaned her head over and rested it on his chest.

"I love Kevin, too. I never knew I'd get so attached to him, but I have. When people ask me if I have any brothers or sisters, I tell them, yes indeed...I have a sister and a brother."

Carol smiled, looked Michael directly in his eyes, and gently leaned in and kissed him. He was hesitant at first, but then the feeling overtook him. Their kiss became more intense, and as it did, he felt her hands pulling on the string of his sweatpants. Once inside, she gently stroked his manhood, which grew by the second. Her hands felt so good, and her kisses had him on fire. Michael stood up and led her to his bedroom.

They sat on the edge of the bed, as he reached for her sweater and pulled it over her head. Her stomach was so smooth. He leaned in to kiss it, while she held his head. Michael loosened the clasp of her red lace bra, exposing the most beautiful breasts he had ever seen. He slowly reached up, and gently nibbled on her large hardened nipples. Her moans of pleasure filled the room. Michael pulled off his sweatshirt, as she undid her jeans and pulled them off, along with her red-laced thong. Carol and Michael both smiled, thinking back to their earlier conversation.

She pushed him back on the bed, as she freed his swelling member from the confines of his sweats. She straddled his waist, leaned in and passionately kissed him. He slipped his hand down to her pussy, which was already moist, hot and ready. He gently laid her on her back, and massaged her hardened button, so he could retrieve his prize. Methodically, he nibbled and sucked each breast. Her nipples grew harder with every flick of his tongue. Her moans became louder with each touch, and she squeezed his nipples, which sent him into his own moans of pleasure. Michael descended down, planting soft kisses along the way, until he reached her valley. She opened her legs wider and exposed the largest clit he'd ever seen.

"Oh, Michael, eat my pussy," she whispered, in pure ecstasy. He obliged her.

Her lips quivered, as he tasted her sweet box, and sucked gently on her swollen pearl. She shuddered and moaned even louder.

"Oh Michael yes. Yes, baby, lick it."

He slid his hands under her firm ass, giving him even more access to her quivering vagina.

"You like that, Carol?" he said, in a muffled tone. "Move your ass, baby, move your ass," he commanded.

Suddenly she screamed out, "I'm cumming!" She panted and moaned, and screamed again. "Michael...oh shit hell yeah!" A gush of her juices came pouring out of her, as he continued to lick and suck...lapping it up like a puppy. "I want you inside of me, give it to me, baby," she said hoarsely.

Michael made a path slowly up to her mouth, kissing her stomach and breasts along the way. He forced his tongue in her hot mouth as far as he could get it, without choking her. He put on a condom, and placed his vibrating dick at the opening of her hole. She grabbed his ass, trying to push him inside of her. He held back a little and continued to kiss her wildly.

"Don't tease me, Michael, give it to me. Please give it to me," Carol whimpered, in his ear.

Michael entered her inch by inch, as Carol moaned in pleasure. Then back out he came. He pushed in a little more, and then out again.

"Damn, you feel good," he whispered.

He couldn't hold back any more, her pussy felt too good. He plunged deeper inside her with all that he had, and her fingernails dug into his ass, sending a sharp pain up his back.

"Oh, yes, give it to me," she ordered, and he was more then willing.

In and out he plunged, deeper and deeper inside of her. She was meeting his every down stroke with an upward push. They were in sync. Her sweetness and his plunging member were making gushing sounds together, that seemed to radiate through the room.

"Do you like this dick, Carol?" Michael asked.

"Yes oh hell yes. I love this dick...don't stop, Michael," Carol moaned.

He withdrew from her hot box, turned her over, and pulled her up on her knees. He wasted no time at all, as he entered her from the back. He was inside of her, and she was slamming her ass back towards him.

"Come and get this dick, Carol. Bring that ass back here," he growled. "Am I hitting this pussy right, am I?" he demanded.

"You know it, baby. Give it here, give it the hell here," she said loudly.

He was knee deep inside her honey pot, reaching under her from time to time, to rub her hardened clit.

He pulled out of her, and said, "Ride me, baby. Come on."

Carol straddled him, while gazing deep into his eyes with a sultry, sexy look. She slowly eased down on his awaiting rod, still moist and glistening from the juices of her dripping valley.

"Oh yes, baby, fuck me," Michael moaned, as her pussy tightened around his dick.

She placed her hands on his chest, and rode him like a jockey in the Kentucky Derby. Faster and faster she wiggled, and plunged herself down onto Michael's hardened tool.

"Kiss me, baby," he said. She leaned down and her lips met his.

Not missing a beat, she cried out, "I'm cumming again, baby!" Her body shook, and her pussy tightened on his rod. But this time, he was joining her in the realm of no return.

"Ahhhhhh shit, Carol!" He slid out of her, holding his tool at the base, turned her on her back, pulled the condom off and exploded all over her stomach and breasts.

He collapsed beside her, as she got on top of him. He put his arms around her, and they kissed and grinded until they came to a stop. Sweat was pouring off the both of them.

"Damn, Michael," Carol gasped. They both began to laugh.

Michael was still throbbing. Juices from her quivering honey pot ran down his shaft, and onto his thighs.

"What did we just do, Michael?" she asked, with a big smile on her lips.

Without a word, he pulled her face to his and kissed her softly, and then harder, more passionate.

"I'm not sure," he said, as they drifted off to sleep.

After a few hours, Michael was surprised to awaken and find Carol gone. She did leave a note:

Michael,

When I woke up, you were sleeping like a baby, so I didn't wake you. I can't explain what happened this morning, but I will say that it was exceptional. Hopefully, it didn't cloud our friendship. I felt the need to release myself, and what better way than with someone I trust. You're a wonderful lover, and I apologize if I made you feel uncomfortable with what we did. I'll talk to you soon.

Carol

"She doesn't have to worry about me feeling uncomfortable about what happened. In fact, I'm ready for it to happen again, but I realize we can't let it happen again. At least I think not. I'd hate to complicate things with Kevin, and our relationship as brothers must not be compromised," he said out loud.

Around three o'clock, Michael headed over to his mom's to take her to her eye doctor appointment.

"Mom, it's me. Are you almost ready?" he asked, walking in the house and calling upstairs.

"I'll be down in a minute," she responded. "The sweet potato pie is in the refrigerator if you want some."

"You know it," he said, making his way toward the kitchen. His mom made the best sweet potato pie.

"Hello, Michael. How are you?" his mom said, walking into the kitchen and kissing him on the cheek.

"I'm alright. How are you feeling?"

"Oh, I'm doing fine for an old lady."

"Please, Mom, you look better than some of these young girls out here," he said, as she smiled.

"Well, I wish you'd tell Arthur that, so he'd get off my case."

"Arthur who?" he asked, not knowing who she was talking about.

"Arthritis, he's one of the *itis* brothers," she said. Michael fell out laughing.

"Mom, get out of here. Listen, I took a piece from the pie that was already sliced. This other one is mine, right?"

"Oh, you're trying to double clutch on the pie, huh?" She smiled. "Yes, the other one is for you to take home."

"Thanks. This tastes good," Michael said, giving her a hug. "I'm going to grab it when we come back."

"Okay. We better be on our way. You know I don't like being late."

"I know. That's why I got here a little early."

While they were driving to the doctor's office, she told him that one of her friends read his book and couldn't put it down.

"Martha read your book, and told me she really liked it. She told everyone down at the beauty salon I had a son that was writing all this hot stuff." She giggled.

Michael laughed along with her. He could just see Miss Martha sitting there, getting all hot and bothered, reading a passage from his book. His mom and Miss Martha were only in their fifties, and he wouldn't consider that old at all. If anything, it would make them want to keep their motors running.

"What you smiling at, boy?" his mom asked laughing, as they pulled up to the doctor's office.

"Nothing Mom"

Chapter 10

BACK at Rivers, Inc., John was preparing to have his regular staff meeting. He stopped by Yvonne's office, to see if she had anything from Michelle that the staff needed to be brought up to speed on.

"Good morning, Yvonne. How's it going?" he said, walking into her office, with his ever-present cup of coffee.

"Good morning, John. Everything is going okay. I see you found the coffee. Did you leave any for the rest of the staff?" she said, smiling at him.

"I may have left a cup, but if they don't get it soon, I'm going to drink that too," he said, as he sipped his brew.

Shaking her head, Yvonne said, "What can I do for you, John?"

"I just came by to see if Michelle had anything she wanted me to tell the staff during our meeting."

"No, she left everything in your more then capable hands. However, I did receive a call from Damon Jennings, who's designing Mr. Ramsey's cover. He said he'd have some designs ready for review on Monday," she told him.

"Alright I'll let Pam know, so a time and date can be arranged for Mr. Ramsey to be here for the review. I'll be in my office if you need me," John said, as he left her office.

"Okay, and stay away from the coffee!" she called out, chuckling to herself.

Making his way to the conference room, John stopped in the staff lounge to get another cup of coffee. He ran into David Hale, who was on his way to the meeting.

"Good morning, John. I'm on my way to the conference room for the staff meeting," David said.

"Good morning, David. We can walk together, and you can tell me how your writing is coming along."

"It's coming along great, sir."

"What I tell you about calling me sir? Oh, never mind. Are you ready to share what you've written with us yet, son?"

"Not quite, but soon," David said, with a wide grin on his face.

"Okay. We're looking forward to reading it," John said, as they reached the conference room. Pam was already there waiting.

"Good morning, Pam. I can't believe we didn't have to send the search party out for you this morning," John said jokingly.

"Good morning, John, David. I'm never that late and you know it," Pam said, with a laugh. "And how many cups of coffee have you had so far?"

"Don't worry about my coffee intake," John said, with a smile. "Let's wait a few more minutes before we get this meeting started," he said. "Let me call Gayle, and see what's holding up the others."

"You know you love us, John," Pam said, with a laugh.

"Hold that thought, Pam," he said, as he dialed his secretary "Hey, Gayle, do you have any messages for me?"

"I was on my way to see you. Brandon's still out sick, Tina's out of town for a funeral, and Elaine's having a breakfast meeting with one of her writers," she said.

"Okay, Gayle, thanks," he told her.

"Will you need me to take notes of the meeting?"

"No, this will be brief. I'll talk to you when I'm finished with Pam and David," he said, before hanging up. Turning to David and Pam, John said, "Okay young David, why don't you go first, since your writer's book comes out this weekend."

"Ms. Carrion's book, *All Halo's Eve*, is being released on Friday. She'll be doing a book signing on Saturday in Morrow. I'll be attending to represent Rivers, Inc. She called me last night all excited, because she received flowers and balloons from the company," he told them.

"Sounds good, David. The flowers and balloons were a nice touch," John said.

"I can't take the credit for them…I didn't send them. I asked Yvonne who sent them when I got in this morning. She told me Michelle told her to send them," David said.

"It looks like our new CEO is on top of things. Okay, Pam. Tell us how everything is going on your end?" John said, glancing her way.

"Everything is right on schedule. I'll be finished editing Mr. Ramsey's book by the end of the day. Ms. Matthews' book is finished, and with the proof-readers for their final review before we send it to the printers," she said.

"That's very good, Pam. I understand Mr. Ramsey is going to have his picture included with this book," John said.

"I didn't realize that," Pam said, looking confused.

"Perhaps it was something he set up with Michelle when they had their meeting. Nonetheless, Yvonne said the artist called and said he'd have something available for review by Monday. I need you to get in touch with Mr. Ramsey, to set up a date and time for him to come down and review them," John said.

"No problem. I'll give him a call today and get that taken care of," she said, a little sharply.

"Does either of you have anything else for me?" John asked.

"No, sir, I believe I'm straight," David said.

"No, that's it for me also," Pam said.

"David, I have a book I want you to get started on. You can pick up the disks from Gayle on your way out."

"I'll get right on it," David said.

"Pam, I have another writer I'd like you to review...C.E. Campbell. This is a new writer, but the manuscript looks quite promising."

"I'll start reviewing it as soon as I wrap up Mr. Ramsey's manuscript. Are the disks with Gayle also?" she asked him, while she scribbled some notes down.

"No. I actually have those disks on my desk. Since neither of you have anything else for me, this meeting is over. Y'all have a good day," John said, ending the meeting.

"You have a good day also, sir," David said, taking his leave.

Pam followed John to his office to retrieve the disks. "Here are the disks for C.E. Campbell," he said, handing them to her. "Have a good day."

"You have a good day also," Pam said.

When she reached her office, she sat for a moment, going over the meeting in her head. *Nice touch Michelle, kissing up to the writers already. I wonder what she's going to send Michael when his book comes out. I can't believe Michael didn't tell me about the pictures, or this artist designing his cover. At least with him having to come down, I'll get a chance to spend some time with him, and maybe we can have a long talk about our relationship,* she thought, as she paced around her office.

After five minutes of pacing, Pam sat down at her desk, and called Michael.

"Good morning, Planning Department. How may I help you?" Sara asked.

"Good morning. Pamela Bryant calling for Michael Ramsey," Pam said.

"I'm sorry, ma'am. Mr. Ramsey is out of the office today. Would you like to leave a message for him?" Sara said.

"Please ask him to give me a call when he gets in."

"I'll give him the message. Have a good day."

That's strange, he's usually in his office at this time, Pam thought to herself, as she dialed his home number.

His answering machine picked up. "Hello, you've reached Michael. I'm unavailable right now, but if you would leave a message, I'll get back to you."

"Hey, Michael, this is Pam. You're not at work, and you're not at home, what's going on? I hope everything is okay. Give me a call as soon as you get this message. We need to talk. I got blindsided in a meeting this morning… about you having pictures done, and some artist designing your cover. Seems the artist will be finished with your cover on Monday, and we need to set up a time and date for you to come down and review them. I also think it'll be a good time for us to spend some time together, and talk about our relationship. Talk to you later, lover," she said, dropping the receiver into the cradle.

I need to get his cell phone number the next time I talk to him. I hate having to wait for him to call me back, she thought to herself, as she tapped her foot.

She then dialed her friend, Sharon, to vent her frustrations with Michael.

"Hello, Sharon? It's Pam. Do you have a minute to talk?" Pam said.

"Hey Pam, what's up, girl? You sound kind of stressed over there," Sharon said.

"It's a lot of little things going on. First, I have to deal with a new boss, and now I can't find Michael when I need him."

"Pam, you need to get a grip. I know you're not still tripping over that man. He doesn't even live down here. How do you expect to keep tabs on him, all the way in Philly?" Sharon asked her.

"I know he feels something for me, and he knows I'm in love with him. I don't know why it's so difficult for him to pick up the phone and call me. It seems like I'm always the one calling him."

"That should tell you something! I told you before, I don't think that man is feeling you like that, but you keep trying to turn it into something else. He fucks you when he comes to town, and then you don't hear from him unless it has something to do with one of his books," Sharon spat.

"It's more then that, Sharon. We spend time together when he comes down here," Pam said defensively.

"Okay, Pam. Tell me this. Have you been to his house?"

"You know I haven't been to Philly yet."

"Has he even asked you to come to Philly, Pam?"

"No, Sharon, he hasn't asked me to come up there!" Pam said, angry by her friend's comments.

"And he probably never will. You need to stop kidding yourself. You're not his woman…you're just someone he has sex with. I keep telling you, you're selling yourself short where these men are concerned. You deserve so much better."

"But I love him, Sharon!" Pam cried.

"You don't know him. Look, I need to get off the phone, and you need to really think about what I'm saying to you. This man isn't in love with you, and I doubt you're in love with him. Remember, you were sleeping with your boss before he died, and would probably still be sleeping with him if he were alive," Sharon reminded her.

"True. But I know how I feel about Michael."

"Okay, Pam. But don't say I didn't warn you when your world comes crashing down. I'll talk to you later, girl."

"Okay, I'll talk to you later."

✳ ✳ ✳

Yvonne was working diligently on the plans for the Christmas party. Finishing up her conversation with one of the caterers, she glanced up to see Gayle waiting on her.

"Hey lady, how are you doing?" Yvonne asked, as she hung up the phone.

"I'm doing okay. I finally got rid of that stubborn cold," Gayle said.

"So, what brings you this way?" Yvonne asked.

"I was headed to *The Grill* for lunch, and would love some company," Gayle said.

"Oh, that sounds like a good idea. We haven't eaten there in a while. How did the meeting go this morning?" Yvonne asked.

"I guess it went okay. John didn't think it was necessary for me to take the minutes, as it was only Pam, David and himself. Brandon's still out sick with the flu, poor thing. Tina's out of town for a funeral, and Elaine were off-site with one of her writers for a breakfast meeting. John said he'd meet with them later. How long is Michelle going to be in New York?"

"She should be back on Wednesday. She said she'd be in the office on Thursday, but out again on Friday…when the movers deliver her things. Speaking of which, I should be receiving a delivery today from Fed Ex."

"Does that mean we have to cancel lunch?"

"Nah, they're usually here by eleven. Why don't we go to lunch at one? That way, I'll have enough time to wrap up things here," Yvonne said.

"That's fine with me. I'll see you later," Gayle said, leaving her office.

After Gayle left, Yvonne settled into inputting information in the computer. Just as she finished the last set of numbers, Michelle's packages arrived from New York.

"Good morning, ma'am. I have a delivery for a Michelle Rivers. Where would you like them?" the Fed Ex guy asked, rolling his cart into the office.

"Good morning. You can place them right through here in the next office," she said, showing the deliveryman where to set the packages. "Is this all of them?"

"Yes, ma'am, six boxes total. I need you to sign right here for them," he said, giving her his electronic clipboard.

Yvonne signed for the packages and the deliveryman left the office.

"It seems they only hire the good looking brothers for UPS and Fed Ex. They better be glad I'm a happily married old woman. Let me call Michelle, and tell her the packages have arrived," she chuckled to herself, as she dialed Michelle's number.

"Good morning, Michelle. This is Yvonne. How are things going with the move?"

"Hey Yvonne everything is going well. The movers left about thirty minutes ago, and Jasmine and I are doing the last walk through before leaving for the hotel. How are things at the office?"

"Everything is going well. I got a call from Damon, and he said he'd have the covers ready for review on Monday."

"That's great. He works fast. Did anyone notify Mr. Ramsey, so he can come back down and review them?"

"I let John know this morning, and he said he'd have Pam get in touch with Mr. Ramsey to set something up."

"Good. Could you please check with Mr. Ramsey to see if he got his pictures done, so we can review those as well, and make a decision for the book?" I said.

"I'll get right on that. But before I forget why I called you in the first place, your packages arrived, and they're stacked in your office."

"Thanks, Yvonne. I'm hoping they got there in one piece. I can't wait to open them, and make sure nothing was broken."

"Would you like me to handle that for you?"

"That won't be necessary. I'd rather wait till I get back, in case one of my figurines is broken, and I can cry about it once," I said laughing. "How did John's staff meeting go today?"

"Gayle said the meeting went fine, and John will update you when you return. I forgot to tell you, David came by this morning and said Ms. Carrion was extremely happy with her surprise. She's looking forward to her book signing on Saturday."

"I'm happy to hear she was pleased with them. I'm looking forward to her book signing as well. Please don't mention to David that I'm coming. I don't want them being on pins and needles at the thought of her publisher being there," I instructed.

"Alright, I won't mention it. I'll see you when you get back on Thursday," Yvonne said.

"If you need to get in touch with me, don't hesitate to call."

"I'm sure everything will keep until you get back, but if I need you, I'll call. Enjoy the rest of your day," Yvonne said.

"You do the same," I said.

After hanging up the phone, I walked over to my favorite window, and reflected on how happy I was when found this condo, and the many special times I spent here with Tony. I remembered showing him the place before signing the agreement to buy it. Dragging him through the door and running to the window. It was a beautiful winter day in December, right before Christmas, and fresh snow had just fallen.

"Tony, look at this view, and how beautiful everything is! I could sit here forever, and just look out the window," I said to him, as he walked up and wrapped his arms around me, resting his chin on top of my head.

That was his favorite thing to do. He said he loved to smell the freshness of my hair, and the smell of my body.

"Michelle, it's beautiful. Almost as beautiful as you are, baby. I can't wait to see it at night, when the stars are out, shining as brightly as our love," he said.

I remembered us walking through all the other rooms, planning a future. We were so happy together. I couldn't remember us ever having any serious disagreements. Perhaps we were too perfect together, but I wouldn't have traded a moment of my time with him.

Looking around, I recalled sitting in the middle of the floor with Tony, and a mountain of decorating books, planning where the furniture would go and the two of us making love on the floor, and then watching the stars from the window. I was so very happy here.

Thank you, God, for giving me that time with Tony. If I never love that way again, I will be forever blessed for having shared what we did share, I thought deeply.

I saw us walking along the park, hand in hand, or him chasing me after I hit him with a snowball, and knocking me down in the snow, then kissing me breathless. Oh, what wonderful memories I have of my life with Tony.

Then I thought about my Uncle Billy and Daddy coming to get me after Tony had died in that car accident. I barely remember calling home to inform them, but the next thing I knew, they were here taking care of me. A single tear spilled down my cheeks as I continued to stroll down memory lane.

When they arrived, I was sitting in the same spot on the couch, looking out the window in shock, knowing I would never see him smile at me again, or hear his voice on the phone. I would never hear him tell me how much he loved me, or feel him pull me close when he slid into bed after a long day at the law firm.

Jasmine walked into the room, to see why I hadn't responded to anything she had said in the last few minutes. She saw the tears that were slowly falling down my cheeks, as I glanced around the room.

"Michelle, are you okay? I've been talking to you for the last five minutes, without any response. Talk to me, baby," she said, walking over and hugging me.

"I'm okay, Jas. I'm just taking a trip down memory lane. I'm going to miss this place, it holds so many memories," I said, wiping the tears from my eyes.

"Yes, I'm sure it does. You were thinking about Tony again?" she asked compassionately.

"You know me so well, don't you?" I said, smiling at my best friend. "Yes, I was thinking of Tony, and our times here." I said.

"Michelle, I understand how you felt about Tony, but life goes on. I know he'd want you to move on with your life. Now, let's get out of here and get our shop on," Jasmine said, with a laugh.

I took a look around, and said, "Yes, let's do that! Let me call the car service, so we can drop our bags at the hotel and then shop till we drop. Watch out New York, Jasmine and Michelle is on the loose," I said, laughing and coming out of my funk.

"No, let's just grab a cab to the hotel. We can call the car service from there," Jasmine said.

"Alright are you ready, girl?" I asked.

"Yeah, I'm ready," she said.

I glanced out of my favorite window for the last time, and then picked up my purse and keys from the breakfast bar. I took one final look around, before walking out the door and locking it for the very last time. We dropped the keys off with the management office, and I said my final goodbye to the security officer on duty, as he hailed us a cab.

"Salaam Muhammad, take good care of yourself," I said.

"Salaam Ms. Rivers you do the same, and good luck in Atlanta," he said, opening the cab door for us.

As we pulled away, I looked around my neighborhood, and smiled at all the happy memories.

"Thank you God, for continuing to bless me and ordering my steps. I don't know what the future holds for me, but I know as long as I carry you, the Divine Creator, in my heart, I'll be okay. Amen," I silently prayed. "Thanks for coming to New York with me. I couldn't have made it through all of this without you," I said to Jasmine.

"If you don't stop thanking me, I'ma hit you over the head with my purse," she said, with a laugh. "You're my sister, and I love you. I wouldn't be anywhere else but by your side, and you better not forget it. Now don't thank me again, or I'ma make you buy me some Gucci boots," she said, laughing again.

"You know, that's not a bad idea. I saw some bad boots the other day in a magazine, and I know just the place for us to get them." I said, looking over at her grinning. "Perhaps they'll have some bags to match at *Angiolini's*. I'm glad we packed light, because I have a feeling we're going to need all the space we can get to take our stuff back to Atlanta," I said.

"Now, that's what I'm talking about. Shopping, here we come," Jasmine said.

Chapter 11

"**D**O you think we're too old to enjoy hot romance every now and then?" Michael's mother asked him.

"Mom, I didn't say that. I just write what I feel, and if anyone, no matter how old, enjoys it, then that suits me just fine," he said smiling.

His mother hit him on the arm and said; "I can just imagine where your head is right about now…with your fresh self."

"Good morning, Mrs. Ramsey. As usual, you're right on time. Dr. Heidelberg is ready for you," Jenny said, when they walked into the doctor's office. She had been Dr. Heidelberg's receptionist for a few years now.

"Good morning, Jenny. This is my son, Michael," his mother said.

"I'm pleased to meet you, Michael," she said, extending her hand. "Let me take your coat, Mrs. Ramsey, and then I'll take you back to the exam room."

After she took his mom back for her procedure, the doctor came out to talk to Michael briefly.

"Hello, I'm Dr. Heidelberg. I'm going to be performing a laser surgery on your mother's right eye. It's a minor procedure, but I wanted to make sure she'd be escorted home," he explained to Michael. "It should take about an hour or so, and she'll be as good as new. Of course, she'll have a patch over her eye to protect it from light. She only has to wear it for about three hours," Dr. Heidelberg continued.

"Thank you, Doctor. I'll make sure she gets home safely," Michael said.

"Very good I'll see you in a little while," he said, as he went to prepare for the surgery.

"I was talking to your mom back in the exam room, and she told me you're a writer," Jenny said. "I thought your name sounded familiar, but I didn't know it was you. You wrote a book called, *Promise of Love*, right?"

"Yes, I'm the culprit. Did you like it?" Michael asked.

"I sure did. It was hot. When is your next one coming out?" she asked.

"Hopefully in about a month or two I'm still working on a few things."

"Well, I can't wait. I wish I had my book here now for you to sign it," she said, with a sigh.

"If you have it when I bring my mom back for her follow-up visit, I'll be happy to sign it for you," he said reassuringly.

"You have yourself a deal," she said.

Michael went over to the waiting area and read the newspaper. While he was sitting there, he thought back to earlier this morning with Carol. He was having second thoughts about what they did. He hoped it wouldn't change their friendship. Michael knew they couldn't let it happen again. But, damn, she was good.

The time flew by, and before he knew it, his mom was heading out of the exam room in a wheelchair.

"We're giving her limo service to your car, Michael," the nurse said.

"Dang, Mom, you look like a pirate with that patch on," Michael said, cracking up.

"That's so funny I forgot to laugh, blockhead," she responded.

"Okay, Mrs. Ramsey. I'll see you back in my office in two weeks. And remember, you have to keep the cover on your eye for the next three hours," Dr. Heidelberg told her.

"Okay, doctor. Thank you very much," she said.

He shook Michael's hand, and then headed back to his office. Jenny said she would make sure she had her book with her when we came back.

"Oh, brother, you have his book too?" his mom asked, shaking her head.

"Yes, I do," Jenny, said. "And your son is going to sign it for me, when he brings you in for your follow-up visit."

Jenny wheeled Michael's mom down to his car, and they pulled off, waving at her.

"Are you hungry, Mom? We can stop and get some dinner if you'd like," Michael suggested.

"As long as it's not a fast food place, I'm with you," she said.

They stopped at an Italian restaurant to eat. When Michael got her home, his dad was there.

"Hey, Dad, how are you doing?" Michael asked.

"Everything is fine. Baby, how's your eye feel?" his dad said.

"It feels pretty good. I'll just be glad when I can take this patch off," she said.

"Dad, she has to keep it on for another two hours," Michael said.

"Oh, you call yourself telling on me?" she said laughing.

"No way Mom, I'm just looking out for my girl," he said, smiling at his mother.

"Awe, that's so cute," his dad said, cracking up.

"I'm going to grab my pie and get on home, Mom," Michael said.

"Okay. Thanks for taking me to the doctor today, and for dinner."

"You're welcome, Mom. Dad, I'll talk to you later."

"Drive safely. By the way, I spoke to Debra today. She said she hasn't talked to you in a while. You better give her a call when you get time," his dad said.

"I will, bye now," Michael said, kissing his mom on the cheek and shaking his dad's hand.

When Michael got home, he had a message from Pam on his answering machine, telling him Damon had a few covers for him to check out. She also said he wanted to talk about their relationship the next time he came down. He didn't know they had a relationship, so to speak. He dialed her number.

"Hello, Pam?" he asked.

"Yes, this is Pam. May I ask who's calling?" she said, rather coldly.

"You know who this is, don't even start that," Michael said.

"It's so hard to catch up with you, I just don't know sometimes."

"Don't know what? Where are you coming from, Pam?"

"Why is it that I can never catch you at home?"

"I'm always on the move, Pam. Between working, writing, and getting with my little brother, I stay busy. What's your point?" he said, rather tersely.

"We need to talk about where our relationship is headed. I'd rather talk to you in person though. The next time you come down, I hope we can get some things straightened out," she said.

"You know what, Pam…never mind, we'll talk when I get there. We need to settle some issues," he said. Michael could feel himself getting ready to tell her off, but refrained. "Is there anything else, Pam?"

"Damon has some cover samples of your new book to show you on Saturday. Can you explain to me why I never knew anything about this?" she asked, sounding like she was ready to explode.

"Pam, this isn't etched in stone, but it's a viable option. Do you have a problem with anything I want to put on my book?" he asked, his voice rising slightly.

"No, I don't. I just thought being your editor I'd be privy to anything pertaining to your book. That's all," she said, sounding a little deflated.

"You are my editor, Pam, and a damn good one. I'm not hiding anything from you, if that's what you're thinking. Michelle had the idea, and I thought it would be a nice touch. I wanted something to grab more attention. And I believe a custom cover will do that," he said defensively.

"You're right, Michael. It isn't a problem. This is your book, and I'm just your editor," she said, rather abruptly. "When do you think you'll get here, so we can meet with this artist?" she asked sarcastically.

"I'd like to make it as soon as possible. I'm busy on Friday. Maybe I can get a flight out first thing Saturday morning, but it may be difficult on such short notice," he said.

"Rivers, Inc. will reimburse you for any expenses you incur," she reminded him.

"If I can get there on Saturday, I'll stay until Sunday afternoon. I'll call you tomorrow to confirm if I can get a flight. In the meantime, see if Damon is available on Saturday and call me back," Michael said.

"I sure will. I'll talk to you later," Pam said, hanging up before Michael could say anything else.

Michael couldn't believe she hung up on him. He was going to remind her about that crap if he saw her on Saturday. Suddenly the phone rang again, and he thought it was her calling to apologize.

"Hello, may I speak to Michael Ramsey, please?" a female voice said.

"This is he…who's calling?"

"Hello, this is Yvonne calling from Rivers, Inc. how are you?"

"I'm doing well, Yvonne. And you know darn well we're past all that formal stuff."

"You're right, Michael. Listen, Michelle wanted me to call to remind you about the pictures," she said.

"She must have a sixth sense, because I had them taken the other day. My proofs should be ready on Friday," he said.

"I think you're right about the sixth sense. She's just like her uncle was… always on top of things. She should be back in town tomorrow, so I'll tell her you've already taken care of it."

"Alright Yvonne, Is there anything else?"

"Nope, that's it. Have a good evening, Mr. Ramsey…I mean Michael," she said, as they both laughed.

"Oh by the way Yvonne, Let Michelle know I may be coming down on Saturday morning to meet with Damon and Pam, if I can get a flight…to see the sample covers for my book."

"I'll do that. Talk to you soon," Yvonne said.

After hanging up, Michael decided to give Debra a call, especially since his dad had said he had spoken to her.

"Hey Deb what's shaking?" Michael said when his sister picked up the phone.

"Michael my favorite writer brother, how are you?" she said.

"Girl, I'm your only writer brother," he said laughing. "I'm doing well, and you?"

"Everything is moving along. There's no sense in complaining. So, you still single over there?" Deb said.

"Listen to you, all in my business. I'm kind of seeing my editor, Pam," Michael said.

"You're sleeping with your editor? Damn, you don't mess around, do you?" Deb asked him.

"I only got with her a few times when I went to Atlanta, nothing serious though. She's just fun to be around for now," he confessed.

"So, I take it she's not the one?"

"You know me better than that. Besides, how can we be serious, when she lives in another state altogether?"

"You've got a point, but it has been done before. I have a girlfriend here who has a boyfriend that lives in Boston. They keep in touch all the time, and he comes to Arizona, or she goes to Boston once a month," she said.

"Well, they must truly be in love…I'm not."

"I hear you, big brother. Well, you be careful. These women today will latch on to you like bees to honey. You'd make a great catch."

"That's nice of you to say, Deb."

"I need to get back to my study group. Thanks for calling, Mike. I love you," Deb said.

"I love you too, Deb. I'll talk to you later."

After hanging up, Michael decided to take a hot shower and turn in early. He couldn't believe Pam was acting the way she was. She was acting as if they were seriously involved or something. He knew he needed to make it clear to her when he saw her they weren't. He just didn't want to hurt her feelings, and screw up the business relationship they had. It was very important for him to have an editor that was on point like Pam. But he knew that he'd made a mistake becoming intimate with her. He had to correct that…and soon.

* * *

The week seemed to fly by after hump day Wednesday. Michael had managed to book a flight for Saturday morning at eight o'clock. Friday after work, he ran home to get ready for the Sixers game. One thing he liked almost as much as writing, was rooting for the Philadelphia 76ers. He stopped by to pick Kevin up.

"Hey, Carol. How you doing? I see Kevin is revved up and ready to go," Michael said, when Carol opened the door.

Kevin was in the living room, pacing back and forth. When he saw Michael, he said, "I'm ready, let's go."

"He's been talking about this game non-stop, ever since you had dinner with us," Carol said laughing.

"Okay, Kevin. Carol, has he eaten yet?" Michael asked.

"No, he was too hyped to eat."

"We can stop and get something before the game. They charge you four dollars for a hot dog at the stadium, and that's ridiculous," he said, as she shook her head in agreement. "I won't have him out too late. Let's go, Kevin," Michael said.

"You guys have a great time," she said, hugging Kevin.

"Okay, Mommy, bye," Kevin said.

They had two hours before the game started, so they stopped by the photography studio after eating to pick up Michael proofs. When they arrived at the studio, Chris was at Belinda's desk.

"Good evening, Mr. Ramsey. And who is this little man?" Chris asked.

"This is my little brother. Tell her your name." Michael egged Kevin on, because he was very cautious around strangers.

"My name is Kevin. What's your name?" Kevin responded politely.

"My name is Ms. Johnson, and this is my photography studio. Welcome back, Mr. Ramsey. Your proofs are ready. Why don't you and Kevin follow me?" Chris said.

She led us into her studio, and once the door swung open, Kevin's eyes lit up like a Christmas tree.

"Oh wow, is all this stuff yours, Ms. Johnson?" he asked, in amazement.

"Yes, Kevin, it's all mine. Do you like cameras and taking pictures?" she asked him.

"I've never had a camera before. Can I look at them?" he asked excitedly.

"Yes. As long as you don't drop anything, you're welcome to look," she said.

Kevin browsed around the studio, admiring everything in sight. *It seems as if we may have stumbled onto something here*, Michael thought to himself, as Chris led him to the table to review the proofs.

"These are absolutely beautiful, Chris. You were working out that day. Half of these poses I don't even remember. I like this one of me smiling and standing with my hand in my pocket. And I love this headshot of my serious side," Michael said, in admiration of her work. "Can I get three 8x10's, and three 5x7's copies of these two proofs?"

"That's not a problem, Michael. The proofs are yours. If you want any more of them in the future, just give me the numbers, and I'll get them done for you. I'd like to get a picture of you and Kevin, if that's alright?"

"That's a good idea, Chris. I don't have any pictures of the two of us together. Kevin, Ms. Johnson is going to take our picture. Come here," Michael said.

Kevin came over, and started striking poses like he'd seen in magazines. She snapped about five or six pictures of us together, and one of Kevin alone. *Carol is going to love that one*, Michael thought.

"Can you show me how to use a camera, Ms. Johnson?" Kevin asked.

"Kevin, this is Ms. Johnson's place of business. She doesn't have the time to teach you how to use a camera. I'll see if your mom can send you to class for that," Michael told him.

"Wait a minute, Michael. If he gets a small starter camera, I can show him a few things. I run a class on Saturdays for children, and one for adults. I'd be more than happy to teach him," Chris said.

"Man, I'm going to learn how to take pictures!" he said, with a big smile on his face.

"Michael, look over the proofs, and if you get back to me quickly, I can have the pictures by Wednesday evening," Chris explained. "You can see Belinda about payment."

"Thank you so much, Chris. You've been very nice, and your work is impeccable. Come on, Kevin, we're pushing it close for the start of the game. Hold this envelope for me." Michael said, as he paid Belinda on their way out.

Michael and Kevin had a blast at the game, and Michael couldn't have chosen a better time to go. Allen had one of those games to remember. Not only did they beat the Spurs, but also Allen had fifty-six points, completely dominating the game in the fourth quarter. Their seats were so good they could see the expressions on the players' faces. At the end of the game, one of the Sixers signed the game program that Kevin had...that made his night complete.

"Carol, you might have a budding Gordon Parks on your hands. We stopped by the photography studio that an acquaintance of mine owns on the way to the game, and Kevin showed more than a passing interest in taking pictures. The photographer offered to teach him how to take pictures on Saturdays, when she has a photography class for children. Think about it, and let me know if it's something you wouldn't mind him pursuing," Michael said to Carol, when he dropped Kevin off.

"Mommy, please, can I go to the classes please...please?" Kevin begged.

"We'll have to see how much it costs first," Carol said.

"Don't worry about that, Carol. If you say he can go, then I got it," Michael said, hoping she would say yes.

"Okay, I'll let you know, Michael. Did you get the message I left for you the other day?" she asked.

"Yes, I did. And I understand where you were coming from. We'll talk," he said.

"Thank you for taking me to the game, Michael," Kevin said, giving him a pound.

"You're welcome, little man. I'll see you later. Bye, Carol," Michael said, as he left.

When Michael got home, he had two messages on his answering machine. One was from Pam, letting him know that Damon would be available tomorrow at two o'clock, and asking him to call her when he got this message. The other was from Michelle, asking him to give her a call, to let her know how everything worked out with Damon. She left her cell phone number. That brought a smile to his face. He thought back to what Yvonne said about Michelle being just like her uncle, and she was right. She was truly on top of things concerning her company.

He decided to give Alex a call, to see what he was doing tomorrow evening.

"What's happening, slice?" Michael asked Alex, once he picked up the phone.

"Michael, how are you, brother?"

"I'm doing well, man. I'll be down there tomorrow to take care of some business with my book. What's going on with you tomorrow?"

"I don't have any plans. Do you want to check out this jazz club while you're down here?" Alex asked.

"That doesn't sound like a bad idea. I may even be able to introduce you to my publisher's friend…if she's available," Michael said.

"I can live with that," he said, as they both laughed.

"I'm going to see if Pam will be picking me up from the airport. If so, we're going to breakfast, to talk over a few things before we meet with the artist, Damon. His spot is in Little Five Points, in the same plaza as the *Natural Food Store*. I should be finished the meeting around four. Do you think you can pick me up, and we take it from there?" Michael asked.

"Sure, that's not a problem. I know where that is. Where you planning on staying while you're here?" Alex asked.

"The Days Inn by the airport," Michael said.

"Not this time, brother. You're staying at my house."

"I don't want to put you out, Alex."

"You must be kidding. You're welcome to stay at my house anytime you're in Atlanta. I'll tell you what, before your meeting, give me a call on my cell, and I'll start getting myself together to head your way. Make sure you hook that up with your publisher and her friend. I'm about due," he said, cracking the hell up.

"You're crazy as I don't know what, Alex. I'll talk to you tomorrow."

"Okay. Have a safe trip."

"I will, brother. Peace," Michael said, hanging up.

The last thing he needed to do was give Pam a call, to see if she could pick him up from the airport. Hopefully, she was in a better frame of mind than when they last spoke.

"Hello, I'm unable to come to the phone right now. Please leave a message after the tone. BEEP," her answering machine said.

"Hello, Pam, this is Michael Ramsey. My flight is arriving in Atlanta at nine-thirty in the morning. It's flight 812 on Delta. Hopefully you can pick me up, and then we can do breakfast. Give me a call if you can't meet me. Good night," Michael said, into her answering machine.

Michael set his alarm for five o'clock, packed his bags and, went to bed.

Chapter 12

YVONNE arrived at work to the sounds of smooth jazz playing, and for a minute, forgot that Billy wasn't with them anymore. She walked up to the door, when she realized it was Michelle playing one of her uncle's favorite CD's.

"Good morning, Michelle. Welcome back. How was your flight in from New York?" she said, knocking on the door to get my attention.

"Good morning, Yvonne. Come on in. I'm happy to be home. New York was cold, but beautiful as always. Our flight was okay. Jasmine and I arrived back in Atlanta around nine last night. I want to thank you again for holding it down while I was gone," I said.

"No need to thank me, Michelle. I was just doing my job," she said, with a smile.

"Yvonne, we both know you always do more then just your job. I don't know what I'd do without you here to guide me, and I want you to know I appreciate all the effort you put in. I brought you something back from New York...I hope you like it."

"Why, thank you, Michelle. You didn't have to bring me anything back, but I'm glad you did," she said with a grin, while accepting the box. "Oh, my God, Michelle! This is a beautiful Gucci bag. You shouldn't have," Yvonne said, after opening the box.

"Yes, I should have. Look inside, there's a wallet to match. Since I didn't know what size boots you wore, there's also a Gucci gift certificate," I said excitedly.

"Thank you. I don't quite know what to say," she said, getting up and giving me a hug.

"Don't say anything, just enjoy them. Now, bring me up to speed with what's been going on around here."

"There's not really much to catch you up on, except for the time and place of Ms. Carrion's book signing for Saturday. And I still haven't been able to secure a place for our Christmas party, but I've worked out a menu."

"That reminds me; let me give you Jasmine's number. As a travel agent, she has connections with many of the hotels. She said she'd be able to help you secure a place. She said she'd call in a couple of favors, because I told her I'd really like to have it at the Embassy Suites near the airport."

"That's great. Will she be in her office this morning?" Yvonne asked.

"Yes. Why don't you give her a call around ten?" I said.

"I'll do just that. Let me go put on the coffee before John arrives. Would you like me to bring you a cup?" she said.

"That would be great," I said

"I'll be back in a few," Yvonne said, still admiring her new purse.

While waiting for Yvonne to return, I made a mental note to ask John how he thought the transition was going.

Yvonne met John in the lounge, coming for his morning cup of coffee.

"Is Michelle in her office?" John asked, as he waited for the coffee to finish brewing.

"Yes she is. And the coffee's almost done," she said.

After a few minutes more, he poured his cup and headed towards Michelle's office.

"Good morning, John. I was just thinking about you. Come right in and have a seat," I said, as John walked into my office with Yvonne.

"If there's nothing else, I'll be in my office, Michelle," Yvonne said, handing me the cup of coffee.

"This will do for now, Yvonne," I said, taking the cup from her.

"How are you doing, John?" I said, leaning back against my desk.

"I'm doing well. How was your trip to New York?"

"It was wonderful. I was able to close up my condo, tie up all loose ends, and do a little shopping, at the same time."

"If you're anything like my wife, you did a lot more than a 'little' shopping," he said laughing.

"Now, now John, you know shopping to us women is like sports to you men…you can never do too much," I said, joining him in laughter. "Why don't we move over to the sitting area, so you can tell me about your meeting?" I said.

"You're just like your uncle, it's almost unsettling. He used to do the exact same thing," John said smiling.

"What did I do?" I asked, slightly puzzled.

"He always wanted to sit over there," John said, shaking his head.

"Wow, that's interesting. I just hope I'm half the businessperson he was. I don't want to let him down."

"Michelle, from what I've seen so far, there's no way you could possibly let him down. Like I said, you're very much like him. Very detailed oriented, you don't miss much at all."

"Thank you, John. That means a lot coming from you. As you know, I'm used to working on my own…being a free-lanced writer. I'm trying very hard not to step on anyone toes around here," I confessed.

"As a publisher, it's your job to step on some toes, Michelle. Everything that goes out of these doors is going to have a direct reflection on you, so don't worry about it," John said, sipping his coffee.

"I never thought about it that way, thank you. Now tell me, how did your staff meeting go?" I asked.

"There were only the three of us at the meeting, but I brought the others up to speed. Brandon's still not a hundred percent, but he came back to work yesterday. The writer he's working with has some re-writing to do, but it shouldn't be a problem, as his deadline isn't until December. Elaine's editing is about a week from being completed for her first writer, and the manuscript by Tyler Bray that she's editing is almost done. Hopefully, it'll be at the printers, and ready for release by the end of November."

"That's our horror writer, correct?"

"Yes, it is," John, said. "Tina's editing is up to speed also. Her writer's book should be ready for release in December. David's writer is doing her book signing on Saturday. By the way, the flowers and balloons you sent her were a nice touch," he acknowledged.

"Thank you. I know I always appreciated it when I received something unexpected at the end of a completed project," I said smiling. "I plan on attending her book signing on Saturday, it should be fun. I want to see the kid's reaction to her book," I said.

"I'm sure she'll appreciate you being there and supporting her," he said, with a smile. "Last, but not least, Pam's nearly finished editing Mr. Ramsey's book, and it will be sent to the printers as soon as the cover is chosen. Which I understand, is being designed by a Mr. Jennings?"

"Yes, Damon Jennings is a friend of mine from high school. I introduced him to Mr. Ramsey when we met. I thought it would be a nice touch to have him design a special cover for his book. In addition, Mr. Ramsey's also having his picture added to the jacket."

"I think that will be a good touch. I asked Pam to give him a call, and set up a time for him to come down and review the covers," he told me.

"I'm sure you'll let me know when that's done," I said.

"I'll be sure to do that. Well, that wraps up my report of the staff meeting. I better get back to my office, "he said, standing up to leave.

"Thank you, John. It's good to be back. And remember, I'll be out the office again tomorrow. The movers will be here with my things from New York," I said.

"Okay have a wonderful day," he said, walking out the door.

Not long after John left, Yvonne buzzed me on the intercom.

"Yes, Yvonne?" I said.

"Michelle, I forgot to tell you I spoke with Mr. Ramsey yesterday briefly, and he said he did get his pictures done, and would be getting the proofs on Friday. He also said he might be in town on Saturday to meet with Pam and Mr. Jennings, to choose the cover for his book."

"Yvonne, that's great news. It looks like everything is shaping up quite nicely for his book."

"Indeed it does," she said, before hanging up.

I sat back, reflecting on what John relayed, when I noticed my packages with my Lladros figurines sitting in the corner. I got the idea to add a corner curio to my office, so I could keep some of them there. Just as I was trying to work out the details, the phone rang.

"Good morning, Michelle Rivers," I said, answering the phone.

"Good morning, Miss Rivers, this is your security company. We have an alarm at your house, and we're dispatching the police to check it out," the person on the phone said.

"Thank you for notifying me," I said, as I quickly hung up the phone. "Why would anybody be trying to break into my house in broad daylight? That doesn't make any sense," I said to myself. "Let me call Daddy."

"Good morning, Rivers speaking," my daddy said, answering the phone.

"Daddy, this is Michelle," I said, in a rush. "I just got a call from the security company, saying there was an alarm at the house, and they were sending the police out. Do you think I should go meet them there?"

"No, Michelle. I'll go meet them at the house. You stay in your office. I'll call you when I get there, to let you know what's going on," he said.

"Daddy, I can't come with you?" I asked.

"No, you can't. Stay put until I call you!" he said forcefully, hanging up before I had a chance to say goodbye.

"But, it's my house!" I said out loud to myself.

Daddy acted like I was still a child. I was going to meet him at the house anyway, and see for myself what was going on. The nerve of him thinking I'll stay put, just because he says so. I grabbed my purse and headed for the door.

"Yvonne, I need to leave the office for a little while. There was an alarm of some sort at my house, and they're sending the police out. Can you ring John and notify him that I'll be gone for a while?" I said, in a rush.

"Hold on one minute, Michelle. I'm going with you. Give me a minute to transfer the lines to Gayle, and let her know what's going on," Yvonne said, picking up the phone.

"Yvonne, that's not necessary."

"I'm going with you, so you may as well wait a minute!" Yvonne said. "Hello, Gayle, this is Yvonne. Michelle and I need to leave the building for a while. Please inform John, and I'm transferring my lines to you. Thanks, Gayle. I'll let you know as soon as we return."

It seemed like it took us forever to get to my house, but it was only about thirty minutes. As soon as we rounded the corner, I saw Daddy's car, and another car I didn't recognize, in the driveway. I parked on the street, and as soon as I opened my door, Daddy stuck his head out the front door.

"Hello, Yvonne. Michelle, I thought I told you to stay at your office until I called you," he said angrily.

"I love you too, Daddy. But I'm not a little girl. You can ask me to do something, but that doesn't mean I have to comply with it," I said, walking up and kissing him on the cheek. "What did the police say?" I asked.

"Well, since you're both here, you may as well come on in the house. Maceo's also here," he said, before answering me. "The police said it looks as if someone tried to open the door, but as soon as the alarm went off, they left. One of your neighbors said they thought they saw a woman at the door, but couldn't be sure. Maceo and I are going to change your locks. We didn't think to do that before you moved in here."

"Daddy, do you really think that's necessary? They weren't able to get in the house, and the alarm was activated," I said.

"We're not taking any chances with your safety, baby," he said. He turned to Yvonne and said, "Thank you for coming with my stubborn child. I should've known she wouldn't stay put and wait for my call."

"It's not a problem, Robert. There's no way I was letting her walk out the office alone," Yvonne replied.

"Y'all act like I'm ten years old, instead of thirty. Where's Uncle Maceo?" I said.

"I'm right here, Michelle," he said, coming around the corner from the kitchen, and giving me a hug. "Hi Yvonne, how are you doing, lady? I add my thanks to Robert's for riding shotgun with my hardheaded niece," he said, smiling at Yvonne.

"I'm doing well, Maceo. And no thanks are needed. Is there anything I can help you all with?" Yvonne asked.

"No, we have everything under control. Robert, let's go to Home Depot and pick up those locks. We'll see you ladies later," Maceo said.

After Robert and Maceo left, I gave Yvonne a tour around the house. I was happy that no one had actually broken into the house. Maybe it was just someone who simply got lost, and got scared off when the alarm sounded.

Whatever the case may be, I knew I'd be perfectly safe with all the new locks Daddy and Maceo were going to install. They had decided to order security doors too, and had convinced them to deliver them the same day the movers were coming.

* * *

Waking up to a sunny Saturday morning, I couldn't believe the week had gone by so fast. I had accomplished quite a few things, and was looking forward to the book signing this afternoon. I hoped Michael got a chance to call, to let me know how things went with picking a cover for his new book. I was almost sorry I couldn't be in two places at once.

No sooner had I finished that thought, the phone started ringing.

"Now where did I put that cell phone?" I asked myself, almost falling out the bed. I grabbed it off the table, before it went to voicemail. "Hello?" I said breathlessly.

"Good morning, Michelle. This is Michael Ramsey. Did I catch you at a bad time?"

"Good morning, Michael. No, you didn't catch me at a bad time. I just practically fell out the bed, trying to remember where I put the phone last night," I said laughing. "Are you already in Atlanta?"

"I just landed not ten minutes ago. I wanted to catch you early, to see if you and a friend could join my friend, Alex, and me for dinner and dancing this evening? You do remember Alex, right?" he asked nervously.

"Yes, I remember Alex. I'll have to make sure my friend is available tonight, but I don't see why not. Why don't you give me a call after your meeting, and we'll take it from there?" I said.

"I'll do that," he said.

"I'll talk to you later," I said, hanging up the phone.

Wow! I couldn't believe Michael Ramsey had just asked me out on a date. I hoped Jasmine wasn't busy. If so, she would just have to cancel whatever she was doing, because she was coming with me. I dialed her number.

"Hello, Michelle," Jasmine said, with a yawn. "Do you realize what time it is, heffa? Couldn't you have waited another hour to call me? What's going on?"

"If you stop asking questions, I'll tell you," I said. "You'll never guess who just called and asked us out on a date tonight? I hope you don't have plans, because if you do, you'll have to cancel them."

"Oh lord, just tell me already," she said, with a groan.

"Michael Ramsey just called me from the airport, and asked if we'd be available for dinner and dancing tonight. Please tell me you don't already have plans?"

"I know you're not asking me to go on a double date with you and him?" Jasmine asked.

"Okay, let me slow down. I'm just so excited right now. Remember I told you he has a friend named Alex, who lives here. Well, it seems they would like to take us out tonight. So, can you make it?" I asked.

"Hmmm, let me check my calendar, and see if I'm available for a double date," she said jokingly. "Yes, I can do it, since I don't have any plans for this evening, Ms. Rivers."

"Thank you, funny lady," I said, laughing at her dramatic act. "What are you doing this afternoon? I have to go to a book signing in Morrow. You wanna tag along?"

"This is for the children's writer, right?" Jasmine asked.

"Yeah," I said.

"Hell no I'd rather stay home and get myself together for this evening."

"Damn, Jas, you didn't have to say it like that," I said. "Why don't you come over around six? That way, we can leave from the same place."

"That'll work. Now, can I please go back to sleep, woman?" she said sleepily.

"Yes. I love you, girl. See you later."

"Bye. I love you too," she said, hanging up the phone.

Chapter 13

AS Michael made his way from the baggage claim, he saw Pam waiting for him. She had a half smile on her face.

"Hello, Pam. Thanks for picking me up," Michael said, as she gave him a halfhearted hug.

"It was no problem, Michael. How was your flight?"

"A little rough in spots, but basically a good flight," he said, as they walked towards the parking area. "Would you like to get some breakfast? I'm starving."

"I don't mind. I know a nice place we can go to," Pam said.

"That's good, because I'm ready to get my grub on," he said.

Michael could sense the chilliness in her conversation, but that was okay. They needed to get on one accord, and that may involve removing the intimacy from their working relationship. Whatever the outcome, he would make sure they were on the same page.

They arrived at the restaurant, after having very little conversation on the drive over. They were led to a table next to a window overlooking Peachtree Street.

"Good morning, folks, and welcome to Mom's. My name is Tanya, and I'll be your waitress. Can I get you some coffee or tea to start?"

"I'll have coffee, a glass of orange juice, and a number five, sunny side up, with wheat toast," Pam said, having already glanced at the menu.

"And what can I get for you, sir, or do you need more time?" Tanya asked.

"That won't be necessary, I see what I want. I'll have coffee, a glass of cranberry juice, a number seven, medium rare, with two eggs over easy, and an English muffin," Michael said.

"I'll be back with y'all coffee in a moment," Tanya said, walking away to place their orders.

"Okay, I can sense the tension with us. Let me ask you something. Why did you hang up the phone on me the other day?" Michael asked, getting right to the point.

"I apologize for that. I was having a bad day, and unfortunately, I took it out on you," Pam said.

"Apology accepted. What's going on, Pam?"

"I'm feeling used right about now, Michael. I thought we were on to something, as far as our relationship goes. I'm feeling some kind of way about you, and I thought the feeling was mutual. I can never catch you when I want to talk to you, or for that matter, when I need to talk to you. I get frustrated when I can't," she confessed, looking him in the eyes.

"Pam, it's not that I don't care for you, because I do. But as far as a committed relationship is concerned, I'm not ready for that at this point in my life. We have a beautiful working relationship, and I'd hate to compromise it for the sake of the physical aspect. I'm not saying I wouldn't like to have you in my life as my lover and friend, but it would be hard to maintain such a relationship from a distance at this particular time. Maybe we shouldn't have become romantically involved, seeing as though we have a business relationship as well. That, after all, comes first. Am I right or wrong?"

"You're right, Michael. Maybe we shouldn't have gotten involved, since business is supposed to come before pleasure. But we did, and I'm telling you that I have strong feelings for you. It's difficult for me to separate the two. Maybe I should get my feelings in check. I just don't want to feel like I'm just a convenient shot for you when you come to Atlanta," she said to him.

"I don't look at you that way at all, but I do feel we should probably take the physical part out of our relationship for now...or until we can both have the same goal in mind. What I'm saying is, this is neither the time nor place to commit to one another. We have to keep everything in perspective. Do I make any sense at all to you?" Michael said.

"Yes, you do make sense, and I'll just have to come to grips with it," Pam said.

"Here are your coffee and juice, folks. Your meals should be up in a minute," Tanya said, placing their coffee and juice on the table.

"Thank you," they said in unison.

"Pam, you're the best editor I know, and the last thing I want to do is make you feel simply like an object of desire. I just feel we have to keep everything on a certain level, and for now, that level will be better served as writer and editor. If you don't agree, tell me," Michael said, very seriously.

"Michael, I'm with you on that. And I apologize if you feel I forced myself on you, but I couldn't help it. You're a sexy man, and your writing does something to me, as I guess it does to any female that reads it. And you're a great lover." We both smiled at one another.

"I'm asking you, are we on the same page?" he asked, wanting to make sure she understood him.

"Yes, we are. Maybe in the future, we'll be able to mix the two businesses and pleasure. Is that a deal?" she asked, raising her glass of juice.

"It's a deal," Michael said, toasting her with his glass.

He felt kind of relieved, but he still sensed a little disappointment in Pam's voice. She tried to disguise it, but he was no fool.

"Okay, let's talk business. I was somewhat surprised at the news about the cover, but I'm over that. Is there anything else you want to add to the project?" Pam asked.

"Actually, there is. I want to put a picture of myself on the back cover, along with a bio. I'd like for my readers to put a face behind the words. Who knows, it may boost sales. What do you think?"

"I agree with you. Since your first book did so well, and your second one made the bestseller's list, this one might do much better. Plus, you are very easy on the eyes," she said, with a hint of a smile on her face. "From what I understand, this artist is supposed to be on point. We'll see when we meet with him today. The waitress is here with our food," Pam said, seeing Tanya coming their way. "So, when are you checking into your hotel?" she asked, after they started eating.

"I'm not staying in a hotel this time. My boy, Alex, is letting me stay at his place. He's meeting me at Damon's studio. You'll meet him when he picks me up," Michael said, though a bite of eggs.

"That's nice. It'll save the company a few dollars," she said. "Don't forget to fax a copy of the airline receipt, so you can get reimbursed."

"Thanks for reminding me. Can I ask you something?" Michael said.

"Sure, what's up?"

"How is it working with Michelle? I mean, are things really going as smoothly at Rivers, Inc. as it seems?"

"So far, I have no complaints. She's not like Bill…I mean Mr. Rivers, but she's pretty fair. Why do you ask?"

"I'm just curious, that's all. Sometimes when transitions take place with companies, it throws the continuity off a bit. I'm just glad everything is working out."

"Yeah, she's covering all the bases, and involved a little more than her uncle was. I guess she feels the need to know as much as she can about everybody. I don't fault her for that. I do, however, think she needs to let me know if she's doing anything new with any project I'm involved with," Pam said.

Michael could sense a little animosity in her comment. It must be a female thing. He also noticed her reference to Mr. Rivers as Bill.

"This steak is done just the way I like it. I'll have to remember this place," he said, changing the subject. "How's your breakfast?"

"It's good. This is normal for Mom's. This place is very consistent. Look at how crowded it's gotten since we got here," she said, looking around.

"Yeah, I see what you mean," Michael said, also looking around.

"Is everything okay?" Tanya asked, walking up to their table. "Would you like more coffee?"

"Yes, thank you. And everything is very good," Pam said.

Michael's breakfast meeting with Pam wasn't as bad as he had anticipated. He thought they had a better understanding of their overall relationship. It remained to be seen what kind of effect, if any, their conversation would have on them working together.

After Pam paid for breakfast, they headed out to Damon's studio. Before they went in, Michael gave Alex a call, to remind him to pick him up in about an hour or so. They arrived a little early, so that gave Pam a chance to admire some of Damon's work. Michael could tell by her silence she was in awe of Damon's talent.

"Michael, would you take a look at this piece over here? I could picture this hanging on my wall," Pam said, which gave him an idea of a gift he could get her, for the hard work she had done on his new book.

"I told you he had mad skills with the brush and canvas," Michael said.

"Good afternoon, Mr. Ramsey, and welcome back. You must be Ms. Pamela Bryant, right?" Damon said, walking up on them.

"Yes. I'm very pleased to meet you, Damon. I can see why Michael chose you to do his cover. Your work is amazing. I can definitely see some of it gracing my walls," Pam said.

"Why, thank you for the compliment. Let's move into my office, so you can review what I have," he said, leading the way. "As you can see, I have four designs that I've worked on. Each one, in a sense, shows a man that's determined to accomplish something, either by the expression on his face, or by his body language. Can you feel any of these pieces?" Damon asked.

"This one, where the man and woman seem to be talking, and she's half turned away from him, while he's holding her hand, stands out to me," Pam responded. "What do you think, Michael?"

"I like that one, and this one, where the woman is standing on a steep hill, with her hands outstretched, and the man is gazing up…seemingly like he's ready to climb that hill. Damon, which one did you get the most feeling out of," Michael asked curiously.

"Well, of course, I like them all. But I put a check mark on the back of the one I thought you would choose," he said.

Michael turned each of them over, and the one Pam felt the most, was the one Damon had chosen as his favorite.

"It's settled, I'm going with the majority. Michelle was right…you're a truly gifted artist. By the way, I received that piece I ordered, and it looks wonderful on my wall," Michael said. "One thing I noticed about these four pieces…is that each man has a striking resemblance to me."

"Ah, they do resemble you, Michael. Damon, you're an incredible artist. Why haven't I ever seen your work at any of the black art expos we have here in Atlanta?" Pam asked.

"I didn't feel I had fully arrived, as far as my work goes, to be displayed like that," he offered.

"I beg to differ. You have arrived, and your work needs to be displayed for all to see. I know one of the organizers of the ATL Gallery Association Expo, which could easily propel you to the forefront of emerging artists from the region," Pam told him, matter-of-factly.

"Now, that would be very much appreciated. I know it started last January, and I had it in the back of my mind to get involved, and possibly join the Atlanta Gallery Association. I'd appreciate that connection, Pam," Damon expressed. "Now, the only thing left to do is place the title on the cover. I can do it with a nice font of my own, or you can have it done by your printer. The choice is yours."

"We're going with you all the way, Damon," Michael said.

"That's fine. I'll place the title on the cover, and have it delivered to Rivers, Inc., to your attention, Pam, along with the bill. Is that okay with you, Michael?" Damon asked.

"That will be fine," he said, extending his hand.

"I'll send you the contact information for my friend at the AGA, Damon," Pam added.

"Thank you. I really appreciate that," Damon said.

When they walked out the studio, Alex was standing by his car, waiting for Michael.

"There goes my brother," Michael said, walking up to Alex. "Pam, I want you to meet my best friend, Alex Black. Alex, this is my editor, Pamela Bryant," Michael said, making the introductions. "I'm pleased to meet you, Alex," Pam said.

"Likewise, Pam. Michael told me his editor was fine, but he left out the word gorgeous," Alex said, in his normal flirtatious way.

"That's nice of you to say, Alex," she said, slightly blushing. "Michael, give me a call this evening if you get a chance," she said, kissing him on the cheek.

"I will, Pam. Bye now," Michael said, walking her to her car.

"Damn, Mike, her body is banging," Alex, said, giving Michael a pound, when he returned to Alex's car. "So, what's the verdict on this evening with your publisher and her friend?"

"She's supposed to call and let me know if her friend is available," Michael said.

"Okay, let's roll back to my spot. The Lakers are playing the Celtics," Alex said.

"That rivalry used to be something back in the day with Magic, Bird, Jabbar and Parrish," Michael said, placing his bags in the trunk. "Both teams are garbage this year. Boston is going to win this game. I know you have a few cold ones, right?"

"You know it, brother. I don't know about the game though. The Lakers still have Kobe," Alex said, as they drove to his place. "Guess who I talked to this past week?"

"I haven't the slightest idea."

"Bob gave me a call, and man, it was good to hear that knucklehead's voice."

"That's right; I gave him your number like you asked. What was he talking about?"

"He told me if I throw that jam next summer, he'd be here with bells on. He also told me y'all gig is looking shaky right about now. What's happening up in Philly, man?" Alex asked.

"Man, they're talking about layoffs. Apparently, the city is hurting some-what. The Mayor made an announcement, that by December 4th, people from all parts of city government, including the police and fire departments, would be affected."

"Damn, Michael. That's some bad news. I hope you two make the cut," Alex said seriously.

"I'm really hoping Bob makes the cut. I have a decent hustle with my writing, but he has a lot of investments that he's gotten into, so he needs his gig badly," Michael said.

"I heard that. I'm going to put you brothers in my prayers," Alex said.

"I've never known you to pray, Alex. When did you get some religion?" Michael asked shocked.

"Man, I pray every day when I wake up, and every night before I go to bed. I thank God for helping me adjust to my new life down here, and for waking me up healthy," he said.

"I hear you. Thanks for the prayer, my brother," Michael said.

"I hope we didn't miss too much of the game. I think it started at four. Those brews should be ice cold by now, and I could use one or two," Alex said, as they pulled up to his house.

They sat, watched the game, and generally enjoyed each other's company. It had been a long time since they just kicked back and relaxed. Alex was anxious to hook up with Michelle and her girlfriend. He was confident his rap would be strong enough to pull Michelle's friend on the first date. Michael kept telling him he didn't think he'd make it to home base on the first date. But Alex said they were from Philly, and that brothers from Philly think they're irresistible to the ladies.

They laughed and joked about the way they used to pull girls back in high school and college. Alex went to Temple, and Michael went to St. Joseph's. Every weekend, they would raid each other's campuses...trying to pull women. Alex reminded Michael of the night they went to this party at Temple, and met three fine ass ladies. They partied until five in the morning that night.

Alex had one girl hemmed up in the corner, running game, and Michael was slow dragging with another. Michael's wood got so hard, and she grinded on him so intensely, that he was about to explode. The girl whispered to Michael that she was ready to feel whatever he was poking her in the stomach with. He glanced over at Alex, and nodded at him, which meant his girl was ready. The third girl that was with their girls had left, and went back to their apartment.

They left the party, and when they got to the girls' apartment, the other girl was sitting on the sofa butt naked, smoking a joint. If that didn't give Michael and Alex a hit of what was coming, nothing would.

All of them were already fired up from drinking and smoking, but the real party was about to start. Michael sat on the sofa next to the naked girl, and she passed him the joint. While he was smoking, she started kissing his neck and chest, while unbuttoning his shirt. The girl he'd been dancing with pulled his pants down, and immediately started sucking his dick. Alex was sitting on the love seat, getting the same royal treatment. Before long, all five of them were on the carpeted floor, with throw pillows scattered around them, getting busy. They used up so many condoms that night; they could've used them for a balloon at the Thanksgiving Day parade. That was the first time Michael had ever had sex with more than one woman...let alone three.

"Michael, I'll never forget that night. There was hot, wet pussy grinding everywhere. Remember when I threatened to knock you out if you shot me with any of your bodily fluids?" Alex said, cracking the hell up.

"Man, you're crazy as hell. Pass me another one of those cold ones." Michael couldn't contain his laughter. "Those were the good old days," he said, laughing at the top of his lungs. His cell phone started ringing.

"Hello," Michael answered, still laughing.

"Maybe we need to come over there. Sounds like you're having a good time," a soft voice said.

"How are you doing, Michelle? I don't think you want to come over here at this moment. We got a hot conversation going on," Michael said.

"I'm doing okay. But I guess there's no need to ask how you're doing. Listen, I hooked up with my girlfriend. You still want to go out tonight?" I asked Michael.

"We sure do. I've been waiting on your call. What time will you ladies be ready?"

"I guess around eight. Do you want to come by here, or meet us somewhere?" I asked.

"You name the place...this is your town," he said.

"There's this nice club named Sambuca's, that my girlfriend, Jasmine, was telling me about in Underground Atlanta. You can meet us there around eight-thirty, okay."   "That sound good, we'll be there. What's the dress code?" Michael asked.

"It's an exclusive spot, so you might want to sport a jacket," I said.

"Michelle, I hope Jasmine looks as good as you do. I don't want Alex to be disappointed."

"Alex won't be disappointed. She's very easy on the eyes." Michael heard Jasmine laughing in the background.

"Tell him I have a big nose and bucked teeth," Jasmine said to me.

"Girl, I'm not telling him that," I said laughing.

"We'll see y'all at eight-thirty. Talk to you later," Michael said.

"Okay, Michael. See you then," I said, hanging up.

"Man, I don't know whether or not you want to meet her friend, Jasmine. She has a big nose and bucked teeth," Michael said to Alex, cracking up.

"Fool, I know you're lying. Remember, birds of a feather flock together. That rule will never change. I already met Michelle, so I know better," Alex said, sipping his beer. "Michael, look in the linen closet in the bathroom and get what you need."

"Thanks, brother. By the way, I told you Boston was going to kick ass," Michael said, getting off the sofa. "Come on, let's go get ourselves together. Do you know where Underground Atlanta is?" he asked.

"I think I've passed it before, but I'll get directions off the computer," Alex responded.

Before long, they were on their way to meet Michelle and Jasmine. Michael couldn't wait to see Michelle again. Ever since he'd met her, her voice had been in his head. He wondered if she had those same thoughts about him. Maybe he shouldn't have those types of thoughts lingering in his head, cause he knew first hand the difficulties mixing business with pleasure could present.

Michael and Alex arrived at Sambuca's around eight-fifteen. Valet parking was available, and the parking area was almost filled. They could hear the live jazz band playing "I Only Have Eyes for you," before they got inside. A slight aroma of basil and garlic could be distinguished, in between the cigar smoke from the walk-in humidor.

"Has Michelle Rivers arrived yet?" Michael asked the maitre`d.

"No, she hasn't, sir. But if you'd like, I can take your coats and seat you now," he suggested.

"Yes, that would be fine. Thank you."

"Right this way, please," he said, leading them to a table off the side of the stage area, where the traffic wasn't too busy, but the band still in view. He handed them two menus. One contained their expansive wine and spirits list, and the other was the dining menu.

"Damn, Michael, I only got thirty dollars with me," Alex said laughing.

"Well, you need to roll up your sleeves and get ready to do some dishes," he responded, smiling at Alex.

"You know I'm just kidding, man. I actually have fifty on me." They laughed again, as Michael noticed a familiar face speaking with the maitre'd. "There they are now, Alex," he said, as they looked at the ladies approaching the table.

"Good evening, Michelle," Michael said standing, along with Alex. He reached over and gave me a hug and kiss on the cheek.

"Michael and Alex, this is my best friend, Jasmine. Jasmine, this is Michael and Alex," I said, smiling at the two of them. They held the chairs for us to sit. "I see we have gentlemen with us this evening, Jasmine."

"Of course you do," Michael responded. "Did you expect anything different?"

"Jasmine, can you give me the name of your plastic surgeon?" Alex asked smiling. "He did a wonderful job on you."

She looked at them, before finally laughing. "Oh, I see you've got jokes." We all started laughing, because he was obviously speaking on the big nose and bucked teeth comment she made earlier. What a great way to break the ice. "I'll be sure to give you the name of my doctor at the end of the night, Alex," she said smiling. "It's good to meet you both."

"It's good to meet you also, Jasmine," Alex responded.

"Good evening. Welcome to Sambuca's. My name is Paul, and I'll be your waiter this evening. Can I start you off with some cocktails from our bar?" he said.

"If the ladies don't mind, I'd like to order a bottle of Cristal for the table," Michael said.

"That's fine by me," Jasmine and I said.

"Good choice, sir. I'll be back shortly with your champagne," Paul said.

"Michael, I didn't take you to be a champagne man. I thought of you as more of a scotch drinker," I said, smiling at him.

"I see you remembered. Well, I thought since this was a special occasion, I'd be a little more versatile," he said, smiling back at me.

"Watch it, Michael. She'll tell you what kind of drawers you're wearing next," Jasmine said, with a sly grin on her face.

"Jasmine, don't give away all my secrets. I bet he wears boxers though," I said.

Alex looked over at Michael, shaking his head and laughing. "Naaaah, he wears pull-ups."

"Alex, you're a funny man. Let me see what kind you're sporting this evening," Jasmine quipped.

"Jasmine, behave yourself! Michael, Alex, you'll have to excuse my friend, she has a warped sense of humor," I said laughing.

At that moment, Paul returned with the champagne. "I see this is a lively table. I like that. Most of the time, the people that come in here are pretty boring," he said, as he poured our champagne. "Are you ready to order, or do you need a few moments?"

"Could you have us a few more minutes, Paul? We're having so much fun, we haven't even looked at the menu yet," I said, smiling at him.

"That will be fine, madam. I'll be back in a moment to take your order," Paul said, walking away.

"They have a very extensive menu here. I know what I want to order," Alex said confidently.

About fifteen minutes later, Paul returned with his recommendations from the menu.

"We have a stuffed chicken breast, garnished with cherries, apricots, and served over fresh vegetables, with a nice herb Berre Blanc sauce. We're also featuring a Filet of Beef with Bleu Cheese and walnut butter, served with fresh vegetables, with a nice Bordelaise sauce. It's very good, I had it for dinner myself," he said smiling.

After placing our orders, another server came over to pour water into our glasses.

"This band sounds really good. I overhead someone say they're local," Michael said.

"They're The Holt Quintet. The sign next to the door mentioned that," Alex said. "So, Jasmine, what type of work do you do?" he asked.

"I'm a travel agent. What do you do?" she asked.

"I work as a buyer for Coca-Cola here in Atlanta. The company moved from Philadelphia last November, and I relocated."

"Michael, would you like to dance while we wait for our food? We can give these two some time to get to know each other," I said.

"That sounds good. I like Sophisticated Lady, it reminds me of you," he said, pulling out my chair.

"Oh, brother, let me get a violin to accompany to two of you," Alex said smiling.

"Michelle, you're looking really good this evening. What's that scent you're wearing?" Michael asked, once we were on the dance floor.

"It's called, Lick Me All Over," I said seductively.

"I'd like to do just that...the way you smell. Be careful what you wear around me," he said, waiting to hear my reply.

"Why, Michael, if you're a good boy, I just might let you do that one day."

"Jasmine, look at those two out there," Alex said, watching us on the dance floor.

"Your friend is pretty smooth. Alex, tell me more about you. How do you like Atlanta?" Jasmine said.

"So far, Atlanta is really nice. I've pretty much adjusted to the more relaxed pace down here. I'm single and not involved at the moment. But that will change soon, I'm sure," he said, smiling at her.

"Oh, so you've met someone who's going to change your single status? I guess I met you a little too late," Jasmine sighed, sipping her champagne.

"You're not too late. How do you know it wasn't you I was referring to?"

"Oh, I see. We'll have to see if you're worthy of my time. You do wear a mean suit, and you're quite handsome too. What else do you have to offer a sister, such as myself?"

"Honesty, a great sense of humor, and I know exactly how to treat a woman that's worthy of my time. Tell me, what makes Jasmine tick."

"Thank goodness, I'm being saved by the waiter. We'll continue this conversation later," Jasmine said, smiling as the waiter came to the table with their food.

"We sure will," Alex said, shaking his head and winking at her.

"Michelle, I could dance with you all night like this. But we should get back to the table, I see our food has arrived," Michael said. We walked off the dance floor, and back to our table.

"Glad you two could make it back, Fred and Ginger," Jasmine said. "We thought y'all would never come off the floor."

"Why, were you bored over here?" I asked jokingly.

"No way, we're enjoying each other's company. It's like we've known each other for an hour or so," Jasmine expressed, as she and Alex laughed.

"I told you she has a warped sense of humor, Alex," I said, laughing at my partner in crime.

The rest of the evening went extremely well. Alex and Jasmine seemed to be hitting it off nicely. They wound up dancing more than Michael and I. I think I was a little different than Michael had expected. The first time we met, I was all about business. But when I'm out on a date, I'm more relaxed and down to earth, with a great sense of humor. Moment by moment, Michael started getting closer to me on a different level.

When the night was over, Michael and Alex walked us to my car, and Michael said, "Ladies, we're going to follow you, to make sure y'all get home safely."

"That's really nice of you, Michael," I said.

As they were following us, Alex slapped Michael a high five for introducing him to Jasmine. He said she was just his type…easy on the eyes, a good sense of humor, and very sexy.

"Man, have you ever felt like you were making love on the dance floor?" Alex asked.

"Yes, I have. What did Jasmine do, make you get hard?" Michael fell out laughing, because that happened to him tonight.

"I see you know exactly what I mean." Alex laughed also.

Chapter 14

"OKAY, Jas, tell me what you think of Michael and Alex? You've gotten a little quiet over there," I said, looking at her out the corner of my eye.

"I was just thinking about how much fun we had with them. I don't remember the last date I was on, where I laughed all night long, and didn't have to find things to talk about. I'm quite impressed," Jasmine said.

"That's saying a lot. I know you're not easily impressed," I said.

"You know how much stuff I've gone through with previous relationships."

"Yes, I know, but you deserve some happiness."

"Michelle, I'm very happy with my life, even without a man in it. But I'm not going to say I wouldn't like someone to share it with. From what I've seen with Alex so far, I can say it looks promising, but we shall see. You know how busy I can get at times, with my job, and the different committees I'm on. We'll have to see if he can hang."

"I feel you on that, girl," I said, with a sigh.

"Okay, what is that sigh about? Talk to me," Jasmine said.

"Jas, I like Michael. I'm really starting to have feelings for him. I thought after our first meeting, it was just that I liked what I was reading in his book. But after tonight, I think it's much more than that."

"Then what's the problem? Oh, I think I understand. It's the fact he writes for your company."

"You're exactly right. I don't want there to be a conflict of interest. But I really like him," I said, with another sigh.

"I don't see a real conflict, since he doesn't actually work for you. If I were you, I'd just go with the flow. It's not like he lives here. You won't see much of him anyway. Just enjoy the time you do spend with him. If he's as good in bed as he writes about, then you've got a winner on your hands. Yes, I did read his book, so you can get that look off your face," Jasmine said laughing.

"You're a mess, but I hear what you're saying. I'll think about it. I was thinking maybe we should invite them in for coffee or a drink when we get to the house. What do you think?" I asked her.

"I think that's a good idea," Jasmine said.

When we pulled up in front of my house, I asked Michael and Alex if they wanted to come in for a nightcap.

"A nightcap sounds good to me," Alex said.

"Nice security door you have here, Michelle. Folks don't have break-ins in this neighborhood, do they?" Michael asked.

"I'll explain the doors when we get inside," I said, opening the garage and pulling the car in.

After I got inside, and turned off the alarm, Jasmine let Michael and Alex in and showed them to the den.

"Would y'all like to listen to some music or watch a movie?" Jasmine asked.

"How about some music. Do you think Michelle would mind if I took a look at her music collection?" Alex asked Jasmine.

"No, I wouldn't mind, Alex," I said, walking into the room barefoot. "Everyone, please make yourselves at home. I put coffee on, but I also have beer, wine and liquor. What's your drink of choice?"

"I'd love a tour of your home, and you can tell me about your doors," Michael said.

"Oh, God, let me tell you about the doors," I said, looking at Jasmine. "Long story short, my father thinks I need more security than the alarm. He and my Uncle Maceo had them put up on Thursday."

"What she's not telling you, is that someone tried to get into the house on Thursday, and they had reason to be worried," Jasmine chimed in.

"Jasmine, I think it was someone who got the wrong house and set off the alarm," I said to her.

"Got lost my foot," she said, under her breath.

"Well, I can understand your father and uncle's concern… better safe than sorry," Alex said, while looking through my music collection. "You have quite a collection here, Michelle. I see stuff I haven't heard in years…like Syreeta, Prince, Jeff Lorber, Donald Fagan, Grover Washington, Stanley Turrentine, and Patrice Rushen. You have a music lover's dream collection."

"Thank you, Alex. I can't take credit for all of it though. A lot of it is from my Uncle Billy's collection. Jasmine, could you turn on the stereo, while I show Michael the rest of the house? Alex, you can help yourself to anything in the bar," I said.

"I'd love to meet your father. He sounds like he's very protective of you, and I can't blame him for that," Michael said, following me out the room.

"You mean overprotective. I'm an only child, and my father often forgets I'm a grown woman...capable of taking care of myself. But I know he does it out of love. This is why I didn't complain too loudly about the doors," I said, smiling at him. "This is my living room. I'm still putting things in their proper place, so please forgive the mess," I said, cutting the light on.

Michael walked over to the curio and picked up one of my Lladro figurines. "This is beautiful. I've never seen anything like it before. The detailing is awesome."

"Those are my babies, they're called Lladros. I must have about thirty of them in my collection. I have ten at the office, and I have a couple of Blackshear pieces, which I haven't unpacked yet. I'm thinking of buying a curio for my office to display them in."

"You said you had some of Damon pieces, are they hung up yet?" he asked. "I'd love to see them."

I told him to follow me upstairs. We could hear Jasmine and Alex laughing, as we proceeded up the stairs.

"Sounds like our friends are having a good time without us," I said.

"Yes, it does sound like they're enjoying themselves," he said.

I could hear Michael catch his breath as I turned on the light, to reveal the painting hanging over my bed.

"From your reaction, I'd say you like my piece," I said, seeing the stunned look on his face.

Michael was in awe, as he walked closer to the painting. "That painting is incredible!" he said, with his eyes fixated. It looks so lifelike...I mean the people look almost three-dimensional."

I walked over to the lounge chair, sat down, and watched the play of emotions on his face. I realized, as I continued talking to him, that I might as well have been talking to myself, because he was lost in thought.

While I sat back, watching his reaction, I heard the soft music flowing through the house. It seemed like Alex found my favorite Kim Waters collection. I loved any music with a saxophone in it.

"I knew the brother had talent, but this painting is amazing! Do you have any other pieces of his? I remember you saying you had quite a few," Michael said.

"Your reaction was a trip. But my mother almost had a fit when she first saw it. She told me to take it off my wall," I said laughing. "I had to remind her this was my house, and I was a grown woman, and if I wanted to have nudes on my wall, it was my choice."

"My mother would've reacted the same way. What did your dad say?" he asked curiously.

"Who do you think hung the picture for me?" I said. "He had a shocked expression on his face when he first saw it, but he just shook his head and hung it up. And to answer your other question, yes, I do have other pieces, but only one is up in the guest room…where Jasmine is staying. So I won't be able to show you that one tonight, but if you follow me to the other room, I'll show you the ones I haven't hung up yet."

"Okay. Then after that, we should get back downstairs, before they wonder what we're doing up here," he said, winking at me.

"Come on, handsome, let me show you the rest of my paintings," I said, walking over to him, grabbing him hand, and leading the way.

When we got to the other bedroom, which was empty, Michael stopped me from turning on the light. He pulled me into his arms, kissed me gently, and then rested his chin on the top of my head.

"I've wanted to kiss you all night. I hope you didn't mind," he said, lifting my chin to look into his eyes.

"No, I don't mind. As a matter of fact, I wouldn't mind if you did it again," I said, reaching up and kissing him until we were both breathless. I could feel his desire for me.

"Lady, you'd better show me those pictures, before we never make it back downstairs," he said, quite seriously.

I kissed him one more time…tempting fate. I then turned on the light, to let him look at the pictures I had lined up against the wall.

Meanwhile, in the den, Jasmine and Alex were having a great time getting to know each other, and discovering they actually had quite a few things in common.

"Jasmine, I still can't believe you actually know how to shoot pool," Alex said.

"Man, I have three brothers, so shooting pool and playing ball is nothing new to this sister. The only time I did any real girl stuff, was when I hung out with Michelle and her mother," Jasmine said.

"What about your own mom? Did she hang out with you too?" he asked.

"My mother spent most of her time on the phone, gossiping with her friends. She thought Michelle's mom was too uppity for her. I guess you can tell we didn't have a good relationship growing up. If it wasn't for the Rivers family, I would've gone crazy, and never achieved as much as I did," Jasmine said seriously.

"I'm sorry to hear that, Jasmine. Are you any closer to your family now?"

"It's okay, Alex. I'm not bitter about it, and my mom died a couple years ago. I'm still pretty close with my brothers and dad."

"Working for a travel agency, I know you take a lot of trips, don't you?" he asked, changing the subject.

"As a matter of fact, I do. I love to travel. I went to Germany this past summer. The countryside was quite beautiful. I've never seen so many amazing castles and churches in my life. I'm thinking of going to Italy next. How about yourself, have you been on any trips?"

"Except for Mexico with friends one summer, I've mostly just traveled to different states. I've thought about going to Jamaica one day."

"Jamaica is wonderful. When you're serious about going, let me know, and I'll hook you up for sure," Jasmine said, with a grin.

"What is that grin about, woman?" he asked, laughing nervously. "Looks like you have something up your sleeve."

"No not really. I was just wondering what you think about nudity?" she said, with another grin.

"I have no problem with nudity. I sometimes walked around my house nude."

"I was thinking more of…if you've ever been naked around strangers… like a nude beach?"

"Umm, Jasmine, are you trying to get me out of my clothes?" he asked, with a wide grin on his face.

"Down, big boy!" she said laughing. "I'm not trying to get you out of them yet. But if you keep looking at me like that, we'll have to see about that soon. How are your oral skills?"

"What did you say…my oral skills? I talk quite well, thank you very much," he said, laughing hard and putting down his beer, before he spilled in on the furniture.

"Now, you know exactly what I'm talking about. Oral skills…as in sexual," she said.

"I knew what you meant. Let's just say, I haven't had any complaints. Why, would you like me to show you?" he said smiling.

"I wouldn't mind if you did, seeing as you do have sensually full lips. But we'll save it for date number two, okay," she said, quite seriously.

"Oh, so this is date number one. Shall we make plans for another date now, and get the ball rolling?"

"Yes, let's do that. Would you like to have dinner at my place or yours?" Jasmine asked, with a sly grin on her face.

"Woman, you don't mess around, do you? Why don't we do it at your place?" he asked.

"Cool, my place it is then. How about next Friday night? I'll cook, and you can be dessert…excuse me…I meant bring dessert."

"I caught that slip of the tongue, and yes, I'll bring and be dessert. I'll make sure I wear the good drawers too," Alex said laughing.

"Why bother with drawers at all? They're only coming off at the end of the night. I'm not wearing any right now. Would you like to take a look at my creamy center?" she asked, watching him closely as his mouth gaped open. "Shut your mouth, big boy. I'll show you next time," she said, with a wink.

"I wonder what could be taking Michael and Michelle so long?" he said, looking rather hot and bothered.

At that moment, we walked in from the kitchen, with coffee and pound cake. We couldn't help but hear the tail end of their conversation.

"Jasmine, I thought I told you to behave yourself while we were gone," I said.

"I was behaving," Jasmine said, with a wink.

"Brother, I know you're not going out like that. You need to make her show you her creamy center," Michael said, cracking up as he placed the tray down on the table.

"I'll wait till a more private moment, brother," Alex said, looking at Jasmine.

"Dang, man, I might have wanted to take a peek also," Michael said laughing.

"You should've asked Michelle for a peek, because she doesn't wear any panties either," Jasmine said, looking at her best friend.

"No you didn't just put me on Front Street, heffa! How do you know I didn't show Michael already?" I said; as everyone turned to look at me, with their mouths wide open. "You three can shut your mouths now," I said laughing. "Would anyone like some coffee and cake? Michael, what time is your flight back to Philly tomorrow?"

"Hell, no! You're not going to drop a bombshell like that and change the subject. Michael, did she show you her creamy center?" Jasmine asked seriously.

"No, but if she had, we would still be upstairs," Michael said, looking at me with a wide grin. "My flight doesn't leave until three in the afternoon. Why, were you planning on taking me back upstairs and showing me something?"

"Alex, would you like some coffee or cake?" I asked again, avoiding Michael's question, although it was quite tempting.

"Yes but could you answer my man's question I'm sure we'd all like to hear the answer," Alex said, with a smug grin.

"Nope, I'm not taking Michael back upstairs tonight," I said smiling, noticing the time.

"Spoil sport!" Jasmine said. "Pass me some cake. I may as well get my grub on, since nothing is getting licked around here tonight. Do you have any ice cream to go with this cake?" she asked innocently, while we all looked at her like she had two heads. "What?"

"Nothing, and yes, there's ice cream in the fridge. Would anyone else like some ice cream?" I asked.

"No, thanks," Michael and Alex said, as Jasmine got up and went into the kitchen.

The evening was a great success. It was going on three in the morning when Michael and Alex finally left to drive to Powder Springs. I hadn't laughed so much in a long time. They were really good company, and I was definitely looking forward to spending more time with them the next time Michael was in Atlanta. Jasmine and Alex seemed to hit it off, and had even made plans for another date. *I'm happy for my sister, and she was in rare form tonight,* I thought.

Earlier that evening, a dejected Pam gave Sharon a call.

"Hey, Sharon, this is Pam. What are you doing this evening?" she asked.

"Hey Pam I don't have any plans. I was thinking of renting a couple of movies. Why, you wanna come over?" Sharon said.

"No, I don't feel like staying in. Come hang out with me, my treat? We can go to McCormick & Schmick's for some seafood, and then check out what's happening at one of the clubs in the area," Pam said.

"What's wrong, Pam? You're offering to pick up the bill, something must be wrong," Sharon said.

"So, are you going to hang out with me or not?"

"Yeah, I'll hang out with you. Are you going to drive?" Sharon asked.

"I'll drive and fill you in. I'll pick you up at eight, and be ready."

"Okay, I'll see you then," Sharon said, as she hung up the phone. "I wonder what that's about She sounds really down. I guess she'll tell me about it when I see her," Sharon said to herself.

Pam arrived at Sharon's apartment at exactly eight o'clock, and blew the horn, not wanting to get out and go upstairs.

Sticking her head out the window, Sharon yelled down, "I'll be right there, give me a minute to grab my coat!" When Sharon came downstairs, and got in the car, she said, "I'm going to excuse you this time, but what I tell you about blowing the horn for me, Pam. That's just plain ole rude."

"I'm sorry, Sharon, I forgot," Pam said.

"What's wrong? I could hear in your voice you were having a bad day. So, what gives?"

"Michael's in town. He arrived this morning on business, and we had a long talk about our relationship...or lack of one."

"Uh oh, that doesn't sound good. I knew he was just after some ass. Damn, Pam, I hate I was right about him," Sharon said angrily.

"I don't know if you were right or not. But he said, right now he needs things to stay strictly business between us," Pam said sadly.

"That's a bunch of bullshit, and you know it. These men aren't about shit. All they want to do is get their dick wet, without the commitment of a relationship. Nah, fuck that," Sharon said, getting madder by the minute.

"I'm the one who feels like she got kicked to the curb, and you're getting madder than me," Pam said. "Let's continue this conversation over drinks and dinner," she said, as she parked the car. They walked across the street to the restaurant.

"Good evening, ladies. Welcome to McCormick & Schmick's. Would you like a table for two?" the hostess asked.

"Yes. I made reservations for Pamela Bryant," Pam said to her.

"Ms. Bryant, please follow me, your table is ready," the hostess said, with a smile and grabbing two menus. "Here you are, ladies. I'll send your waiter right over," she said, handing them their menus before walking away.

Looking around, Pamela saw that it was quite busy. She wasn't the only one in the mood for some good seafood.

"Good evening, ladies. My name is Mary, and I'll be your server tonight. Can I get you something from the bar before you order?" she asked.

"I'd like a Long Island Iced Tea," Pam said.

"I'll have the same," Sharon said.

"Very well, ladies. I'll be right back with your drinks," Mary said.

"Alright, now finish telling me about dude," Sharon said, as soon as Mary walked away.

"There's not much more to tell. He came to Atlanta to approve a cover for his new book. He decided over breakfast, although he enjoys kicking it with me, he doesn't really have time for romance. He wants to keep things strictly business between us, so as not to complicate things."

"I know you didn't just roll over and play dead. What did you say when he handed you that nonsense?"

"I had no choice but to agree with him," Pam said, when she saw the look on Sharon's face. "Hold up, don't give me that look. Yes, I'm upset about it. I actually thought there was more besides sex between us, and I still think that. But its important there is no conflict between us. I'm his editor, and if we have conflict, I could get pulled off his books," Pam said, with a sigh.

"Damn, Pam. I didn't even think about it in those terms. Although I think dude was just after some ass, it still doesn't make it right. You're my girl, and you deserve better," Sharon said.

"Ladies, here are your drinks. Are you ready to order yet?" Mary asked, placing their drinks on the table. "May I first tell you our specials for this evening?" As they nodded their heads, she continued. "We have a delicious Salmon, roasted on a cedar plank, and fresh Nantucket Bay Scallops. The red snapper is quite entrancing, and we also have Florida grouper, that's out of this world."

"Mary, I'll have the scallops," Sharon said.

"And you Miss?" she asked Pam.

"I'll have the salmon," Pam responded.

"Those are very good choices, ladies. Let me get those menus out your way, and I'll put in your orders. I'll be back with your salads," Mary said.

"Thank you," Pam said. "Sharon, what gets me the most, is that I had my mind set on what I was going to say to him. But after he said his piece, all I could do was agree with him, when I really wanted to curse him out. I was just that mad."

"I understand. Men aren't about shit," Sharon said, with a frown.

"Damn, he had some good dick. The brotha could blow my back out, that's for sure. He's the first man I ever looked forward to going down on. I would be sucking on it right now, if he hadn't decided to stay with his friend this time," Pam said, with a sigh.

"I don't remember describing a dick quite like that before," Sharon said laughing. "So, you're saying the brotha could really put it down like that? You should've told him to find another editor, and kept the dick. I'm just kidding."

"Yeah, girl, he was that good and then some. Michael doesn't fuck you, he makes love to you," Pam said, with another sigh. "He takes his time, making sure you get yours. The oral pleasure he gave was so on point, that he had me squirting and climbing walls. When he made love to me, I could feel every delicious inch of him up inside of me."

"Damn, Pam. You should've shared that man. I would've even done a threesome to get some of that. Okay, let me stop lying, because I'm just not that freaky," she said, with a sly grin on her. "He sounds like he practices what he writes about. I wonder how many women he has running after him in Philly, because there has got to be a few, if he's putting it down like that."

"I don't even want to think about him with other women. I feel like such a fool for letting myself get emotionally involved with him. I originally thought I could just hit it and quit it. But he treated me so well whenever we were together. I just lost my head over him. Oh well, it's over and done with now. I'll just have to learn to detach myself emotionally, and keep it business from now on," Pam said sadly. "Okay, enough of this woe is me stuff, here comes Mary with our food."

Chapter 15

"**M**AN, I have got to give it to you, Jasmine, is all that. I can tell she's a freak," Alex said, giving Michael a pound.

"I hope you can handle her, my brother. She's fine, and can talk big shit... just like you," Michael said, as they were riding home, after leaving Michelle's house.

"You know where I'm from Philly's in the hizzouse." He laughed.

"Good luck on your date next week. Hit it once for me, okay?" Michael said.

"Oh don't worry I'm going to make a lasting impression, that's for sure."

"I think you already did. Both of you were laughing like you were old friends," Michael said.

"She was very easy to talk to, and I felt comfortable with her. I thought you and Michelle were getting it on, as long as you two took upstairs," Alex said.

"Nah man, I was admiring the artwork she has hanging in her bedroom. The same artist that's doing the cover for my book did it. Anyway, she's not the type of woman to give it up on the first date. She has more class than that," Michael said, in a serious tone.

"I bet you were admiring her artwork alright. She has a fine brown frame." Alex laughed.

"That she does, brother. But you know I have a feeling this can get very serious. She's definitely wife material."

"Say it isn't so, Mike! She's got you sprung!" Alex said, laughing hysterically. "Slow down, brother. You have to spend some quality time with her first, before you start thinking like that."

"Man, don't get it twisted. I said she was wife material, I didn't say she was *my* wife material. I'm not even sure if dealing with her on that level is a good idea. I just got out of a similar situation with Pam. Working with someone and becoming lovers is a trip," Michael confessed.

"I can't say I really know what you mean, because I've never been involved with anyone I've worked with. But I will say this, since you just broke it off with

Pam, you better be careful dealing with Michelle. Women can be vicious when it comes to stuff like that," Alex said, making a lot of sense.

"You're right, man. I'm sure Michelle will keep quiet about any possible relationship between us. At least until any feelings Pam has for me dies down."

"Just be careful. You know I love you, and would hate for you to go through any bullshit because of this," he said, putting his hand on Michael's shoulder.

"I will, man. Thanks for the advice," Michael said, as they pulled up to Alex driveway.

It was four in the morning, and they were beat. They talked a little longer, and then crashed. They didn't have long to rest up before Michael had to catch his plane. His flight was schedule to leave at three, and Alex was going to drop him off at one, so he could get through security.

✳ ✳ ✳

Michael and Alex were both shaved and showered by ten o'clock. They shared a quick breakfast at the pancake house before heading to the airport.

"Okay, my brother. Have a good flight back to Philly. Give me a call when you get in," Alex said, pulling up in front of Jackson-Hartsfield International Airport.

"I'll do that. Thanks for letting me crash at your place," Michael said, getting out the car, and retrieving his luggage from the trunk.

"Don't even try it…my house is your house," Alex assured him.

"Don't forget to let me know how your date with Jasmine goes," Michael said, smiling and giving him a brotherly hug.

"Don't worry, I'll give you a call, and tell you all about it. Take it easy, Mike."

"Peace, my brother," Michael said, walking into the airport.

✳ ✳ ✳

Surprisingly, Jasmine and I didn't sleep late on Sunday. I thought we would both be tired, after staying up till after three in the morning with Michael and Alex.

"Good morning, Michelle," Jasmine said, lying across my bed. "What would you like to get into today?"

"Well, since we're both awake, how about we go out to breakfast, and visit my parents when they get home from church," I said.

"That sounds like a plan. I wonder if your mom is cooking today, and if she baked one of her pound cakes? I can taste it now," Jasmine said, smacking her lips.

"Well, let's call them and see," I said, reaching for the phone, as Jas turned on the TV to catch the news. "Good morning, Daddy. How are you doing this beautiful Sunday morning?" I said when he picked up the phone.

"Good morning, baby. You sound all bright and chipper. I'm doing well, waiting on your mother to get done in the bathroom, so we can get to church on time. I have to usher today. What are you up to?" he said.

"I'm just relaxing right now, and watching Jas channel surf. She spent the night with me, and we're calling to see if Mom is cooking today. We were going to come over after y'all get home from church."

"Hey Daddy I love you!" Jasmine yelled out.

"Tell Jasmine I love her too, and yes, your mother is cooking. So, I guess we'll see you girls, excuse me, ladies later," he said.

"Yes, you will, Daddy. Love you. Kiss Mommy for me," I said, before hanging up. "Daddy says he loves you too, Jas. Now, where do you want to go for breakfast?" I asked Jasmine.

"Let's go to *Front Page News* in Little Five Points. It's been a while since I've been down there, and I want to pick up some oils and incense from the mini mall," she said.

"That's fine. I could use some more oils and incense myself. Michael seemed to be really turned on by the one I was wearing last night."

"Girl, you could've been wearing dog shit, and that man would've still been turned on by you. You have his nose wide open, that's for sure." Jasmine fell out laughing.

"Oh, please. It's not that deep between us," I said, also laughing at her assessment of Michael.

"Michelle, I saw how he was watching you, when he didn't think anyone else was looking. That man's definitely feeling some kind of way about you, but I'm not sure he realizes it yet," she said, quite seriously.

"Jasmine, it's strange, because I'm feeling something for him also. But he writes for my company, and lives in Philly," I said, with a sigh.

"We talked about this before, woman. There's no conflict of interest, as far as him writing for your company. And you both can travel back and forth to see each other. Hell, if you make the arrangements with me, I can get you some discounts. So, hush up and just go with the flow."

"You're right, Jas. But let's talk about you and Alex. Girl, please take it easy on that man," I said laughing. "And give him a chance. I think he may be just the man for you."

"Damn, I'm not going to hurt him, relax," she said. "I'm just going to blow his back out a little bit, to see if he can keep up. He does look delicious, but we'll have to see if he's worth keeping," Jasmine said.

"Oh, Lord, I feel sorry for Alex. I saw how you two clicked, and I think, given a chance, he could be what you need in your life."

"We'll see just how good for me he is on Friday, when he comes to dinner and becomes my dessert," she said, with a devilish smile on her face.

"Alright, I've heard enough! My virgin ears can only take so much. Get out my room and go get dressed. I'm getting hungry," I said, throwing a pillow at her head.

* * *

We had a great time at breakfast, and with my parents. Jasmine acted a fool, as usual. My mom baked a pound cake, and I couldn't believe that Jasmine ate three slices, and still took some home for later.

"Jasmine, you must be taking that cake home to share with Alex." I laughed.

"He'll get none of this cake, trust me," Jasmine answered, with a smile on her face. It was a good thing Jasmine didn't put on weight, or she would be big as a house by now, as much as she ate.

Dad said he was in heaven, having all his girls under the same roof again. I must admit I have some of the coolest parents in the world. It does me good to see how much they still love each other, after more than forty years of marriage. I pray I find someone who I love as much, to spend my life with one day.

After dropping Jasmine off at her house, I called and left a message for Michael when I got home. Then I took a long relaxing bath, reflecting on the weekend and the week ahead. Everything seemed to be working out fine so far, and I knew Uncle Billy would be proud of how I was handling things.

* * *

Michael's flight back to Philly was nice, even though there was a change in the flight number, and an hour delay because of it. When he got home, it was a little after seven that evening. He took a quick shower, and gave Alex a call to let him know he made it home.

He had a few messages on his answering machine. One was from Kevin, telling Michael he missed him, and wanted him to call. His mom called, to remind him that Tuesday was his dad's birthday, and she was going to have a few people over for dinner. And Michelle called, to tell him how much she and Jasmine had enjoyed their company. He made a note to give her a call on Monday.

He watched Sports Center, to catch up on the Eagles. After he finished checking out all the football scores Michael decided to give Kevin a call.

"Hello, Carol," he said, when she answered the phone.

"Michael, how are you?" she said.

"I'm doing fine. I was in Atlanta over the weekend, getting this book stuff in order."

"That's great. Kevin missed you. That boy loves him some Michael," she said laughing.

"I love him too. Is he in bed yet?" Michael asked.

"No, but he's heading that way. Let me get him for you." He heard her shout, "Kevin, pick up the phone. It's Michael!"

"Hi, Mike," Kevin said, picking up the phone.

"Hey Kevin, what's happening?"

"Nothing much, except I had this dream about you on Saturday. Where were you when I called?"

"I thought I told you I was going to Atlanta this weekend. So, tell me about your dream," Michael said.

"I had a dream that you moved away from Philadelphia, and I never saw you again," he said, his voice starting to crack.

"Kevin, we'll always be together. You're my little brother, and I'm going to be around, bugging you about school and college, even when you grow up and get married. So, don't you worry about that," he said, trying to reassure Kevin.

"Are you sure Mike?"

"I'm positive, little man. I'm coming by on Wednesday, so we can go to *Friendly's* and talk man to man, okay?"

"Okay, Mike. I'm going to bed now. I'll see you then," Kevin said.

"Good night, little man," Michael, said, hanging up.

"That was one hell of a dream Kevin had," Michael said to himself. He called it a night, so he could get a fresh start in the morning.

* * *

"Good morning, Sara," Michael said, walking into his office on Monday morning.

"Good morning, Michael. How was your weekend?" she said smiling, while tapping her desk with a pencil.

"It was fine. I picked out a cover for my book. I'm waiting for the photography studio to finish my pictures to add to my bio page."

"Do you mean the ones that you took here?" she asked.

"Yeah. They should be ready by Wednesday, and then I'll submit them to the publishing company. After that, my book will be ready to go live," Michael, said proudly.

"Now that you've told me about your book business, give me the real scoop. You know what I want to hear. Don't start none won't be none," Sara said.

"What on earth are you talking about, detective Sara?"

"Man, I'm going to pop you right upside your head."

"Alright Sara Damn, you're persistent. After I met with my editor and the artist that's doing my cover, Alex picked me up, and we went to his house."

"So, while you were in Atlanta, you never got with Ms. Rivers I guess, huh?"

"Later that evening, Alex and I met her and a friend for dinner. That's all that happened. It was strictly all about business."

"Business is what you're giving me right about now," she said, shaking her head. "But you know I know better, don't you? You and your homeboy, Alex, went on a double date, and it was all business, huh?"

"Yes it was, and I enjoyed it. Let me get in my office and see how much work I have to catch up on," Michael said, smiling and easing away from any further interrogation.

He had a desk full of paperwork to get finished, and there were two meetings scheduled with the city planner. His day was going to be a full one. There was a knock at the door.

"Come in, it's open," Michael said.

"Hey Michael, how are you doing, bro?" Bob said, walking into his office.

"I'm doing okay, Bob. What's shaking? Is there any word on the layoffs?"

"Man, I'm trying not to think about that shit. So far, there has been no announcement of any change in the December 4th deadline, so how as your weekend? Did you get a chance to get with Alex's crazy ass?"

"I stayed at his place," Michael said.

"And what about your editor, slash spare shot?" Michael shook his head and laughed when Bob said that.

"Man, you're sick. I met with her, and went over my book. I also let her know we had to chill out on our sexual liaisons. I told her we needed to keep things on a business tip for the time being. The funny thing is, she agreed," Michael said.

"Well, that's what you wanted, right?"

"Yeah, but she was acting kind of strange afterwards. She could barely keep focused during our meeting. I hope we can still work together. She's the best at what she does. Now, here's the kicker…and you have to keep this between us," Michael said.

"Man, you know how I roll," Bob assured him.

"I'm feeling my publisher. I mean really feeling her. Alex and I went out with her and one of her girlfriends Saturday night. Alex and her friend hit it off from the jump."

"That figures with him," he said laughing. "So, what happened with you and the publishing chick?"

"Let's just say I can see her in my future," Michael said.

"Man, you better be careful. You're playing it kind of close with that other sister," Bob said.

"That's the same thing Alex told me. I have to see where this can lead. She had me feeling all giddy inside, and that's unusual for me."

"She's got your nose wide opened. I have to meet this woman," Bob said, shaking his head.

"Maybe you'll get a chance to meet her if Alex has his big bash in the summer. But right now, I have to get into this pile of work. I'll check you out later," Michael said.

"Okay, I'll get back with you. Peace," Bob said, leaving Michael's office.

It wasn't as busy a day as Michael thought, especially since the meetings were postponed until a later date, but It was steady. Before he knew it, four o'clock was staring him in the face, and it was time for him to leave. As he was heading out the door, Sara stopped him.

"Michael, I forgot to ask you to give me Debra's cell phone number. I misplaced it," she said.

"I have it in my cell, hold on a minute. My mom told me she'd be home for Thanksgiving. So, you know we're having a big dinner," Michael said.

"Oh, don't worry, I'll be there. This time I'm bringing my Tupperware." We laughed, because Michael's mom always cooked more than enough food.

"I need to give her a call myself. I'm glad you reminded me. Here you go," he said, giving her Debra's number.

"Thanks. I'll talk to you later," Sara said.

Michael stopped at the liquor store on his way home to grab a six-pack. For a change, he decided to cook something instead of getting takeout. He had taken out a couple of salmon steaks that morning.

When he got home, he cooked those, along with linguine in claim sauce, garlic bread and a salad. He was so glad his mother had made sure that he and his sister learned to cook. After eating, Michael gave Debra a call.

"Hello, Sis," he said, when she picked up the phone.

"Michael how you doing" Debra asked.

"I'm doing good, baby girl. What's happening?"

"I'm finishing up my last presentation for class. You need to send me a commission check, the way I'm pushing your book over here. These women love you," she said laughing. "When is your next one coming out?"

"Hopefully, it'll be ready within the next two months. I did something a little different with this one."

"What's that?"

"I'm going to have my picture on the back cover, and the front cover was designed by an artist."

"That sounds nice. Now I'll really have to beat these women down. They'll be trying to meet you for real after this," she said.

"Maybe I can do a book signing near your campus.

Are you familiar with any bookstores around there?"

"There's an African-American bookstore that's very popular here. Since I know the owner, maybe I can set something up for you," she said.

"That would be great. If you can pull that off, I'll make sure you get a nice cut."

"You're on. I'll get on that as soon as possible," she said.

"Thanks, you know I love you," Michael said.

"I love you too, Michael. Now, tell me, what else is going on with you? I heard through the grapevine you took your new publisher out on a date."

"That damn Sara has a big mouth," he said.

"Somebody has to keep an eye on you since I'm not there. So what gives?" she persisted.

"There's not much to tell. I was in Atlanta to meet with my editor and the cover artist. Later that evening, I spoke to Michelle Rivers, and we decided to hook up and do dinner. I took Alex with me, and she brought along a girlfriend of hers."

"How is Alex doing since relocating?" Debra asked.

"He's adjusting well. He has a nice house and everything. He loves Atlanta, although he says Philly will always be home."

"So, are you feeling this woman?"

"I am a little. She's a nice lady. You'd like her," Michael said.

"So, whatever happened with your editor? I thought you were doing a little something with her?"

"I was, but she was getting too close. She was talking about having babies and what not. I had to cut the physical part out, and stay strictly business with her."

"I see. So, now you want to get with her boss? Um, Michael, you better watch yourself with these women. They can be dangerous, when it comes to love interests," Debra said seriously.

"Man, Sara and Alex told me the same thing. So I understand where you're coming from, but I'm not worried too much," he said.

"When you broke it off with Pam, what did she say?" Debra asked.

"She said she understood us not mixing business with pleasure. I told her I hoped we could still maintain our professional relationship. She said we could, and that was that."

"You know as well as I do, that won't be that. She's probably very upset, and if she finds out you and her boss might have something going on, all hell is gonna break loose. Did you tell this new chick you had something going on with one of her employees?"

"I don't think it's necessary, because we haven't gotten to that point. You know…a relationship."

"Hmm, well, you could be right. I'd hate for you to get all involved, and then wham, all your stuff gets put out on Front Street. I think, depending on how serious you two get, you might want to tell her you were involved with Pam briefly, and see what she says. If she's serious about being with you, she'll appreciate you being up front with her. If she doesn't, then you'll know she's not worthy of you anyway."

"You're right, Sis. Thanks for the sisterly advice. When will you be coming home for Thanksgiving?"

"I'll be home on the 22nd. I can't wait to see you guys. Remember what I said…be careful, okay?" she said seriously.

"I will. Do you need any money or anything?" he asked.

"What college student do you know that doesn't need money?" she said laughing. "Why, do you have some for me?"

"If you need it, and I have it, you know you got it," he said.

"I'm cool until I get there. I could use a couple hundred though," she said.

"I have your back. I'll see you when you get home."

"Thanks Mike. I'll talk to you soon. Love you," she said.

"I love you too," Michael said, hanging up.

It was funny how, even though Debra was Michael's little sister, she gave him some very grown up advice.

Chapter 16

I arrived at my office a little later then usual on Monday. I stopped at Krispy Kreme to pick up some donuts for the office. When I arrived, Yvonne was busy typing at her desk.

"Good morning, Yvonne. How was your weekend?" I asked her.

"Good morning, Michelle. My weekend was wonderful, and those donuts smell delicious," she said.

"Yes, they do! I had to eat one before I arrived. Can you put them in the break room? I need to get ready for my meeting with John. Has he arrived yet?"

"I'm sure John's in his office, but I haven't seen him yet. Can I bring you some coffee?"

"No, thank you. I'll have some of your wonderful coffee later. Before I forget, Jasmine mentioned she'll be stopping by this morning to meet with you, to go over the plans for the Christmas party," I said.

"I don't know why I didn't think of calling her first, since she's been handling some of the travel arrangements for the company for a while now. Let me go drop these donuts off. I placed the reviews from last week on your desk, along with your schedule for this week. I'll send John in as soon as he arrives," Yvonne said.

"Thank you, Yvonne. I appreciate all your extra efforts," I said. When I walked into my office, I saw the fresh flowers on my desk.

I have the best assistant in the world. I can't believe she brought me flowers. As I went over the reviews, I noticed the editing for Michael's book was just about finished. I figured if everything went well with the copy write and production, we should be ready for release of his book in December. We'll definitely tie his book release in with the Christmas party. I'll have to run it by Yvonne and Jasmine later, to let them know it's a definite.

"Good morning, Michelle. How are you doing today?" John said, as he knocked on the open door to get my attention, before coming into the office and dropping into the chair in front of my desk.

"Hey John I'm doing fine. Aren't you looking kind of spiffy this morning... all dressed up in a suit and tie," I said, smiling at him.

"I always look good, young lady, even when I'm dressed casual," he said, with a grin.

"Yes, you do, John," I said, winking at him. "How was your weekend, and how is the family?"

"The family is doing well, and I had a wonderful weekend. I ran into your father on Saturday at the shelter, and did a little barbecuing on Sunday. How was your weekend?" John said.

"I had a wonderful weekend. I hung out with some good friends, and then spent time with my folks on Sunday," I said, smiling at the memory. "Well, we better get down to business. I just finished reading the reviews from last week, and I see Mr. Ramsey's book is nearly complete. Please tell Pam I said, thank you for the excellent work she's doing on her edits. I'm hoping we can get his book released in December. What do you think, John?"

"It may be too soon, but I'll check with production, and see what else they have coming down the pike. And I'll check with Pam, to see if we have the cover design ready, and relay your message," he said.

"Do you remember that we have that publishers' conference to attend starting next Wednesday in Philly?" I asked.

"It completely slipped my mind," John admitted. "Are we flying in that Wednesday morning or Tuesday evening?"

"It looks like Yvonne has us scheduled to fly out Tuesday evening. That's not going to be a problem for you, is it?" I asked.

"It shouldn't be a problem. I know how detailed Yvonne and Gayle are. They probably have everything planned out to the minute," he said laughing.

"Yes, they are," I said, joining him in laughter, and passing the schedule to him.

"Just as I thought, they have everything planned out, even lunch and dinner," he said, grinning as he passed the paper back to me. "I don't have anything else to report that you aren't on top of, Michelle. I must say Billy would be proud of how you're handling things. So am I."

"Thank you, John. I'm happy to know you feel I'm doing a good job. I was a little worried at first, but I'm getting the hang of it, and I'm grateful for all of your help."

"Well, I'm out of here, young lady. Have a good day," he said, getting ready to leave.

"You do the same, and try not to drink too much coffee," I said laughing.

"You may as well tell me not to breathe. I got to have my coffee…it's like breathing air," he said, walking out the door laughing.

Shaking my head at John's statement, I walked over to the window and looked out at the beautiful day. I thought about the good time I had this past weekend with Jasmine, Michael and Alex. I should let him know I'll be in Philly next week, and see if we can have dinner or something together.

"Excuse me, but is this what all busy publishers do with their time…look out the window, instead of work?" Jasmine asked, as she entered my office and sat behind my desk.

Laughing, I turned around and stared at her. "Well, good morning to you too, lady. Are you comfortable in my chair?"

"As a matter of fact, I'm quite comfortable. So, tell me, what were you daydreaming about, and don't deny it. I know you, Michelle," she said, giving me a direct stare.

"Didn't you come to meet with Yvonne? Why are you in my office, all up in my business?" I asked, avoiding her question for now.

"Yes, I'm here to meet with Yvonne. If you're not busy, I'd like you to sit in on the meeting, so we don't have to repeat things," Jasmine said.

"I don't have anything else scheduled, so I guess I can sit in on the meeting. Where's Yvonne?"

"I'm right here, Michelle," Yvonne said, walking into my office. "Can I get you ladies some coffee before we get started?"

"No, thank you. I'm fine," I replied.

"Yes, I'll have some," Jasmine said.

Before long, Yvonne returned with Jasmine's coffee.

"Thanks, Yvonne. Mmmm, this is good!" Jasmine said, taking a sip. "What brand of coffee is this?" she asked, taking another sip.

"It's a Columbian blend, with a hint of almond extract," Yvonne said, with a smile.

"You'll have to tell me where you bought this from," Jasmine said.

"There's a coffee shop in Little Five Point that sell all kinds of coffees and teas from around the world," Yvonne said.

"I wonder how I missed that store, as much as I go down there. I have to pay closer attention," Jasmine responded.

"Okay, let's get this meeting started," I said.

"I was able to get the Embassy Suites for the second Saturday in December.

I also had them block off twenty-five rooms for that night. Do you feel that will be enough?" Jasmine asked.

"I think twenty-five rooms should be adequate," Yvonne said.

"I agree, but could you ask if we could have five of them for the entire weekend?" I asked.

"No problem. I'll handle that," Jasmine said, scribbling in her notebook. "The hotel does some nice catering, all we have to do is decide on a menu. We can set up a meeting with them. I'd like to request we have a sit down dinner, as opposed to a buffet, and have the desserts set up buffet style. Is that okay with you, Michelle?" Jasmine said.

"I defer to Yvonne, because this is her baby. I'm going to just sit back and listen," I said.

"I like the idea of a sit down dinner, especially since we're thinking of doing this semi-formal. Of course, your word on the caterer is good enough for me," Yvonne said smiling.

"Great. Now, were you thinking of having a band or a disc jockey?" Jasmine asked.

"I was thinking more along the lines of hiring a DJ," Yvonne said. "I know a few, unless you already have one in mind."

"I do have one in mind. He has whatever kind of music you prefer," Jasmine said. "Do you have a color scheme in mind, or will you leave that up to the hotel?"

"We can leave it up to the hotel. The only request I have is that they have a Christmas tree in the banquet room," Yvonne said.

"I like that idea, that's a nice touch," I agreed.

"That's easy enough. Now, would you like to have an open bar, or just fountains of champagne and ice tea?" Jasmine asked.

"We can do both," Yvonne said.

"I'll take care of that. Okay, ladies, I think that about wraps it up on my end, unless y'all have something else to add?" Jasmine said.

"I don't have anything else. Do you, Michelle?" Yvonne said.

"I was thinking of doing one other thing. Mr. Ramsey's book should be ready for release, barring any problems with production. I'd like to tie it in with the party, as a surprise. What do y'all think...would that be too much?" I asked.

"I think that's a great idea!" Yvonne said.

"I have to agree with Yvonne. But how do you plan to pull it off?" Jasmine asked.

"I'd like to have his book cover blown up and placed on an easel. I was also thinking of inviting his family down for the party," I said.

"Wow, Michelle, I like how you think. So, you don't plan on telling Mr. Ramsey about the release prior to the party?" Yvonne asked.

"No. We would be the only ones who know about it, except for John, before it goes live in bookstores the following Monday."

"That sounds good. How do you plan on getting his family here?" Jasmine asked.

"I haven't thought about that yet. Do y'all have any ideas?" I asked them.

"I'll come up with something. We still have a little time," Yvonne said.

"Okay, if there's nothing else, I say we adjourn this meeting. I'll meet with the hotel management about the things we've discussed, and get back with Yvonne in a week or so," Jasmine said.

"Thank you, Jasmine and Yvonne. I'm getting excited about this party," I said.

"So am I. I'll go type up these notes, and Jasmine, I'll fax them over to your office this afternoon," Yvonne said, getting up to leave.

"That'll be fine," Jasmine said.

As soon as Yvonne left, Jasmine looked at me and grinned.

"What is that look about?" I asked her.

"Don't play cute with me, Ms. Rivers. That's a nice idea you have for Michael," she said.

"Jasmine that is business and nothing more."

"If you say so," she said grinning. "Let me get out of here, and back to my office. Let's do lunch on Wednesday or something."

"That sounds workable. Jas, thank you for taking this on, I really appreciate all your help. Now get your butt out my chair and office," I said.

"Just pay my bill, that's all the thanks I need," she said, winking and giving me a hug before taking her leave.

After she left, I couldn't wait to get home, kick my shoes off and relax. When five o'clock rolled around, I decided I'd had enough for the day.

"Leaving on time for a change, I see," Yvonne said; as I walked pass her desk.

"I'm a little drained after the weekend I had, so I decided to be the first out of here, instead of my usual," I said.

"I don't blame you. I'm right behind you," she said.

"Well, have a good night, and I'll see you in the morning," I said.

"You do the same," she said.

I stopped by my favorite Chinese restaurant for some takeout, and before I knew it, I was relaxing at home. I had a message on my answering machine.

Hello, Michelle. I can see you're not in yet. I know I said I'd call you after five, but I just wanted to hear your voice. I'll call back later. Bye, Michael's said.

Hmmm, I wonder why he didn't just call me at work, I thought to myself. I'll have to remember to ask him when I return his call after I eat. After eating, I must've nodded off, because the ringing phone startled me.

"Hello, Michael," I said, in low tone, after looking at my caller ID.

"Huh, how did you know it was me?" he asked surprised.

"Well, this is the 21st century, and caller ID has been around for a few years now," I said laughing.

"Oh, yeah, that's right. How are you? You sound like you were sleeping," he said.

"I'm good. How was your trip back to Philly?"

"It was good. I had thoughts of you all the way back home," he said.

"Good thoughts, I hope," I said.

"What other kind could I possibly have? I had a great time with you. I appreciated your hospitality."

"You're quite welcome. I had a wonderful time too. It's been a while since I've been out on a date. Jasmine really liked meeting you and Alex. I see you two are really close."

"Yeah, he's more like a brother to me. He told me he thought you and Jasmine were the bomb. I know they're planning on going out again. That's good, cause he needs some female companionship."

"What about you? Would you like to go out with me again?" I asked.

"Michelle, that goes without saying. I like everything about you so far. The way you talk mesmerizes me. The way you smell entices me. And you have a warm and caring personality. You felt so good in my arms when we danced. And your kiss knocked me off my feet. I wish you were here with me right now, so I could hug you. Excuse me for rambling," Michael said.

"Just hug me, Michael?" I asked laughing. "I'm feeling you also. It's been a long time since I've given any serious thought to wanting someone in my life on this level, but you intrigue me."

"Intrigue you…how?" he asked.

"We never seem to run out of things to say to each other, and you really listen to what I have to say. We have a lot in common. We laugh at the same things, if that makes sense. I'm totally relaxed in your company," I told him.

"Being relaxed is a good thing. I was actually a little nervous at first…being with you in a more casual setting," he said.

"Would you like to spend more time with me soon?" I asked him.

"That would be nice. But I won't be back down your way for a while," he said.

"What if I told you I was coming your way next week? Would you be available to spend some time with me?" I asked.

"I'd make time for you, Michelle. What's going on next week?" he asked.

"There's a publishers' conference in Philly. John and I will be there Wednesday through Friday, and I could stay over for the weekend," I said hopefully.

"You ain't said nothing but a word, Of course I'll be available," he said, happy to know he'd be seeing her again real soon.

I could hardly contain the excitement in my voice. "Great, I'll make plans to stay over the weekend. I'm really looking forward to this. This will be my first conference, and then I get to spend some quality time with you as a bonus," I said.

"Where is the conference being held?" Michael said.

"We'll be staying at the Marriott Convention Center. I'm sure you know where that is."

"That's in downtown Philly. You'll be close to everything," Michael said.

"Great. I don't have the schedule in front of me, but keep Thursday evening open, if you can. I want you to have dinner with John and me. It's about time y'all meet one another."

"It'll be nice to finally meet him. Tell me, would you have a problem staying at my place over the weekend?" he asked.

"Do you have room for me?"

"I have an extra bedroom, if that's what you mean," Michael said innocently.

"Then I don't see why I couldn't stay with you. If you're sure you want to share your private space with me," I said.

"I'd love to share my space with you…among other things," he said, smiling to himself.

"What other things do you have in mind, Michael?" I asked laughing. "Never mind, don't tell me or I may not stay with you."

"My lips are sealed. I don't want to scare you away. Well, give me a call when you get to Philly, and Thursday belongs to you. As a matter of fact, I'm supposed to pick up my pictures on Wednesday. I'll hold onto them, instead of sending them down to Atlanta. We can pick the one to use for the book together on Thursday," Michael said.

"That's great. I'll call you after I get settled on Wednesday, and I'll see you on Thursday evening," I said, before hanging up.

Michael guessed the decision had been made. Once Michelle came to Philly next week, it was going to be on. He wanted her…there were no two ways about it.

He called and made reservations for three at the Samson Street Oyster House. That was one of his favorite seafood spots.

* * *

After a long and productive hump day Wednesday, Michael left work and made his way down to Chris studio. Her secretary had called yesterday to remind him the pictures were ready for pick up. He was really starting to get excited. This would be the final step towards getting his book completed, and ready for the public.

"Hello, Belinda," Michael said to Chris secretary.

"Hello, Mr. Ramsey," she said, with an impish grin on her face. "I'll let Chris know you're here. Could you do me a big favor?"

"If I can. What's up?" he asked, curiously.

"I have two more copies of your book that my girlfriends picked up. Do you think you could sign them? One is for Candace, and the other is for Gail." Michael laughed, as she pulled out two crisp copies of his book.

"Sure, I'll sign them, no problem." Michael worded each of them differently.

"Thank you, Michael. I'll let Chris know you're here," Belinda said, buzzing Chris.

"Good evening, Michael," Chris said, coming out her office.

"Hello, Chris. How are you?" Michael said.

"I'm doing well, thank you for asking. I've got something to show you." She motioned for him to follow her into her office. "Here are the two portraits you picked out from the proofs."

"Chris, these are beautiful. You're the best, that's for sure," he said, admiring the pictures of himself.

"These extras I just threw in." His eyes lit up, and the biggest smile he'd ever had seemed to become chiseled on his face. There was a huge 20 x 14 picture of Kevin and him. She also had one pose of Kevin by himself, and one of him fidgeting around, looking at her different cameras.

"Wow, Chris, these are really nice," he said. "You can look at this picture of Kevin and me, and just feel the love we have for one another. Your work is truly amazing."

"It's funny you'd say that. I felt the exact same way when I was developing it. It just spoke to me and said, 'I'm the one you want to enlarge'."

"I like the way you caught Kevin just being himself. How much do I owe you for these," Michael asked, reaching into his wallet.

"Oh, you don't owe me anything. You already paid for them on the back end." They fell out laughing. "No, I'm just kidding. But you can do something for me, and I'll consider us even. When your new book comes out, I want an autographed copy."

"That's a deal, Chris." They shook hands to confirm it. "I'll make sure you get your props on the book as well."

"See what I mean. You can't buy that sort of advertisement. This is the first time I've done a picture for an author's book," she said.

"I'm sure it won't be the last. I'd love for you to do the photography for any future books I write. Your work is that special, and that good," Michael said seriously.

"Thank you. I appreciate the work. Listen, has Kevin's mom decided on whether or not he can start taking classes with me on Saturdays?" she asked him.

"She hasn't decided yet, but I'm on my way over there now to find out. I'm sure he'll have permission though. I'll give you a call, and maybe I can bring them both over here to sign him up," he said.

"I see you're always thinking. I need her to sign a permission slip anyway. Just let his mom know the class only runs for two hours…from noon to two. I'll explain what we do when she signs him up. He'll also need a starter camera for the class. Don't get anything too expensive," she said.

"I'll pick up a camera from Target," Michael said.

"Okay. You have a good evening," she said, as they shook hands.

"I will, and thanks for everything," he said, as he winked at Belinda on his way out.

Michael left her studio, feeling like he was one cloud nine. Very rarely did you find a professional like her, who would throw in extra stuff. When his book came out, he was going to present it to her and throw in a little gift.

On his way over to Kevin's house, he stopped at Target to pick up a camera, and to see if he could find a nice frame for the picture of Kevin and him. Afterwards, Michael pulled up to Carol and Kevin's house.

"Hello, Michael. Come on in and have a seat," Carol said, opening the front door.

"Is Kevin home?" he asked.

"He's next door doing homework with his friend. I'll call him in a minute," she said.

"Have you given any more thought to Kevin taking photography classes at my friend's studio? She holds the classes on Saturdays from noon until two."

"Yes, he has my permission. I think he'd enjoy that. I like to keep him busy, if you know what I mean," Carol said.

"I sure do. There are too many deterrents out here. I stopped by Target and bought him a starter camera for the class," Michael said.

"You just knew I was going to say yes, didn't you?" Carol asked, shaking her head and smiling.

"Kinda…sorta." They laughed.

"I also wanted to apologize again for my actions. I felt good and bad at the same time after we made love, Michael. It felt good, because you're a damn good lover, and I was in need of some sexual release. On the flip side, I felt bad that it happened, because I was being selfish. For that moment, I only thought of me and my wants and needs, not yours or Kevin's. You're a good man, Michael. You're a loving man, and I don't want what happened between us in any way to affect you and Kevin's relationship. Which I was afraid might've happened afterwards. Can you feel me on this?" she asked, in a somber tone.

"I feel you, Carol. My take on it is this…I wanted it to happen. I wanted to make love to you. If I didn't, it never would have happened. I'm not ashamed of what happened. But it can never happen again, because I could easily fall for you. You're attractive, a good mother, a great lover, and a no nonsense type of woman. As far as Kevin is concerned, I'm truly in love with the idea that I have a little brother. He's a very important part of my life, and I'm lucky to have him in it. I'm lucky to have both of you, and I wouldn't what to jeopardize what we have going on here." Carol came closer to him and they hugged. Michael kissed her cheek, and she returned the gesture.

"So, are all minds clear?" she asked.

"Yes, all minds are clear. I'm glad we had this chance to talk about it. I feel much better now," he said.

"So do I, so do I," Carol said.

Suddenly the door flew open, and Kevin came running over to Michael. "Mike!" he shouted. "I missed you. How are you?"

"I'm doing fine, little man. Boy, you're getting heavier and taller every time I see you," Michael said, as he hoisted Kevin in the air.

"Kevin, do you still want to learn how to take pictures?" Carol asked.

"Yes, Mommy, I really do," he said anxiously.

"Well, I'm going to let you start taking classes, but under one condition. Your grades have to be good, or else the classes will stop," she said.

"Mommy, my grades will be good, I promise. A's and B's only…no C's," he said.

"Kevin, here's something for you to get started," Michael said, handing him the bag from Target.

"Look, Mommy, I have a camera!" He was so excited.

"Carol, I'm going to take him to Friendly's to have dinner. Do you want to go with us?" Michael said.

"No, thank you. I need to finish up some paperwork I brought home. You boys go and enjoy yourselves. Just remember, it's a school night," she said.

"No problem. I almost forgot, you have to take him down to the studio on Saturday, so you can fill out his permission slip. The class is already paid for. Here's the address to the studio. Can you make it?" he asked Carol.

"We'll be there at noon on the dot," she said.

"There's one more thing. The photographer was nice enough to give me these." Michael showed her the two 8 x 10 pictures of Kevin, and the 20 x 14 picture Kevin and him.

"Oh, these are beautiful, Michael! Kevin, come look." Kevin momentarily stopped pretending he was taking pictures, and looked at the pictures.

"Those are nice, Mommy. See, I look like a photogramer on this one, don't I?" he said, admiring himself.

"You mean photographer, Kevin," Carol corrected him, as she and Michael cracked up at his pronunciation. "That was very nice of her. We'll be sure to thank her when we see her on Saturday," she said.

"Let's get going, Kevin. I have a taste for a Friendly's ice cream sundae," Michael said.

"See you later, Mommy," Kevin said, rushing out the door.

"Thanks again, Michael," Carol said, smiling once again and closing the door.

"So, Kevin, how's school coming? Have you had any more problems with that boy you had the fight with?" Michael asked him, once they were seated in his car.

"Nope, he's one of my friends now," Kevin said.

"I told you that would happen, didn't I? I'm still going to teach you how to protect yourself better."

"I can't wait," Kevin said.

They had a good time at Friendly's. Kevin's appetite was growing as much as he was. Michael got him back home by eight-thirty, and then went straight home to bed.

* * *

On Saturday evening, Kevin called Michael, all excited.

"Mike, Mommy and I went to the photography class with Ms. Chris today. I had a lot of fun. I learned how to load my camera with film. We then went to the movies and saw Sponge Bob. I wish you could've been there," he said.

"That's great, little man. Maybe next time I'll go with you, okay? Then afterwards, we can pick up those boxing gloves, and I can start teaching you how to defend yourself," Michael suggested.

"Okay, Mike. I'm going to take some pictures before I go to bed," Kevin said.

"Have fun, and I'll talk to you later."

"Alright, Mike. I'll see you later," Kevin said, hanging up.

Kevin sounded like he was having a good time with his new camera. Michael had decided to just sit back and relax this weekend. There was a double header on the tube...the Sixers were playing the Celtics, and the Spurs the Lakers. Later on that night, he found himself wondering how Alex had made out on his date with Jasmine. He didn't have to wait long for his answer, because his phone rang shortly thereafter. He answered it on the second ring.

"Hey Michael, what's up?" Alex sounded liked he was in rare form.

"Yo Alex. What's shaking?" Michael asked.

"Man, I just left Jasmine's house a little while ago," he said.

"Get out of here. You've been over there since Friday?"

"Yeah, man. What can I say? That girl is a freak!" he said laughing.

"You don't say," Michael said, like he didn't already have an idea. "Give me the scoop, brother."

Chapter 17

THE rest of the week went by pretty quickly. Before I knew it Saturday afternoon was almost gone, and I was at home, listening to Jasmine tell me about her evening with Alex.

"No, you didn't tell me he just left your house," I said, reclining in my chair.

"Yes, I did, and he was good too," she said laughing. "Girl, I turned his ass out. Or did he turn me out? It doesn't matter…all I know is that it was good. I can't wait to get together with him again."

"Okay, Jasmine, back up and start from the beginning. Don't leave out any details," I said, laughing and being nosey.

"Hmmm, let me see. He arrived around seven, with dessert in hand, along with a bottle of wine and some beautiful flowers," Jasmine said, sounding impressed.

"That was very thoughtful of him," I said smiling.

"He was impressed with my condo, of course," she said. "I cooked chicken with shrimp in hollandaise sauce over pasta, a salad on the side, and plenty of garlic bread. He brought some Italian pastries, which we didn't get a chance to eat till this morning. Let's just say, after dinner and some wine by the fireplace, he became dessert. And damn, was he delicious, just as I thought he would be.

"I had him singing my name before we reached the bedroom. If my rug could talk, it would have some stories to tell," she said, laughing at the memory. "Michelle, that man can eat some pussy. But first, let me finish telling you about what I did to him. After dinner, we lit the fireplace and were drinking wine and talking. I couldn't take my eyes off his full lips, and before I knew it, I was kissing him. I slowly started removing his clothes, and when I was pulling down his pants, I noticed he remembered what I said about no drawers."

"No, he didn't!" I said, interrupting her.

"Oh, yes, he did. Girl, he had one of the most beautiful dicks I've seen in a long time, and I just had to taste him," she said.

"Jasmine, you didn't suck that man's dick," I gasped.

"Yes, I did. And stop interrupting my story, or I'm not telling you the rest," she said laughing.

"Oh, yes you will tell me or I'll get in my car and come the hell down there."

"Like I'm going to let you in."

"Oh, how soon they forget. Remember, I have keys to your house. Now, tell me the rest. Don't leave me hanging. This is better than a book or movie. Maybe I should pop some popcorn," I said.

"Where was I? Oh yeah, after I sucked his dick, and had him screaming my name, we took a shower together. Where he returned the favor, and had me literally climbing the fucking walls. Girl, he was that good," Jasmine said breathlessly. "Then we did each other on the bathroom floor, before making it to the bed. Where he proceeded to fuck me so hard and good, I saw stars. We had sex so many times, I can't remember the number or positions we used," she said, with a sigh. "Michelle, I was so sore this morning when we finally woke up, but that didn't stop me from riding that dick again until we were both totally satisfied."

"Damn, Jasmine, sounds like y'all had some night over there. When is he coming back again?" I asked.

"We haven't made any plans, but I know he'll be back for some more of this pussy," she said, with confidence.

"I just know he will. Damn, girl, you don't play around. I wonder what he'll tell Michael?"

"I'm sure he'll tell him pretty much the same thing I told you, except about him screaming my name," she said. We both started laughing.

* * *

"Man, that sister tried to work a brother. She wasn't lying when she said I would be dessert. She worked my body over like I was a creamsicle," Alex said, laughing on the other end of the phone. "You know I handled her Philly style, right?" he bragged. "Her honey pot was tight and juicy, just the way I like it. You want to talk about a wood worker? She went down on me so well, I was seeing stars."

Michael fell out laughing when Alex said that, because Jasmine looked like she was a true freak.

"You just better had taken care of her, if you want a recall," Michael said.

"Man, I tried to tattoo my name on her walls. I had her crying my name... oh Alex, Alex!" he said. "I left a lasting impression on Jasmine, that's for sure.

We'll be hooking up again, you can bet on that. But in all seriousness, she's a really nice woman. We'll see where this goes."

"Well, alright now, Starchild's here." Michael had to laugh at his own George Clinton imitation. "I'm glad you had a good time together. Is she someone who you might pursue on a full time basis?"

"Well, my friend, things like this take time. I'm going to see if she has that type of potential," Alex said.

"Just don't dog her out, or else I'll be hearing about that shit from Michelle, and I don't need anymore headaches," Michael said.

"Mike, have you ever known me to dog a woman?"

"Well, there was the time when…no, I'm just kidding, bro."

"You got that right. Look, I'll talk to you later. I'm going to take a shower and hit the sack. My ass is beat," Alex said.

"Take care of yourself" Michael said hanging up.

Michael sat back and chilled out for the rest of the day, watching sports on the tube, and contemplating on his next book. He had an idea, and needed to start putting it down while it was fresh on his mind.

On Sunday, he decided to surprise his mom, by going to church with her. She was always getting on him, not about only going with her to church, but going in general. He remembered when he used to go every Sunday when he was little. He called her around eight that morning, to see what time she would be ready.

"Good morning, Mom," Michael said, when she answered the phone.

"Good morning, Michael. What's wrong now?" she asked, kind of surprised to hear his voice so early in the morning.

"Nothing's wrong, Mom. I was wondering if you're going to church this morning?"

"Of course I am. Don't tell me you want to come with me?" she asked, totally surprised.

"Yes, that's why I'm calling. I wanted to see what time you wanted me to pick you up," he said.

There was silence on the other end of the phone. He knew she was shocked to hear him say he wanted to go to church with her.

"My, my, do you know how long it's been since we've gone to church together?"

"I know it's been a while. So, what time do you want me to pick you and Dad up?"

"You know your father likes to drive his big Cadillac to church, so be here by nine. It's about time you decided to come back to church. Reverend Thomas will be glad to see you. He always asks how you're doing."

"Okay, Mom. I'll be there by nine," he said.

"I'll see you when you get here," she said, before hanging up.

Michael knew he had made her day. He could hear it in her voice. He grabbed a shower, fixed himself a sausage and egg sandwich, put on a suit and tie, and headed out the door. When he got to his parents house, they were just coming out the door.

"Michael, that's what I call perfect timing," his dad said smiling.

"Hi, honey. You know I like to be on time," his mom said, as he got in the car.

"Yes, I do. How's your eye feeling?"

"It's doing better now. So, I guess the spirit popped you upside the head this morning?" she asked.

"I just wanted to be with my family this morning. The only person missing is Debra," Michael said.

"She'll be home soon. I talked to her yesterday," his mom said.

When they got to church, Michael's mother went into her matchmaking mode, pointing out all the single women. She called them, Good Christian Women. He had to admit there were a lot of fine looking women in church this morning.

When the service was over, Reverend Thomas was standing at the door, greeting everyone as they were leaving.

"Hello Brother Ramsey and Sister Ramsey. Michael, it's been a long time. How are you?" the Reverend said.

"I'm doing well, Reverend Thomas. You preached a very good sermon today," he said.

"Thank you. I'm just thankful you were here to receive the Word. How's your writing coming along?" he asked.

"Oh, Lawd, don't tell me you read his books too?" his mom asked, shaking her head and grinning shyly.

"Yes, I have. It's not everyday I get to say I know an award winning writer. Keep up the good work, Michael," he said, extending his hand. "I hope to see you in church more often."

"I will, Reverend, and I'll get back more often." Hearing this brought a smile to his mother's face.

"Hello, Michael Ramsey," a strange, but sexy, voice called to him. "You don't remember me, do you?"

"You do look kind of familiar. Did we go to school together or something?" Michael asked, looking at her closely.

"Yes, we were in a school play together. I'm Melissa Jones. I used to sit behind you in English class. You remember the girl with the retainer?" she asked.

Michael smiled, as it came to him. "Yes, now I remember. How are you doing? That was a long time ago," he said.

"It was back in the day." She laughed.

"What have you been up to?" he asked her.

"I own a bookstore in town. Have you heard of MJ's True Black down in the Gallery?" she said.

"Yes, of course I have. I've been there before. I didn't know you owned that store. It's very popular," he said.

"Yes, and it's doing rather well. In addition to the one in the Gallery, I have one in Germantown, and another in the Northeast," she said proudly. "I must congratulate you on your latest book. It was an excellent read. I remember saying to myself, I wonder if this is the Michael Ramsey I knew from school. Then I heard someone in church talking about it, and I knew it was you."

"That's nice of you to say, Melissa. I have another one almost ready to hit the market. Maybe I can arrange to do a book signing at one of your stores?"

"I'd be happy to host you at my Gallery store," Melissa said, handing him her card.

"I'll definitely give you a call soon. You take care, and it was nice seeing you again after all these years," he said, placing her card in his wallet.

"Yes, it was. Bye now," she said, making her way down the steps.

"I see you ran into a friend," his mom said, shaking her head, as they got into the car.

"Yes, Melissa and I went to school together. She owns a few bookstores, and offered to host a book signing at her main store downtown," Michael said.

"It's a small world, isn't it?" his dad asked. "Did I hear Reverend Thomas say he read your book?" he asked.

"Yes, you heard right." They both laughed. "Come on, Mom, he's allowed to read something other than the Good Word, from time to time," he said, after seeing the look on his mother's face.

"Oh, hush." She couldn't help but join in the laughter.

"Why don't we go to dinner tonight after the football game...my treat?" Michael asked, once they got to his parents house.

"That sounds good. What time is the game over?" his mom asked.

"It's an early game today, so it should be over by four. Bob's coming over to watch it with me, so I'll pick you up by four-thirty. We can go to *Ruth Chris'* for dinner. How does that sound?"

"We'll see you then," his mom said. "Don't be late!" They both laughed, as he left their house.

After the game, and a very nice dinner with his parents, Michael returned home, wrote a few ideas down he had for his next writing venture, then settled in for a good night's sleep.

The early part of the following week was pretty uneventful. As Wednesday rolled around, the thought of finally seeing Michelle again was on Michael's mind. He figured she should be calling him soon.

Sure enough, when Michael got home from work, there were a couple of messages on his answering service. One from Michelle, and one from Pam. Michael wondered why Pam was calling him now...of all days.

Hello, Michael. I was just calling to see how you were doing. I hope everything is going well with you. I received the cover for your book. All that is needed is the picture of you to go with your bio, and it'll be ready for printing. Give me a call, to let me know if you've sent the picture already. Talk to you soon. No matter what, I still have love in my heart for you. Bye.

He told himself he'd return her call on Friday. She almost had him guilt tripping, over deciding to keep it strictly business between them. Damn, she was good, but just a little bit too possessive. If she knew he had eyes for her boss, she would have a fit.

The next message was the one Michael couldn't wait to listen to.

Hello, this is Michelle. We made it into town safely. I'm staying at the Doubletree Hotel on Broad Street. Give me a call on my cell when you get a chance. I can't wait to see you for dinner tomorrow. I'll talk to you soon.

She can't wait? She doesn't know the half of it, Michael thought, as he dialed her number.

"Good evening, Michelle," he said.

"Hello, Mr. Ramsey. How are you?" I said.

"I'm great. What's with the Mr. Ramsey stuff? How was your first day in Philly so far?"

"I'm just kidding, Michael. The Doubletree isn't far from the convention center, and John knows Philly pretty well. We had breakfast at the hotel, and then walked over to the conference. John introduced me to so many publishers and editors, that it had my head spinning. That man knows everybody," I said.

"It sounds like you've had a full day up to this point," Michael said.

"This evening, we're having dinner with a group from the Association of Black Journalists. Afterwards, I'm going to just sit back and relax. We're still on for tomorrow, right?"

"There's no doubt. I already made reservations at a nice seafood restaurant. I hope John likes seafood."

"Are you kidding? Anytime he sees food, he wants some." We both fell out laughing.

"I see you got jokes. I'm going to tell him what you said," John said.

"Go ahead, I'll tell him myself, and have on many occasions. Well, let me get out of here and get to dinner. How are we going to connect tomorrow?"

"I'll come and pick the two of you up around six. Our reservations are for seven. Meet me in the lobby, and we'll take it from there."

"Okay, I'll see you then. Have a good evening," I said, before hanging up.

"I'll see you tomorrow."

After hanging up with Michelle, Michael had one more call to make.

"Hey, Carol. How are you doing?" he said, when she picked up the phone.

"I'm doing fine, Michael. How are you?" she said.

"I'm hanging in there. Can I speak to little man?"

"Kevin is sleeping right now. He was a little under the weather today. He had a fever when he came home from school," Carol said.

"I'm sorry to hear that. Does he have the flu or something?"

"I think it's just a cold. I gave him some medicine to bring his fever down, and then he went to bed. He'll be fine," she said.

"Well, tell him I called, and that I hope he feels better. I was thinking of coming by on Saturday and taking him to photography class. Is that okay with you?"

"Of course it is. Kevin will love that. I'm sure he'll be okay by then," she said.

"I'll see you then," Michael said.

"Okay," Carol said, hanging up.

Michael felt bad his little brother wasn't feeling good. Hopefully, he would be doing better by Saturday. He was hoping that Michelle would get a chance to meet his ace while she was in town.

* * *

On Thursday, Michael finally finished up his project, and gave it to Sara to type up. After that, it would go to the City Planner for his approval. Michael hoped he would be impressed by it, and then he could present it at the meeting scheduled with the Overbrook Neighborhood Association. It was important for the youth, and the more established citizens of that area, to work together on strengthening the neighborhood.

"Michael, you did a great job on this proposal. By next week, it will all come to fruition," Sara said proudly, after putting her finishing touches on it. Bob agreed when he read it later that day.

"Brother, your contribution, along with the rest of our department, is what made it happen," Michael said to Bob. "The group from Overbrook worked hard also, by convincing the neighbors in the area the building that would take place would be completed as swiftly as possible. I'm just glad to be a part of it. I'll bring the point home with a nice presentation next week, and I know the Mayor will sign off on it," Michael said, as he, Sara and Bob slapped each other high fives. "Well, folks, I'm going to get out of here. Bob, I'll see you in the morning. Sara, you're still going away tomorrow for the weekend, right?"

"That's right, boys. I'm headed to Jamaica with a couple of my girls for the weekend," she said, with a huge smile on her face. "I hope it's not too chilly here for you guys," she said laughing.

"Awe, shit, they're about to hurt Dexter for sure!" Bob said, as the three of them fell out laughing.

"Well, have a safe trip, Sara. Bring me back a key chain or something, okay?" Michael said.

"I sure will. Take it easy," she said.

On his way home, Michael stopped and grabbed a few bottles from the liquor store to beef up his bar, and then got ready for dinner with Michelle and John.

When he pulled up to the Doubletree Hotel, he saw a brother named Cliff that Debra used to date, doing the valet parking. Michael asked him to pull his car over for him, while he went inside to meet Michelle and John.

"You know I got you, Michael. How's Debra doing? Is she still in school?" he asked.

"Yeah, she'll be finished soon though. How's your family doing, Cliff?"

"Everyone is fine. Thanks for asking," he said.

"Thanks again for watching my car, man. I'll only be a few minutes," Michael said.

He went into the lobby, and at first, he didn't see Michelle. Then the elevator doors opened, and he saw her talking with this gray haired gentleman and another woman. A big smile came across my face as I focused in on Michael.

"Hey Michael, how are you?" I asked, giving him a hug and kiss on the cheek.

"I'm doing fine," Michael said, returning the hug and kiss.

"Let me introduce you to a couple of people. Michael, this is Donna Jenkins, an editor from Essington Publishing, and John Masters, Executive Editor of Rivers, Inc. Donna and John, this is Michael Ramsey," I said, making the introductions.

"I'm pleased to meet both of you," Michael said, extending his hand to them.

"So, this is Michael Ramsey," Donna said. "I've read your last book, and let me tell you, it was a very nice effort."

"Thank you, Ms. Jenkins," he said.

"How in the world did Rivers, Inc. snatch you up from down in Atlanta, and we're right next door in New Jersey?" Donna asked.

"I don't know. Maybe the magnet was stronger down in the ATL," he said smiling.

"Well, you three enjoy your dinner. I have to hop in a cab and head out to dinner myself. It was nice meeting you, Michael," Donna said.

"Bye, Donna. I'll catch up with you in the morning," I said.

"Michael Ramsey, it's nice to finally meet you. I've heard a lot about you from Pamela Bryant, and my boss here." John chuckled.

"The pleasure is mine, sir," Michael said.

"Forget all that sir crap. We're family, okay?" John said.

"Okay. I'm parked right outside. Let's get going," Michael said, walking out the hotel. "Thanks for taking care of me, Cliff," he said, giving him a five spot for his troubles.

"Not a problem, Michael. Tell Debra I said hello when you see her," Cliff said.

"I'll do that," he said.

Michael held the door open for me then he and John got in. The *Oyster House* wasn't too far from the hotel, so it only took us about ten minutes to get there.

"Hello, we have a reservation for three for Ramsey," Michael said to the hostess, who greeted us when we entered the restaurant.

"Yes, it's for seven o'clock. Your table isn't quite ready yet. Would you like to wait at the bar?" she asked.

"That'll be fine," Michael said. "This place is packed this evening. The food is great here," he said, after they found seats at the bar.

"Yes, it is. I've been here once a few years back," John admitted.

"John, I don't believe there are many places you haven't been," I said.

"Well, since my children are grown, Karen and I have been able to travel all over the place. In addition, Bill and I used to travel all over the country to these conferences. Excuse me, I see a friend I haven't seen in a while. I'll be right back," John said, walking away from them.

"He knows people everywhere," I said. "So, Michael, are you ready for me this weekend?"

"Of course I've been thinking about you visiting me ever since you told me you were coming to Philly. The question should be...are you ready for me?" he asked, looking directly into my eyes.

"That depends on what you have in mind." I smiled at him.

At that moment, Michael leaned in and kissed me on the lips, before saying, "I want to make sweet love to you."

"Well, I guess this will be a very nice weekend," I whispered to him.

"Nice is probably an understatement," he said.

"Excuse me, sir, your table is ready. If you would follow me, please," the hostess said, just as John came back to the bar.

"You have perfect timing, John. Our table is ready," I said, as we all followed the hostess to our table.

"Here are your menus. Your server will be Dominic, and he'll be with you shortly," she said, after we were seated.

"Thank you," Michael said.

"What's good, Michael?" I asked, looking at the menu.

"Everything, if you want to know the truth. I'll be having the smoked salmon and the oyster sampler from the raw bar," he said.

"I think I'll join you with those oysters, Michael. They sound good. I'm also going to have the broiled seafood combination," John said.

"You guys go right ahead with your oysters. I'm having the lobster," I said, wrinkling up my nose.

"This is a small world. I ran into a woman I went to college with. She teaches at a high school here in Philly," John told us.

"They had colleges back then?" I asked, almost choking on my drink.

"Oh, I see you have jokes this evening," John said, smiling and shaking his head. "Michael, I heard your next project is almost ready to go."

"Yes, it is. The printers are just waiting for the picture that I have to go with my bio," Michael said proudly.

"I read the manuscript, and quite frankly, I enjoyed it more than your last one. There's no telling how big this one will be," John said.

"Thank you. I sure hope it does well," Michael said.

"How could it not, with your picture on it? All the ladies will probably be flocking to the bookstores to pick it up," I said grinning.

"I guess you're saying I don't look like an ogre," Michael said in jest.

"You look slightly better than that," I snickered. "The point is, with your face on it, the readers will be drawn to it. Don't you agree, John?"

"I believe it will boost the sales of your book especially with your last book going on the bestsellers list without a picture."

"I apologize for the delay. My name is Dominic, and I'll be your server this evening. Can I freshen up your cocktails?" he asked, walking up to our table.

We all agreed to go ahead and order. The rest of the dinner went smoothly. I insisted on picking up the tab. Michael wanted to take us to a jazz club after dinner, but John had other plans.

"Instead of the jazz club, how about going to a spot a friend of mine owns? I told him when I made it to Philly I'd check him out. You don't mind, do you?" John asked, as we left the restaurant.

"No, go right ahead, John," Michael said, handing him the keys to his car.

John drove to a club in West Philly called the *Top Shelf*. Michael had been there once or twice before.

"John, you're something else. Is there anywhere that you don't know someone?" I asked.

"If you live as long as I have, you'll meet a lot of people from all over. Let me see if my man is in here," John said, as they walked into *Top Shelf*.

The club was pretty packed, and sure enough, John's friend was there. There was a nice jazz band playing.

"I know you didn't just sneak into Philly without giving me a call first. John, what's going on, man?" a heavyset guy, with a handlebar mustache, shouted from behind the long oval shaped bar. He came from behind the bar and gave John a hug. "It's so good to see you, my brother," he said, as they shook hands.

"It's good to see you too, James. Let me introduce you to a few people. This is my boss, Michelle, Bill's niece, and this is Michael," John said.

"I'm pleased to meet you both. Michelle, I'm very sorry about your uncle. I wasn't able to get down to Atlanta for his home going, but I did send a card," James said.

"You must be James Cook. I remember reading a card from someone from Philly," I said.

"That's me. I used to ride with John and Bill," he said.

"Ah, so you're a motorcycle man too," I said.

"Yes, indeed. I still ride occasionally. Come on over and sit at my table. Sonja, these folks money is no good here!" he shouted, to one of the barmaids.

"Thanks, Jimmy," John said.

We ordered a round of drinks, and the four of us talked, listened to jazz, and had a really nice time.

"Damn, John knows a lot of people," I said to Michael. "That's the Masonic brotherhood. They travel all over together, and they stick together. Have you ever thought about getting into the organization?" I asked him.

"It crossed my mind before. But you have to be committed…as far as time goes. Right now my time is limited. But I may consider it one of these days," he said.

"Well, James, we need to get moving. I have a meeting in the morning, and before you know it, it will be time to get back on the plane to Atlanta," John said.

"It was nice meeting all of you, and John, make sure you tell Karen I said hello. Michelle, I hope you have continued success with your company. I know Bill would be proud of you. Michael, don't be a stranger," James said to us.

"I won't, and take care," Michael said, as he shook James' hand.

When we got back to the hotel, John said, "Michael, take it easy, and I'll see you the next time you make it down to Atlanta. I'll see you in the morning, Michelle."

"Okay, John. Have a safe trip back," Michael said, as the elevator closed.

"Well, I had a wonderful time, Michael. Thank you so much." I reached up and kissed him on the cheek.

"I had a good time also. You and John had me rolling all night. What time do you want me to pick you up?" Michael asked.

"Let's see...I check out at one. How about two o'clock?" I said.

"That's fine. I'll see you then. Good night, Michelle." This time he grabbed me gently by the shoulders, pulled me toward him, and gave me a deep, passionate kiss.

Michael left the hotel with a very good feeling. He came to the conclusion that Michelle was definitely a woman he'd like to spend a lot of time with. She had everything a man could possibly want. She was mentally strong, and possessed a great sense of humor. She was confident, independent, and fine as wine. The one thing he hoped was that she would understand, after he told her about Pam and him.

Chapter 18

THE morning came quickly, and since he had to pick Michelle up at two o'clock, he was only in the office for half a day.

"Bob, I'm leaving a little early today. Thanks for helping me get this project together. Tuesday is show time with the committee. On Monday I'd like to run my presentation by you one more time," Michael said.

"That's fine, bro. I'm not doing anything after work on Monday. Would you like me to stop by your place?" Bob said.

"That's cool. I'll even cook you some dinner for helping me out," Michael said.

"You got yourself a deal," Bob said, extending his hand.

"Okay, I'm out of here. Enjoy your weekend."

"You too don't hurt nobody," Bob said, as Michael left the office.

He pulled up to the hotel about one forty-five, and I was waiting in the lobby with my bags.

He walked into the lobby and said, "Good afternoon, Michelle. How was the rest of your night?"

"Let's just say your kiss stayed with me," I said.

"Let me get these bags for you. Damn, what do you have in here, anvils?" Michael asked, after he picked up my bags.

"No, but I did manage to pack the kitchen sink. Are they too heavy for you?" He didn't even respond, he just stuck his tongue out at me, and took my bags out to the car.

"How was the rest of the conference?" he asked, as we pulled off.

"It went quite well. I got a few ideas for some small changes I might incorporate at Rivers, Inc."

"That's good. I know you got a chance to meet a lot of people."

"I did meet a few publishers, but what I noticed is there aren't a lot of black women running things," I said, with a grimace.

"A rare breed, I'm sure, but you represented no doubt."

We left the center city area, and Michael pointed out the Post Office, and this well lit building across from it.

"Over there is 30th Street train station. They just remodeled the building. It's state of the art now, and has so many shops and restaurants, it'll make your pocketbook spin."

"Hmmm, you mean it's kind of pricey? Perhaps you could spend your big royalty check on me there. I'm just kidding…you can take that look off your face. I wonder if it's as expensive as some of the places in New York or Atlanta."

"Have you ever traveled by train? I have a few times, because there was a time when I was scared to fly, and would only travel by train or car," Michael said, making conversation.

"Yeah, I used to travel by train quite a bit when I lived in New York. I don't know if you remember, but I'm a free-lance writer, and would travel all over the place. Traveling by train gave me a chance to relax, sit back and reflect on my pieces before putting them on paper. So, tell me, why were you afraid to fly?"

"I used to be afraid of heights when I was younger. It took an emergency for me to finally get on a plane. When my grandmother passed away in Seattle, we had to get on a plane to go to her funeral."

"Wow, I can't imagine being afraid of heights. And I'm sorry for your loss. I never knew my grandparents…they were deceased before I was born. I guess that's why I was so close to my uncle."

As we got on the expressway, Michael pointed out a few more sights.

"Take a look over there, Michelle. That's Boathouse Row…that's where the different college rowing teams store their boats," he said.

"Do you ever bring your little brother down here? Kevin is his name, right?" I asked him.

"Kevin loves this place. It looks really nice at night…when the houses are lit up. He's taking a photography class, with the photographer that took my pictures for the book. You'll meet him while you're in town. Don't forget, we need to pick out the picture for my book also," Michael said.

"Great, I'd love to meet Kevin. If we have time, maybe we can bring him down here at night when it's lit up. I'm sure it's quite breathtaking and cold. Forget I asked…we can do it when I come back to visit again when it's warmer." I laughed.

"That sounds like a winner," Michael said.

About ten minutes later, we were exiting the expressway, and turning onto Michael's street.

"Well, that's my house on your right, with the bay window and the wind chime," Michael said, pulling into a parking space in front of his house.

"I love your house…the bay window is beautiful. Is that beveled glass?" I asked, getting out the car, and admiring the outside of his house.

"I see you have a great eye. Yes, it is. When I bought this house, I had all the windows replaced, and the bay window put in," he said.

Michael grabbed my bags out the trunk, and when we got inside, he sat them on the steps leading upstairs.

"Can I get you something to drink?" he asked me.

"I'll have whatever you're having, as long as it's not beer. Do you mind if I look around?"

"What you got against my brewskis?" he asked laughing. "And no, I don't mind if you look around," he said, heading toward the bar. "Do you have anything against having seafood again for dinner?"

"I don't mind, and I have nothing against beer, I'm just not a big beer drinker."

"Well, make yourself at home, and I'll get dinner started," Michael said, going toward the kitchen. "Let me know if you see anything you like."

"You have a very well kept home, for a bachelor. I love the fresh flowers… they're a nice touch. I keep fresh flowers around my home, and at the office. This fireplace is elegant too," I said, walking in the kitchen. "I'm going to take my bags upstairs and freshen up a bit. Do you mind?"

"Not at all my bedroom is in the front," Michael said.

"Oh, I see you've got Damon's artwork hanging over your bed. This is beautiful," I yelled from upstairs.

"Yeah, Damon is the man. You'll see a lot more of that picture," Michael yelled back.

A short time later, I eased back downstairs unnoticed. "Hmmm, and just what did you mean by that?" I asked, walking up behind Michael.

"You'll see exactly what I meant a little later," he said smiling.

"Something is starting to smell good. Can I help you with anything?" I asked.

"Nah, I'm okay…dinner's just about ready. On second thought, you can set the table. The plates are in the breakfront, along with the silverware," Michael said.

"I think I can handle that. Should I use the water goblets, or are we drinking just wine with dinner?"

"Whatever you prefer, Can you grab two salad bowls while you're at it?"

"Is there anything else I can do to help?" I asked.

"Michelle, I don't mess around when I'm in the kitchen. Everything is ready. We're having fettuccine alfredo with crabmeat, lobster tails, salad and garlic bread. I bought a pineapple cheesecake for dessert."

"What, no oysters?" I asked, with a frown on my face and laughing.

"I ate enough last night to last me for today," he said, winking at me.

"I bet you did," I said, blushing at his innuendo. "Michael, let me help you fix the plates."

"Okay, that's cool," he said, passing me a serving fork for the pasta.

"This all looks so good. Where did you learn to cook like this?" I asked. But before answering, he blessed the food.

"I learned from my mother. She made sure her children learned their way around the kitchen."

"Well, you tell her she did a fine job. I may have to keep you around for a minute," I said, putting a fork full of pasta into my mouth. "This is really good."

"I'm glad you're enjoying it. You may get a chance to tell her yourself. I was thinking of introducing you to my parents before you left town. Do you think you'll feel up to meeting them?"

"I must be kind of special, if you want to introduce me to your folks. I'd love to meet them," I said, touched that he wanted me to meet his parents.

"You're alright," he said, smiling at me.

After dinner, I offered to help Michael with the dishes. This time, he took me up on my offer. He made a pot of coffee to go with dessert. After the dishes were done, we sat in the living room relaxing. He lit the fireplace and put some *Jazz Crusaders* on.

"It's been a long time since I've felt this comfortable with a man. I'd love to spend as much time with you as possible," I said seriously.

"You're very special to me, Michelle. Ever since we talked in your office, I knew you were a different type of woman," Michael said, pulling me closer to him.

As we sat in on the floor in front of the fire, he motioned for me to put my head on his chest. He gently traced little designs on my face and arms with his finger. He could hear me softly sighing, as his fingers moved closer to the buttons on my blouse.

"I'm falling for you, Michelle. Not only because you're here at this moment, but I feel all warm and tingly inside every time we talk. Now that we're together, it's getting hotter by the minute. I need and want you in my life so much, that I need to tell you something that's been on my mind," Michael said seriously.

"What is it?" I responded, in a soft, soothing voice.

"Pam and I shared some intimate moments together. Even though that's in the past, I wanted to be upfront with you," he said.

Michael waited for me to pull away from him, but it never happened. I turned towards him, and pushed him down on the plush carpet we were sitting on. His head rested on one of the throw pillows, as I straddled his waist, leaned over and kissed him. It was such a hot and fulfilling kiss, that he closed his eyes and seemed to drift off into another world for a moment.

"Michael, the fact that you felt the need to tell me about you and Pam, proves you're someone I want in my future. Most men would've kept that to themselves, and then when, or if it ever came up, they would've been lost in explanations. At least we don't have to worry about that now," I said.

The look in my eyes mesmerized Michael. I began to unbutton his shirt, and my body went into a slow grind. The feel of my hands, as I explored the light dusting of hair on his chest felt good. As if on cue, the O'Jays, *Let Me Make Love To You*, began to swirl from every corner of the room.

I kissed my way from his face, down to his chest and stomach. I raised up long enough for him to unzip his pants and remove his briefs. At the same time, I removed my blouse, and turned so Michael could unsnap my white lace bra. I stood over him with a sultry smile on my face, and stepped out my jeans and white lace panties. We were completely naked in front of the cozy fire, and lust filled the room. I lowered myself down near his fully erect dick, so that it was just touching my freshly shaven valley.

I kissed Michael's stomach, slowly moving down to his awaiting tool. I then began to fondle it, before letting it enter my warm wet mouth. Michael's body writhed in pleasure from the feel of my mouth. I licked and sucked his dick, until soft moans escaped the confines of his mouth.

"You like that?" I asked, as if he really had to tell me.

"Oh, yes…you feel so good," he said.

I turned my body around, so that my legs straddled his shoulders, and my honey pot was within a breath of his tongue. As I continued to suck and lick his throbbing wood, he slowly inserted his tongue into my moist hole, sending my body into a tremor.

"Oooh, Michael," I whispered, as he nibbled and licked my spot, until I could barely take it. "I want you inside of me...I want you inside of me now."

I turned again and straddled his waist, lowering myself, inch by inch, onto his rod. The lips of my tight valley sent him into his own world. I slowly went up and down, while my hands rested on his chest. He met each of my downward movements with upward strokes of his own. I threw my head back, and rode Michael like I was in a rodeo, busting broncos.

Michael cupped both of my breasts with his hands, and gently squeezed my nipples, provoking sighs from my luscious lips. I achieved my first orgasm, as my juices ran down his dick, onto his thighs.

"Yes, Michael...oh yes," I moaned.

He motioned for me to turn on my back. I slowly lay down, and Michael wasted no time reaching for my breasts, to suck on my large nipples. He nibbled and licked them until they were hard, then slowly and deliberately eased himself into my moist hole. Slowly he advanced into my tight pussy, and then out. Finally, the pace quickened to a fevered pitch, until we both reached the point of no return.

"I'm getting ready to cum, baby. Where do you want me to cum?" Michael asked breathlessly.

"Cum on my breasts...ooh please, cum on my breasts," I moaned.

No sooner had I got the last word out my mouth, Michael withdrew, straddled my stomach, and shot his hot load all over my breasts.

"Damn!" I shouted, almost out of breath, as the last shot emptied from his rod.

We both smiled at each other, as he lay beside me. He reached for a blanket from off the couch, and laid it over us, before we drifted off to sleep.

When Michael woke up, the fireplace was still burning, and he could smell the scent of fresh coffee brewing. I walked into the room with one of his robes on, smiling.

"Good morning, Mr. Ramsey. You're finally awake," I said, leaning down and kissing him on the lips.

"Yes, I had one of those nights to remember. Do you know what I mean?" Michael asked, smiling at me.

"I sure do. You did pretty well for the first time." I laughed.

"I can smell breakfast, that's always a good sign," he said, picking up a pillow, and hitting me over the head.

"By the time you go and grab a shower, breakfast will be ready," I said.

"Come here, woman," he said, reaching out for me in a warm embrace. "Last night was wonderful, Michelle," Michael said seriously.

"Yes, it was, and I'm looking forward to many more like it. Now you need to go shower, so we can eat."

"You sure I can't just have you for breakfast?" he asked, laughing and kissing my neck gently.

"No, Michael. But if you're good, perhaps you can have me for a snack later," I said, grinning at him.

"Alright then, let me get a quick shower. I'll join you in the kitchen in a few minutes," he said, getting off the floor.

"Michael, how do you like your eggs?" I asked.

"I like them over easy or omelets, but I'll make them when I finish in the shower," he said, grabbing another quick kiss before heading upstairs in the nude.

No man should look that good this early in the morning, I thought to myself, as I began straightening up the living room. I added more wood to the fireplace, so it would keep the ambience going.

Looking around, I decided to set up the coffee table, so we could eat in front of the fireplace instead of in the kitchen. I used cloth napkins to cover the surface, and Michael's best china. I hope he had a bottle of champagne, so I could make mimosas. I was feeling so happy I didn't know what to do.

After Michael took his shower, he came downstairs, and stood back reminiscing. Last night was better than he could have ever dreamed. When Michelle didn't get upset when he spoke about Pam, it was a relief, and the way they made love…was just fantastic.

"Michelle, would you like me to make you an omelet to go with whatever you have smelling so good in my kitchen?" Michael whispered in my ear, as he kissed me gently on my neck, and playfully grabbed my ass.

"Michael, you scared me! How long have you been back downstairs?" I asked laughing. "That'll be fine with me. I fried ham and sausage; cooked some grits, and the biscuits are in the oven. If you don't stop feeling me up, we're going to be eating a cold breakfast, mister. Do you want the biscuits to burn?"

"I'm burning up right now looking at you, woman. But so you don't think I just want you for your body, I'll pull back until after breakfast," he said, winking at me. "Let me start the eggs, and then we can plan out the day," he said, getting a frying pan out the cabinet. "I have to pick up my little brother for photography class around eleven. Do you want to tag along, or would you rather stay here? You can always go shopping, you know."

"I'll just stay here, if you don't mind. I want to use your computer to do a little work, and of course, I brought a book with me. Can you leave me an extra key, because I may take a walk around the neighborhood?"

"Baby, that's fine with me. I just don't want you to feel neglected," Michael said.

"I'll be fine. I'd rather just relax while you're gone. Have fun with your little brother, and if his mother doesn't mind, maybe you can bring him back with you, and we can have an early dinner together," I said.

"Okay. I'll check to make sure Kevin's mom doesn't have any plans for him when I pick him up. The eggs are ready. Look in that cabinet next to the fridge, and pull out a tray."

We settled in front of the fireplace, had breakfast, and just enjoyed being with each other. The soft music playing in the background made the atmosphere just right.

"Michelle, I'm glad you decided to stay over for the weekend. I'm really enjoying spending time with you," Michael said.

"Yes, this is nice. I thought I'd be nervous at first, but I'm totally comfortable with you."

"I know exactly what you mean, baby. I must admit, you haven't been far from my thoughts since the first day we met."

"So, do you like playing the field? Love them, and keep it moving," I asked.

"Actually, no I don't. I've never been the casual lover type person. Not to say I haven't had a couple of casual flings, but that hasn't been the norm with me. I guess it comes from my upbringing, and the fact I have a little sister. I wouldn't want some dude getting with her, and then leaving her, so I try to set a good example," he said, quite seriously. "I can't begin to tell you how many people, women mostly, who've read my books and think I'm like the characters I write about. I have more women coming on to me than I can count, but they don't try to get to know the real me…the real Michael Ramsey. I feel comfortable with you, Michelle. Maybe it's because you're taking the time to get to know me, see me for who I am. I love the feeling I'm experiencing. You're a very special lady," Michael said.

"I didn't realize it was like that. I'm just being me, nothing special. This is the only way I know how to be," I said.

"Ummm, and I love that about you, baby. I've never met anyone like you before. Not only are you beautiful, but you're equally as intelligent, as well as nice."

"Stop, Michael…you're making me blush. Now will you help me take these things to the kitchen, so I can get to these dishes? You need to get out of here, so you're not late picking up Kevin," I said, smiling at him.

"By the way, what time is your flight back to Atlanta tomorrow?" he asked, following me into the kitchen.

"My flight leaves at three in the afternoon," I said.

"Would you consider changing it to Monday morning? I'd love to spend as much time with you as possible."

"I'll see if I can change my reservation," I said, grinning at him and stepping into his arms to kiss him gently. "Now get dressed, or you're going to be late."

"I'll get dressed as soon as I help you clean up the kitchen," he said.

"No, I can handle this on my own. Go get dressed and get out of here," I said, smiling and pushing him out the kitchen.

"Okay, okay, I'm going," he said laughing. "A man can't even help clean up his own kitchen. Women are always trying to take over and what not."

"You need to stop," I said, laughing as he went to get his clothes on. "That man is a riot," I said to myself, as I started straightening up the kitchen.

This weekend was turning out to be better than I expected. I thought there would be a lot of awkward moments between us, but we seemed to be quite comfortable with each other.

I was so deep in thought I didn't hear Michael come back into the room, until he walked up behind me and kissed me on the neck.

"I turned the computer on for you in the den upstairs, and the extra key is beside it. I was thinking I'd take you and Kevin to *Geno's* in South Philly for cheese steaks. So don't eat too much today, okay?"

"I doubt I'll eat anything more than a salad…if I eat anything at all. That big breakfast should hold me for a while."

"Make sure you dress warmly. It's supposed to be in the sixties today, and after we stop at *Geno's*, I wanted to take y'all down to Penn's Landing. It's on the river front, so it'll be a little cool, with the breeze blowing off the water," Michael said.

"I have jeans and a thick sweater. I'll be ready when you get back. Now stop worrying and get out of here, before you're late. I don't want Kevin disliking me, before he even meets me, because I held you up."

"He would never do that, but I'm going. I'll call you if I'm going to be late," he said, kissing me again, before walking out the door.

After Michael left, I grabbed a shower, got dressed, and spent some time on the computer, typing up some ideas I got from the conference. I wanted to implement some of them at Rivers, Inc. I also had a few ideas for the Christmas party to go over with Yvonne. I was able to change my flight back to Atlanta without any problems, and decided to call my parents and Jasmine to let them know, so they wouldn't be worrying.

"Hi Mom and Dad, sorry I missed you at home, but I wanted to let you know I won't be back on Sunday night as originally planned. I'll be home on Monday morning. I'll be going straight to the office, and will call you then. You can reach me on my cell phone if you need me. I love you both, bye," I said, leaving a message on their answering machine. "Now let me call Jasmine."

"Hey Michelle, what's up, girl?" Jasmine said, answering on the second ring.

"Hey, Jas. Were you sitting on top of the phone or what?" I said laughing. "Everything is good. I'm just calling to let you know I decided to stay another night in Philly."

"Is the dick that good, you have to stay an extra day?" she asked.

"Yes, it's that good, but that's not the reason I'm staying over. Michael asked if I'd stay an extra night so I could meet his parents tomorrow."

"He wants you to meet his parents?" she asked, cracking up. "What the hell did you do to that man?"

"Jasmine, behave yourself," I said, laughing with her. "I didn't do anything to him. I'm as surprised as you are, but that's what he said this morning."

"So, how do you feel about it?" she asked, in a serious tone.

"I'm a little nervous, but looking forward to it actually. It'll be interesting meeting the people who raised such a talented man. He can cook too, Jas," I said.

"Whoa, sounds like he's pulling out all the stops for you. But, Michelle, please take things slowly. I don't want to see you get hurt, cause then I'll have to come to Philly and kill somebody's son."

"Don't worry, I'm taking this slow. This is the first time we're spending any real time together, and who knows, I may find out he has warts or something. So, you can put away your gun for now," I said. "But thanks for having my back, girl."

"No problem. You know someone has to look out for your softhearted ass. By the way, do your parents know you're staying with Michael for the weekend?"

"Jasmine, I'm a grown ass woman," I said. "And, hell no, I didn't tell my parents I was staying with Michael for the weekend. They only know I was staying in Philly after the conference," I said laughing.

"Grown woman my ass," she said laughing. "I didn't think you had told them that part."

"Let me get off this phone, heffa. Michael should be coming back soon with his little brother, and he's taking us out for the day. I'll call you when I get settled at work on Monday morning. As a matter of fact, I have some ideas for the Christmas party I need to go over with you and Yvonne. Perhaps we can set up a meeting for early next week."

"I'll check my calendar and let you know which day works for me on Monday. Have a good time with Michael, and I want all the dirty details when you get back, and I mean everything."

"Jasmine, you're a mess, girl. Bye, I love you," I said, hanging up.

Chapter 19

WHILE Michael was driving to pick Kevin up, it occurred to him that he had never let a woman stay at his place alone. His mind and heart kept telling him that Michelle was the one he had been waiting for. He could just imagine how his mom was going to act. She'd always been very critical of any woman that he had introduced to her. He guessed being her only son was the reason.

When Michael pulled up to Kevin's house, Kevin was in his usual spot in the window...waiting for him.

"Hi, Michael," Kevin said, opening the front door and leaping into his arms.

"What's up, Kevin. I heard you were sick. I'm glad to see you're feeling better," he said.

"I had a fever, but it's all gone now. Are you taking me to the studio?" he asked anxiously.

"I sure am. Where's your mom?"

"She's in the basement washing clothes. I'll go get her," Kevin said, running to the basement steps. "Mom, Michael's here!" he yelled down to her.

"Hello, Michael. How are you?" Carol asked, coming into the living room, and giving him a hug.

"I'm fine, Carol. After his photography class, I want to take him out with a friend of mines from Atlanta for cheese steaks. Did you have any plans with him?"

"No, he can go with you. I'm in the middle of washing, so it's not a problem."

"I won't keep him out too late," he said.

"You guys have fun. Kevin, don't forget to put your sweater on. I don't want you catching another cold," Carol said.

"I have it on, Mommy. Come on, Mike, let's go," Kevin said, grabbing his camera case and heading out the door.

"See you later, Carol," Michael said. "Kevin, you really like this photography class, huh?" he asked, as they walked to the car.

"Yes I have so much fun. Ms. Carol is teaching us a whole lot about taking pictures. I've been taking pictures of everything."

"I bet you have. When can I see them?"

"After they get enveloped you can see them," he said.

"You mean developed, don't you?" Michael said, laughing at his pronunciation.

"Yeah, that's what I mean," Kevin said, pushing Michael's arm and smiling. "Ms. Chris is going to show us how to develop them today. I have three rolls of film already."

"Wow, you've been taking a lot of pictures," Michael said.

* * *

"Good afternoon, Chris," Michael said, upon entering her studio.

"Hello, Michael. I see you brought one of my photographers with you," she said, rubbing Kevin on the head.

"Yes, I did. Do you mind if I sit in on your class?" he asked.

"No, I don't mind at all. By the way, how did your publisher like your pictures?" she asked Michael.

"I haven't sent them yet, but I'm sure they'll like them. I have the task of choosing one for my book, which will be hard, because they're both nice shots."

"I'm glad you liked them. Why don't you have a seat and I'll get the class started," she said. "Good afternoon, class," she said, turning her attention to her eight students.

"Good afternoon, Ms. Chris," the children answered in chorus.

"Did everyone bring their roll of film to be developed?" she asked.

"Yes, Ms. Chris," they all answered.

Michael could tell she was a great teacher, along with being a fantastic photographer. All of the children were so attentive and focused on her every word. He was very impressed, and learned a few things about photography himself. When the class was almost finished, he stepped out to give Michelle a call, to make sure she was ready to go.

"Hello, Michelle. How's it going?" Michael said.

"Hello, Michael. Everything is going great. How's the class?" I said.

"It's almost over now, but it went well. I enjoyed the class just as much as the children. I was calling to see if you'd be ready in about twenty minutes."

"I'll be ready. I got a little work done on your computer, and took a little stroll around the neighborhood. It seems like a nice area. What part of town is this called?"

"Wynnfield It's a mixed area as far as ethnicity goes, and it's a nice mix of young couples and older, more established citizens. I lucked up on getting my house, because most of the people don't move once they move in. From the neighborhood meetings, I think I'm one of only a few single people in the immediate area. I know I am on my block."

"This brotha that lives across the street from you was washing his car, and asked me if you were home. He said his name was Bob," I said.

"Oh, that's my co-worker and one of my friends," Michael said.

"He looked kind of surprised when I told him you weren't in."

"I bet he did," Michael said, laughing in the phone. "I don't usually have any females staying at my place."

"Well, he asked me to tell you to give him a call when you get a chance."

"Okay, that's fine. We should be home in a few, so be ready, okay?"

"I will, honey."

Damn, she sounded good saying that, Michael thought. "Bye now," he said, hanging up.

The class was ending when he went back into the room, and all the children had contact sheets with their pictures on them.

"Look at my pictures, Michael! Look, look!" Kevin said, all excited.

"Oh, these are nice, Kevin. I see you took pictures of cars, a dog, and birds in the park, and you even have some nice shots of your mom. She's going to like these," he said, giving Kevin a hug for a job well done.

"This group of children has some real talent," Chris said to Michael. "Class, next week we're going to take the contact sheets and develop them as single pictures, okay," she said.

"Yes, Ms. Chris," they all responded in unison.

"Pass in your sheets, and I'll have them ready for you to work on next Saturday. Make sure you put the sticker with your name on the back of the sheet," Ms. Chris told them.

They did as she asked. The children passed them up to her and the class was over. The lobby was filled with parents waiting to pick their children up. One little girl spoke to Kevin and waved.

"Bye, Kevin! I'll see you next Saturday," she said smiling.

"Bye, Mya," he responded, with a smile as well.

"I see you've made some friends in your class," Michael said, as they started on their way.

"Mya was in Ms. Chris class before, so she's been helping me out," Kevin said.

"That's nice. We're going by my house to pick up a friend of mine."

"What's his name?" Kevin asked.

"Her name is Ms. Michelle," Michael said, as Kevin turned to look at him with a strange look on his face.

"Your friend is from Atlanta?" Kevin asked.

"Yes, she is. She owns the company that publishes the books I write."

"Why is she staying at your house?" he asked, with that same strange look still on his face.

"She's my friend, and I let her stay there so she doesn't have to pay to stay at a hotel."

"Is she your girlfriend?"

"I guess you can say that. She's nice, you'll like her."

Since Michael had been Kevin's big brother, he had never introduced him to any of his dates. He just hoped Kevin didn't start thinking he was going to move to Atlanta and leave him, like in the dream he told him about.

They pulled up to the house, and Michael came inside to get me. I was sitting in the living room, ready to go. I had a bag sitting beside me on the end table.

"How was the class, baby?" I asked, kissing Michael.

"It was a lot of fun. Chris has those children mesmerized, and I see why. She has a small class of only eight children, so she gets a chance to interact with each one closely. So what's in the bag?" Michael asked me.

"It's none of your business. You're so nosey, Michael Ramsey."

"Inquiring minds want to know," he said laughing. "Are you ready for a cheese steak?"

"Sure, let's go. Kevin is going with you, right?"

"He's waiting in the car," Michael said.

"Well, we might as well go and break the ice," I said smiling.

When we got outside, Kevin had hopped in the back seat. He had kind of a serious look on his face.

"Kevin, I want to introduce you to my friend, Ms. Michelle. Michelle, this is my little brother, Kevin," Michael said, once we got in the car.

"I'm pleased to meet you, Ms. Michelle," Kevin said, with a half smile.

"I'm pleased to meet you too, Kevin. Michael has told me so much about you," I said.

"Really, what did he tell you?" he asked, as his face brightened up.

"Well, he told me that he loves you very much, that you like to take pictures, and that you're really doing well in school." Kevin was grinning like a Cheshire cat when he heard that. "I saw something I thought you'd like while I was at the bookstore today," I said, handing him the bag.

Kevin looked at Michael to make sure it was all right to accept it. Michael nodded his head, and Kevin tore the package open.

"Look, Michael, I have a book about photography. It's called, *The History of Cameras and Photography.* Thank you, Ms. Michelle," he said.

"That's nice, Kevin," Michael said, smiling at me.

As we made our way to South Philly, Kevin got into his book and was really quiet.

"Michelle, that was nice of you to get him that book," Michael said, glancing at me.

"While I was taking a walk around your neighborhood, I saw that little group of stores on City Avenue, and it had a bookstore that I couldn't resist going in. I figured the book would be a nice way to break the ice with your little brother," I said.

"I guess you broke the ice, cause Kevin hasn't said a word since you gave it to him," Michael said. "Well, here we are," he announced, pulling into a parking space in front of *Geno's.*

"Yeah, cheese steaks!" Kevin said all excited, looking up and seeing where we were.

"Have you ever had a cheese steak, Michelle?" Michael asked.

"I've had cheese steaks before," I said to him.

"Well, get ready, because you've never had one like this before. I'm talking Philly cheese steaks," he said.

"We'll see about that," I said, as we got out the car.

We walked up to the window, and there was a small line waiting to order. The line was moving swiftly, so we didn't wait long.

"Hey, Michael, how's it hanging?" came a familiar voice, from inside the restaurant.

"Wow! Vincenzo Vento! What's up, man?" Michael asked, as Vincenzo came outside to give him a hug.

Vincenzo was a short, muscular Italian guy that Michael went to high school with. He still looked the same as he did back then.

"How you been doing?" Vincenzo asked.

"I've been doing well. This is Michelle and my little brother, Kevin," Michael said.

"I'm pleased to meet you, Michelle," he said, as he shook her hand. "Pleased to meet you too Kevin."

How long have you been down here, man?" Michael asked.

"My grandfather opened *Geno's* back in 1966, and when he passed away, he left it to his grandchildren to run it. So I moved back to South Philly, and here I am," Vincenzo told him.

"You own a landmark, Vinnie. *Geno's* is the spot. It's been a while since I've been down here though," Michael said.

"We still make the best steaks in Philly. Hey, Joey, their steaks are on the house!" Vincenzo shouted, as he headed back in. "I'm making yours myself. What will you have, Michelle?"

"I'll leave that up to you," I said.

"I want provolone on mine, Mr. Vinnie!" Kevin shouted.

"Okay, little man, and what about you, Mikey?"

"Do your thing, Vinnie. Wrap them up though. We're going down to the waterfront to eat," Michael said.

We grabbed three fountain sodas while we waited, which wasn't long, because after a few minutes our steaks were ready.

"Here you go. The peppers, pickles and other stuff are on that table in back of you," Vincenzo said, in his heavy Italian accent. "Yours has your name on it, Michelle. You folks enjoy your sandwiches, and Michael; let's catch the Sixers one day. I own a club box down at the Wachovia Center."

"Thank you, Vinnie. I'm going to get with you on that. See you later," Michael said.

We got our condiments, then got in the car and headed down to Penn's Landing. We parked near a bench that was situated so we could enjoy the view of the ships docked along Delaware River.

"This is a nice view, Michael," I said. "Kevin, are you going to take some pictures of the ships?"

"Yes, Ms. Michelle, just as soon as I finish eating. Can I take a picture of you and Michael too?"

"Of course you can," I said smiling.

After we finished eating, we strolled along the waterfront and talked, while Kevin took pictures of everything in sight. There were a few beautiful tall ships of Portuguese registry docked along the river, which were open for visitors to view. Kevin took pictures of the ships and few of Michael and me alongside them. A young couple walked by, and I asked them if they'd take a picture of the three of us.

"I'll be glad to take a picture of you all," the young man said.

We stood beside the ship with the name, *Portuguese Lady* above our heads.

"Everyone say cheese!" the man said, as he snapped the picture. "This should turn out nice," he said, handing the camera to Kevin.

"Thank you, mister," Kevin said politely.

"You're welcome, young man."

As the day moved along, it started getting a little chilly, so we decided it was time to head home. Michael asked if we had to use the restroom, because he did.

"Ms. Michelle, is Mike going to move down to Atlanta with you?" Kevin asked, out of the clear blue sky, while we waited for Michael to come out of the restroom.

I responded, "No, Kevin. We're just friends, and I don't think he'd come to Atlanta, because his family and friends are here. Besides, I know he wouldn't want to leave his little brother." Kevin looked at me with a half smile on his face.

"I don't want him to leave and move to Atlanta. I love him, and I need him to finish teaching me stuff," Kevin said.

"That's exactly why he wouldn't move away. You're very important to him, and he loves you too. I like you, Kevin. Maybe when it gets warmer, you can come down with Michael and visit me. And when I come back to visit, I want to make sure I get a chance to see you." His face brightened up, and he gave me a really big hug.

"I'm glad to see you two have become friends," Michael said, as he returned to loving scene.

"Ms. Michelle said I can come down to Atlanta to visit when you go, Mike," Kevin said.

"That's nice. I heard they have a Six Flags down there just like the one we have in New Jersey. That sounds like fun, doesn't it?" Michael said.

"It sure does. I can't wait," Kevin said, as we got in the car.

"I can just imagine the conversation you two had while I was gone," Michael said, smiling at me

"There's no doubt he loves his big brother," I said.

After we pulled up to Kevin's house, we all got out and said good night to each other.

"Kevin, I had so much fun meeting you. Can you send me a copy of the picture of all of us?" I asked him.

"Yes, Ms. Michelle. And thank you for the book. I like you, you're a nice lady," he said, with a big smile on his face, as he gave me a big hug.

"Thank you, Kevin," I said, getting back into the car.

"I'll be right back, Michelle," Michael said, walking Kevin to his front door.

When Michael walked Kevin into the house, Carol was sitting in the living room reading.

"Hello, guys. Did you have a good time, Kevin?" she asked.

"Mom, I had fun today. After class, we went to *Geno's* for cheese steaks, and then went down to look at the tall ships along the river. I took so many pictures. Mike's friend, Ms. Michelle, gave me a book about photography," he said excitedly, showing her the book.

"That was nice of her. I'm glad you had a good day today. Are you hungry?" Carol asked.

"Not now, Mommy. I'm going upstairs to finish reading my book," he said, giving Michael a hug and then heading up the steps.

"So, who's this mystery friend of yours from Atlanta?" Carol asked, as she walked Michael to the door.

"That's my publisher, Michelle Rivers. She was in town for a conference, and I figured I'd show her around Philly. Would you like to meet her?"

"No, maybe the next time she's in town. Tell her I said thanks for buying Kevin the book," she said, waving to Michelle.

"Well, let me get out of here. I'll talk to you later, and tell Kevin I'll call him later on," he said, as they hugged.

"I will, Michael. You take it easy," Carol said, as he walked down the front steps.

"Carol told me to thank you for buying Kevin the book," Michael said, once he got in the car.

"That was nice of her, but it was my pleasure. Kevin's a fine boy, and no doubt with you as his big brother, he'll grow up to be a fine young man. I'll tell you one thing, he sure loves you." As we drove towards Michael's house, I explained what I meant. "While you were in the men's room, he asked me if you were going to move down to Atlanta with me. He told me he didn't want you to move away, because you have to finish showing him stuff while he's growing up. That sounded so cute."

"And what words of wisdom did you give him?" Michael asked.

"I told him you wouldn't move to Atlanta, because your friends and family were here, and especially him. I said whenever I come back to Philly to visit, I'd make sure I got to see him."

"My lil brother is something else," Michael said laughing. "He's my main man."

Michael asked me if I wanted to stop and grab a cocktail before heading in. I told him I would rather just chill with him at his house. When we got back to his house, we sat by the fireplace and watched a movie. Then he called his parents, to see what they were doing tomorrow. After all, he did want them to meet me.

"Hey Dad, How's it going?" Michael said, when his dad answered the phone.

"Hey son, everything is going okay over here. How are you?"

"I'm doing well. Listen, are you and Mom going to be home tomorrow?"

"Yes, we'll be home. What's up?"

"I wanted to bring a friend of mine over for you two to meet."

"Well, we're not going to church tomorrow morning. Your mom's eye has been bothering her a little."

"Is she okay?" Michael asked concerned.

"She got something in it while she was cleaning, but she'll be fine."

"That's good. I'll see y'all around two o'clock tomorrow."

"We'll see you then."

"Well, that's done. We'll head over there around one tomorrow. Did you want to go to the mall or something in the morning?" Michael asked, after hanging up.

"I'd like to get something to take over to your parent's house," I said.

"You know you don't have to do that."

"Michael, when you're invited to someone's home, it's customary to bring a gift. That's how I was raised," I said.

"You're right. I was taught the same thing. I just didn't want you to feel like you were obligated. Let me give you a little heads up. My mother has been known to be standoffish, so don't let her intimidate you."

"Oh, I'm not easily intimidated. We'll be just fine," I said grinning. "All mothers are like that about their sons. I'll probably be the same way with mine, if I'm blessed to have any."

"How many children would you like to have one day?" he asked.

"I don't know, maybe two or three. That's a good sized family, isn't it?" I asked.

"Yes, it is. Two is what I'd like to have one day."

It was starting to get late, so we finished straightening up the living room and went upstairs to Michael's bedroom. He could tell I was a little nervous about finally getting a chance to lie in his bed. I moved about rather deliberately, going through my suitcase, looking for something to sleep in.

"Are you okay, baby?" he asked, as he turned the stereo on to a smooth jazz station.

"Yes, I'm fine," I said.

I grabbed some clothes from my bag, and went into the bathroom to freshen up. Michael stripped completely naked and got under the covers. He was just about to nod off when I appeared dressed in a black see-through shirt and black thongs.

"Do you like it?" I asked, standing in front of him like a runway model. "Michael, do you like it?" I asked again.

Damn, she's a sexy sight, he thought to himself, as he opened his eyes. "Oh, yes I do. Come here and let me show you how much," he said, pulling back the covers, revealing his erect throbbing member.

"I can see you do like it," I said, easing in beside him, and kissing him passionately on the lips.

The rest of the night was…well, very interesting. Let's just say this time we were more in sync with each other, as far as making love went. We made love in every position imaginable, and then drifted off to sleep in each other's arms.

We woke up pretty early on Sunday morning. It was a beautiful, sunny morning for November. It wasn't too cold, but it was jacket weather. Michael decided to take me out to breakfast to one of his favorite spots, *The Southern Inn.*

* * *

"Good morning, Michael," a familiar voice called out to him from behind the counter. "I'll be with you two in a minute."

Ms. Madeline was one of Michael mom's friends from way back in the day. She had opened this restaurant back when Michael was about eight years old. The breakfast was voted one of Philadelphia's best by one of the magazines in the city. Everyone who has ever eaten there knew it was much deeper than that. The atmosphere was like being at home.

"Good morning, Ms. Mattie." Michael greeted her and gave her a little smooch on the cheek.

"Who is this lovely lady, Michael?" she asked, as a bright grin came over my face.

"This is my lady, Michelle. Michelle, this is Ms. Madeline." An even bigger smile came over my face, upon hearing Michael introduce me as his lady.

"Baby, you can call me Mattie," she said.

"I'm pleased to meet you, Ms. Mattie," I said.

"Are you having your usual, Michael?" she asked.

"Yes, ma'am," he said.

"What can I get you, Michelle?" she asked.

"I'll let you decide that. Let's just say I'm hungry," I said, as we both laughed.

"What will you have to drink?"

"I'll have some orange juice and a cup of tea," I said.

As Ms. Mattie turned to walk away, she looked at Michael and winked her eye. That must be the wink of approval or something. After a few minutes, one of the waiters came over with our breakfast. Michael had sausage, eggs, grits and wheat toast. I had sausage, eggs and three pancakes.

"Do you think that will fill you up, honey?" Mattie asked me, walking up to our table.

"It looks good, Ms. Mattie. I know it will do the trick," I said.

After breakfast, we went to the Gallery in Center City before heading to Michael parents' house. When we pulled up to their house, Michael's dad was wiping his car off. Michael told me that was his customary Sunday ritual. He was a stickler for keeping his car shined. He always told Michael that your car, among other things, is a direct reflection of you.

"Good afternoon, Dad," Michael said, as we approached him.

"Hello, son," his dad said.

"Dad, I'd like you to meet Michelle. Michelle, this is my dad, Purnell," Michael said.

"Well, hello Michelle. I'm pleased to meet you," he said, extending his hand.

"I'm pleased to meet you also, Mr. Ramsey," I said.

We all walked into the house, and Michael called out, "Mom…Mom! Let me take your jacket, baby." He took both of our jackets, and while hanging them up in the closet, his mom appeared from the kitchen.

"Good afternoon, Michael," his mom said. She walked right past him to hug me. "So you're Michelle. I'm so glad to meet you, baby."

"I'm glad to meet you too, Mrs. Ramsey," I said, glancing at Michael, smiling and sticking my tongue out. I could only assume after we left the restaurant, the chat line must've been hot. Ms. Mattie probably got on the wire and called his mom to tell her about me.

"Oh, forget that Mrs. Ramsey stuff, you can call me Mom. Come on with me into the kitchen so we can talk," she said, grabbing my hand. "Michael, you go on in the living room and watch the game or something." She didn't even give him a hug.

Michael walked into the living room, grabbed the remote control and turned on the Eagles game. Soon after, his dad came in the house.

"Do you want a beer, Michael?" his dad asked him.

"Sure Dad."

"Where's Michelle? Don't tell me, your mom came in, snatched her up, and took her to the kitchen, right?"

"You got that right. She did it with the quickness too," Michael said. They both laughed.

"You know Mattie called here and told her you had a nice young lady with you," his dad said.

"I kind of figured that," Michael said.

"Mattie doesn't mess around. I'll be right back," his dad said, walking into the kitchen to get their cold ones. His dad came back into the living room, and said, "Seems your mom likes Michelle. They're in there getting dinner together, laughing and talking. That's a good sign, because you know she's hard when it comes to any ladies that you've brought here."

"I warned Michelle that Mom would be grilling her about me," Michael said.

"I doubt the grilling even took place. You know women can just vibe on each other from the beginning, and she must be all right. You said she works for your publishing company, right?"

"No, she owns the company," Michael said.

"That's nice. So, how do you feel about her? It's not everyday you bring someone around for us to meet," his dad said.

"Dad, I think Michelle may be the one. I just have to give it more time to be sure, but all the signs point to it. We communicate so well, and she's a pleasure to be around, and she's very intelligent. Her uncle passed away in September and left her the company. She's been full steam ahead ever since. Plus, she knows how to make a man feel real good," Michael said, smiling and slapping his dad five.

"I hear you, Michael. Just be careful. Sometimes these women can be nice and sweet, doing everything the way you like, and then bam, they switch up on you as soon as they think they've got your nose completely opened."

"Well, I'm not rushing into anything, Dad. I'm going to take my time and make sure she's everything I think she is. You raised me to not take everything at face value."

"I haven't really talked to her yet, but she's very easy on the eyes," he said, smiling at Michael.

"Yes, she does look good," he said.

Just then we walked into the living room and then upstairs. "Taking her on a tour of the house I see?" Michael's dad said.

"Awe, you just hush up and get back to your game," Michael's mom said, as we both laughed.

When we finished the walking tour, and came back into the living room, I said to Michael, "That's a nice GI Joe collection you have up there."

"I can't believe she showed you that. Mom! And yes, I'm very proud of that collection. It's probably worth some money by now," Michael said, cutting his eyes at his mother.

"You're probably right, especially the ones with the lifelike hair." Everyone fell out laughing at the way I said it.

"I see you've got jokes today, Michelle," Michael said.

"You know I always keep one or two ready to go," I said.

"It'll be time to eat dinner after we set the table, so go on and get washed up," his mom said, as we headed back into the kitchen.

"Yup, your mom likes Michelle. That hurdle has passed. Now you know she has one more hurdle, right?" his dad said, as they went to wash up.

"I know, Debra," Michael said.

"She'll be home for Thanksgiving, so maybe if Michelle isn't busy, she'll get to meet her then," his dad said.

"I think since this is the first holiday without her uncle, she'll probably have dinner with her family. Then again, there's always Christmas," Michael said, full of hope.

You would've thought it was Thanksgiving now with the spread that Michael's mom had for Sunday dinner. She had prepared a roast chicken, string beans, macaroni and cheese, candied sweet potatoes, rice and gravy, tossed salad, home made iced tea, and for dessert, she made her world famous sweet potato pie. His dad blessed the table and welcomed me into the fold. I felt so relaxed and at home around Michael's family.

"This food is so good, Mom," I said. "I wonder if you'll give me the recipe for your macaroni and cheese. Everyone can't make it like you do," I said.

"I might make an exception to my no share policy…just for you," she said, smiling at me. "Michael, when are you going to bring her back to see us?"

"Whenever she comes back to visit, we'll make sure to come by," he promised.

"This is the last girl I want to meet, Michael," his mom said, looking him in the eye. "This is my future daughter-in-law." Michael almost choked on his iced tea as I looked at him, smiling.

"What did I tell you, Michael?" his dad said.

"Yes, you hit the nail on the head, Dad."

"What are you boys talking about?" his mom asked, looking suspicious.

"Nothing much, I just told him that you liked Michelle, that's all," his dad said.

"Well, it's about time Michael settled down and brought me home some grandchildren."

Again, Michael just shook his head, while I looked at him smiling.

"One day, Mom, you will have some grandchildren," he said.

The evening wore on, and it was approaching eight o'clock. His mom and I had finished cleaning up the dishes, and then went into the living room, where Michael and his dad were relaxing.

"Well, Mom and Dad, we're getting ready to get out of here. Michelle has to catch an early flight back to Atlanta in the morning. Thanks for dinner, it was great, as usual," Michael said.

"Yes, it was Mrs. Ramsey…I mean Mom. Thank you for sharing your recipe too," I said.

"Oh, you're welcome, baby. And you don't need an invitation to come back," Michael's mom expressed, as we hugged each other.

"Would you mind if I sliced a piece of this pie to take with me on the plane?" I asked, pointing to the dining room table.

"I'll tell you what, you can have a slice, and I'll get one from the freezer that you can take home with you. How 'bout that?" she said, as she headed to the kitchen.

"Hey, wait a minute. You're taking from my stash," Michael said laughing.

"Don't leave it at Michael's house. He'll have it for lunch on Monday," his mom said.

"It sure was nice meeting you, Michelle. I hope to see you again one day," his dad said smiling.

"Okay, Mom and Dad, I'll call you later in the week," Michael said, kissing his mom on the cheek, and giving his dad a pound.

We grabbed our jackets from the closet, and were on our way. Overall, I think the evening went well. As we drove home, Michael just looked at me and shook his head.

"What did I do?" I asked, smiling at him.

"You two were a mess in there. Mom sitting talking about grandchildren, and you off to the side, grinning like a Cheshire cat."

"You have to admit your mom was on a roll. I wasn't going to try to stop her," I said laughing.

"You both had me cracking up, but I'm glad you all hit it off so nicely."

"Both of your parents are nice. Your father is a very charming man. Now I see where his son gets it. They say the apple doesn't fall far from the tree."

We pulled up to his house around nine, and we were both beat. There was one thing left to do. We had to pick out the picture to go with Michael's bio page. We went inside, and he fixed both of us some tea to go along with the pie. We sat down and looked over the pictures Chris had taken.

"I like this picture of you...the one of you looking directly at the camera smiling. It looks so distinguishing. What do you think?" I asked.

"I was leaning more towards this one of me gazing off into the sky, but I do like the one you picked also. Either one is fine with me," he said.

"So, we're gonna go with the one I like, okay?" I asked.

"That's fine with me."

"Then it's settled. Let me pack it away in between these two books I have, so it won't get messed up."

Afterwards, we took a warm shower together, taking turns washing each other's back. There was no question that Michael was a man I could see myself spending the rest of my life with. We toweled off and headed to bed for a well earned rest.

* * *

Monday morning rolled around before we knew it. I was already in the middle of dressing when Michael got up. The coffee was on, and he decided to make us both egg and cheese sandwiches for the ride to the airport.

Michael was so glad he took off from work, because he was still tired. The excitement of having me with him for the entire weekend had taken its toll.

"We had better get moving. Philadelphia International can be a trip on Monday mornings," Michael said.

"I've got everything all packed away. I even took the frozen pie out of its tin and put it on a plastic plate I found in your kitchen and rewrapped it. I'll carry it on the plane with me," I said.

"Damn, them clever Chinese," Michael quipped, as I playfully hit him on the arm. He turned me around and pulled me into his arms. He gave me a long passionate kiss. "I really enjoyed having you with me, Michelle."

"I enjoyed being with you, baby. But...uh...we better get moving."

We talked about our weekend, and me finally meeting Kevin and his parents as we drove the ten miles or so to the airport. When we pulled up, there was some serious hustle and bustle going on.

"Okay, baby, you have a safe trip back home. Call me when you touch down in Atlanta, okay?" Michael said, as he walked me to the security checkpoint.

"I will, and thank you for showing me such a wonderful time."

We hugged and kissed once more before I walked through security to catch my flight. This was truly an amazing weekend.

Chapter 20

I loved traveling first class. It seemed as soon as I arrived at the gate, they started boarding my flight. I stored my carry on and buckled my seat belt, then started reflecting on my time with Michael. The weekend went better then I could have ever imagined. He had been so attentive, and we had communicated so well with each other.

I was a little surprised that he told me about his liaison with Pam, but I was glad he did, as opposed to me finding out later on.

I was so deep in thought I didn't even realize we were airborne, until the stewardess asked if I would like something to drink, which I declined. I just wanted to reminisce about my time with Michael. Our lovemaking was wonderful. It was almost as if our bodies were made for each other.

His parents were wonderful. I couldn't believe how fast his mom took to me. You could tell she thought the world of her son, although she likes to pretend she's unimpressed with his writing. Her pride for his success shines in her eyes when she talks about it. His father was too funny, teasing his wife every chance he got.

Soon they were announcing our arrival at Hartsfield-Jackson Airport. As soon as I deplaned, I took the train to baggage claim. While waiting on my luggage, I decided to call and let Yvonne know I was going to be late. I hadn't called to leave her a message, and knew she had to be worrying and wondering where I was by now.

"Rivers, Inc., Yvonne speaking," she answered.

"Hello, Yvonne, it's Michelle," I said.

"Hi Michelle I was just about to call and see if you overslept or something."

"I decided to stay over in Philly until this morning, and forgot to call you. I'm waiting on my luggage now, and will be coming straight to the office from here."

"Okay. I'll see you then. I'm just glad everything is alright," she said.

"I'll see you soon," I said, before hanging up.

As luck would have it, I didn't have to wait long for my luggage to appear, and was soon on my way to the parking garage to reclaim my car. Rush hour was over, so it didn't take me more than thirty minutes to reach the office.

"Good morning, Ms. Rivers. What a beautiful day we're having," Curtis the security guard said, as I walked to the elevator.

"Yes, it is a beautiful day, Curtis," I answered, with a smile.

When I walked into the office, Yvonne said, "Good morning, Michelle. You look absolutely beautiful. Philly must've agreed with you."

"Hi Yvonne, Thank you, and you're right, I had a wonderful time in Philly. Give me a few minutes to get settled, and I'll tell you about my trip. Is there anything that needs my immediate attention?"

"No, there's nothing pressing. Your mail is on your desk, along with the production reports and a few phone messages. Can I get you a cup of coffee or tea?"

"A cup of tea would be wonderful," I said, going into my office.

"I'll bring it to you in a few minutes. Welcome back," Yvonne said.

As soon as I sat down at my desk, the phone rang. I started laughing as soon as I glanced at the caller ID and saw the name.

"Dang Jasmine, Can a sister get settled in before you call for the 411?" I said laughing, when I picked up the phone.

"Don't play with me, heffa! Now spill it, I want every juicy detail, and you better not leave anything out," she said.

"Jasmine, just in case you've forgotten, I'm at work. I'm not giving you any details of my trip until later this evening. So, you'll just have to wait, but trust me, it'll be worth it. How was your weekend?"

"My weekend was fine. I worked most of it, ran some errands, talked to ole boy on the phone, and made plans to see him this weekend, nothing special. What time are you leaving the office? How about I come over for dinner, and you can feed me and tell me all about your weekend?"

"What makes you think I want to cook for your nosey ass?" I said. "Meet me at my house at six o'clock, and if I'm not there, use your key and let yourself in. Look, I just arrived at the office, and I have some work to catch up on. I'll see you later this evening. Bye, Jas," I said, hanging up as Yvonne walked into my office with my tea. "Thank you, Yvonne. Please have a seat and fill me in on what's been happening around here while I was gone. I've yet to even glance at any of the notes you left me."

"Everything went smoothly while you and John were in Philly. I got a chance to see the picture for Mr. Ramsey's cover. Damon did a fantastic job, and I wouldn't mind him doing a family portrait for me."

"Why don't you give him a call, and see if he can do one for you. I'm sure he wouldn't mind," I said.

"I'll have to give it some thought. I hate taking pictures. But back to Mr. Ramsey's book. I believe as soon as they receive his picture for the bio page, they'll be ready to move to production. Of course, that's after he approves the galley, which should be ready by the end of the week. After he goes over it, and makes whatever changes he deems necessary, it'll go to the printers. From past experience with Mr. Ramsey, I'm sure the changes, if any, will be minimal and he'll have everything back to us fairly quickly," Yvonne said.

"I've been hearing from everyone that Mr. Ramsey is a perfectionist, and his stuff is mostly edited before we get it, so I'm sure it will be just fine. Also, please have Pam come see me sometime today. Mr. Ramsey gave me the picture for his bio while I was in Philly," I said. "How are the plans for the Christmas party going?" I asked.

"Everything is going great. Jasmine and I met with the hotel banquet staff on Friday, and worked out all the details. We completed the menu, which is on your desk. We also hired the DJ Jasmine recommended. The only thing left to do is to have the invitations printed up, and to go over the guest list once more."

"Sounds like you've been busy, Yvonne. I'm getting excited about this party. I have some ideas for special gifts. I ordered some angels from Blackshear to put on the tables that everyone can take as keepsakes to hang on their trees. Speaking of trees, did you find out if the hotel could supply the ones we were talking about for the room, or do we need to purchase some?"

"They said they wouldn't have a problem supplying us with the two extra trees for the ballroom," Yvonne said.

"Great. Let me know when you're ready to go over the guest list for the invitations, and then we should be all set," I said.

"I'll have some samples of invitations for us to choose from by Wednesday. We could all meet at one on Wednesday and finalize everything, if that's okay with you. I've already spoken with Jasmine, and she's available at that time," Yvonne said.

"That sounds fine, but you know my schedule for this week better than I do," I said laughing.

"I guess you're right about that. And I'm having a wonderful time working with Jasmine. She's very detail oriented and a lot of fun," Yvonne said.

"That's my Jasmine. Thanks again for all your hard work, I really appreciate it. I'm going to look over the notes you left me, and if I have any questions, I'll let you know. Please don't forget to ask Pam to come and see me sometime today," I said.

"I'll do that right away. Welcome back again," Yvonne said.

"It's good to be back," I said smiling, as Yvonne got up to leave my office.

When she left, I decided to call my mom to let her know I had made it back safely. But as usual, I got the answering service, so I left a message. She was probably at the church, and I bet dad was at work. I gave him a call.

"Rivers speaking," my dad said, when he answered the phone.

"Hey Daddy, It's your other woman calling to check in. How are you doing?" I said.

"Hey, baby. Your old man is doing fine. Did you have a good time in Philly?"

"I had a wonderful time. The conference went well, and I got some ideas I may try at Rivers, Inc. I also made contacts with other publishers. I'm glad John was with me, he knows everybody, and was a great help. I'm learning quite a lot from him."

"Johnny has been with the company from the start. Billy said he's the best editor in the business, and he helped put Rivers, Inc. on the map. He wanted to make him a partner in the company, but John said he was happy with the shares he owns and being the Executive Editor. He's quite an asset to the company."

"That he is, Dad. I tried to reach Mom at home, but of course, I got the answering machine. If she calls you, please tell her I made it home safely."

"You know she's probably at the church, and there's no use calling her cell phone, because she never has it on anyway," he said laughing.

"What's the use of her having one if she doesn't turn it on?" I said, laughing with him.

"You know your mother…she says it's only for emergencies."

"What am I going to do with you two?" I said. "I'll talk to you later, Daddy. I love you."

"I love you too, baby. What are you doing for dinner tonight? Why don't you come by the house and tell us about your trip?"

"I'll have to take a rain check for later in the week. Jasmine is coming over for dinner for the same reason. All of you are just plain nosey," I said. "Bye, Daddy," I said, hanging up before he could ask any more questions.

They were all too funny, but I loved each of them. I know Jasmine will be full of questions tonight. I had one more call to make before I got lost in my work.

"Hello, Michael, this is Michelle," I said, when he picked up the phone.

"Hey, lady. I was waiting on your call. How was your flight back?" he said, sounding happy to hear my voice.

"It was good. I was so lost in thought, before I knew it, the plane was landing," I said.

"Hmmm, and just what were you thinking about," he asked, with a slight chuckle.

"You're asking me a question you already know the answer to. Let me get off this phone and do some work. I was just calling to let you know I made it home safely. I'll call you later, honey. Have a wonderful day," I said, preparing to hang up.

"You have a wonderful day also, baby. Bye," he said, hanging up.

After we hung up, I realized how good it felt hearing his voice. I was so happy at this moment, I could scream. I looked up at the clock hanging over the door, and couldn't believe it was almost noon. Where did the time go?

"Michelle, I'm about to order some lunch. Can I get you anything?" Yvonne asked, through the intercom.

"Yes, would you please order me a salad with chicken strips, honey mustard dressing, and a iced green tea? Thank you," I said to her.

"You're welcome. I'll let you know when it arrives," Yvonne said.

I decided to eat lunch in my office. I put on some smooth jazz and started reading a manuscript that one of the editors had just finished. I loved the extra perks of being able to read a book in its raw form, just as the writer thought it out, and then re-reading the finished product. Just as I was getting into the first few pages, there was a knock on the door.

"Hey, Pam, come on in," I said, looking up from the manuscript.

"Hi Michelle, Yvonne said you wanted to see me," Pam said, entering my office.

"Yes, I have the picture you need for Mr. Ramsey's bio page. He gave it to me while I was in Philly. Please have a seat while I get it out of my bag."

I can't believe he gave her the picture. Just wait until I talk to him. Now I'm not sorry for what I did. I just hope she doesn't notice while I'm in her office, Pam thought to herself.

"Here it is. Are you okay, Pam? You have this strange look on your face," I asked her.

"I'm okay, just an upset stomach. I don't think the pizza I had for lunch agreed with me," she said.

"I have some Tums if you think that would help," I offered.

"Thank you, but I took something before I left my office. I'll make sure this pictures gets to production," Pam said, tucking the photo in her notepad.

"I was wondering if you've met with C.E. Campbell yet? I understand from John that you're doing the editing for his new book."

"Not yet, but we've been corresponding by e-mail. I have an appointment to meet with C.E. Campbell on Friday night," she said.

"Well, I look forward to hearing how your meeting goes," I said.

"I'll be sure to let you know next week. Well, I better get back to my office. Have a good evening, Michelle."

"You too, Pam, and I hope you feel better soon."

That was certainly strange. I hope Pam's okay, and just has an upset stomach and not food poisoning, I thought to myself after she left my office.

I started to bring things to a close for the day. I knew Jasmine would beat me to my house. Since I didn't feel like cooking, I decided to stop by my favorite Chinese place to pick up some take out.

"This is sure to be an interesting evening," I said to myself, as I headed out the door.

"Good night, Yvonne. I'll see you bright and early in the morning," I said, as I walked by her desk.

"Good night, Michelle. I'm right behind you. I have one more letter to type up. Have a good evening," she said.

As I was driving home, I thought again about my weekend with Michael. I couldn't believe my luck with him. It just goes to show that you can't take what you read in books literally. I would've taken him for the playboy type, but he's quite the opposite. The love and patience he has for his little brother, shows what a great father he will be one day.

Just as I thought…Jasmine had made it to my house before I did. She was sitting on the porch, waiting patiently. Nosey heffa couldn't wait to grill me about my weekend.

"It's about time you got here, woman. Give me that bag and get in here," Jasmine said, as I as getting my suitcase out the trunk of my car.

"Dang, heffa, get the Chinese food out the car, and give me a chance to get in the house at least. And it's good to see you too," I said, giving her a hug.

"Yuck, get your hands off me. Don't be hugging me. How was your day?" Jasmine laughed, getting the bag of food out the car.

"You know you love my hugs," I said laughing. "My day was long, but okay."

"I bet it was long after you just flew in from Philly. And I bet your ass didn't get much sleep last night," she said, as we walked into the house.

"I did too get some sleep, Jas! You need to stop with your nonsense," I said, cracking up as I was taking off my shoes. "Can I at least take a shower before you get all up in my business?"

"Yeah, but just don't take too long. I'll get the food on the table, and we can get right to it as soon as you come back downstairs."

"Nosey ass," I said under my breath, as I went upstairs.

"I heard that!" she shouted up after me.

"I just bet you did," I said to myself, as I undressed and got in the shower to wash away the weariness, that all of a sudden came over me.

I knew I would be getting a good night's sleep tonight, but first I had to tell my nosey friend about my trip. Who was I trying to kid...I wanted to talk about it as much as she wanted to hear about it.

Slipping on a gown and robe, I headed back downstairs to the kitchen, where Jasmine had set the table with my best china and lit some candles.

"It looks quite cozy in here, woman," I said smiling. "Let me get the glasses and a bottle of wine from the fridge. How was your day?"

"My day was good, but we're not here to talk about me. We're here to talk about your weekend in Philly, so don't try to be slick," Jasmine said, wanting me to get to the point.

"Can't put anything over on you, can I," I said laughing, as I took a seat at the table. "Let's say grace. Dear Lord, thank you for the meal we're about to receive, and thank you for the beautiful company with which to share it with. Amen."

"Amen. Now start talking, heffa," Jasmine said, waving a fork in my direction.

"Dang, a sister can't even eat. Okay, okay, my weekend with Michael was wonderful. He picked me up from my hotel on Friday, and took me sightseeing on the way to his house."

"Michelle, I swear I will beat you if you don't stop stalling and get to the good part. Can he fuck?"

"Oh, my God, no you didn't," I said laughing. "But to answer your question, yes, brother man can fuck and make love too. The sex was incredible between us...almost as if we had been sharing the same bed for a while. Although we never made it to the bed that first night," I said grinning.

"Whoa, don't stop there. Why didn't y'all make it to the bed?"

"Well, first let me tell you about his confession," I said.

"Oh, what confession is that?"

"If you shut up, I'll tell you," I said. "Well, it seems that he and one of my editors had something going on for awhile."

"Excuse me, come again?" Jasmine asked.

"Michael told me he'd been involved with his editor, Pam. They had a sexual relationship, but he had broken it off with her, and he wanted to tell me before we got any more involved."

"Well, I'll be damned. How do you feel about this confession? That's a stupid question...you must be okay, since you stayed the weekend with him. But are you really okay with it?"

"You know what, Jas, I surprised myself, because I'm okay with it. I figured if he took the chance on telling me, then it must not have been that serious. You know what I mean?"

"Did he tell you before y'all got horizontal or after?"

"He told me before, and then I was the one who made the first move."

"No the hell you didn't, girl," she said surprised.

"Yes I did, and it was wonderful. Right there on his living room floor in front of the fireplace. After I finished savoring the dick, I decided to do some riding, and I have to say I missed that," I said, smiling at the memory.

"I know you aren't saying you ain't had a dick since Tony died, because I know better."

"No, that's not what I'm saying. Of course I've had sex, but it's quite different when you connect mentally with the man you're having sex with."

"This is getting too deep for me. Michelle, please tell me you aren't falling in love with this man. You just met him."

"Jasmine, I may have just met Michael, but I feel as if I've known him all my life. I'm not saying I'm in love with him, but I'm feeling some kind of way about him. I'm just going with the flow right now. I'm not trying to define our relationship at this point."

"I just don't want to see you get hurt. I'd hate to have to take a baseball bat to the brotha."

"What am I going to do with you, woman?" I said laughing. "And do you know he even introduced me to his parents."

"Excuse me, what did you say?" Jasmine asked, nearly choking on her Moo Shoo Pork.

"Remember when I talked to you on the phone, and told you he was going to introduce me to his parents? Well, he did and let me tell you, his mom and I got along right from the start. As a matter of fact, she gave me her phone number and address, and asked me to keep in touch with her. By the way, would you like a slice of sweet potato pie? She gave me one to bring back home with me."

"If it's as good as your mother's, then yes, I want a slice. But damn, he really took you home to meet the parents? This is serious, men don't usually take you to meet their mother right away."

"It was funny, as soon as we got to his parents' house, his mother came out the kitchen, gave me a hug, and took me away from Michael," I said laughing. "Michael had taken me out to breakfast to a place owned by one of his mother's friends, and she must've called before we got there and gave her the thumbs up. His parents reminded me a little of my own…they have this secret look they give each other."

"Oh, no, not the infamous look," Jasmine, said laughing. "I know exactly what you're talking about. The way they look in each other's eyes and smile, like they're sharing a secret no one else is a part of."

"That's exactly what I'm talking about. I thought I would be nervous, but I wasn't at all. They invited me to come back for Thanksgiving, but you know I can't this year. I thought about inviting them here for the Christmas party, as a surprise to Michael. What do you think about that?"

"That's a great idea," Jasmine said, as she heaped more food on her plate. "But we need to finalize this arrangement soon. Thanksgiving is next week, and then we have three weeks before the party."

"Wow, where has the time gone? It seems like I just got here from New York, and here we are already talking about Christmas. I haven't even started any shopping," I said.

"Well, we can start shopping this weekend. No, on second thought, we can't because I'll be doing Alex this weekend," she said grinning.

"Damn, Jas, I thought y'all were just getting together for dinner, and now you talking about him staying the weekend."

"I know you're not talking, Ms. Just Returned From A Weekend In Philly," she said laughing. "His mom stepped in this pie. It's almost as good as your mom's," she said, after eating a slice of the sweet potato pie.

"You didn't hear it from me, but it's better than Mom's pie. Mom still makes the best cakes in the world. I doubt anyone can touch her there," I said.

"You'll get no complaints from me. Pass me the pie, I want another slice and I'll wrap one up to take home too," Jasmine said.

"Just because I love you, I'll give you half the pie. Now help me clean up the kitchen and put this stuff away. I'll make us some coffee, and we can finish talking about my weekend."

"Yes, because I want to know if Michael knocked off all the cobwebs."

"I know you didn't just go there," I said, throwing the dishrag at her. "But if I had any cobwebs before this weekend, they're all gone. He has a gifted tongue, and knows how to use it!" I said, flashing back to the way Michael feasted on me like a ripened peach.

"Hurry up and throw this stuff in the dishwasher. This I got to hear," she said, snatching stuff out of my hand. "Forget the coffee, grab another bottle of wine. Hell, I'm staying over, I can head out in the morning with you," Jasmine said.

Chapter 21

THAT night, Pam was sitting at home working on C.E. Campbell's manuscript.

"This is one hot writer. I can't wait to meet with this person on Friday," she said to herself. She still wasn't sure if Campbell was a male or female.

This mystery is killing me, she thought to herself. She also couldn't help but to think about Michael. It had been a few weeks since he decided to break off their personal relationship, but that didn't keep her from loving him. She still felt some kind of way about him. What bothered her more was that now it seemed like Michelle was involved with his work.

"It's almost as if she's taking over my job. I wonder if she's also taken over being his lover too. She probably went to Philly to do more than just attend a conference. She handed me that picture like there was nothing to it. Humph... how convenient," Pam said out loud, with tears running down her face.

Suddenly the phone rang. It was Sharon.

"Hey Pam, What's going on, girl?" Sharon said.

"Hey Sharon" Pam responded, trying to cover up her sniffling.

"What's wrong, Pam? I can hear in your voice that something's wrong. Don't tell me you're over there thinking about that man again?"

"I can't help it, Sharon. I still have feelings for him. And now it seems like Michelle has taken over his book and she's probably fucking him too. She went to this conference in Philly last week, and I bet she got with his ass then."

"How can you be so sure?"

"When she got back today, she called me into her office and handed me a picture of him. She told me it was to go on his book, and that she got it from Michael while she was in Philly."

"Oh, she's a slick bitch, I see," Sharon said.

"She thinks she's all that. She doesn't realize I was there way before she was. If my baby Bill hadn't died, and left the business to her, she wouldn't be shit. She thinks she's Miss Big Stuff, with all her little expensive knickknacks scattered all around her office. I'm glad I grabbed one of them off her display and broke another one," Pam said angrily.

231

"Damn, girl, she has you all upset over there. Maybe we need to do a good old fashion beat down on her ass. Nobody can mess with my girl like this. That damn writer you were sexing is just as guilty. You do know that, right? I told you not to get involved with them slick talking Philly brothas. But I'm not going to do that I told you so crap."

"What the hell does that mean?"

"I mean I'm not going to say I told you so, because you already know that," Sharon said.

"Well, say that, bitch! I'm already mad about Michael dicking someone else down, and you're talking in riddles and shit. I know you were right all along, but it's too late now. I'm in love with his ass," Pam said sadly.

"Yeah, it's too late, but you shouldn't be over there dwelling on this nonsense. What you need to be doing is finding yourself another man, a man that cares for you just as much as you care for him. You just need to get over Michael and move on with your life. One day she'll get hers, I promise you that," Sharon said seriously.

"Listen, girl, I need to go to bed. I have a long day tomorrow. I'm meeting this new author whose work I've been editing, so it should be interesting," Pam said, changing the subject.

"Alright, I'll talk to you later. And stop worrying about that man. You take it easy."

"Okay, Sharon. I'll talk to you soon. Bye," Pam said.

After hanging up Pam sat and had a conversation out loud with herself "Maybe she's right. I need to get out a little more. That bitch, Michelle, still needs to be taught a lesson. She helped ruin a good thing between Michael and me. I know she's the reason he decided to stop seeing me outside of business. I think I'll read a little more of Campbell's work, to take my mind off of those two slick asses before I turn in. Whoever this person is, they have some serious writing skills. I'll be glad to finally meet them, and get this script off the ground. Now where was I?"

Paul reached back to get a better grip on the bedpost, as Kim worked his dick like she was the originator of fellatio. He felt himself coming to the point of no return, when suddenly she stopped.

"What's wrong, baby? I was almost there," he asked, with his body still gyrating.

"This is what's wrong." Kim reared back and slapped him in the face so hard, his cheeks turned a shade darker.

"What the hell did you do that for?" he asked.

"Turn your ass over now and get on your knees. I've got something for you. Shut the fuck up!" Kim screamed, at the top of her lungs.

For some odd reason, he felt intimidated and did as she asked. While on his knees, she reached underneath him and slowly began to massage his throbbing wood. Then he felt the heat of her mouth blowing around his ass. He felt her warm wet mouth kissing his firm butt cheeks.

"Do you like this?" she asked. When he started to respond, she interrupted. "Didn't I tell you to shut the fuck up?" He almost answered, but then he refrained.

The motion of her hand wrapped around his dick was turning him on. It almost reminded him of when he's alone and masturbating. Suddenly, he felt her tongue slide into his hole, as she licked all around it, making it wet from her warm mouth and constant licking. As his mind drifted off into another world from the sensation of having his salad tossed, and the steady motion of her hand on his dick, he was abruptly disturbed by what he thought was her finger. It indeed was an insertion, but of a miniature dildo.

"Oh, hell no!" he thought to himself, but then he started moving his hips from side to side, as she penetrated slowly and deeply.

He moaned with pleasure, as she forcefully smacked his ass a few times. Slowly he was beginning to like the feel of this anal intrusion. She continued massaging his throbbing dick, and slowly pushing the invader in and out his ass, until he couldn't take it anymore.

"I'm getting ready to cummmm!" he screamed, as she quickly got underneath of him to suck the juices from his dick.

Streams and streams of fluid were launched into her mouth, and she guzzled every drop. It felt like he shot a pint of his cum into her mouth.

"I've never experienced an orgasm like that before," he said to Kim, as they passionately kissed.

"Damn, this is hot," Pam, said, as she felt the wetness forming in her panties. There was only one other writer that had gotten her worked up like this before, and that's... Before she uttered Michael's name, she put the manuscript down, headed to the bathroom to shower and change into her gown for bed.

The next day after work, David prepared to go down to *The Marquis*

Steakhouse, to meet Pam for dinner. She had e-mailed C.E. Campbell to meet her there for their first meeting. Secretly, he'd had a crush on her ever since he started working at Rivers, Inc., but he kept that fact to himself. He knew Pam would be totally surprised to find out it was him who had written the manuscript that she had been working on. Who would've ever thought that David, who has been a children's literature editor since coming to Rivers, Inc., would write some steaming erotica? To say that he was a little nervous would be an understatement, but it was time for the fact to be known.

"Good evening, sir, and welcome to *The Marquis Steakhouse.* Do you have a reservation?" the maitre`d inquired.

"I'm meeting Pamela Bryant for dinner. Has she arrived yet?" David asked.

"No, she hasn't, but her table is ready. Follow me, please."

"No, thank you. I'm trying to surprise her. I'll get a drink at the bar and wait for her to arrive," he said.

"Very well, sir."

The reservation was for eight o'clock, and it was seven forty-five, so he had some time to get a drink to relax before Pam arrived. Shortly after he was served his vodka and orange juice, she arrived.

"Good evening and welcome to *The Marquis Steakhouse.* Do you have a reservation?"

"Yes, I do, a table for Bryant," Pam said.

"Yes, your table is ready, please follow me." After the maitre`d seated her, he mentioned that a gentleman was already here asking if she had arrived. He told her that he was seated at the bar, but he wasn't there when he turned to point him out. "He must've stepped out for a moment," he said.

"That's okay, he'll be here soon I'm sure." *Well, at least I know it's a man,* she thought to herself.

"Hello, my name is Donte, and I'll be your server this evening. Can I get you a cocktail from the bar, or are you ready to order?" he said, walking up to the table.

"I'm waiting for someone. I'd like a glass of white zinfandel in the meantime, please," Pam said.

"Very well, I'll be back shortly," Dante, said, walking away to get her drink.

Pam was glancing over the menu and sipping on some water, when she glanced up and saw David walking towards her table.

"Hey David fancy seeing you here. Are you having dinner with someone this evening?"

"Yes, I am, as a matter of fact," David, said.

"So am I. I'm supposed to be meeting a new author this evening…C.E. Campbell."

At that moment, David sat his drink on the table and then had a seat. "Am I late?" he asked, with a smile on his face. "I'm C.E. Campbell."

Pam almost choked on her water after his last statement. "Yeah right, stop joking, David," she said, in disbelief.

"I knew you wouldn't believe me, that's why I brought a copy of the last e-mail you sent me about this meeting," he said, handing it to her.

"I can't believe this, David. Why did you keep this such a big secret?" Just then Donte arrived with her cocktail.

"Here you go. Would you like a few more minutes to go over the menu?" he asked, placing her drink on the table.

"Yes, please," she said.

"Okay, I'll be back shortly," he said, walking away.

"So, David, why were you so closed mouthed about this?" Pam asked, once Donte was out of earshot.

"Well, I didn't know how everyone would take me writing erotica with my background in working with the children's authors. You know the difference is like night and day," David said.

"That may be true, but you're one heck of a writer. This book is good. It has me pretty warmed up just thinking about it. Especially the scene you wrote involving Paul and Kim…now that was hot," she said, fanning and smiling. "It doesn't matter what type of writer you are, as long as it's quality work. You know that already, you're one of Rivers, Inc. finest editors."

"Thanks, Pam. I'm glad you think it's a quality piece. One day it just came to me and I started writing."

"Where did the name C.E. Campbell come from?" she asked curiously.

"C.E. means 'Come Enjoy', and Campbell is my mother's maiden name. So I figured I'd use it as my pen name. Before I let it slip my mind, you look ravishing this evening."

"Why, thank you for the compliment. Your pen name is very original. Let me flag down the waiter so we can order. I'm starving. I just can't believe this… you're C.E. Campbell," Pam said, signaling for Donte.

The meeting went very well, once Pam got over the shock of her discovery. David's nervousness was a thing of the past. Whether it was the screwdrivers he was drinking, or just getting the mystery out…who knows. All he knew was that he enjoyed finally being with her. He was also glad she was the one assigned to his manuscript.

After dinner, Pam picked up the tab with her company card, and they walked outside. She was a little tipsy from the several glasses of wine she had, and David wasn't ready for the evening to end yet.

"Listen, David, would you like to go to my place, so we can finish discussing your manuscript?" Pam asked.

"That sounds good. But I think I should drive you home, cause you're a little tipsy." They both laughed.

"I'll be fine getting home if you have other plans," she said.

"I don't have any other plans. And I'd feel better if you'd let me drive you home," he said.

"I don't live that far away, I'll be fine," she insisted.

"Okay, I'll follow you," he said, as he turned and walked to his car.

Once they got to her place, he was amazed at her entertainment system and her collection of CD's and DVD's.

"Damn, you have a lot of music here, and that system is all that. I bet it set you back a knot?" David said.

"Well, I love my music, and I only wanted the best to play it on. Would you like to hear something?" Pam asked, kicking off her shoes.

"Yes, do you have any old school stuff...like Luther Vandross?"

"Just press the play button. You may be surprised," she said.

David pressed the play button on her remote, and Superstar filled the room. It was almost as if Pam was a mind reader. While he was browsing her music and film collection, Pam eased away, changed into a pair of black silk pajamas, poured them each a drink, and had placed the manuscript on the coffee table.

"Damn, was I that preoccupied? I didn't even hear you leave the room," he said, smiling at her.

"I get like that myself when I'm into something...like music or work. Have a seat right here, and let's talk about this manuscript for a moment," she said, as she patted a spot on the sofa next to her and passed him his drink. "I noticed that your character Paul seems to be pretty shy in regards to the women he runs across. Would this book be about your life?" The question caught him off guard.

"You're so inquisitive, Pam. To answer your question honestly, yes, it is in a way. I haven't been involved with many women, but the ones I have been involved with have never taken me seriously, for some reason. One in particular has never given me even a glance, but I've always wanted her."

"That's interesting, because one of the women in your story seems kind of familiar to me."

"She should sound familiar, because I'm talking about you." He looked at her smiling, and her sultry brown eyes seemed to smile back at him.

"I'm flattered, David. You wrote about me in your book?" Pam asked amazed.

"I've always had a crush on you. When I first came to Rivers, Inc., I was in awe of your beauty, and the way you carried yourself. I dreamed of one day being able to sweep you off your feet and make sweet love to you, but I never got up the nerve to ask you out."

To say that Pam was speechless would have been an understatement. She was in a frozen trance, with a warm smile on her face. She grabbed David's drink and sat it on the table, and leaned in to kiss him. He was hesitant at first, but then he succumbed to his innermost desires, and leaned in to receive her advance. She pushed him back on the sofa and began unbuttoning his shirt, exposing his firm chest. She gently kissed his nipples, which became harder with each flick of her tongue. Slowly her hands moved down to his pants, and she unbuckled his belt and tugged on his pants. He lifted up his ass to help make it easier for her. As she removed his pants and boxer briefs, his manhood sprung up to attention.

"Oh, I know what to do with this," she said, as she grabbed his dick with her hand and slowly engulfed it with her hot mouth.

David's eyes rolled back in his head. He was in another world. She worked his rod up and down with a ferocious appetite, as he thrust himself deeper into her mouth. He felt himself coming closer to the point of no return, when he suddenly pulled her up towards him.

"I want to taste you," he said, as she stood to let her silk pajamas fall to the floor.

She had the perfect body, just as he had imagined she would. She lay down on the sofa, and he slowly began kissing her neck. He then deliberately worked his way slowly down to her firm breasts, encircling each of her large nipples with his wet tongue. His hand found the way to her freshly shaven valley, and he slowly inserted his finger into her warm, wet vagina.

"Oh, yes David, that feels so good," she whispered, as her body writhed in ecstasy.

He continued working his way towards her moist valley, kissing her smooth stomach along the way. She moaned when he finally reached his prize. He parted her pussy lips, exposing the largest pearl he'd ever seen. He gently kissed her clit, and then began sucking and flicking it with his tongue. She arched her back and began to tremble, as she reached her first orgasm. He lapped up every drop of juice that oozed out of her cavern like it was honey.

"David, I want you inside of me," Pam moaned, as she parted her legs and he proceeded to grant her wish.

He placed the head of his throbbing dick at the opening of her slick hotbox, and slowly penetrated her opening. David moved slowly as he entered her, until he was fully inside. In and out he went, working his body like a piston engine. She clawed at his back, and screamed for him to go harder. He obliged, as sweat poured from his head like a faucet.

"Oh, yes, baby right there…right there," Pam moaned thickly, as David worked her over. Their bodies were in sync. She met his every thrust with upward strokes of her own.

"Yes, Michael, yes baby…fuck me! Oh, David, yes…yes do me, baby!" she screamed, as she was met by another orgasm.

She felt his body tremble, and she tightened her pussy around his dark warrior, until he felt he was about to release.

"I'm almost ready to cum, Pam. where do you want it, baby?" David asked.

"In my mouth…I want to taste you." He withdrew from her hot valley, as she sat up to receive his load. "Give it to me…give it to me," she said, as he reached that point of no return.

"Oh shit!" he screamed, as his hot cum shot into her mouth, almost causing her to gag.

She sucked and licked his dick until every last drop of cum had been exhausted. He lay beside her on the sofa, and they kissed hungrily as they drifted off to sleep.

David woke up to the smell of breakfast cooking. He got up and walked to the kitchen, and Pam was dressed only in his dress shirt. He walked up behind her and kissed her on the neck. She smiled and turned around to kiss him.

"Good morning, David," she said, as they both laughed. "I left a towel and washcloth out for you in the bathroom, and some cocoa butter lotion on the sink. By the time you finish showering, breakfast will be done."

"You thought of everything, didn't you? I'll be right back," he said.

While he was showering, he thought about what happened last night, and how good Pam had made him feel. Being infatuated with her for so long, and then finally having a chance to make love to her, absolutely blew his mind. He would've felt even better if he hadn't heard her call out another man's name.

When he returned, they talked about the night and how they had surprised each other. Pam never knew that he even took notice of her, other than them working together.

"Pam, I had a wonderful night last night," David said.

"So did I, David. Do you want some coffee?"

"Yes, I would, thank you. Who's Michael?" he asked, as she damn near poured hot coffee on his lap.

"W...w...why do you ask?" she asked stuttering.

"While we were making love, you called out his name," he said.

Suddenly she sat at the table, and broke down in tears. He didn't expect that reaction, but then again, he didn't know what to expect. David slid his chair next to hers and gave her a big hug.

"What's wrong, Pam? Tell me. I'm here for you. I promise."

"I don't want to bore you with my problems. I like you too much," she said, between sobs.

"Did this Michael person hurt you?" he asked concerned.

"Michael is someone I used to go out with. We just recently stopped seeing each other."

"Oh, I see," he said.

"Let me start from the beginning. The Michael I'm talking about is Michael Ramsey."

"What!" David shouted, in disbelief. "You were sleeping with Michael Ramsey, the writer? You're his editor, aren't you?"

"Yes, I am, and I was in love with him," she said, her voice cracking and more tears gathering in her eyes.

"But was he in love with you?"

"I think so. But he was unsure of what he wanted, or how he felt about me. When I finally asked him what he wanted to do with our relationship, he said he wanted to stop seeing me on a personal level, and keep it strictly professional between us."

"That sounds reasonable enough to me. So, why are you crying?" he asked.

"Michelle Rivers had something to do with it," she said, as her tone turned to anger.

"Michelle? How can you be so sure?" he asked.

"Ever since they had a lunch meeting a couple of months ago, he's changed towards me. I think when she went on her trip to Philadelphia last week she slept with him."

"Come on, you don't have any proof of that."

"I just know they did, and it hurts. She's the reason we broke up, and she's going to pay for it."

"Pam, forget about him. I love you and I always have."

"That's sweet, David, and last night was wonderful but…"

"But nothing, I want you, Pam. You deserve someone who can love you unconditionally, and I can be that person," David said, cutting her off.

"I don't know. I think we'd be better off as friends," Pam said.

"Listen to me, you may think we're better off as friends, but I don't. I'm in love with you, and have been for some time now. I know I'll be better for you than Michael Ramsey could ever be, if you would just give me half a chance."

"David, you're a sweetie, but I'm still in love with Michael. I don't want to hurt you…you're a good man."

"Okay, we'll try it your way for now…just friends. But I won't let you forget that I'm here for you," he said sincerely.

He knew the only way he would be able to have Pam's full attention and love would be for her to forget about Michael. The fact that she was so hurt by Michelle's interference in their relationship, if that's what it really was, upset him also. He felt a certain type of bond with Pam…almost like he was her protector.

"David, let's talk about your book. I'll let everyone know on Tuesday, at the editors meeting with John, who C.E. Campbell is. What do you think about that?" Pam stated.

"I guess that's as good a time as any. I can just see everyone's face," he said smiling. "They'll all be surprised."

"You may be right, especially since we're all so close. They'll wonder why the big secret. Your book is good, and it's an honor for me to be editing it. I'm confident that it will do well," she told him.

"Thanks for the vote of confidence, Pam. Since it's my first effort, I hope it will be well received," he said, getting nervous.

✳ ✳ ✳

At Tuesday's editorial staff meeting, John went around the table and asked everyone for a progress report on the submitted manuscripts.

"Good morning. I'm going to start with you, Elaine. How's your project coming along?" John asked.

"My work is almost completed on Tyler Bray's book, *One Bloody Night*. It's the story of a morgue attendant, who's haunted by the ghost of a man, which he not only saw murdered, but also was in charge of doing the autopsy. It's not your typical blood and guts horror book, but it has quite a bit of mystery in it. The galley will be ready by the end of this week for Tyler to review."

"That's very good, Elaine. It's your turn, Brandon," John said, sipping his coffee.

"I'm halfway done with *The Negro Baseball Leagues, The True Story*, by John 'Slim' Johnson. It's a heck of an historical perspective on the lifestyles and the obstacles that he and other Negro baseball players had to endure, just to provide for their families. He played for the Chicago American Giants, and they were some of the greatest ballplayers to ever play the game. No wonder the white teams never wanted blacks to participate in the major leagues. If so, they surely would've taken over America's greatest pastime," Brandon said.

"I had an uncle that played for the Atlanta Black Crackers. He used to tell us stories of his life in the league. I wonder if they know each other," John said.

"When his book is ready, he'll be in town, so you'll get a chance to ask him then," Brandon said.

"Great job Brandon. Tina, what's going on with your project?" John said.

"The manuscript I've been working on is entitled, *I Can Hear Him Calling Me*, by Marion Johnson. It's the story of a woman's spiritual transformation from a hooker, who didn't believe that anyone cared for her. She became a Christian, and had a near death experience at the hands of one of her johns. It also talks about her friendship with a reformed hooker, which strengthened her belief in the almighty creator. It's a very good read...to say the least," Tina said.

"David, a new manuscript was just submitted by a writer named Jonathan Smiley called "*When I Grow Up*." I want you to get to work on it," John said.

"Okay, John," he said.

"Pam, how's the progress coming with the Jackie Pollard script?" John asked.

"After reading it thoroughly, I sent it back to her for some re-writes. It has potential, but a few things I suggested to her need to be ironed out. She agreed, and will be re-submitting it soon," Pam said.

"So, how did your meeting go with your mysterious writer, C.E. Campbell?" he asked.

"It went very well actually. I have a surprise for all of you. The book is entitled, *Enlightened.* It's the story of a shy nineteen-year old young man, and his growth into adulthood. It's a wonderful voyage of the young man's discovery of his sexuality. I think this book has a world of potential," she said.

"Okay, spill the beans. Who is this mysterious writer?" John asked.

"It's none other than our very own David Hale," Pam said smiling.

Everyone looked at David with a surprised look on their faces, and then slowly they all began to clap their hands in approval.

"David, why didn't you tell us you had submitted your work? Why was it such a big secret?" Tina asked.

"I just didn't know how a book such as this would be received, since you all know I specialize in children's literature. I guess I was a little embarrassed," he said shyly.

"Embarrassed? We're family around here, son, and you know anyone can write anything about any subject. It's called free speech. I can't wait to read the finished product. C.E. Campbell is your pen name, huh?" John asked.

"Yes, it is. C.E. means 'Come Enjoy'. And Campbell was my mother's maiden name," David said.

"That's very original, David. Good luck with it," John added. "Okay, if there are no other concerns, this meeting is adjourned."

Everyone gave David hugs and pats on his back as they left John's office. When David walked into the break room to get a cup of coffee, I was there making myself some tea.

"Good morning, David," I said, in an upbeat tone. "How's your day going?"

"It's fine. I'll talk to you later," he said rather abruptly, as he left the room.

"I wonder what his problem is?" I said to myself.

Chapter 22

WHEN I walked back to my office, I decided to ask Yvonne if she had knowledge of any problems that David may be having.

"Yvonne, did you talk to David this morning?" I asked her.

"Yes, I saw him when he came in. Why do you ask?"

"He seemed like something was bothering him a minute ago. He didn't seem like his usual happy go lucky self," I said.

"Well, we all have days like that, don't we?" Yvonne reminded me.

"Yeah, you're right about that. I just hope everything is okay with him."

"I'm sure everything is okay, but if it isn't, we'll find out about it soon enough," Yvonne said. "I just finished typing up the invitation list, do you want to look it over one more time before I start sending them out?"

"Yes, I'll take it in my office and look it over. I also want to make sure that Mr. Ramsey's parents and sister get an invitation. I thought it would be a good idea to invite them, since we're going to announce the release of their son's newest book."

"Would you happen to have Michael's parents address?" Yvonne asked.

"As a matter of fact I do. His mother wrote it down for me when I was in Philly," I said.

As I was about to leave Yvonne's office, John walked in with his ever-present cup of coffee, all excited.

"Good afternoon, ladies. I'm glad you're both sitting down, because I have something to tell you that will blow you away," he said, grinning from ear to ear.

"What is it, John?" we both said at the same time.

"Remember we received a manuscript from a mysterious writer named C.E. Campbell?"

"Yes, I remember that manuscript. Pam told me she was meeting with the author," I said.

"That's correct. She had the meeting, and it turns out that C.E. Campbell is none other than our own David Hale," he said, as our mouths dropped open. "You heard me right, ladies, so you can close your mouths now."

"Well, I'll be damn," Yvonne, said, recovering from the shock of his announcement.

"Our children's editor David But why the pen name" I asked.

"He seemed to think we wouldn't have taken him as seriously if he had submitted it under his own name, so he decided to use the pen name," John explained.

"How did he come up with C.E. Campbell?" Yvonne asked.

"Well, wait till you hear this, C.E. means 'Come Enjoy', and Campbell is his mother's maiden name," he said laughing. "Quite creative of the young man I must say."

"Yes, it is quite creative, and I guess that explains his strange behavior earlier when I ran into him," I said, and explained after seeing John's puzzled look. "I ran into David a little while ago in the break room, and he was rather abrupt with me."

"He was probably afraid of what you were going to say about him submitting his manuscript under a different name, not realizing at the time you didn't know yet," John said.

"That's probably it, and if I remember correctly from the little bit I read before passing it on to you, it was a good read. I'll have to read it again when Pam has finished editing it," I said. "Is there anything else you needed to go over with me?"

"No, that's all for now. Gayle will be sending you the minutes from my meeting with the editorial staff later. I have some loose ends to tie up myself before the Thanksgiving holiday next week. Do you ladies have any special plans?" John asked.

"My children will be coming home for the holiday, so I have quite a bit of cooking to do. And, of course, I'll be out shopping the next day," Yvonne said.

"I'll be spending it with my parents and Jasmine, of course. Knowing my mom, she's probably invited a few extra people. And the next day, she'll drag me out shopping with her," I said groaning. "I love shopping, but the crowds on Black Friday are a bit much, and she likes to get there when the stores open."

"Glad I don't have to go shopping. Well, you ladies have a good day," John said laughing, as he winked and walked away.

"Well, if that doesn't beat all. Imagine David writing an erotic novel," Yvonne said in wonder, as I walked back into my office, deep in thought.

While I was going over the invitation list, I couldn't help but think of Uncle Billy, and wondered if he would be pleased about all the things that had happened since I'd taken over the company. At least we're still in the black, but I knew that wasn't what was important to him. It was all about putting out quality books people couldn't wait to read. Holding the Rivers, Inc. family together was also a top priority of his. I was going to miss him at Thanksgiving dinner this year.

"Is this what all publishers do, sit around and daydream on the job?" Jasmine asked, as she walked into my office like she owned it.

"Good afternoon, lady. How's my favorite travel agent doing today?" I said.

"If I was any better, I wouldn't be able to stand my damn self," she said laughing. "What's up?"

"Nothing much I was just sitting here going over this invitation list and thinking about Uncle Billy."

"I hope you're not going to get depressed on me and shit," Jasmine said.

"No, Jas, I'm not going to get depressed, but I do miss him. I find myself always wondering what he would think about the company's progress. And you know this will be our first Thanksgiving without him at the table."

"Heffa, don't make me beat your ass. This is your company now, and from where I'm standing, you're doing a great job and he knows it. He lives through you, so get over yourself," she said, as only Jasmine could. "And I understand what you mean about missing him. I won't have anyone to fight with over the pound cake this year."

"You know this is why I love you so much, you always give it to me straight with no chaser. I'll fight with you over the pound cake if you'd like," I said laughing.

"You know you going to lose," Jasmine said chuckling.

The Fed Ex man knocked gently on my open door. "I have a delivery for Michelle Rivers," he said. "No one was in the outer office."

"Come on in. She's Ms. Rivers. Fed Ex should know better then to hire such fine brothas to deliver their packages, damn," Jasmine said.

"Jasmine, behave yourself! But I have to agree, you are fine, my brotha. Do you need me to sign something?" I asked.

"Yes, ma'am," he said, handing me the clipboard, while shifting his eyes between Jasmine and I. "Where do you want me to put your packages?"

"Over by the sofa is good, thank you," I said.

"Well, I'll be going now. Thank you for the compliment, ladies," he said.

"You're very welcome, hmmm," Jasmine said, as she watched him walk out the door. "Damn, did you see the ass on that man?"

"Alright, you've embarrassed that man enough," I said. "But he was fine!"

Yvonne walked into my office after hearing all the laughter. "You ladies sound like you're having a good time in here," she said.

"I know you just saw that fine ass Fed Ex guy, so I'm sure you understand. Ummm, let's get down to work before I go after him," Jasmine said. "Michelle, what's in the packages?"

"It should be the Blackshear pieces I ordered for the Christmas party," I said, as I opened the first box.

"These angels are beautiful, Michelle! How long have you been buying Blackshear pieces?" Yvonne asked, admiring the mini sculptures.

"Someone dear to my heart…Tony started me collecting. I started collecting Lladros, and then when he saw these, he started buying them for me. Jasmine, would you look behind you on the shelf and show Yvonne the 'Tickle Tickle' piece, please."

"Oh, Lord, you've got her started. She loves these pieces like they were her children. I bet she has almost every piece Blackshear has made," Jasmine said, handing the piece to Yvonne. "Michelle, did you know that 'The Guardian's' wing is broken?"

"Jasmine, please tell me you're joking. I bought that piece right after Tony died," I said, walking over to examine it for myself. "Damn, I wonder how this happened? I better look to make sure nothing else is broken. That was one of my favorite pieces. I can't believe this. Oh, shit, it looks like one of my circus pieces is missing also," I said with tears in my eyes, while holding 'The Guardian'.

"Do you think you can replace them?" Jasmine asked, as Yvonne looked on with concern.

"I don't know. I'll have to check into it. A lot of his pieces are limited editions. I just pray I can at least replace 'The Guardian'."

"Michelle, would you like me to see if I can get it repaired for you?" Yvonne asked.

"No, I'll take it home and try to repair it, but thank you for offering," I said, wiping my eyes.

"I know you aren't crying over a couple pieces of porcelain, Michelle?" Jasmine said.

"Jasmine, you know they're more than that to me. As far as I'm concerned, they're priceless. I'm angry about it, but hopeful I can replace them," I said, taking a deep breath to compose myself. "By the way, the guest list is perfect,

Yvonne. I'd like to extend an invitation to a reporter I know from *Creative Loafing Magazine*, since we're also going to unveil Mr. Ramsey's book as a surprise."

"I think that's a good idea," Yvonne said.

"I agree, and it's a great way to get free publicity for the book too," Jasmine said.

"I'll give you his name and address, Yvonne," I said. "Ladies, it looks like we're all set for the Christmas party. Yvonne, could you confirm with the limousine company we use, that we're going to need them to pick up our out of town guests at the airport. I'd also like to keep two of them on reserve for the evening, in case anyone drinks too much and needs a ride home."

"I'll take care of that this afternoon," she said.

"I think that's a great idea…keeping the limos on reserve. No need taking a chance of anyone driving under the influence," Jasmine said.

"Those were my thoughts exactly. I guess that about wraps it up. Yvonne, it's almost five, so why don't you clean off your desk and get out of here. I'll lock up, cause I have one more phone call to make," I said.

"I don't mind waiting, in case you need something," she said.

"You've done enough for the day. If there's anything else, it'll wait until tomorrow. Enjoy your evening, and I'll see you bright and early in the morning," I said.

"Okay, I'm gone. Bye, Jasmine. You two have a good evening," Yvonne said, leaving out my office.

"Bye, Yvonne, be careful driving," Jasmine said. "Michelle, I'll wait and walk out with you."

"Jasmine, you don't have to wait on me. But if you are, why don't we go out to dinner?" I said, looking at her.

"That sounds like a good idea. Let's go to *Justin's*, since it's not far from here, or would you prefer the *Atlanta Fish Market* in Buckhead?"

"*Justin's* will be fine. Let me get this phone call out the way, and then we can be out of here," I said.

"Then I can tell you all about my evening with Alex," Jasmine said, with a smirk of a smile on her face.

"Whoa, when did this happen? You've been holding out on me! I'm going to wring your pretty neck."

Jasmine started laughing, walked away to sit behind my desk, and started twirling around in my chair.

"Spill it, woman! I'm waiting on the details," I said, while watching her closely.

"Well, let's just say we were both in need of some company, and didn't want to wait for the weekend. I cooked dinner and invited him over. Don't look at me like that, I was going to tell you soon enough, nosey. Before you say something smart, I did let the man eat his food before dessert this time," she said, cracking up.

"Jasmine, you're so bad. Get your ass out my chair, so I can make my phone call. I want to hear the rest over dinner, or do I need an empty stomach for this?"

"It wasn't that bad. In fact, it was quite good."

"I think I'm having a heart attack," I said. "Damn, you don't ever do anything halfway, do you? I can't wait to hear this story."

"Calm your ass down, woman, and make your damn call."

"I just have to call Michael's parents, and then we can be out of here," I said, as she looked at me in shock. "Oh, hush, I'm just calling to issue them an invite to the Christmas party," I said, picking up the phone.

"Okay, you had me going there for a minute," Jasmine said.

"Hello, Mrs. Ramsey. How are you doing? This is Michelle Rivers," I said, when Michael's mother answered the phone.

"Hey, baby, and I thought I told you it was okay to call me Mom. I'm doing okay, can't complain," she said.

"I'm glad to hear that, Mom," I said, and almost dropped the phone at the look Jasmine gave me when she overhead that. "I was calling to invite you and Dad to our company Christmas party on December 17th. If you can make it, all expenses will be taken care of on this end. One thing though, this is a surprise for Michael, so he doesn't know I'm inviting y'all."

"A surprise for Michael, huh? I'd love to come, but his sister, Debra, will be home on Christmas break, and I'd hate to leave her behind," she said.

"She's more than welcome to come with y'all," I said.

"Let me talk it over with Purnell tonight, and I'll give you a call tomorrow," she said.

"You have my home and cell numbers, right?"

"Yes, baby. I'll let you know by tomorrow at the latest," she said.

"I'll talk to you then. Bye, Mom," I said hanging up, and mentally preparing myself for Jasmine's questions.

"Oh hell no, I didn't just hear you calling her mom," Jasmine said.

"I knew I wouldn't have to wait long before you'd say something about that," I said laughing. "Yes, you heard me call her mom. She insisted I call her that when I was in Philly. I thought I told you about that when I got back."

"You may have told me, but hearing it is a different story."

"Let's get out of here," I said, clearing my desk. "Give me a minute to lock these packages in the closet, so nothing else is broken or missing when I come in tomorrow."

"This conversation isn't over, not by a long shot believe that" Jasmine said.

"Now why would I have thought that?" I said, under my breath.

"I heard that," she said.

"I'm sure you did, and while you're at it, come help me move these packages," I said, looking at her with my hands on my hips.

"Oh, don't get smart, woman. I can still take your old ass down a peg or two."

I started laughing, with tears rolling down my cheeks, at the memory of the first and only fight Jasmine and I ever had.

"Do you remember when we were in the eighth grade, and we both liked the same boy, James Mack? Damn, was he good looking," I said to her.

"I can't believe you brought that up," Jasmine said, as I tried to catch my breath.

"Do you remember Uncle Billy asking which one of us won, and then laughing after we both said I did?"

"How could I forget?" Jasmine was laughing just as hard as I was.

"We were slinging snot all over the place. I wonder whatever happened to him. He's probably potbellied with gold teeth," I said laughing.

"Oh, Jesus, I hope not. That would be a waste of a fine man," Jasmine said.

"Well, this is Atlanta…he could be gay, or worse, on the down low," I said, doubling over in laughter. "Let's continue this conversation over lunch at *Justin's*."

Since it was a beautiful day, and *Justin's* wasn't too far from my office, we decided to walk. As usual, Jasmine attracted a lot of attention. A guy tried to holla at her from a passing car. She just continued walking and talking like she didn't notice.

"Jasmine, I know you heard that brotha trying to holla at you from that car," I said.

"He was riding on the passenger side, so I didn't hear a thing. You know scrubs get no love from me," she said, trying to be serious, but smiling.

"That scrub could've been rich and hung, and *TLC* is going to sue you for stealing their lyrics," I said laughing.

"I've got a man that's hung in the right place. Thank you, but no thanks, and forget *TLC*," Jasmine said.

"No, you didn't just claim Alex!" I exclaimed, stopping in the middle of the sidewalk.

"Maybe I did, maybe I didn't. Bring your ass on, woman, I'm hungry," she said, glancing back at me over her shoulder, as she got to the door of *Justin's*.

"Good evening, ladies. Welcome to *Justin's*. Will you be joining us for dinner, or would you like to sit at the bar?" the hostess asked, as we walked in the door.

"Yes, we'll be joining you for dinner," I said.

"Table for two, or are you expecting other people?" she asked.

"A table for two will be fine, thank you," I said.

"Very well, ladies. If you will follow me to your table," the hostess said. "Here we are. Your server will be April, and she'll be with you in a minute. Can I get you something to drink while you wait?" she asked, as she handed us our menus.

"Yes, I'd like an Apple Martini," I said.

"I'll have the same, thank you," Jasmine said.

"I'll send your drinks right over," she said, as she walked over to the bar.

"I wonder if we'll see Puffy tonight," Jasmine said, looking around.

"Okay, woman, spill it. What's the deal with you and Alex?" I asked.

"Did I tell you I called your mom, and asked her if it was okay if I brought him for Thanksgiving?" she said, talking fast. "I thought it would give me a chance to see how he reacts around family."

"I swear before God, I'm going to jump over this table and beat you down," I said laughing.

"Here's our drinks right on time," Jasmine said grinning.

"Good evening, ladies. Here are your cocktails. My name is April, and I'll be your server tonight. Are you ready to order, or would you like to hear our specials?"

"I already know what I want," Jasmine said. "I'd like the Cape Cod salad with house dressing on the side. And may I also have some water, with plenty of lemons, also on the side? Thank you."

"I'd like the Blackened Chicken salad with honey mustard dressing on the side. And water with lemon on the side, also. April, thank you," I said, handing her our menus.

"Very well, ladies. I'll be back soon with your orders," she said, walking away.

"Okay, the server is gone, so you can finish telling me about you and Alex. How is it all of a sudden he's staying over during the week, and getting invited to Thanksgiving dinner? I talked to my mother this morning, and she didn't say a thing about it," I said, looking at her closely.

"Your mother doesn't have to tell you everything," she said, quite amused by this time. "To answer your questions, a girl has her needs, and Alex is quite skilled at what he does. I just called him up, and told him I felt like having some company and would feed him, and feed him I did," Jasmine said.

"You are so nasty," I said laughing.

"Oh, don't act like you weren't feeding Michael while you were in Philly, because I know different. It's all good," she said, twirling her finger around her drink. She licked her finger and grinned at me.

"Jasmine, you're a mess and I love you, my sister. I can tell you're enjoying Alex. Oh, Lord, did I just say that?" I said, and fell out laughing. "So, are you really bringing him to Thanksgiving dinner?"

"Yeah, and I know your dad will do his lawyer thing, and rake him over the coals a little. I just wish Uncle Billy was still alive to help," she said.

"I know what you mean," I said, with a sigh. "It's going to be a little rough for all of us. But with Alex coming, it will be a good distraction for Daddy. Maybe he'll be too busy grilling him to notice the void."

"I doubt it, but it'll help. Is Maceo coming with his family?" Jasmine asked.

"I don't know whose coming. You know how my mom is…anyone is liable to show up for dinner."

"You're right. Your mom is the kindest woman I know. I remember when she invited my whole family, and didn't blink an eye when my mom got drunk. She just took her in the kitchen, and asked her to sample this new coffee she had bought."

"I forgot all about that. Yes, my mom is one of a kind, and she loves her some Jasmine…as we all do. But back to Alex," I said smiling. "How do you really feel about him?"

"It's still a little too soon to be talking about commitment, but I like him. It's been a long time since I've been with someone who's the total package. He can hold a intelligent conversation, looks good, and can fuck too."

"What am I going to do with you?" I said, laughing at her last statement.

"Just love me, girl, just love me. Hmmm, on that note, here comes our dinner," Jasmine said, as April walked up to the table.

Chapter 23

"HEY, baby. How was your weekend? I can call you baby, right?" Michael asked me.

"You can call me anything you want, as long as you call me. My weekend was good. It would've been even better had you been here to share it with me. If I'm not mistaken, you had a presentation to do last week, didn't you?" I asked him.

"Damn, you remembered that? It went well. The Neighborhood Association and the Mayor really came together on this. All that has to be done now is for it to pass through city council, and the project will be underway," he said proudly.

"I'm so happy for you, Michael. From what you told me, you worked really hard to get it done."

"I can't take all the credit, it was truly a joint effort," he said.

"Yeah, but you were the point man, so you should be very proud of yourself."

"Thank you. You want to know something?" he asked.

"Yes, I do. Tell me something good, baby," I said.

"I thought about you a lot this past week."

"And what were you thinking?"

"I had help, believe me. My parents really like you. They asked me when you were coming to visit again. I was with Kevin this weekend, and well, let's just say that book really made an impression. That's just for beginners. He kept bugging me about Ms. Michelle."

"I'm glad your parents liked me, I like them as well. Please tell your parents and Kevin I'll be back to visit soon. I'm happy Kevin's enjoying the book. So, what else were you thinking?"

"How much I enjoyed being with you. I just wish the weekend could've lasted longer," he said.

"I enjoyed being with you too. It's as if you've awakened a part of me that has been asleep for a long time. And I agree, the weekend wasn't long enough, but there will be other weekends," I said.

"What are your plans for Thanksgiving?" he asked.

"I'll be spending it with my family and Jasmine. What about you? Is your family doing a big dinner?"

"My parents are having a big dinner at their house. My sister will be in town from Arizona, so it'll be a nice reunion of sorts. I know this will be a rough one for your family since Mr. Rivers isn't physically with you. I just want you to be strong, and remember that he'll be sitting right there with you."

"Thank you, Michael. This will be the first time he hasn't been with us, and I'm praying we all get through it. I don't know if Alex has told you, but he'll be breaking bread with us."

"What? That knucklehead didn't tell me about getting invited to dinner." Michael laughed.

"I was as surprised as you are. Jasmine just casually mentioned it the other day, but I think she's really feeling him."

"Well, that's good. He's a positive brother, and he deserves someone equally as positive in his life."

"I feel the same way about Jasmine. She has a heart of gold, but she plays hard and doesn't let many people get too close. I have a good feeling about the two of them, and I'm pulling for them, but don't tell her that," I said.

"Don't worry, your secret is safe with me. By the way, I received your invitation to the Christmas party," Michael said.

"I was wondering whether or not you had received it yet," I said.

"It was delivered this morning."

"I hope you'll be able to make it."

"There's no doubt about it. I'll be there with my jingle bells on. So, tell me what's new at Rivers, Inc.?"

"Something kind of strange happened the other day. I got a delivery from Blackshear, and when I started showing Yvonne my collection, we discovered one was broken and another was missing," I said.

"You mean the prized possessions that you had on the curio in your office?"

"Yes, my babies. I'm thinking of taking them home, but I like having my things around me," I said sadly.

"I wouldn't go that far. Why disrupt your comfort level in your office? Does anyone have access to your office after hours, besides the cleaning people?" he asked.

"Actually everyone does. We don't lock our doors, but I guess I'll have to start locking my door now. Security turns off the elevators when we all leave for the night."

"That's a good idea. Check with the cleaning people, to see of someone accidentally broke them. I can't imagine anyone breaking or stealing anything from your office on purpose," he said.

"I'll do that. Thank you for understanding and not laughing at me," I said.

"I wouldn't laugh. I understand about prized possessions. Remember my G.I. Joe collection? I value them a lot," he said.

I laughed and said, "Yes, baby, I remember the G.I. Joes. You have so many of them...especially the ones with the lifelike hair. Have you started Kevin on collecting anything like that?"

"I see you've got jokes. I haven't started Kevin off on anything like that, but he does show an interest in my G.I. Joes. He always plays with them when we go to my parents' house. I may pass them down to him...well, maybe not all of them."

"I'm sorry for laughing, baby. I was just remembering the look on your face when I came downstairs from your old bedroom...it was priceless. Your mother took such pleasure in pointing them out to me," I said.

"I can always depend on my mother to stir things up," he said, as we both laughed. "Well, baby, I hope you have a nice holiday, and don't eat too much turkey."

"Okay, Michael, I'll talk to you soon. You enjoy your holiday, and tell everyone I said hello. Bye now," I said.

"Bye, Michelle," he said, hanging up.

After hanging up, Michael thought to himself *that's odd. First, the alarm incident at Michelle's house that Jasmine had spoke about. Now it's the missing and broken artwork in her office. It's probably nothing to worry about.*

✳ ✳ ✳

Later that evening, Michael drove to the airport to pick Debra up. It was so nice to have her home for the holiday. He knew once she and Sara got together, it was all over for him. When he pulled up to the airport, he saw Debra standing at the curb.

"Hey, big brother," Debra said, giving him a big hug when he got out the car. "Thanks for picking me up. Did you have to drive around the terminal?"

"Not this time, baby girl. We got the timing just right. How was your flight?" he asked, while putting her bags in the trunk.

"It was good. I'm just glad I wore this wool jacket. It's cold out here," she said.

"The weather started changing on Sunday," Michael said.

"So, I heard you brought your publisher by to meet Mom and Dad."

"I see the wire is still working to perfection," he said, shaking his head.

"Of course it is. Mom said she was a very nice woman. But I need to meet her and see for myself. Is she going to be here for Thanksgiving?"

"No, her parents are having dinner at their house. It will be their first Thanksgiving since she lost her uncle. Maybe she'll be able to visit around Christmas. You can meet her then, if she does," he said.

"Okay, that sounds good. What's going on with you and your editor friend? Anything new with her since you ended your relationship?" she asked, with her eyebrows raised.

"It wasn't really a relationship, but everything seems to be okay with her. Anyway, Michelle and I are taking it slow for now. But I'm sure everyone will know after a while that we're close. One thing though, I really like her, Debra."

"I gathered that, since you felt the need to introduce her to Mom and Dad. Just be careful, big brother. I don't want you to get hurt by any of these women out here."

"That's enough about me. How's it going with you?" he asked, changing the subject.

"I have a friend I'm dealing with, nothing serious though. By the way, do you know when your book is coming out? I've arranged a book signing for you when it does," she said.

"That's great, Deb hopefully, it'll be ready by next month…in time for Christmas. I'll let you know as soon as it drops."

"That would be good if it comes out by then. It'll sell nicely…with everyone doing their Christmas shopping," she said, as they pulled up to the driveway of their parents' house.

"Hey, baby girl," their dad said, hugging Debra as they walked in the door. "How was your flight?"

"It was good, Dad. I'm glad to be on a little break," she said.

"You don't have much longer now. Your mom and I are so proud of you."

"There goes my puddin'," their mom laughed, as she came in from the garage. "How are you, Debra?"

"I'm doing fine, Mom," she responded, with a big hug and kiss.

"Folks, I need to be getting home. Debra, I'll talk to you a little later, Mom, Dad, you take it easy," Michael said, preparing to leave.

"See you later, son," his dad said, as he walked him to the door.

After Michael left, his mother said, "Listen you two, Michelle Rivers has invited us to her publishing company's Christmas party on December 17th. She said that Rivers, Inc. will take care of everything, so something special must be happening. Would you like to go, Purnell?"

"Of course I'd like to go. I don't have to work that weekend." They all laughed, because he was enjoying his retired life. "Debra, do you think you'll be able to make it?"

"I don't see why not. Christmas break will have started, and I'd love to travel to Atlanta. You can count me in," she said.

"That's good. So, are we going to stay for the weekend?" she asked them.

"I don't have a problem with staying for a couple of days," Debra said.

"I told Michelle I'd call and let her know if we all can make it. Let me give her a call now." Michael's mother picked up the phone to call Michelle. "Hello, Michelle, this is Mom." Debra looked at her, smiling and shaking her head. "I'm just calling to let you know we can make the party."

"Oh, that's great, Mom! Did you all want to stay for the entire weekend or just overnight?" I asked.

"We're going to stay for the weekend."

"I'll arrange everything. Your airline tickets will be at the ticket counter, and I made reservations at the Embassy Suites by the airport."

"Wow, you've thought of everything, haven't you?" Michael's mom said sounding impressed.

"Well, I can't take all the credit for his. My secretary and best friend actually made all the arrangements. I'll call you next week with the details," I said.

"Okay, honey. Enjoy your Thanksgiving. Bye now," she said, hanging up.

* * *

While Michael was driving back home, he decided to do something a little different this year for Thanksgiving. He was going to take Kevin to the Thanksgiving Day Parade. He hadn't been to the parade in years. By the time it was over, dinner would be just about ready, and the football games would be rolling. When he pulled up to his house, Bob was getting out of his car.

"How's it going, Mike?" Bob called from across the street.

"It's going well, Bob. What's up with you?" Michael said.

"I was just getting ready to fix a couple of steaks and watch the Sixers game. They're playing the Heat tonight. Have you eaten yet?"

"No. Let me put my things in the house, and I'll be over" Michael said.

"I'll leave the door open for you," he said, as he went into his house.

When Michael got in the house, his answering machine was blinking. He went upstairs to change into jeans and a sweatshirt, while he listened to his messages.

Hi, Mike, this is Kevin. I just called to say hello, and I'll see you on Thursday at Mom Mom's house.

He decided to call Kevin back after he finished listening to his messages, to see if he wanted to go to the parade.

Hey, Michael, what's shaking? You won't believe this when I tell you. Jasmine invited me to Thanksgiving dinner over Michelle's parents' house. Man, I'm handling some serious business down here, brother. Give me a call when you get a chance. And thanks for hooking me up with her.

Michael couldn't contain his laughter at Alex's ass. Alex tried to tell him his nose was wide open, but it sounded like his nose was Mack truck drivable. Still laughing at the message Alex had left, he dialed Carol's number.

"Hello, Carol," he said, when she picked up.

"Michael, how are you?" she asked.

"I'm doing well. I was thinking about taking Kevin to the Thanksgiving Day Parade. Is that okay with you?"

"You must've been a fly on the wall in here. Kevin said to me yesterday he was going to ask you to take him to the parade. Of course it's okay with me. Plus, it'll give me a chance to finish baking the two cakes I'm bringing to your parents' house."

"Yummy, why kind are you baking?"

"She asked me to bake a carrot cake and a pineapple upside down cake," she said.

"Oh, this dinner is going to be the bomb," Michael said, his mouth beginning to water. "Can I speak to Kevin?"

"Hold on a second. Kevin, pick up the phone, it's Mike!" Carol said, yelling upstairs to Kevin.

"I got it, Mom. Hi, Mike," Kevin said, picking up the phone.

"Hey, little man. How are you?"

"I'm doing fine."

"Would you like to go to the parade? I already asked your mom, and she said if you wanted to go, that you could."

"Yippee! I'm going to the parade, I'm going to the parade!" Kevin sang happily.

"I'm going to pick you up early Thursday morning, around seven, so we can get a good spot, okay."

"Okay, Mike. I'll be ready, I promise. I'm going to take my camera too," he said.

"That's good. You should be able to get some nice pictures down there. Make sure you ask your mom to get some more film and batteries for your camera. I'm going to take some hot chocolate down there with us," he said, getting excited. "Okay, I'll see you early Thursday morning."

"Okay, Mike, bye. Mommy, I'm going to the parade!" Michael heard Kevin shout, as he was hanging up.

He grabbed a six-pack from the fridge, and headed over to Bob's to get his grub on.

"Yo, Bob, I'm coming in," he said, to let Bob know he was coming through the door. He didn't want to surprise him and end up getting shot.

"Come on in, Mike. I'm in the kitchen!" Bob shouted. "Let me grab one of those cold ones. You can put the rest in the fridge. So, tell me, what's up with that fine sister from Atlanta? I haven't had time to get with you about her."

"Man, she's the bomb. I'm still getting to know her better, but I think she might be the one, brother," Michael said.

"She must be, if you let her stay at your crib. That's a first…that I know of," Bob said, shaking his head. "I was shocked when I saw her coming out your house that afternoon. You know when Sara and Debra get a chance to meet her, they're going to grill her," he said laughing.

"I know, but she's more than capable of handling them. I'm telling you, Bob, she's all that."

"Is she coming to your mom's house on Thursday?"

No. She's having dinner with her parents, but she may be visiting during the Christmas holiday. I introduced her to my parents, and they loved her."

"That's good. Well, you know I'll be at your mom's house for dinner. I haven't missed one of those big throw downs in years," he said laughing. "These steaks are ready, bro. Let's move this party in the family room and watch the game," he said, putting the steaks on paper plates.

* * *

Just as Michael was settling into a deep sleep, his phone rang out, piercing the quiet of his toasty home.

"Huh…what? Who in the world could be calling me at five-thirty in the morning?" he asked, with his eyes barely focused on the phone. "Hello?"

"Wake up, Mike! It's Thanksgiving Day! It's time to go to the parade!" Michael smiled, after realizing it was Kevin.

"Good morning, Kevin. Boy, you're up early this morning," Michael said, sitting up in the bed.

"I sure am. You said we had to leave early in the morning to get a good spot for the parade."

"Okay, little man, I'm up. I'll be over to pick you up in an hour, okay? Tell your mom I'm on my way."

"She made us some egg sandwiches to take with us. Hurry up. I love you, Mike," Kevin said.

"I love you too, Kevin."

Michael got up and went downstairs to fill the kettle up with water for the hot chocolate. By the time he was dressed and hitting the bottom step, the kettle was whistling. He had put two portable fold up chairs in his car last night. When he pulled up at Carol's, she had their breakfast sandwiches bagged and ready to go.

"We'll see you at my mom's house after the parade, Carol. Thanks for the breakfast. Let's go Kevin," Michael said.

"Okay, you guys have a great time," she said, hugging Kevin.

"We will, Mommy," Kevin said, running to get into the car.

Parking down around the Philadelphia Art Museum, where the main entertainment would be located, was impossible. So Michael parked his car about three blocks away, and they walked to the museum area. Kevin carried their sandwiches, and he carried the two chairs and thermos. Kevin had even remembered to bring his camera, which Michael had no doubt he would.

Once they got settled in their chairs and ate the sandwiches, the first of the marching bands were coming by them. There were so many floats, clowns, tumblers and huge cartoon character balloons that it would make any grown person feel like a child again. Kevin was in awe of how many people it took to hold onto the big balloons. He was snapping away with his camera. And when a 60-foot tall balloon of Darth Vader floated by, he stopped what he was doing and just stood up, with his mouth wide open.

"Wow, Michael, look at how big he is," he said, bright eyed as I had ever seen him.

"He's huge," Michael said. "Where is my light saber?" he asked laughing.

As the weather started to warm up a bit and the parade festivities were drawing to a close, Santa Claus made his appearance. All the children started cheering and clapping, as Santa made his way to the top of the Art Museum, waving and tossing tee shirts and candy canes to all the happy children from his sleigh. Kevin even caught one of the tee shirts. This was truly one of the best parades Michael had ever been to. Kevin hugged him in appreciation, as they made their way back to Michael's car and headed to dinner.

When they walked inside Michael parents' house, the aromas coming from the kitchen filled the air and blasted their nostrils like a cannon.

"Is it time to eat yet? We're starving," Michael, said, as they hung up their coats in the closet.

Dad, Bob and Mr. Ted were in the family room watching the football game. The children were in the basement playing video games and watching television. All of the ladies were hustling in the kitchen, putting the finishing touches on the Thanksgiving feast. Michael's dad always cooked the turkey and ham during the wee hours of the morning, so that he would be out the way when Michael's mom reclaimed her kitchen. The dining room table was all set, and the desserts were placed on the server, looking delicious.

"Did you have a good time at the parade, Kevin?" Carol asked him.

"I sure did, Mommy. I took a lot of pictures, and once they get developed, you'll see just how much fun we had. Look, I even caught a tee shirt from Santa Claus!" Kevin said, all excited.

"Oh, that's nice. I'm glad you had a good time," she said, smiling at Michael.

Before long, Michael's mom was calling everyone to the table to bless the food. His dad stood at the head of the table, and asked Michael to offer a blessing. They all held hands and Michael began:

May we bow our heads?

Most glorious and everlasting God, the author of all wisdom, goodness and mercy. We want to thank you Father for last night's down lying, and this morning's up rising. We want to thank you for bringing this gathering of family and friends together to give thanks to you for this feast we're about to receive. Please bless those that are here within the sound of my voice. Bless those that are on their way, and give them traveling mercies. Bless those that are not with us, my Father. Bless those that are sick and afflicted, my Father. Heal them and let them know that with your powerful hands, you will make things right. Bless the food we are about to receive for the nourishment of our bodies. Bless those that prepared the food. And, my Father, when my praying days are over, when my tongue sticks to the roof of my mouth, I will pray that You will have a place over there where Job declared that the wicked will cease from troubling and the weary shall find rest. These and all other blessing we ask in your son, Jesus', name. Let us all say Amen.

Michael looked around the table, and noticed quite a few faces with tears in their eyes.

"That was beautiful, Michael," his mom said, as she hugged him. "You need to be a deacon at the church," she said smiling.

"Amen," said Ms. Mamie, Mr. Ted's wife.

"Mom, I will never forget how to pray," Michael said.

Needless to say, the meal was fantastic. It seemed every year the dinner outshined the one from the previous year. There was everything you could imagine on the table. They had turkey, ham, roast beef, stuffing, giblet gravy, candied sweet potatoes, collard greens, string beans, potato salad, macaroni and cheese, and all kinds of pies and cakes. It was pure heaven.

"Man, your mom knows how to put it down, Michael," Bob said. "I told you I'd never miss one of your parents' throw downs."

"Carol, that carrot cake was on the money," Michael said, as his dad nodded in agreement.

"Why, thank you, gentlemen. I'm glad you liked it," Carol said.

Later on that evening, everyone was getting their doggie bags together, and beginning to make their way home. Even Sara had her Tupperware, just as she said she would. After Michael helped with the clean up, he decided to head on home with his plates as well.

"Hey, Deb, let me talk to you for a minute. What are your plans for tomorrow evening? Would you like to go out to a club or something?" he asked his sister.

"That sounds great. Give me a call tomorrow, so we can get together on a time. You know, Mom, the girls and I are going to hit the malls in the morning," she said.

"I figured that," Michael said, shaking his head. "How much money do you need?"

"I could use about four hundred, if you have it."

"You need four hundred dollars? Damn," he said, smiling and handing her an envelope with four hundred dollars in it.

"How did you know I was going to say that amount?" she said, when she looked in the envelope.

"Deb, I've known you all your life…I know what my little sister is thinking," he said smiling.

"Thank you, Mike. I sure can use this."

"No problem, baby girl. Why don't you call me when you get back home and settled?"

"Okay, I will."

"Mom and Dad, I'm going to call it a night. Thanks for a good dinner," he said, giving both of them a hug.

When he got home, he decided to give Michelle a call to see how everything went on her end.

"Hey, baby, how are you?" Michael asked, when I picked up the phone.

"I'm good, Michael. I've been thinking about you today. How was your Thanksgiving?" I asked, happy to hear his voice.

"It went well. It started out with Kevin waking me up at five-thirty in the morning," he said. "He woke me up early so we could go to the parade. He was so excited."

"That sounds like fun."

"I think I enjoyed it more then he did," he said, as I laughed. "The dinner at Mom's was its usual fantastic event. How did you make it through your day?" he asked.

"It went smoothly, and just like yours, the food was great and plentiful. I remembered what you said about my Uncle Billy being right there beside me, and you know what, it felt just as you said. He was in all our thoughts, but I was cool. Alex came over with Jasmine, and was the life of the party. He said he had a really good time. My father and Uncle Maceo gave him the once over," I added, with a chuckle. "Your boy pulled through it okay. They really liked him."

"I told you he's a good man. I'm glad you all enjoyed yourselves, in spite of your uncle not being there physically. Listen, I've had a long day, so I'm gong to turn in early. I'll give you a call sometime this weekend, okay?"

"Okay, baby. Good night and I'll talk to you soon," I said.

Chapter 24

AFTER hanging up with Michael, I decided to turn in also. I wanted to be up early the next morning to go shopping with my mother and Jasmine. Unlike previous years, I was actually looking forward to going shopping with them. I wanted to find a new gown to wear for the Christmas party, something that would make Michael sit up and really take notice.

I was happy his family was coming to the party. It was going to be interesting to see how our families got along. I had to admit I was nervous about meeting his little sister. I remember how protective Tony's sisters were when we finally met. They would make good lawyers themselves, with all the questions they asked. *I should call them so we can catch up*, she thought. *It's been much too long since I've talked to either of them, and I miss them.*

The next morning, I heard the dull buzz of the alarm clock. "It's time to get up already?" I groaned, as I turned over to turn off the alarm. It seemed like I had just went to sleep. I was having such a wonderful dream about Michael. Oh well, perhaps another time.

Just as my feet hit the floor, the phone started ringing off the hook.

"Hello, Mom. I'm up, I'm up!" I said, answering the phone, without even looking at the caller ID.

"Good morning, baby. Jasmine will be here in ten minutes. I made sandwiches for all of us, and we'll be there to pick you up shortly, so make sure you're ready," my mom said.

"Okay. Did you remember to make mine ham?" I asked.

"Yes, I remembered you don't like leftover turkey, baby. Now get off the phone and get ready. We'll be there soon," she said, and hung up before I could remind her she was the one who called me.

I jumped out of bed and grabbed a shower. Just as I was pulling on my boots, I heard the house alarm beeping and then being turned off, signaling they had let themselves in.

"Michelle, you had better not still be in the bed!" I heard Jasmine shout, as I got to the top of the stairs.

"No, I'm ready and dressed. I even have on my shoes, woman." I said laughing. "Let me grab my jacket. Good morning," I said, as I came downstairs and gave both of them a hug and kiss.

"I guess I lost the bet, Mom." Jasmine laughed.

"Oh, don't tell me you two were betting I wouldn't be ready?" I asked, as I turned around from the closet with my jacket in hand, laughing at them.

"Yes, baby, we did because usually I have to drag you out the bed to come shopping with us on Black Friday. Let's go, I want to hit Lenox Mall first, and you know how hard it is to find a parking space up there," Mom said.

"We can always valet park," Jasmine said, as we were walking out the door.

"Y'all must be planning to do some serious shopping, since you brought Daddy's truck," I said, laughing when I saw it.

"You know your dad's truck holds more packages than either of our cars," Mom said, as Jasmine got into the driver's seat and she got in the passenger seat. "Here's your sandwich. I brought bottled water, I figured we could get coffee at the mall."

"Thanks. So, do you have an attack plan ready?" I asked, as Jas and I both fell out laughing.

We knew my mom had a list of stores and merchandise she wanted to get. She was one of the most organized people we knew.

"I don't know why y'all laughing. You both know I'm always prepared," she said, smiling like the queen she was.

"Yes, Mom!" we both said in unison, and started laughing again. Mom shook her head and turned the radio to the gospel station.

Just as Jasmine suggested, we took advantage of the valet parking, and were soon shopping away. After leaving Lennox Mall, we headed to two other malls before stopping for lunch.

"Jasmine, Dad and I really enjoyed meeting and getting to know your friend, Alex. You'll have to bring him around more often," Mom said, after we were seated in a restaurant.

"I will, Mom. He enjoyed meeting you all too. Dad and Uncle Maceo invited him to the Falcons' game on Sunday," Jasmine said grinning.

"You know they're trying to size him up, right?" I said to Jasmine.

"I know, but trust me, he can handle himself. After all, they're just practicing until they can meet Michael. That's when it's going to get really interesting," Jasmine said.

"Hmmm, Jasmine, what was your impression of Michael? I only got to speak to him briefly when we ran into him and Alex at the mall that time," my mom said.

"Oh Lord," I said groaning, as Jasmine looked at me and smiled.

"I think he's okay, Mom," she said, and stuck her tongue out at me. "I'm sure you'll get to talk to him at length when he comes down for the Christmas party. He is coming, right Michelle?"

"Yeah, he'll be there," I said, shooting daggers at Jasmine, as she smiled and continued talking to my mom, as if I wasn't there.

"He's quite handsome, don't you think, Mom?" she asked, and continued talking, as Mom agreed. "From the little time I've spent with him, he seems quite intelligent. I think they'll make some pretty babies," Jasmine said.

"Hold up!" I said, as I sat up straighter and started choking on my iced tea. This started the two of them laughing. "Can we at least get to know each other a little better, before y'all start talking about babies and shit?"

"Michelle, how do you really feel about him? You know we only want the best for you, and it has been a while since anyone has caught your attention," Mom said.

"I know, Mom. I was still mourning Tony, I guess. I really like Michael, but I'm going to take my time. Besides, he lives in Philly and I live in Atlanta," I said.

"Like that's a big problem. Like I said before, it's not like either of you can't afford to fly back and forth, so don't use the distance as an excuse," Jasmine said.

"I'm not. I was just stating a fact. Have you both bought your gowns for the Christmas party?" I asked, changing the subject.

"Notice how she changed the subject," Jasmine said to Mom. "No, I haven't bought a new gown yet. I was hoping we could look today."

"I don't need a new gown, but I'll help you girls find one. You know I have more gowns than the law allows…with all the Eastern Star and Mason events Dad and I attend. I'm going to choose from one of them," Mom said.

After a day full of mall hopping, I was never so happy to see a day end. Jasmine and I found beautiful gowns to wear to the Christmas party. We pulled up to my parents' house around three, and walked in to find Dad sitting in his favorite chair in the den.

"Hi Daddy, My feet hurt," I said, sounding exhausted as I sat down on the ottoman in front of him.

"Hey, baby. Did your mother leave anything in the store, or do I need to get a second job?" he asked smiling.

"She did go a little overboard, but I don't think you'll need a second job," I said. "How you doing, Daddy?"

"I'm doing good…enjoying the quiet while it lasted. But now that you all are back, I'm sure your mother will find something she needs me to do," he said.

"I heard that, old man. You can relax today, but I have plans for you tomorrow," my mom said, walking into the room with Jasmine behind her.

"You two are just too cute," I said, smiling at my parents. "Jasmine, are you ready to go? Let's stop and pick up some Chinese food on the way to my house, unless you have other plans with Alex this evening."

"We have plenty of leftovers. You two could join us for dinner," Mom said.

"Hmmm no thanks, I have a taste for Chinese tonight," I said, as Dad laughed and Jas looked on smiling.

"I don't have plans with Alex tonight, so Chinese sounds good. Let's hit the road, Thelma," Jasmine said, and laughed at her own joke.

"I'm ready, Louise. Love you, Mom and Dad. We'll see you later," I said, kissing them both as we left.

Jasmine and I spent a wonderful evening together, reminiscing and talking about how we achieved most of our dreams. The future was looking bright for the both of us in the love department.

* * *

It seemed the weekend sped by, and before I knew it, it was Monday again, and the start of a new business week. I made my usual stop by *Krispy Kreme*, and bought donuts for the office, to go with Yvonne's wonderful coffee.

"Good morning, Ms. Rivers. Let me get that door for you," Curtis said, as he saw me coming through the door with all my packages.

"Good morning, Curtis. Thanks for getting that door for me. Please take the box off the top. It's for you and your fellow co-worker."

"Thank you, Ms. Rivers. We appreciate your kindness," he said.

"You're welcome, Curtis. Have a wonderful day," I said, as I walked to the elevator.

Once I reached my floor, I walked into the break room and placed the donuts down, before going to my office.

"Good morning, Yvonne. I see you've beaten me into the office as usual," I said smiling, as I walked into our suite of offices. "How was your holiday and weekend?"

"Good morning, Michelle. My holiday and weekend were very good. My kids were home for the holiday. It was good seeing them, and I did some shopping and a lot of baking. How was yours?" she said.

"It was wonderful. I spent most of it with my parents and Jasmine. You know my mom; she invited quite a few people over for Thanksgiving. It was a full house, with plenty of food, and somehow we still had leftovers," I said grinning "How does my schedule look for today?"

"It looks pretty light. You have a meeting with John at ten. I'll have the production reports ready for you to go over in about thirty minutes."

"Okay, thanks. I bought donuts and put them in the break room."

"You're going to have us all fat, if you keep this up," she said smiling, as she got up to go get one. "Can I bring you some coffee or tea?"

"Not right now, thanks. I think I'll settle for some cranberry juice," I said, as I went into my office.

No sooner had I sat down at my desk, the phone rang.

"Good morning, Rivers, Inc., Michelle speaking," I answered.

"Good morning, baby. It's Michael. How are you doing?"

"I'm great. This is a pleasant surprise," I said grinning.

"I needed to hear your voice before I started my day. I missed talking to you over the weekend. It seemed we kept playing phone tag," he said laughing. "My sister was giving me strange looks, when I complained that I had missed your call on Saturday night when we went clubbing."

"Poor, baby. I can just imagine," I said, laughing to myself at the visual.

"No you can't. She teased me all the way to the airport...talking about you had my nose wide open," he said, sounding pitiful.

"You need to stop, Michael," I said laughing. "I can't wait to meet your sister. I bet she's a lot of fun."

"Yes, she is...spoiled brat that she is, which is partly my fault. But enough about my sister, how was your weekend?"

"Good. I went shopping with my mom and Jasmine, did some things around the house, plus found time to read a couple of books. I picked up a beautiful gown for the Christmas party. Have you sent Yvonne your RSVP yet?"

"No, I thought I'd just call and let her know I was coming. I can't wait to see you again, baby," he said.

"I'm looking forward to seeing you also. I'll give Yvonne your message. It doesn't make sense for you to call her directly, when I can just tell her myself."

"Yes, you do that, and I'll try to give you a call this evening. Have a wonderful day, baby, and think of me," Michael said.

"You do likewise, baby. I'll talk to you later," I said, hanging up.

My day had gotten off to a good start. I was so happy that Michael had decided to call. He must've read my mind, because I had wanted to hear his voice also. I couldn't wait to talk to him later tonight.

About five minutes later, I heard a gentle knock on the door.

"Come on in, Yvonne," I said, looking up as she entered.

"I love that song you're playing. Who is the artist, I don't think I've heard her before," Yvonne said.

"That's Maysa. She's the lead female vocalist for Incognito, and the song is called *Blue Light*. I was lucky enough to see her perform in person once, and she put on a great show. She actually sounds better live. I have an extra copy of this CD at home, so I'll give you this one at the end of the day."

"You don't have to give me your CD, but I'm not going to turn the offer down," she said laughing. "Here are the production reports and the mail. I've gotten over thirty confirmation calls for the Christmas party, and I'll give you a list of whom by the end of the day."

"Sounds good. I have about ten minutes to go over these reports before John gets here. Please send him in when he arrives."

"Okay, will do," she said, as she left my office.

Looking over the production report, I saw that in addition to Michael's book, we had one other book almost ready for release in December, and another two that would be ready in January. That's not bad, not bad at all. Putting the report aside, I started going through the mail. I saw what looked like a personal letter addressed to me, and not the company. I opened it, and it read:

Hello Bitch,

You really think you have it all now, don't you? Well, we'll just have to see about that. Watch your back, because I have a surprise for you, Michelle Rivers, and it's a good one too. It's time to knock you down a peg or two, bitch. Watch your back!

"What the hell is going on around here?" I said aloud, turning the envelope over and noticing no return address.

"What's wrong, Michelle?" John asked, walking into the office, and over-hearing what I said.

"It seems I'm now getting hate mail, John. I don't know what's going on around here. First, someone tries to break into my house, and then some of my Blackshear's are either broken or missing, and now this," I said raising my voice, with tears in my eyes.

"What's going on? I can hear you in my office," Yvonne said, running into my office.

"Come in and have a seat, Yvonne. Michelle, let me see the letter," John said, walking to stand behind me.

"Michelle, are you okay?" Yvonne asked.

"Something is very wrong here. Why didn't you tell me about the missing items?" John said, before I could answer Yvonne.

"It happened right before the holiday, and I really didn't think about telling you. I didn't think it was that big a deal," I said.

"Well, we're going to get to the bottom of this mess, because now it's getting personal. Yvonne, I want you to call Gayle, and tell her to call all of the staff together in the conference room right away," John said. "Michelle, I want you to call your father and Maceo, and ask them to come to the office."

"John, is that really necessary?" I asked.

"Yes, it's necessary. I'm not taking anyone threatening you lightly, and you shouldn't either," he said.

"John, do you think we should call the police?" Yvonne asked.

"And tell them what? I don't really think we have enough to take to the police, but we'll see what Robert has to say about it. Michelle, call your father and Maceo now!" he said, looking at me until I picked up the phone.

"I'll go call Gayle now," Yvonne said.

I picked up the phone and called my father. "Hello, Daddy, this is Michelle," I said.

"Uh oh, I know your voice, baby. What's wrong?" my dad said.

"Daddy, I received a threatening letter at the office, and John thought I needed to call you to come over here. He wants me to call Maceo too."

"Damn right you needed to call me. I'll be right there, and I'll call Maceo myself. Where's John?" my dad asked.

"He's standing right behind me," I said.

"Put him on the phone."

I handed John the phone, and then I got up from my desk, walked across the room and looked out the window in deep thought.

"John, what the hell is going on over there?" my dad asked.

"I have no idea, Bobby, but I intend to find out. She seems to be holding up okay. I'll see you soon," John said, hanging up the phone. "Michelle, your father is on his way. Will you be okay while I go speak with the staff?" he asked. "Michelle, did you hear me?"

"I'm sorry, John. Yes, I'll be okay. Go ahead with the meeting. Speaking of meetings, we never had ours."

"We'll have it later. Michelle, please stay here until your father and Maceo arrive, okay?"

"I know how to take care of myself," I said, looking him in the eye.

"I know you do. But until we know exactly what we're dealing with, I want you to humor me and be careful," John said.

"Okay, I'll stay here," I said, giving him a hug.

After John left, I walked over to my desk to look at the letter again, but realized it wasn't there. I guess John had taken it with him.

"I brought you some tea. Why don't you sit down, while we wait for your father to arrive? Jasmine's on her way also," Yvonne said.

"Oh hell, Yvonne, I wish you hadn't called Jasmine. My father and Maceo are bad enough, but Jasmine will turn this place upside down," I said.

"I didn't call her, she called me, and I told her what was going on. I'm sorry if I did the wrong thing, Michelle," Yvonne said sincerely.

"It's okay. Just don't say anything to my mother about all this. Maybe it's someone's idea of a sick joke. Did you get anymore calls about the Christmas party?" I said, trying to focus on work.

"Yes, I received five more calls. I don't see many people turning down our invitation. It's going to be a beautiful party," she said smiling.

"I agree. I'm looking forward to it, and thank you again for all the extra effort you've put into making this a success. I appreciate it."

"I had a lot of help. Jasmine's a dream to work with, but thanks for the praise just the same," she said.

"Did I hear someone mention my name?" Jasmine said, as she walked into the office. "Okay, what the hell is going on around here? Let me see this letter."

"Hey, Jas. Thanks for coming over, but you didn't have to," I said.

"Save it," she said, holding up her hand. "Where's the letter?" she asked again.

"John has it. He took it with him when he left the office," I said.

Meanwhile, in the conference room, everyone was assembled except Pam when John arrived. Everyone looked up when he entered, and knew right away that something was wrong by the look on his face, and the lack of his ever-present cup of coffee.

"Hello everyone I'm glad you could all make it on short notice. Have a seat…and where's Pam?" John said.

"I'm right here, John. Sorry I'm late; I was finishing up a call. What's so important that I was told to drop everything and come to the conference room right away?" she asked.

"Have a seat, Pam," John said abruptly. "I'll get right down to the reason for this meeting. Someone sent a threatening letter to Michelle this morning, and I plan to get to the bottom of it," he said, as everyone gasped. Holding up his hand for silence, he continued. "A couple of strange things have happened since she has taken over Rivers, Inc., and I want to make sure none of you have anything to do with it, because there will be hell to pay if I find out differently."

Just then the door opened, and Maceo walked into the conference room. Without a word, John handed him the letter in question to read. After reading it, Maceo handed it back to John.

"I'm going to ask this once. On second thought, I'm not going to ask anything. I'm going to tell you, if anyone in this room has an issue with how this company is being run, or has a personal issue with Michelle being in charge, I strongly suggest you resign. Do I make myself clear?" John stated.

Everyone looked around at each other and nodded yes.

"John, was the letter that bad?" Brandon asked.

"Excuse me, what did you ask?" Maceo asked, saying something for the first time since entering the room.

Brandon swallowed hard and repeated his question.

"Yes, the letter is that bad, when you take into account some of the other things that have been going on since Michelle has taken over this company. By the way, just in case some of you don't know who I am, my name is Maceo Cunningham, and I'm on the board of directors of Rivers, Inc., as well as a personal friend of the Rivers family," Maceo said.

Both Pam and David looked at each other, before glancing away quickly.

"John, is there anything special you want the security staff to do? I'd be happy to walk Ms. Rivers to her car in the evening," Curtis said.

"That's a good idea, Curtis. I'd like to meet with you after this meeting to solidify our security procedures," John said.

"Yes sir, I'll make sure everyone who isn't here is briefed of your request," he said.

"Sir, is Michelle okay?" one of the staffers from the printing department asked.

"Yes, Nathaniel. I think she's more disappointed than anything else. If there are no more questions, let's get back to the business of publishing," John said.

Everyone began to file out, when John stopped Pam. "Pam, I'd like to speak with you for a few minutes before you return to your office," he said.

John took Maceo aside and asked if he'd see if Robert was here yet, and for the both of them to meet him in his office.

"Curtis, give me five minutes, and I'll come downstairs and speak to you in your office," John said.

"Okay, I'll meet you there," Curtis replied.

"Alright John. What can I do for you?" Pam asked, after Curtis had left the conference room.

"Pam, please don't take this the wrong way, but I need to know something. I know you had a problem when Michelle first took over, but I hope you're not responsible for any of this," he said, as soon as the door shut behind Maceo. He watched her closely for her reaction.

"John, I'd never think of doing such a thing. My God, you can't possibly think I'd stoop so low!" she said, in a shocked tone.

"I had to ask Pam, so you'll have to forgive me. God help whoever is doing this shit," he said angrily. "You can go now, but if you hear of anyone who may have a problem with Michelle, please let me know."

"Yes, I will," she replied, and left as quickly as she could.

Robert finally arrived and met Maceo in the hallway, as he stepped off the elevator on his way to Michelle's office.

"Hey, brother, I see you made it here before me. How's my daughter?" Robert asked.

"She was being well taken care of when I got here by Yvonne and Jasmine.

I didn't speak to her yet though. I sat in on John's staff meeting, to get a feel for the staff," he said. "Let's go check on our girl now."

Looking up, I saw my father and Maceo walk into the suite of offices, and knew it was going to be a long day.

"Hey, baby. Are you okay?" my father asked, as soon as he walked in the room and sat down in front of me.

"I'm fine, Dad. Everyone didn't need to come over here. I'm more then capable of taking care of myself," I said, looking at Maceo as he burst into laughter. "Hey, Uncle Maceo, you should know I don't break that easily. After all, you're the one who taught me self-defense."

"Damn right, and you were good too," he said.

"What do you mean was? I'm still good," I said, looking around at all the faces in my office. "I appreciate everyone's concern, but I'm okay. Y'all can go back to work."

"We don't work for you, so you can save that, Michelle," Jasmine said. "I, for one, am not going anywhere until we figure out what the hell is going on."

"I'll be at my desk if anyone needs anything," Yvonne said, leaving my office.

"Thank you, Yvonne, for everything," I said.

"Okay, let's all have a seat. I want to see this letter," my dad said.

"I want to see it too," Jasmine said.

"John still has the letter," I said.

"Okay, I'll look at it when we meet with him. Has something else been going on that I should be aware of?" my dad asked me.

"One of my figurines are missing, and one was left in the display broken," I said.

"You mean the Blackshear pieces that you're always talking about? Why didn't you tell me about this, Michelle?" Dad asked.

"There was so much going on, I just didn't think to tell you. It happened right before the holiday. I figured it was probably an accident from when they were cleaning the office."

"It was an accident my foot," Jasmine said under her breath, which caused Maceo to laugh.

"Listen baby. We all love you, and I don't like the idea of anyone threatening you, so you'll have to excuse us for being overprotective. And yes, we know you're grown, but we're concerned just the same," my father said. "Maceo and I are going to meet with John, and we'll be back soon."

"I'll stay here with her, Dad. I can do my work from here today," Jasmine said, looking at me.

"Good. We'll be back soon," he said, giving me a hug and kissing Jas on her forehead.

"Don't be giving me any looks, heffa. You're stuck with me for the day, so you may as well get used to it," Jasmine said, sitting behind my desk as if she owned it.

"Can I at least get my production report off the desk before you take over?" I asked, as I walked over and snatched them up, which started Jasmine laughing.

"I love you too, Michelle," she said.

Pam was sitting in her office, thinking about the staff meeting that took place a little while ago. *I can't believe John all but accused me of sending that shit to Michelle. I wonder what was written in that letter. It seems I'm not the only one who dislikes her. I wonder if David had anything to do with it. I'll have to ask him,* she thought, as she tried to calm her nerves. She picked up the phone and called Sharon.

"Hey, Sharon, this is Pam. What are you doing for lunch today?"

"Hi Pam, I hadn't given it any thought yet. Do you want to meet me at the *Grill* or something?" Sharon said.

"That sounds perfect. How about in half an hour? I can leave now and get us a table," Pam said.

"Okay, I'll see you in a few," Sharon said, before hanging up.

Pam arrived at the *Grill* before Sharon and got a table near the window. It was such a beautiful day outside…not too cold for November.

"Hey girl, how have you been doing? I missed talking to you since I've been out of town the last week or so," Sharon said, once she arrived and sat down.

"I've been okay, but wait till I tell you what happened at work today," Pam said.

"What happened?" Sharon asked.

"Let's order, and then I'll tell you all about it," she said.

After they ordered lunch, Pam began to tell Sharon about the happening at Rivers, Inc. "You'll never believe what happened this morning. It seems someone decided to send Michelle Rivers some hate mail, and we all got called into a conference about it."

"Wow, what did they say? How did she look?" Sharon asked.

"She wasn't at the conference, just my boss, John. One of the board members who said he was a friend of the family came in during the meeting. John just told us about the letter, and said if anyone had a problem with her running things to resign."

"Damn, girl. So you think it's one of the employees that wrote the letter?"

"Oh, it gets worse. At the end of the meeting, John asked if I'd stay for a minute, and then asked me straight out if I'd written the letter."

"What, you've got to be kidding!" Sharon said shocked.

"I wish I was. Of course, I denied it because I didn't write the damn letter," Pam said angrily.

"Of course you didn't. I can't see you doing anything like that," Sharon said.

"Well, I'm glad someone believes in me."

"Of course I believe in you, you're my girl. Forget about that shit. I guess you aren't the only one who doesn't like the bitch," Sharon said.

"I guess not. So, tell me about your trip to California. Did you meet anyone?"

"No, girl, it was mainly a business trip. I did get to go out to a club with a few co-workers," Sharon said.

Chapter 25

ROBERT and Maceo walked towards the editorial offices, talking about the threat made to Michelle. Gayle was at her desk typing.

"Hello, Gayle. Is John in his office?" Robert asked.

"No, he isn't. He called a moment ago, and said for you two to go right in and have a seat. He'll be with you in a moment. Would you care for some coffee or tea while you're waiting?"

"Yes, I'd like some coffee," Maceo said.

"I'm fine for now," Robert responded.

"Okay, I'll be back shortly. Please make yourselves at home," she said.

"Okay, Bobby. Give me your gut feeling on this," Maceo inquired, once they were alone in John's office.

"The thought crossed my mind about the alarm incident at Michelle's place, and the pictures we found of Billy and Pam. She's a suspect unfortunately, but we have no proof that it was her. I don't think we should mention it to John right now. I'd hate for him to accuse her of anything based on the photos. So, for now, we'll keep that between us," he said.

"I agree with you on that, Bobby."

Suddenly the door opened, and John came in a little out of breath. "Hello, my brothers. I apologize for holding you up. I was down with security, going over a few things with the lead officer, Curtis," he said.

"Not a problem, brother," Maceo said, as they all shook hands.

"I think in lieu of what has happened, we need to get with Brother Jennings and hire one more security guard for the building. That'll give Rivers, Inc. a total of five. Currently, we have four guards, working twelve-hour shifts. The extra guard will straddle the other two shifts for eight hours, covering the parking garage."

"I think that will work out just fine," Robert said. "It probably wouldn't be a bad idea to have a camera system installed as well. Since we're still trying to find out who's behind this, it should be installed during the night, when the building is relatively empty."

"Let me give Jennings a call. I'm sure he'll give us a deal with the installation of surveillance equipment," Maceo suggested.

"Here's the letter, Bobby," John said, handing him the evidence.

"This shit just doesn't make any sense at all. Did you two notice the postmark on this envelope?" Robert asked, with his eyebrows raised. "It was mailed from Dallas, Texas, which is odd. Who in Texas would have a beef with my baby? Unless it was mailed by someone from here who recently took a trip down here" Robert wondered. "I'll ask Michelle if she knows anyone in Texas."

"Whoever it was really thought this one out," Maceo added.

"I'll put my feelers out there, to see if anyone from the company has taken a trip down there recently," John said.

"John, has anyone here had any kind of issues with Michelle since she's taken over…that you know of?" Maceo asked.

"When Michelle first came on board, one of my editors did have a little issue with Michelle, but I squashed that immediately."

"Who was that?" Robert asked.

"That would be Pamela Bryant," John said, as Robert and Maceo stole a glance at each other.

"Does she have access to Michelle's office at all? The reason I ask is, remember some items were missing and broken in her office recently."

"I just heard about that this morning when Michelle mentioned it. No one would've gotten past Yvonne without her knowledge. Besides, I asked Pam if she knew anything about the letter point blank, and she looked me square in my eyes and said that she didn't. To be quite honest, it's not her style. She also hasn't been out of town either. I'm going to have Yvonne get with the cleaning company, to see if maybe one of their staff accidentally broke anything in Michelle's office," John said.

"Okay, that's a good idea John," Robert said.

"Don't worry, Bobby, we'll get to the bottom of this. We're not going to let anything happen to Michelle. Trust us," John and Maceo assured him.

Just then, Gayle buzzed John on his intercom. "John, you have a call from Michelle on line one."

"Thank you, Gayle."

"Hello, Michelle," John said.

"I hope I didn't disturb you gentlemen," I said. "Could you have my father come by my office before he leaves?"

"He was headed right over, Michelle. How are you feeling?" John asked.

"I'm still a little uneasy, as I guess you can imagine."

"Your dad is coming right over…and Michelle, don't worry, we're on the case," John said.

"That's nice to know, John. Remember, we still need to meet before the day is over."

"When you're ready, just call and I'll be right over. Bye now," he said, before hanging up. "Okay, brothers, we know what has to be done. If anything comes up, or if I hear anything, I'll put a call in to you two first thing," John assured them.

"Alright, I'm going to go see my daughter. You two take it easy," Robert said, as he left John's office.

"I'm right behind you, Bobby. I'm going to stop by Brad Jennings' office to get this security situation ironed out, instead of calling. Later, John," Maceo said, as he left.

While on his way to Michelle's office, Robert stopped to ask Yvonne for a favor. "Hello, Yvonne," he said.

"Hello, Mr. Rivers," she said.

"Can I ask you for a quick favor? Will you make a copy of this letter for me, please?"

"Sure, give me a second," she said, moving towards her copier. "Here you go. Is everything okay?"

"Oh, it will be. Can you let Michelle know I'm here?" he said.

"Go right in, she's expecting you," Yvonne said.

"Daddy, I know you three have come up with something, so tell me about it," I said anxiously, when he walked into my office.

"First of all, how are you feeling?" he asked.

"I'm still a little shaken by all of this, but I'm okay. I'm just trying to figure out who would do such a thing, or for that matter, what I could've done to warrant such hatred."

"Well, this is the deal. There are a few changes in security that the board feels need to be implemented. Of course they would need your approval. The first thing is for you to hire at least one more security guard, who will work eight-hour days, and mainly patrol, the garage area. They would act as back up for the other two on duty during the day. Also, my lodge brother, Brad Jennings, has a security firm that deals with video surveillance. We'd like to get a system in here. Maceo's getting in touch with him to come out and give an estimate."

"I remember Mr. Jennings. He used to be an FBI agent, right?" I asked.

"Yes, he's retired from the FBI, but he has his own security business now. I guess he got bored with all of that retirement money," he said smiling. "Another thing is this letter. Did you notice the envelope was postmarked from Dallas, Texas?" he asked, showing Jasmine and me the envelope.

"I hadn't noticed that," I said.

"Can I see that letter?" Jasmine asked. "This is crazy," she said, after reading the letter and passing it to me.

"Do you know anyone in Dallas that might have a beef with you?" he asked.

"No, I don't know anyone in Dallas, but I do know a few people in Houston. But I've never had any problems with them. As a matter of fact, I haven't seen them in a few years."

"John told me that you had some sort of run-in with one of the editors when you first took over. Is there still a problem?" my dad asked me.

"No, John squashed that problem right away, and there have been no problems since," I said.

"One more thing, make sure you get with the building maintenance people, to see if maybe someone broke your figurines and forgot to mention it. By the way, once Jennings gives you his estimate, let me know, and if you approve, I'll pay for it myself," he said.

"That won't be necessary, Daddy. The company will pay for it," I said.

"Michelle, will you let me take care of that, please?" he said, rather firmly.

"Okay, I'll let you know what the bill is…if I approve it."

"Thank you. I had Yvonne make me a copy of the letter and the envelope for future reference. I need to get back to the office now. I have to meet with one of the Atlanta Hawks that I represent. You girls take it easy. Take care of Michelle for me, Jasmine," he said, giving both of us a hug before leaving.

"Oh, I will, Dad. Don't worry," Jasmine responded. "I'm willing to bet you this Pam person had something to do with what's been going on around here," she said, with a hint of anger in her voice. "She probably walked in your office when Yvonne was away from her desk and smashed the Guardian, and then grabbed one just for spite."

"I doubt that, Jas. I don't think she's brave or stupid enough to chance coming in this office, with the possibility of getting caught. I just don't see it."

"Well, I'd keep my eye on her anyway. Don't forget that she and Mike used to have a thing going on, and she might think you're the reason he's not seeing her anymore."

"You have a point there, but that doesn't explain the letter coming from Texas. Nor does it say she was the one who tried to get into my house," I told her.

"Think about it for a minute, Michelle. Didn't you tell me you saw some pictures of her and your uncle in some rather risqué positions? Maybe she tried to get in the house to get those pictures back. She had to have known her way around that house, and she probably had keys."

"You could be right, but I'm not sure how deeply involved he was with her anyway. I'll just keep my eyes and ears open. I'm also going to run this letter by Michael when I talk to him later this evening."

"I think the surveillance cameras are a good idea. Most businesses have them now," Jasmine added. "When you tell Michael about the letter, see if he thinks Pam could've stooped so low as to do something like this," she said.

"Girl, I'm glad you're here with me. I couldn't have held it together if you weren't," I said, hugging my friend.

"Save it, Michelle. We're sisters, and I wouldn't be anywhere else but by your side."

"I appreciate the support just the same," I said, before hitting up Yvonne on the intercom. "Yvonne, could you call John and see if we can meet in his office?" I asked.

"Okay, hold on a minute," she said, dialing John's number. After a minute, she came back on the line and said, "He said that would be fine."

"Thank you, Yvonne. Jas, I'm going over to John's office for a meeting. Are you staying here?"

"No, I'm going to fax something real quick, and then I'm going to head back to my office, if you're sure you'll be okay," she said.

"I'm good. Thanks for coming over and staying with me. I love you, girl," I said, as we hugged again. "I'll give you a call when I get home this evening."

"I'll talk to you then, Michelle. Please be careful, okay? Bye," Jasmine said.

While walking over to John's office, I could sense the tension in the air, as I walked by a few of my employees. It was as if they wanted to say something, but didn't know how to express themselves. Everyone I passed just said good afternoon with scripted smiles. When I walked into the editorial offices, Gayle and Elaine greeted me.

"Good afternoon, Michelle," Elaine spoke first. "If it helps at all, I hope that whoever is doing this gets caught soon."

"So do I, Elaine. I just can't imagine who would be so hateful," I said.

"John is expecting you. Go right in, and I'm with you all the way, Michelle. If there's anything I can do to help, just let me know," Gayle said, as she hugged me.

"Thank you, Gayle. I appreciate that," I said, as I went into John's office.

"Good afternoon, Michelle. Please have a seat," he said.

"So, tell me what's going on with your editorial staff?" I asked.

"Well, we should have three books ready by the end of the year. Michael Ramsey's book is due to go live by the second week in December, along with Taylor Bray's horror novel. The book Brandon's working on, about the negro baseball league, should also be ready by year's end," John said.

"That's very good, John. We'll have three books published before the year is out. I'd say we're rolling right along," I said proudly. "John, would you say that the scripts are coming in more frequently now?"

"Yes, I'd say that. Why do you ask?"

"I remembered that you said we could use one or two more editors on staff when I first came on board. Do you still think there is a need for them?"

"Honestly, I feel that if we had one more editor on board, we could get more work out there," John said.

"Let's bring another editor on staff then. You work out all the details, and I'll sign off on it. Also, do we have anyone on staff that has experience building web pages? I'd like to get our site up and running to start the New Year off."

"It's funny you should mention that. There's a young lady that works down in the printing department that's a Webmaster. I'll get a list of some of the sites that she's built for you to peruse."

"John, if you've seen them, I'll go with your decision. Just get with her and see what her fee would be for building a website for us. Then you and I will take a look at it, and if it looks good, we'll get it online as soon as possible."

"Okay, I'm on it. It's nice to see that, in spite of the day's events, you're still focused on what needs to be done. I swear you're just like Bill."

"Life goes on, John. I realized that, in spite of what's happening around me. It's important to the family of Rivers, Inc. that everyone sees I'm being strong through this ordeal. By the way, you'll be at the company Christmas party, won't you? I asked.

"Of course, my wife and I will be there," John, said emphatically.

"Now, unless you have something more, I'm going to head home." I said.

"I think we've covered everything. And don't worry, we'll get to the bottom of this mess as quickly as possible," he said.

"Okay, John. Have a good day, and I'll see you in the morning."

While walking back to my office, I saw Pam heading into her office. For my own curiosity, I was almost tempted to go and confront her about the letter I received, but thought better of it. Instead, I just headed to my office, to gather my things and head on home.

"Yvonne, I'm going to call it a day. I'll see you in the morning," I said to her.

"Okay. But please do me a favor, and don't take any work home with you tonight. Just take yourself a nice bubble bath and relax for the rest of the evening. If you feel like talking, give me a call," she said.

"I think I'll do just that. I'll see you in the morning."

When I stepped off the elevator, Curtis greeted me. He took his job and the threat that I had received very seriously.

"Good afternoon, Ms. Rivers. Are you leaving for the day?" he asked, noticing my briefcase.

"Yes, I am, Curtis. You have a good evening," I said.

"Let me walk you to your car, Ms. Rivers," Curtis said.

"Thank you, but that won't be necessary."

"Ms. Rivers, I'd feel better if you let me walk you to your car," he said.

"Okay then, thank you." I reluctantly gave in to his request, realizing it was for the best. Plus, it was his job.

It was three o'clock when I arrived home. I made myself some tea and tried to eat a sandwich, but ended up wrapping it up for later. I turned on the stereo and went through my mail, and then decided to run a nice warm bubble bath. This was the first time since I had been at the helm of Rivers, Inc. that I had taken some time out to just simply relax. It was a shame that it had taken a day like today for me to do it.

I wasn't sure if I wanted to even bother Michael with details of my day, but for some reason, I needed to talk to him about it. After all, I felt comfortable talking to him about anything, and today shouldn't be any different. I picked up the phone and dialed his number.

"Hello, Michael," I said, when he answered his phone.

"Hey, baby. How are you?" he said.

"I'm doing okay, considering. I wasn't feeling very good, so I decided to leave work a little early today."

"Awe poor baby, what's wrong?"

"Today, while I was opening my mail, I received a threatening letter," I said, as my voice started to crack.

"You got hate mail? What did it say?" he asked, as his tone became somewhat louder.

"I'll read it to you," I said, retrieving it from my briefcase.

Hello Bitch,

You really think you have it all now, don't you? Well, we'll just have to see about that. Watch your back, because I have a surprise for you, Michelle Rivers, and it's a good one too. It's time to knock you down a peg or two, bitch. Watch your back!

"Get the hell out of here! Someone mailed that to you through the post office?" Michael asked shocked.

"Yes, and it's rather strange though. It has a Dallas, Texas postmark on the envelope."

"Dallas? Who do you know down there?" he asked.

"That's just it, I don't know anyone down there, let alone anyone with that much hate towards me to send me this," I said, as my voice began to crack even more.

"It's okay, baby. You'll be all right. Did you tell your dad or John about this?"

"John was on his way into my office when I received it. I called my father to tell him about it, but only after John insisted. Michael, I need to ask you something. Do you think this is something Pam could've done?"

"I know what you're thinking. Even though Pam and I have stopped seeing each other, why would she send you hate mail? She doesn't have any knowledge of us seeing each other, right? And if she did, why would it have come from, of all places, Dallas? Has she gone down there recently for something?"

"I asked John the same thing, and he said she hasn't left Atlanta, as far as he knows. She's been busy finishing up your book, and another one she's been working on."

"Does anyone else from Rivers, Inc. know we're seeing each other, besides maybe John?"

"No one knows we're seeing each other. I just wanted to get your opinion on it, that's all," I said.

"Well, I'll be talking to her soon about the release date for my book, and I'll keep my ears open, just in case I hear anything," Michael said.

"Now that you've seen how good my day has been, how is everything going with you?" I asked, with a slight chuckle.

"I've been okay. I'm just waiting with the rest of the city to hear if we'll have jobs or not. The Mayor said he would send out the pink slips by tomorrow, December 1ˢᵗ."

"Wow, I forgot about that. I hope you and Bob make the cut. I know it's a hard market out here right now."

"Yes, it is, but, but..." Suddenly a loud burst of applause, and the sounds of people cheering could be heard coming from the office and throughout the hallway. "What's going on, Michael? Is everything alright?"

"Baby, the Mayor just made some sort of announcement. Let me check it out. Can you hold on a minute? Sara, what's going on out there?" Michael yelled out to her.

"The Mayor just announced that no layoffs are needed! The State gave us the money necessary to help keep the city services going for the next four years!" Sara said, with a look of relief on her face.

"That's great! Hello, Michelle?" Michael said, getting back on the phone.

"I'm here. I overhead the good news," I said.

"Yes, that's exactly what it is. But getting back to you and your situation, I'm sure that John and your father will find out who's behind this madness. I don't want you to worry yourself. Remember, I'm here for you, and if need be, I'll try to take some time off and come spend it with you."

"I appreciate that, baby, but I'll be fine. Well, I'm going to lie down for a while. I'll talk to you later, and tell your parents I said hello."

"I will baby. I'll call and check on you later this evening," Michael said, before hanging up.

After hanging up, I hit the remote to set my house alarm, laid across the bed, and slowly drifted off to sleep.

Back at Rivers, Inc., everyone was walking around with these quizzical looks on their faces. They had to be wondering to themselves, who would've sent such a letter to their CEO. Everyone liked her...well, almost everyone.

"Pam, what are you doing after work today?" David asked, stopping by her office.

"I don't have any plans. What's on your mind?" she said.

"I need to talk with you. How about we meet at my place around seven o'clock?"

"Okay, that sounds good. Are you cooking for a sista?"

"I'll feed you, don't worry," he said laughing.

"Then I'll see you at seven," she replied, with a smile.

After leaving work, David stopped and grabbed a couple of seafood plat-ters from *Ocean City* on his way home. When he arrived home, he straightened up a little, set the table and waited for Pam to arrive. A few minutes after seven, she arrived with a bottle of wine, to go with whatever they were having for dinner.

"I thought you liked being on time for everything," David said, while looking at his watch.

"Awe, man, I'm only a few minutes late. What are we having...I'm starving," Pam said.

"I grabbed some seafood on the way in from work." He took the bottle of wine, and poured them each a glass. "So, what did you think about the meeting we had this morning?" he asked.

"It blew my mind. I'm still trying to figure out why John asked me if I had sent that threatening letter to Michelle."

"Oh, he asked you that?" David asked, with his eyebrows raised.

"He sure did. After the meeting, he pulled me to the side...very diplomati-cally, I might add...and asked if I had sent it," she said, getting visibly upset. "It's true that I don't care for her much but not enough to threaten her in any way. I don't know who would do such a thing."

"Well, to be honest with you, I thought that you did it as well, especially after you told me about her possibly interfering with you and that writer. I'm just glad it wasn't you. It's not worth losing your job over," he said.

"I appreciate your honesty, David, but I had nothing to do with it. I'd like to know who sent it too," she said.

"So would I. I saw how you glanced at me during the meeting, so I'm letting you know it wasn't me," David said.

"I had no doubt in my mind about that," Pam said.

After dinner, they began discussing his book. Pam was more than three quarters of the way through editing his manuscript. She was really enjoying reading his work.

"David, your book is fantastic. It's a very good read, and it seems so real. To tell you the truth, there is very little editing that needs to be done with it. It could possibly be ready for a January release…at the earliest."

"I'm happy to hear that. Just imagine, my first book is well on its way to becoming a reality. I'm getting excited just thinking about it, and I'm glad you're the one working on it," he said.

He leaned over and unexpectedly kissed her on the neck. She smiled and returned a kiss on his lips.

"We better stop before we wind up in the middle of something," she said. But when he leaned in to kiss her again, she realized she wanted to make love to him again.

* * *

Later that evening, Michael and Bob were celebrating the news from the Mayor's office at Bob's house.

"I'm so relieved about our job situation," Bob said.

"I told you not to worry about it. I had a feeling all along the city would work something out," Michael said.

"Yeah, you did," he said, toasting with a cold beer. "I just kept thinking about all this new crap I just bought. I was thinking to myself I might have overdone it. Now I'm going to pay this shit off as quickly as possible," he said laughing.

"I'm just glad no one had to get laid off, especially when it's this close to the holiday. Only twenty-six days left before Christmas," Michael said.

"Don't remind me. I need to start my Christmas shopping," Bob said.

Chapter 26

I woke up to the phone ringing. I glanced at the clock, and saw that it was after seven in the evening. When I checked the caller ID, and saw my parents' number, I grabbed the phone and rolled over on my back to face the music.

"Hello, Mom," I answered, without opening my eyes.

"Hello, baby. Daddy told me what happened today. Why didn't you call me? Are you okay?" she asked.

"Yes, Mommy, I'm okay. I didn't call because I figured you were at church, and I didn't want to worry you. Telling Dad was hard enough," I said.

"Michelle, you're our only child, and it would devastate us if anything were to happen to you. So, please be careful. I'm praying this is someone's idea of a sick joke."

"So am I, Mom. What did you cook for dinner?" I asked.

"I cooked a meatloaf, garlic mashed potatoes, green beans and rolls. But don't think I didn't notice you changed the subject, Michelle Rivers."

"I could never put anything pass you, Mom," I said giggling.

"Yes, you better know…you couldn't then, and you can't now," she said, laughing with me.

"Mom, hold on a minute, my other line is ringing," I said, before clicking over. "Hello. Oh, hey Jasmine. I have Mom on the other line," I said.

"Do you want to call me back in a few minutes?" Jasmine asked.

"No, hold on for a minute, while I finish my call with her," I said, before clicking back over to my mom. "Mom, I'm going to talk with Jas. But please know that I love you and Daddy, and I know you both are concerned about this letter. I'm a Rivers, and I won't let someone's idea of a sick joke derail me from my mission of making our company the best publishing house possible."

"Okay, baby, I get your point. I'm happy to hear the strength in your voice. I won't promise not to worry, because that's my job as a mother. I love you, and will talk to you tomorrow. Good night, baby," my mom said.

"Good night, Mommy," I said, before clicking back over to Jasmine. "Jas, sorry I kept you holding so long."

"It's okay. I just read a book while I waited," she said laughing.

"I want to thank you for dropping everything and coming to my aid earlier today," I said seriously.

"Hush that noise, girl. You would've done the same thing. I just wish we had some idea of the coward behind that letter. Did you talk to Michael and ask his opinion?"

"I talked to him this afternoon, and he doesn't think it was Pam either. Since she doesn't have any knowledge of our involvement, she wouldn't really have a motive."

"That's debatable, but I'll hold my peace until we know differently. Now tell me, how are you holding up?" Jasmine asked.

"I'm angry, Jas. I don't like the idea of some unknown person threatening me, and not knowing why. But I'm not going to let it handicap me from doing my job."

"Good, I'm proud of you. I knew you wouldn't let that letter keep you down for long."

"Don't get me wrong, Jas...I was scared for a minute. A cold chill ran down my spine when I first read those words, but I won't lay down for anyone!"

"You will for Michael, I bet," she said, cracking up.

"You're so nasty," I said, and started laughing with her. "Speaking of which, how are things going with Alex?"

"Girl, that man curls my toes. I actually look forward to our time together. And it's not all about the sex either, so don't even go there," she said, in a serious tone.

"I'm really happy for you, and I hope he feels the same way. I know it's been a while since you've been in a serious relationship. I love hearing the happiness in your voice when you talk about him," I said.

"That's because I'm really happy with how things are going with Alex. I'm not saying we're in love or anything, but he calls me as much as I call him. He's even started text messaging me in the middle of the day, just to say he was thinking of me."

"Awe, that's so sweet," I said, with a sigh.

"Awe, shut it up, heffa. Don't act like you don't have similar feelings for Michael," she said laughing. "Isn't it ironic that we both fell for Philly men?"

"Yes, it's ironic. I was a little apprehensive at first about the distance thing. But it's like you love to point out...it's not like we can't afford to travel back and forth."

"Sure you're right," she said.

"But on a serious note…the Christmas party is next weekend, and Damon is supposed to be coming by my office tomorrow to deliver the painting of Michael's cover. I was thinking it would be better if I had him deliver it to you, as opposed to the office, so that it remains a surprise. What do you think?"

"I think that's a wise decision. You don't want anyone walking into your office to be tempted to look at it. Did you buy an easel?"

"No, I haven't. I'll have Yvonne ask the hotel if they have one. If not, I'll bring one from home."

"Speaking of paintings, don't tell me you haven't hung the rest of yours yet, woman?"

"Okay, I won't tell you," I said laughing. "I haven't spent that much time at home since I moved here. I've just been too busy to worry about hanging them."

"Well, you need to hang them soon, or I'm coming to relieve you of one or two of them," she said.

"Oh no you won't, I'll buy you one when you get married." I could hear Jasmine coughing after I made that statement. "Jasmine, Jasmine…are you okay over there?" I asked giggling.

"Whew, I'm going to get you for that one!" she said, in between coughs. "And on that note, I'm calling it a night. Remember, it's going to be a brighter tomorrow."

"Good night, Jas. I'll remember that," I said, before hanging up.

After talking to my best friend, I did something I hadn't done in ages… wrote some poetry and said my prayers before going back to sleep.

In the morning, I saw the message light blinking on my phone, and realized I must have slept through the ringing. Upon listening to the message, I was happy to know Michael had kept his promise to call.

* * *

Later that morning, when I turned into the parking lot at Rivers, Inc., the first person I saw was Curtis.

"Good morning, Ms. Rivers. It looks like a beautiful day on the horizon," he said, as I got out the car and set the alarm.

"Good morning, Curtis. Are you planning to be here every morning when I arrive?" I asked.

"Yes Ma'am…just following my orders."

"I don't think it's necessary, but I do feel safer." I said, as we walked into the building. "Have a nice day, Curtis."

"You too, Ms. Rivers," he replied, as I got on the elevator.

"Good morning, Yvonne. How are you doing this morning?" I said, as I entered our suite of offices.

"I'm doing well, Michelle. A better question would be how are *you* doing?"

"I'm having a brighter tomorrow," I said, with a smile. "You can't keep a Rivers down for long," I said, with a wink.

"That's what I like to hear. I put yesterday's production reports on your desk, along with your phone messages. Now would you like coffee or tea to start off your morning?"

"Your coffee would be wonderful. Could you also order me a bagel with cream cheese and strawberry jam from the deli? I hardly ate anything yesterday, and now I'm famished," I said smiling.

"I'll order it right away, and will bring your coffee in a few minutes," she said.

"Thank you," I said, as I walked into my office.

I had just hung my jacket in the closet, and was about to sit down, when John knocked on my door. "Good morning, Michelle. How are you doing today?" he asked.

"Hey John, I was going to call you in a few minutes. I'm doing better today."

"I'm glad to hear that. Now, what were you going to call me about?" he asked, taking a seat in front of me and sipping on his coffee.

"I'd like to call a staff meeting at ten, to let everyone know I'm okay, and that we need to get back to the business of publishing."

He started grinning and said, "Okay, Billy Jr., I'll personally alert the staff their presence is requested in the conference room."

"You're very funny, John." I said, as he laughed and walked out my office, where I heard him greet Yvonne.

"I see John's in a great mood this morning," Yvonne said, as she handed me my coffee. "Your bagel will be here in a few minutes. Is there anything else I can get you in the meantime?"

"No thank you, Yvonne. Please sit down for a minute. I asked John to gather the staff together in the conference room at ten. I'd like for you to be present, but it's not necessary to take notes," I said.

"Okay. If you don't mind, I'll walk down with you," she said.

"No problem."

After Yvonne left to go back to her desk, I settled down to finally go over the production reports. I made a couple of notes, and returned some phone calls. I also put in a call to Damon, to let him know of the change in delivery of the painting of Michael's book cover. He said he'd deliver it personally to Jasmine.

On the way to the conference room, I informed Yvonne about the change of delivery. "I was talking to Jasmine last night, and decided to have Damon deliver the painting of Michael Ramsey's book cover to her instead of here. I don't want to take a chance of anyone spoiling our surprise."

"That sounds like a good idea. Would you like me to call him?" she asked.

"No, I've already done that, but thank you."

By the time we arrived, everyone was assembled.

"Good morning everyone thank you for coming on such short notice. I won't keep you long," I said. "I'd like to thank everyone for your concern, and to let you know that although I was upset to have received that threatening letter yesterday, I'm still determined...rather, *more* determined...to make Rivers, Inc. the best publishing house possible. I will not let some coward's letter deter me," I said.

I had to pause to let the applause die down before continuing.

"I will need every one of you to make this happen. There's been a lot of tension around here, and I don't want anyone on pins and needles about speaking to me. I still have an open door policy here, and I won't change that. We have three novels coming out in the next few weeks, that I feel will be bestsellers," I said, and had to pause again for the applause. "Thank you everyone. As I was saying, we have three bestsellers coming out, and the best staff in the business. In another week, we'll be having our Christmas party, and I expect to see all of you there. Have a wonderful day," I said, and turned to leave as more applause broke out.

"Alright everyone, y'all heard the lady. Let's get back to work," John said.

As soon as John got back to his office, he put in a call to Robert.

"Rivers here," Robert said, answering his private line.

"Hello, my brother, John here. I just wanted to let you know that your girl is back on top. She just called a meeting and told everyone she's not laying down for anyone," he said laughing.

"That's my girl!" Robert said proudly. "Thanks for letting me know, John."

"No problem, brother. You know she's like my daughter also, and I'll keep my eyes open, and my ear to the ground."

"I appreciate it. Maceo spoke with Jennings yesterday, and he'll be out tonight after business hours to look over the site. And the new security guard will be in place tomorrow."

"Good. I see you brothers haven't wasted anytime getting everything in place," John replied.

"You know how we do, John. I'm going to give Michelle a call, to inform her of the changes before my next client gets here. Stay blessed, my brother," Robert said.

"You do the same, Bobby," John said, as he ended the call.

Down the hall, David and Pam were having their own conversation about the meeting.

"Well, Pam…you have to admit Michelle was quite impressive in that meeting," David said.

"I'll give her that. I don't know if I'd have held up as well, if some unknown person was threatening me, or if I would've publicly called them a coward," she said.

"I guess I better get back to my office. Would you like to have lunch with me around one?" he asked.

"Lunch sounds good. I'll see you then," Pam said, as her phone rang. "Hello," she said.

"Hey, girl," Sharon said.

"I just got back from a meeting. What's going on, chick?"

"I was wondering what took you so long to return my call. What are you doing for lunch?" she asked.

"I'm having lunch with one of the other editors. Sorry, if I had known, I wouldn't have accepted," Pam said.

"It's cool. We can do it another time. So, what was your meeting about this time?"

"Remember me telling you about our publisher receiving hate mail? Well, she wanted to let us know that she wasn't going to let some coward have any effect on her work environment."

"Wow! She said all that?"

"Not in those exact words, but yes," Pam said, smiling at the thought.

"You sound like you were kind of impressed or something. What's up with the change in attitude?" Sharon asked.

"No change, but I can't help but be a little impressed at how she's handling all this…she's a strong woman," Pam replied.

"Okay, Pam. I have to run, but call me tonight, so we can set up a time to have dinner or something soon."

"I'll do that, Sharon. Bye."

* * *

Meanwhile, I concluded my call with my father, and then went over the expense report for the month, and signed off on the end of the year bonuses for the staff. Things would be pretty quiet around the office after the Christmas party, with most of the staff being on half-day schedules, and the rest, including myself, on vacation. I was looking forward to spending Christmas in Philly with Michael.

I was just about to pick up the phone to call Michael, when Yvonne came in with this beautiful vase of yellow and white roses.

"Oh, those are so beautiful," I said to her.

"They were just delivered for you," she said, placing them on my desk.

"Thank you, Yvonne," I said, as I removed the card to see who had sent them. "Here's the approval for the year end bonuses. Would you make sure that the board gets a copy?"

"I'll do it right away," she said, as she exited my office.

I opened the card, and saw that the roses were from Michael.

Hey, Baby,

I just wanted you to know I was thinking about you, and wanted you to have something beautiful to glance upon after your trying day yesterday.

Michael

Excitingly, I picked up the phone to call and thank him for the wonderful surprise. Noting the time, I called him at his office.

"Hello, Sara, this is Ms. Rivers calling. Is Mr. Ramsey available?" I asked.

"Hold on one minute, Ms. Rivers. I'll check," Sara said, putting me on hold.

"Hello baby, Did your receive the flowers?" Michael asked, as he came on the line.

"Yes, they're beautiful," I exclaimed.

"I can't believe you sent two dozen roses!"

"Well, I couldn't decide between the yellow or white roses…so I just sent them both. I'm glad you're happy with them. How's your day going so far?" he asked.

"It's going well. I called a staff meeting this morning…to let everyone know I was okay."

"Good, baby. I'm glad to know you're handling your business."

"I'm doing my best. So, tell me…how are things going with you? I'm sorry I slept through your call last night."

"That's okay, you probably needed the rest. Everything is going great here. We're all still on cloud nine, after the threat of losing our jobs was lifted from our shoulders. I'll even be able to buy you a decent gift for Christmas," he said, half jokingly.

"Michael, you know you need to stop. I guess I need to start thinking about what I'm going to get you for Christmas also."

"Your being with me will be gift enough, baby," he said.

"Thank you…I feel the same way. And on that note, let me go. I'll give you a call this evening," I said.

"Okay, baby. I'll talk to you then. Bye."

No sooner had I finished talking with Michael, my private line rang. Glancing at my caller ID, I saw that it was my father calling.

"Hello, Daddy. I just talked to you. Are you missing your other woman already?" I asked giggling.

"Hey, baby. I see you got your sense of humor back. I guess things are going well today."

"Everything is under control. No worries, mon," I said, with a fake Jamaican accent.

"Good. Now the reason I called was to let you know that everything is set with Mr. Jennings. He'll be coming out tonight after business hours to walk through the site. He'll fax both you and me his recommendations for the security cameras."

"Okay, Daddy. That was fast."

"Not fast enough, if you ask me. But after you approve the plans, he can get to work installing the cameras," he said. "Another thing…the new security guard will be starting tomorrow. And we have our year-end board meeting on

Monday. Don't forget that we're having the meeting at your office this time," my dad said.

"Yvonne has it marked on my calendar for four. I'll have some refreshments catered to hold you all over until dinner," I said.

"Please don't forget Yvonne's delicious coffee," he said laughing. "Would you like to go out to dinner after the meeting?"

"That sounds like a plan, Daddy. Just make sure Mom doesn't have anything else planned for you beforehand."

"I'll just tell her I have plans with my other woman, and she'll be cool. Besides, she has me all to herself all weekend; one night away won't kill her."

"Daddy, you're too much. We both need to get back to work. I'll talk to you later. Love you, Daddy. Bye," I said.

"I love you too, baby. Bye."

Glancing at the clock, I saw the morning had flown past, and I had gotten quite a few things accomplished.

"Yvonne, when you get back from lunch, would you please come to my office with your pad...as well as the notes for the Christmas party?"

"I can come right now, Michelle, if you need me," she answered.

"That's okay, enjoy your lunch and come see me afterwards," I said.

"Would you like for me to order something for you?"

"Thank you, but no. I brought a sandwich from home, and I'm going to catch up on some reading."

"Okay, I'll see you soon."

I grabbed a juice and my sandwich from the refrigerator, and grabbed the horror manuscript to read while I had the chance.

It was a cold and rainy night...the wind was blowing something fierce outside my window, and the house was making strange noises.

I hope Jason hurries up and comes home soon, I thought, as I sat in my room with a flashlight, after the lights had gone out in the house.

I remember how happy we were when we first bought this house. The owners seemed to be in a hurry to sell it. They claimed they got homesick for the city, after living this rural country life for so long.

I was beginning to think they were afraid to stay here any longer. I was scared to stay here alone at night myself. Jason thinks I'm imagining thing, but I swear I see things move in the shadows. And although neither of us smokes, I smell smoke when I wake up every morning.

The other day, I started to notice that things were mysteriously being moved around in the house. Jason swears he didn't move them, and I know I didn't.

"Jason, thank God you're finally home," I said, as I walked to the top of the stairs, after hearing someone downstairs. "Jason, Jason? This isn't funny. Jason, are you down there?" I asked.

Getting no answer, I ran back in my room and locked the door. I started feeling around on the bed for my cell phone, and it fell on the floor. Damn!

As I reached down to pick it up, something brushed up against my hand, and I started screaming bloody murder.

"Michelle? Michelle, are you okay?" Yvonne asked, as she came into the office.

"Oh, Yvonne, you scared me half to death!" I said, putting my hand over my heart and laughing.

"I'm sorry. I was calling your name, but you didn't answer. That must be a good manuscript," Yvonne said.

"It's a scary one, that's for sure. I'm not much of a horror fan, and I certainly won't be reading this at night," I said.

"Good thing you don't have to edit it yourself," she said smiling.

"You're right about that." I said laughing. "We would never have any horror books at Rivers, Inc. if I had to edit them."

"I brought the list you requested, along with my writing pad. Are you ready for me?"

"Lord, yes! I don't think I can read anymore of this, or I'll be screaming like the character in the book," I said, taking the papers from her. "Oh great, it looks like everyone we invited is going to make it."

"I had no doubt they would come out for a Rivers, Inc. event," she said proudly.

"You sound as excited about this as I am. You and Jasmine did a wonderful job planning this."

"I think the surprise you have in store for Mr. Ramsey is special."

"Now all we have to do is keep him from running into his family before the party," I said.

"I have that covered also," Yvonne said smiling. "Since his family is aware that we're trying to surprise him, they've agreed to order room service until they come down for the party."

"Great! You've thought of everything. They'll all be surprised when we reveal the book cover for his latest effort," I said, smiling at the thought.

Chapter 27

"SO, Pam, how's it going with the editing of my manuscript?" David asked, like he didn't already know the answer. They were sitting at a table in a diner around the corner from Rivers, Inc., having lunch.

"The fact that you're an editor, leaves very little work for me to do. At the rate I'm going, your book will be ready for the printer by next month," she said, smiling with confidence.

"That's great. It's taken me a while to finally get the confidence to have my work published. I'm very excited," he told her.

"As well you should be. David, the book is good. I promise you it's going to be well received by readers." She smiled at him, as the waiter brought them their lunch.

"Have you heard anything new on the letter Michelle received?" he asked.

"No. I think it was just some jerk trying to put a scare into her," she said.

"Well, it must've worked. I see they've hired another security guard," he said.

"Yeah, I met him this morning. He's cute, too!" she said, looking for a reaction from him.

"Yeah, right, but I think you need to be flirting with me instead," David said, shaking his head.

"The food here tastes better when you eat in. Have you noticed that?" she asked, enjoying her corned beef special, and conveniently changing the subject.

"I don't know about that. But I do know they give you a little more than they do when you order take out," David said, between chews. "And don't think I didn't notice you changing the subject. So, tell me something…have you given any more thought to what I asked you the other night? Before you answer that, let me say I swear if you just give me a chance, I can prove I'm the man for you. I think about you every day. I didn't take what happened between us lightly."

"Neither did I, David. It was beautiful, but…"

"Baby, listen to what I'm about to say to you, and listen closely," he said, cutting her off. "Whatever you had going on with Michael is over. He was never the man for you…I am. You can reach out and touch me whenever you need too. I love you, and no other man will ever love you more. I may not be what you think you want, but I swear to you that I'm the man you need. Just give me a chance to share all this love with you," he said.

Pam lowered her head, as tears formed in her eyes. David slid closer to console her. He placed his hand under her chin, and slowly raised her head. He gently kissed her on the forehead, as he dabbed her eyes with a white handkerchief that he carried in his back pocket.

"Excuse me, folks…is everything alright?" the waiter asked, with a concerned look.

"Everything is fine, thanks. Could you bring a glass of water and the check, please?" David said.

"Yes sir."

"I do need you, David. Please be patient with me and never let me go," Pam softly whispered.

* * *

As Michael laid in his bed, deep in thought, he was amazed at how, even the thought of Michelle, or the whisper of her name, seemed to mesmerize him so. From the first moment he laid eyes on her, she had been a constant entity in his thoughts. Could it be that he had finally found the Ying to his Yang? Was it a blessing that he had finally found a woman to love him for what he possessed inside? Had his soul mate surfaced, after all the years of writing and dreaming about what true love would feel like? She touched parts of him that had never been touched before, without even being near him.

He looked at the time, and realized he had better get up before Kevin thought he wasn't coming to pick him up for photography class. He had missed their usual Wednesday time together for the past couple of weeks. He had been so busy trying to make sure his book was ready to be released, and wondering about the layoff situation at his job. After he showered and put on some clothes, he called Kevin to see if he was ready for class.

"Hello," Carol said, answering the phone.

"How are you, Carol?" Michael asked.

"I'm doing great for a change, Michael. How are you?"

"I'm doing well. Is Kevin ready to go to class?"

"Michael, you're not going to believe what I'm about to tell you," she said, with a hint of happiness in her voice.

"Try me," he said.

"Kevin's uncle called me on Tuesday, and asked if it was alright for him to take Kevin to New Jersey to spend the weekend with him. He stopped by on Wednesday, and we talked for hours. He apologized for all the years of not being involved in his nephew's life after his brother passed away. It seems he blamed me in some crazy way for his death," she said.

"Wow...that's something else, Carol. So, what turned him around from those weird thoughts?"

"He told me he searched his soul, prayed a lot, and realized that a greater being has control over all things, especially life and death. He asked if he could start off on the right foot and get him for the weekend, to start getting to know him better. Of course, I had to make sure he was serious, and after hours of conversation, he convinced me. I asked Kevin how he felt about it, and he was okay with it."

"That's so nice, Carol. I'm happy for the both of you, but especially Kevin. He needs to know his father's side of the family, as well as yours."

"I apologize for not calling you," she told him.

"That's okay. I've been so busy with my book and job, that Kevin and I missed our day. But I'm glad that he's with his uncle. I guess I'll go and try to get some of my Christmas shopping out the way. Kevin gave me his Christmas wish list. I'll let you know what I've gotten for him, so we don't duplicate anything," Michael said.

"That's a good idea. I'll talk with you later," Carol said.

"Okay. Bye, Carol," Michael said, hanging up.

Now that's some really great news, he thought to himself. Even though Kevin seldom talked about his father's family, when he did, you could tell he missed getting to know them better. He had a few cousins around his age, which Michael knew Kevin would love to get to know better.

He decided to give Debra a call, to let her know about the book signing that she had arranged for him in Phoenix.

"Hello, I'm unable to come to the phone. Please leave a message," Debra's voicemail message said.

"Hey, Deb, this is Mike. I'm just calling to let you know I spoke with your friend, and postponed the book signing. Since my next book is due to be released in a couple of weeks, I think it would be better to plan the signing for after the first of the year. Get back with me when you can. I love you. Bye."

He then decided to give his dad a call, to see if he wanted to do some

Christmas shopping with him. It had been a while since they'd had some father and son time together.

"Hello?" his dad said.

"Hey Dad, How are you?" Michael asked.

"I'm doing fine, son. How are you?"

"I could use a little company. Are you busy?"

"Not really. I was going to make a run to the hardware store in a few minutes. What do you have on your mind?"

"I was going to hit the mall and do a little Christmas shopping. There's a Home Depot right next to the mall. Do you want to take a ride with me?"

"That sounds good. I need to pick up a few things myself. I'll come by and pick you up in about twenty minutes."

"Okay, I'll see you soon."

As Michael waited for his dad, he had thoughts about Pam. He hoped she had nothing to do with the threat that shook Michelle up so badly. But he couldn't imagine her being responsible for such a thing. No one knew that he and Michelle were involved except for John, and he wasn't the type of man to spread gossip.

Michael heard a car pull up, and looked outside, just as his dad put his flashers on. He grabbed his jacket and went outside.

"How do you feel, Dad?" he asked, as he got in the car.

"I'm cool as a cucumber, and groovier than a ten cent movie," he said, as they laughed at his old school terminology. "So, what else do you have on your mind, son?" he asked, with a slight grin on his face. "You've been my son for thirty-four years, and I know when something is troubling you. Spill it."

"I guess I could never play poker very well," Michael said, as his dad looked at him out the corner of his eye. "It's about Michelle. She called me the other day, and told me that someone sent her some hate mail, and that some things were stolen from her office."

"Really what kind of coward would threaten a woman as nice as she is?" his dad asked.

"I haven't a clue, and neither does she. But to be on the safe side, they stepped up the security force, and installed some surveillance equipment in the building."

"Well, that's good. In today's society, businesses need that added security anyway," his dad, said.

"That's true. The only person I know of that might have a reason to send a threatening letter is my editor, Pam. She's been acting differently ever since Michelle took over the company."

"What, one of her own employees? Okay, give me the real deal, Mike. What's going on?"

"I slept with my editor a few times, and when I saw she was starting to get kind of possessive, I decided to break off that part of our relationship. We both decided that it was the right thing to do." His dad just shook his head.

"Damn, son. Did she get wind that you and her boss are seeing each other?"

"No, we've kept our relationship quiet for now. The only one who knows is John, the executive editor at Rivers, Inc. But he's too thorough to go and run his mouth."

"Wow…you and Michelle had better be careful, son. Some women can be pretty vindictive if they feel they've been dumped for another woman. And the fact that it's her boss can complicate matters even more," his dad said seriously.

"I know. But I can't turn back the clock, and make the fact that I slept with my editor disappear."

"I agree with you there. Just be careful. I do have one question for you… was she good?" They both fell out laughing when he said that.

"Dad, you're crazy. Thanks for lending me your ear."

"Anytime, that's what I'm here for. Now let's go and get our women some gifts," his dad said smiling.

"I want to go to *Toys R Us* and pick up some games for Kevin's Play Station 2. He gave me a list of five games that he wanted, and he wants a remote controlled Hummer also," Michael said.

"That's good. I'll get a couple games for my little son, too," his dad said. They were going to make sure that Kevin had a nice Christmas.

After they left *Toys R Us*, they walked to *Sbarro's* and grabbed some lunch. After they ate their full of pizza and salad, they had a few more stops to make.

"So, what did you want to get Michelle for Christmas, son?"

"I figured that all women love diamonds, and I saw a nice tennis bracelet in the newspaper that was on sale at *Macy's*. It's down at the other end of the mall," Michael said, as they started walking in that direction.

In the center of the mall, there was a long line of parents with their children, waiting to get their picture taken with the man of the season.

"Dad, do you remember when I found out who Santa Claus really was?" Michael asked, as they walked by Santa Claus.

"Yeah, I remember. I dropped a wrench on the floor while I was putting your bike together that year. Your mom went upstairs to see if you woke up. You were pretending that you were sleep." Michael looked at him and started laughing.

"How did you know I wasn't sleep?" he asked.

"Because when your mom went upstairs, you had left one of your GI Joes on the steps, and it wasn't there earlier." Michael almost choked, he laughed so hard. *And all this time, I thought they had no idea.* "Hey, isn't that Carol over there?" his dad asked. "Mike who's that with her holding her hand"

"You know, I think you're right. Wait a minute…awe, man, that's Bob walking with her. I'd know that head anywhere," Michael said laughing.

Carol and Bob had stopped in front of *Victoria's Secret* and were looking in the window.

"Might as well go in and get something nice," Michael said, walking up behind them. They both turned around and laughed.

"Hey, Mike…hey, Dad," Carol said, giving them both a hug.

"What's up, Mr. Ramsey…Michael?" Bob said smiling, and giving Michael a pound.

"I'm surprised to see you two together," Michael said, with a little smirk on his face.

"I'm not. I saw them at dinner on Thanksgiving…making eyes at each other. I told your mother they would make a nice couple," his dad said, as both of them blushed and smiled like two teenagers.

"Well, what can I say…Carol is good people," Bob expressed, and she chimed in, agreeing that Bob was a good brother.

Michael was very surprised by this discovery. He had this funny feeling inside…almost like he was jealous of Bob. But deep down inside, he was also very happy for the both of them. Two wonderful friends of his, who he loved dearly, he hoped they would do well together.

"Well, since I ran into you, let me tell you what I got Kevin. We bought him seven Play Station 2 games and a remote controlled Hummer," Michael told Carol, sounding as excited as he knew Kevin would be.

"Wow, Michael! You didn't have to go all out like that. Those games, I know for a fact, go for like forty dollars apiece," she said.

"He's my little brother, and I want to help him have a nice Christmas. Plus, I can't take all the credit, Dad insisted on picking a few of them up."

"He's blessed to have a big brother like you, Michael," Carol said, as Michael smiled and gave her a hug.

"Well, we need to be going. Victoria has a secret she wants to tell us about," Bob joked, as they all burst out in laughter.

"Well, you two take care," Michael, said, giving Bob a pound.

"Bye, Mike...Dad," Carol said, as they headed into the store.

The funny feeling that Michael had when he saw the two of them together had disappeared. He knew they both were in good hands.

"Come on, son, we need to head into *Macy's* and finish fighting with this crowd," his dad said anxiously.

Michael bought Michelle a nice diamond tennis bracelet, and his dad bought a nice anniversary ring with diamonds, with Michael and his sister's birthstones in it. His dad always had good taste.

"Mike, what are your plans for next weekend?" his dad asked.

"It's funny you should ask that. I'm going down to Atlanta on Friday evening. Rivers, Inc. is having a Christmas party on Saturday," he said.

"That sounds like it's going to be a good time. But I know you really want to see Michelle again," his dad said grinning. "You really are feeling her, aren't you?"

"How could I not feel her? She looks good, is independent, has her own company, and she cares about me. It would be nice if you and Mom could make it down with me."

"Your mom and I have plans of our own. We're going to a dinner that a friend of hers is having. You just go on and have a great time with your woman. I want to hear all about it when you get back. When is your next book supposed to be coming out?"

"It's actually done. It just has to go to the printer. I'm really excited about this one. I'm going to have my picture on the book for a change, and the cover was drawn by an artist."

"That's different. I wish you the best of luck with it. Your mom and I are so proud of you and your sister's accomplishments. The one thing we always prayed about when we started our family was that our children would put forth their best effort to achieve their goals in life. And our prayers have been answered."

"It's really nice to know you feel that way, Dad. I know Debra would agree that we were blessed with two of the best parents in the world. You two are our role models, and for that, I want to say I love both of you," Michael said seriously.

"Is this a hallmark moment or what?" his dad asked, and then began to laugh.

"Dad, you're absolutely crazy. Let's go, so I can buy you a drink before we head back?"

"Where do you want to stop?"

"Let's stop at the *Hideaway*. We can get a couple of platters to take home. Mom isn't cooking tonight, is she?"

"Are you kidding? The kitchen hardly gets used on Saturdays. It's 'go for what you know' day."

* * *

When his dad dropped him off at home, Michael got all of his travel arrangements together the weekend, and then he gave Alex a call. He was going to be staying with him on Friday. That way, he would be out of Michelle's way while she was doing her last-minute running around for the party. He could also get the scoop on what his man and Jasmine had been up to.

"It's your dime," Alex's laughing voice said, answering the phone.

"Man, you got issues," Michael responded.

"Hey, Mike. How you be?" Alex said.

"I'm hanging tough, brother. What have you been up to?"

"I've just been hanging in there. Man, I want to thank you again for turning me on to Jasmine. She's off the hook, man!" Alex said, sounding as if he was ready to give up his player's card.

"Damn, bro! You sound like you're hooked for real. So, things are going okay for the two of you?"

"Yeah she's a good woman, and we click like you wouldn't believe. I'll tell you more when you come down here this weekend," Alex said.

"That's one of the reasons I called. My flight's arriving on Friday at six-thirty. Will you be able to pick me up?" Michael said.

"You know it, homey. I'll be waiting on you. Are you staying with me on Friday?"

"Yeah I figure with the Christmas party, Michelle will be busy getting everything together, and I'd just be in the way. Plus, I get to hear all the details of how you've been waxing that ass down there." Alex cracked up.

"Yeah, brother, I've been handling my business down here. Mike, I meant to ask you whatever happened with the layoffs."

"The city got bailed out by the state financially, so our jobs were saved," Michael said happily.

"That's a blessing. I was worried about you brothers up there. I know Bob was really worried. He called me a couple of weeks ago, talking about some investments he'd made, and how the layoff thing would hurt if it was to happen," Alex said.

"Well, we're all okay, at least for the next four years. Listen, man, I have a platter of food from the *Hideaway*, and I'm about ready to get into it. I'll give you a call on Thursday, so you won't forget me."

"Michael, I got you, trust me. You take it easy, and tell your folks I said hello."

"Okay, Alex. You take care, and don't hurt yourself with Jasmine," Michael said laughing.

Alex sounded like he was enjoying himself down there in Atlanta, especially since he connected with Jasmine. He needed to find a good woman to help occupy his time, and Jasmine seemed to have done just that. Michael wouldn't be surprised to hear they were going to hook up permanently.

Michael was sitting back, watching a movie on the satellite, enjoying his fried chicken, greens and potato salad platter, when the phone rang.

"Hey, Mike," Debra said, when he picked up the phone.

"Baby girl, how are you?" Michael asked.

"I'm doing fine, big brother. I got your message earlier. I've been so busy with finals, that I haven't had time to touch base with you. The cancellation is fine, because all of the details with the bookstore weren't finished anyway. And this way, both of your books will be available at the signing," she said.

"I'm shooting for after the first of the year, so see if you can plan it for sometime in early January. I understand about finals. Just handle your business, and make us all proud. You're coming down the homestretch now."

"I sure am. I can't wait to finish up. How's it going with you and your friend? What's her name again?"

"Michelle and I are doing fine," Michael said laughing. "I'm going down there this weekend, as a matter of fact. The publishing company is having their Christmas party on Saturday."

"That sounds like a good time. I'll be partying myself on Saturday. A friend of mine is having a Christmas party," she said. "So, have there been any problems with the other chick?"

"No problems, sis. It's business as usual."

"Well, I'm glad to hear that. You still need to be careful, Mike."

"I will. You're still coming home for Christmas, aren't you?"

"Yes, I'll be on the first flight out on Monday morning. Can you pick me up from the airport?" she asked.

"Just let me know what time and I'll be there," he said.

"Okay. Kiss Mom and Dad for me. I love you," Debra said, before hanging up.

"I love you, too, Deb. Bye," Michael said.

Chapter 28

WHAT *a beautiful day I have ahead of me*, I thought, as I got up the day before our big Christmas party. I was so excited.

Glancing at my gown hanging on the closet door, I couldn't help but wonder what Michael would think when he saw me in it. And I prayed my father didn't have a heart attack when he saw the back...or *lack* of a back," I said, laughing to myself, as I got out of bed.

After a quick shower, I dressed in my favorite green suit with the long skirt, a black turtleneck sweater, and a pair of knee high black boots. I grabbed my briefcase and purse, and was almost out the door when my phone rang. Glancing at the caller ID, I saw it was Michael.

"Hey, baby, you just caught me," I said smiling. "I was walking out the door."

"Hi yourself beautiful, I just wanted to let you know I'll be arriving in Atlanta around seven tonight. Alex is going to pick me up, and I'll be staying with him tonight, unless you've changed your mind and want me to stay with you," he said half jokingly.

"Now, you know I'd love to have you stay with me, but I'm going to be busy taking care of last-minute party business. Plus, I know you boys want to have time to catch up with each other," I said.

"You're right about that, but you can't blame a brother for trying," he said laughing. "And this will probably be our only chance, since I'm sure you and Jasmine have plans for us," Michael said.

"You can always spend the weekend with Alex if you want," I said laughing, because I knew I was lying.

"I don't think so, baby. It's been much too long since I've had you in my arms. And on that note, I better let you get to work. I'll give you a call tonight when I get there," he said.

"Okay, Michael. Have a safe flight. I'll see you soon," I said, as I hung up.

When I arrived at the office, I found Yvonne talking with John.

"Good morning, Yvonne and John," I said smiling. "John, you're here early today."

"Now, here are two of my favorite women. One makes the best coffee this side of heaven, and the other one brings the best donuts," he said, grinning and relieving me of the donuts I had picked up.

"John, you make sure you leave some of those for the rest of the staff," I said laughing, as he lifted two out of the box and inhaled deeply. "Now, I know you weren't waiting around for donuts…so what's up?" I asked.

"I was just bringing my report to Yvonne for your perusal, and to see if you had any last minute instructions before you started your vacation," he replied.

"Excuse me, Michelle, let me take these donuts to the staff lounge before he inhales the rest of them," Yvonne said laughing, as he grabbed another one out the box. "The reports are on your desk," she said.

"Thank you, Yvonne. Come on in my office, John, and have a seat," I said, as he followed me. "I don't have any last minute instructions for you. I know you're more than capable of running things without me."

"I may be, but I don't look as good," he said laughing. "I'll get out of your way, since this is going to be a short day for all of us. Everyone is looking forward to the party tomorrow night."

"I'm looking forward to it also, John," I said grinning.

As John left my office, I could hear him joking with Yvonne.

"That man is a mess!" Yvonne said smiling, as she entered my office and handed me a cup of coffee.

"Indeed he is, and thanks for the coffee," I replied. "Now tell me, what's on the agenda for today?"

"Jasmine will be here at ten, and we're going over to the hotel to finalize the arrangements and pick up the room assignments. We're also going to take the angels over for the tables," she said. "I spoke with the limousine company earlier, and gave them everyone's name and flight information."

"That's great. It looks like you have everything under control," I said. "I'm going to go over these reports, and then I'm out of here until after the first of the year. Could you please make sure Gayle has my cell number in case of an emergency, since you'll also be gone?"

"I've already taken care of that, and made sure both she and John have the new access code to our offices," she replied.

"As usual, you're on top of things. I'll see you before I leave. Thank you again, Yvonne," I said smiling, as she walked out of my office.

* * *

"Damn, the answering machine. I'll have to leave a message…I hate talking to machines," Pam said to herself.

"Hey, Sharon…this is Pam. Don't kill me, okay? I know it's short notice, but I'd like you to go with me to our Christmas party tomorrow night. This will give you an opportunity to check out everyone for yourself. It's semi-formal, and I know you have something to wear, with all the company bashes you attend. Please give me a call back as soon as you receive this message. I'll be in my office until noon, and then I'll be headed to *Paris* to get my locs tightened up," she said, into Sharon's machine.

∗ ∗ ∗

Michael's plane landed in Atlanta at six-thirty in the evening. As usual, Alex was waiting outside to pick him up.

"What's up, my brother?" Michael asked, as he walked out of the airport.

"How you be, Michael?" Alex asked, grabbing Michael's garment bag, and giving him a pound.

"Everything is everything," he said.

While they were walking towards the parking lot, Michael asked Alex where his car was, because damn if it didn't feel like they had walked a country mile to get to it. Suddenly Alex hit his key remote, and the back door of this black 2006 Envoy SLT popped open.

"No, you didn't get a new ride! Is this you?" Michael asked.

"Yes indeed brother. I decided to treat myself to a new car. I never had a brand new car before…I always inherited someone else's problems. Now I can create my own," he said proudly.

"This joint is nice, Alex," Michael said, in admiration.

"I'm glad you like it. This baby is loaded, too."

"How much did this bad boy set you back?"

"I got a pretty good deal on it. The saleswoman is the sister of one of my co-workers, and she hooked me up big time. It ran me thirty-seven grand, and as you see, it has everything," he said, as Michael tinkered with the DVD player on the inside roof.

"I need to get me a new car. I'm still driving my 1999 Subaru," Michael said, as they both started laughing. "I've been checking out the new Continentals. I may hop on one before the year is out."

"Yeah, now is the time to cop one, because automobiles aren't selling too well right now," Alex said, as they drove towards his house. "Anyway, 'Mr. Bestselling Author', you can afford to buy anything you want. I'm so proud of you, my friend. You're doing exactly what you said you would be doing back in the day," he said smiling.

"And now that you have a woman, you don't have to tell women that you know *me* to get a date anymore," Michael said.

"I know...Jasmine is as shy as can be one minute, and then aggressive the next. Shit, I have at least three women rolled up into one with her. Plus, she's fine! Listen, let's stop at this soul food spot called *Big Daddy's*, to get some grub to take out."

"Come on with it, I'm starving. Those peanuts on the plane didn't do nothing but make me mad," Michael said.

Big Daddy's was one of Atlanta's best soul food restaurants. They had every-thing...from fried okra to chitterlings. Michael settled for the steak smothered in onions and gravy, okra and tomatoes, cornbread, and for dessert, peach cobbler. Alex got the fried catfish, macaroni and cheese, string beans and corn-bread. They both got a large sweet iced tea to wash it down. Hell, for twenty bucks, they both ate like kings.

"So, are you ready for the big bash tomorrow night?" Alex asked, as they sat in his dining room eating.

"Oh yeah, I'm ready. I bought a black tuxedo for the occasion. I hope I'm not overdressed," Michael said, sipping on his iced tea.

"It's a semi-formal party, so you're in the house, my man. I rented my tux. I'll show it to you after we finish eating," Alex said.

* * *

As Michelle slept peacefully, she was awakened by the sound of the steadily ringing phone. She almost fell out of bed trying to find it.

"Hello?" she answered sleepily.

"Get your behind out of bed, heffa. It's Saturday and I'm pulling into your driveway now. I brought coffee. Hop in the shower, and don't forget to brush your teeth," Jasmine said laughing. "I'll let myself in."

Groaning, I hung up the phone, without saying a word, and headed to the bathroom. *Damn Jasmine, for being so bubbly early in the morning.*

When I came downstairs, Jasmine was dancing around my kitchen, singing along with Luther Vandross and preparing omelets. It had been so long since I'd heard her singing that I forgot my girl could actually sing.

"Wow, she's cooking and singing too. Is there anything I can do to help?" I asked smiling.

"Good morning, beautiful lady. It's so good of you to join me for breakfast. You can make the toast to go with our eggs, pour the coffee, and if you would be so kind as to pour me some orange juice, I'd appreciate it very much," she said smiling.

"Yes ma'am, I think I can do that," I said, laughing and mumbling under my breath...that this was my house. "I swear you're worse than my mother. Neither of you sleep in or let a sister get her rest. If you get up early, you figure everyone else should get up too."

"I heard that, and you're damn right! You'll miss half the day if you're lying around in the bed, and we have things to do," Jasmine said.

"Excuse me, but what do we need to do this morning?" I asked.

"Nothing, it was just a figure of speech," she said giggling. "Sit your ass down and let's eat."

"Bossy this morning, aren't you," I said laughing, as I took my seat and dug into my breakfast. "Did you bring your clothes over with you for this evening, or are you going back home after you finish torturing me?"

"No, I brought them with me, so I have all day to torture you," she said, sticking out her tongue at me. "By the way, I spoke to Alex this morning, and he's going to bring Michael to the hotel around five o'clock, so they can both get dressed and chill out before the party."

"Okay. I was wondering what time they were going to check in. Michael's parents and sister will be checking in around one. Their flight gets in about noon, and the limo will be picking them up," I said.

"I know, Yvonne and I went over the schedule and room assignments yesterday while at the hotel. The hotel was gracious enough to give us early check-in for five rooms and not charge us extra. Of course, that was after I reminded them that we had reserved twenty-five rooms, and it was the least they could do," Jasmine said.

"Alright, Ms. Businesswoman, handle your shit," I said half-jokingly.

"You know I got this," she said, cracking up. "All jokes aside, this is going to be a classy affair. I love how they set the tables up, and with the addition of the angels and place cards, it's going to be beautiful."

"Seven o'clock can't get here soon enough. I'm so excited," I said smiling.

As we were eating, the phone rang.

"I bet that's Michael calling you now," Jasmine said smiling.

"Good morning," I said, answering the phone.

"Good morning, baby. How are you doing?" Michael asked.

"I'm doing good, and you? How was your flight?" I said, looking at Jasmine.

"My flight was cool and on time. Alex picked me up at the airport, and we went and grabbed some grub, and then sat around shooting the breeze. I'm looking forward to seeing you, baby. It's been too long since I've held you in my arms," he said.

"I'm looking forward to seeing you too, Michael. This evening can't get here soon enough," I said, blushing as Jasmine looked at me and smiled.

"Can I convince you to see me sooner, baby?" he asked.

"No, Michael. If we get together now, we'll never make it to the party. Besides, Jasmine's listening to my side of the conversation…nosey heffa that she is," I said laughing.

"Hello, Michael!" Jasmine yelled out.

"Tell her I said hello back," he said laughing. "Okay, I'll see you later, baby. I'm going to see if Alex wants to run some ball to work off some of this energy."

"Michael says hello back, Jasmine," I said to her. "Alright, we'll see you guys this evening. Jas and I should be checking in around six. I'll hit you up when we get there."

"Bye, baby," he said, hanging up.

Sighing, I turned around and faced Jasmine.

"How sweet, let's get this kitchen cleaned up and chill in the den. We have a busy night ahead of us," she said.

"Sounds like a good idea," I replied. "I need to take a nap, since someone woke me up all early and whatnot."

* * *

Later that evening, Jasmine and I arrived at the hotel, and after talking to the front desk, we learned that all the out of town guest had checked into their rooms. We decided to look at the ballroom before going to our room to get dressed.

There was a sign outside of the ballroom, which read: *Welcome to the Rivers, Inc.'s Christmas Party*. When I walked inside the room, I was blown away. It was simply beautiful. They had placed two Christmas trees, as we requested, in the room. They placed one near the podium, and the other near the bar. Each tree was decorated in different colors, and the tables were draped with white linen, sparkling crystal stemware, and fine china. They used the angels to hold the place cards, and had put little silver gift bags behind them.

"Good evening, ladies," DJ Hollywood said to us.

"Hey Hollywood, It's good to see you're getting set up, and I love your tux. You're looking good," Jasmine said.

"Thank you, Jasmine," he said, going back to setting up.

"Jasmine, you and Yvonne did a wonderful job," I said walking around, glancing at the cards to see who was placed where. "It's more beautiful then I had imagined."

"Thank you ma'am, we aim to please," Jasmine said smiling. "As you noticed, although Michael isn't sitting at the same table as you, he's nearby," she said.

"Yes, I noticed that, and thank you for putting him close enough for me to touch," I said laughing. "I like the place cards that say special guests at his table. I'm sure everyone will be wondering who they are."

"They won't have to wonder long. I'm going to personally escort his family down around seven-thirty, during the 'Meet and Greet'. I can't wait to see the look on Michael's face when he spots them," Jasmine said. "We need to go upstairs and get dressed. Good thing we showered and did our make-up at your house."

"Yeah, that was a good idea," I said, as we linked arms and left the ballroom.

When Alex and Michael came downstairs, the first person Michael noticed was his baby standing near the bar, talking to John and another man. She was more breathtaking then he remembered, with her hair curled all over, and poured in a silver gown with no back...to speak of.

"Oh, my God, is that Michelle?" Alex asked, as he spotted her when she turned around. "Damn, man, you better go get her before some other man claims her in that dress."

"I know what you mean, man. I feel like taking her upstairs and undressing her right now. Let's go greet our hostess," Michael said, as they walked over.

Out the corner of my eye, I saw Michael and Alex approaching, and felt the butterflies starting to stir in my stomach.

"Good evening, gentlemen. Don't you both look spiffy," I said smiling. "Daddy, I know you remember Alex, but I'd like to formally introduce you to Michael Ramsey. Michael, this is my father, Robert Rivers," I said proudly.

"Good evening everyone," they both said.

"It's a pleasure to finally meet you, Mr. Rivers," Michael said, extending his hand.

"Likewise, young man, I've been hearing a lot of good things about you," my dad answered, while shaking Michael's hand.

"Hello, John. How are you doing, sir?" Michael said, extending his hand to him next.

"I'm doing well, Michael, and you can cut the sir stuff," John said laughing. "Let me go find Doris before she thinks I'm neglecting her. Nice meeting you, Alex," he said, walking away.

"How long will you be in town, Michael?" my father asked.

"I'll be here until Monday, sir."

"Good, that will give us a chance to sit down and talk. I'll see you young folks later, I'm going to mingle," he said, walking away.

"Where's Jasmine?" Alex asked me.

"Here's your lady now and damn if she's not drop dead gorgeous," Michael said.

Slowly turning around, Alex said, "Wow!"

"Close your mouth lover boy, before you catch something," Jasmine said, as she walked up to us.

"I'd love to catch your tongue in my mouth," Alex said, and then drew her to him for a kiss.

"Excuse us. Michael, come let me introduce you to some of our other authors, and leave these two lovebirds alone. They need to go find a bed somewhere," I said, grabbing his hand to lead him away.

"Don't tempt me, heffa. There are some perfectly good beds upstairs," Jasmine said laughing.

Standing in shock in the doorway was Pam. She saw Michael put his arm around my waist, causing Sharon to walk into the back of her.

"I can't believe what I just saw," Pam said.

"What," asked Sharon obviously confused "You almost made me break my heel stopping like that"

"I can't believe I saw Michael with his arm around my boss' waist, is what I'm taking about," she said, pointing to where we had walked off to, while trying not to be too obvious.

"So, that's the famous writer Michael Ramsey. I see why you're a little bent out of shape. The brother is fine," Sharon said. "Well, don't stand here in the doorway staring, introduce me to them."

Passing a waiter on the way over, they each grabbed a glass of wine.

* * *

"Good evening everyone. I'd like to introduce you to Michael Ramsey. Michael, this is David Hale, our children's editor, and Ms. T. Carrion, one of our children's author," I said.

"I'm very glad to meet you, Miss Carrion. I bought two copies of your latest book, All Hallo's Eve. One for me, and one for my little brother," Michael said laughing. "David, I've heard so much about you. From what I've seen, you're a fantastic editor."

"I've read all your books also, Mr. Ramsey, and my name is Theresa, but all my friends call me Terri," Ms. Carrion said.

"Michael, I forgot to mention that David will be giving you some competition soon on the bookshelf. We'll be publishing his book soon also," I said.

"That's wonderful, David. There's always room for another talented writer," Michael said, holding up his glass for a toast.

"I feel the same way, Michael. Congratulations on your bestseller," David said.

"Hello everyone," Pam said, as she walked up behind us. "Very nice party you have going on, Michelle. The DJ is wonderful. I'm really feeling these oldies," she said, snapping her fingers. "This is my best friend, Sharon. Sharon, this is my boss, Michelle Rivers. Michael Ramsey is next to her. And this is Ms. Carrion, our children's writer, and my co-worker, David Hale."

"Hello everyone, it's good to meet you all," Sharon said, as the waiter walked up to us with a tray. "Those shrimp rolls look delicious, may I?" she asked. The waiter handed her a napkin, so she could help herself.

"Yes, they are very good, and I better stop eating them, or I'll have no room for dinner," Terri said laughing.

"Pam, you're looking very nice this evening," Michael said, as she paused for a moment.

"Thank you, Michael, and so do you," she said.

"Oh wow, that's my jam the DJ is playing. Sharon, would you care to dance?" Michael asked which caught Sharon off guard.

"Yes, I'd love to dance, Michael," Sharon answered, after glancing at Pam.

"I have to agree with Michael, Pam you look stunning in that black gown," David said.

"Thank you, David," Pam said.

"Excuse me, ladies. Michelle, would you care to dance? Jasmine seems to have abandoned me," Alex said, as he walked up.

"Terri, Pam and David, this is my friend, Alex. Alex, this is everyone. Excuse us while I show this man how to dance," I said.

"Woman, please, I hope you brought your A game, because you're about to be Soul Trained by a Philly brother," Alex said laughing, as he playfully did the robot.

"So Michael, I can see why Pam loves to work with you," Sharon said, pausing a moment while they were dancing. "I've read some of your work and it's hot," she said, smiling at the perplexed look on his face.

"Thank you, Sharon. You're a great dancer. Are you sure you're not one of those video dancers?" he asked, as she blushed.

"No you didn't say video dancer. You're too funny," she said, cracking up.

"Alex, you better stop before you break something," I said, laughing at him doing the robot on the dance floor.

"Oh shit is that Michael's parents?" Alex asked, doing a turn. "And Debra's here too. My boy didn't tell me they were coming."

"That's because your boy didn't know they were coming," I answered smiling.

At the same moment, Michael spotted his family walking into the room, and stopped dead in his tracks.

"Excuse me, Sharon, but my family just walked in. I can't believe this," he said, as his sister walked up to him.

"Hey big brother, nice party isn't it?" she said, hugging Michael.

"I can't believe this," Michael exclaimed, as he walked over to where his parents were standing. "Mom and Dad, this is one heck of a surprise," he said, hugging both of them, as he watched me walk up to them. "Michelle, you pulled a fast one over on me, but I'm so happy you did. Dad, you played me… telling me you and Mom were going to a function."

"Well, we're at a function, aren't we? I just didn't say where the function was going to be held," his dad said grinning. "Hello, Alex, it's good to see you again, and Michelle, come on over here and give me a hug."

"Michael, you look quite handsome in your tux. I'm proud to say you're my son," his mom said. "Michelle, where's the rest of your dress, young lady?" she asked, grinning as the DJ announced that dinner would be served in ten minutes.

"Thanks, Mom. I just don't know what to say," Michael said. "You really surprised me. Let me introduce you to Michelle's parents before they start serving dinner," he said. As we all started to walk over to where my parents were sitting, Michael turned to me and said, "Woman, I'm going to get you for this later." He gave me a huge hug and kiss, which caught Pam and Sharon's eyes. They looked at one another, and walked over to their table.

"Can I depend on that?" I asked, as he winked at me.

"Robert and Mary Rivers, I'd like to introduce you to my magical parents, Purnell and Christine Ramsey, and my sister, Debra," Michael said, as we all laughed at his magic reference.

"It's a pleasure to meet you all," Mary said, as Robert stood to shake Purnell's hand. "You have a very talented son," she said.

"Thank you, Mary. We're very proud of him," his mom said, smiling at Michael. "I can see where Michelle gets her beauty. I enjoyed spending time with her while she was in Philly."

My father looked at me a little closer, after overhearing that, as did Pam, who overheard the conversation from the next table. Soon after, everyone took their seats, as the catering staff started serving dinner. Michael introduced everyone to his editor and her friend.

"Pam and Sharon, I'd like you to meet my parents, Mr. and Mrs. Ramsey, and my sister, Debra. Family, this is my editor, Pamela Bryant, and her best friend, Sharon," Michael said.

"I'm pleased to meet you, Pam. I've heard so much about you," Debra said, looking directly into her eyes.

"It's nice to finally meet the family of such a gifted writer," Pam said, with a slight grin on her face.

"So Pam, tell me how you like working with my brother?" Debra asked, as Michael gave her a look.

"I have no complaints. Your brother is quite easy to work with," she answered, with a smile.

"Did you say my brother was easy to work with? Are we talking about the same Michael Ramsey?" Debra asked smiling. "I'm just joking."

"Debra, you need to behave yourself," Michael said, as everyone started laughing.

"You ladies will have to ignore my children," Mr. Ramsey said. "They sometimes forget they are grown up now."

"My family acts the same way," Sharon said, and smiled as everyone was served dinner.

"If they don't remember, I'll have to take them upstairs and show them Daddy's belt," Mrs. Ramsey said, which caused everyone to laugh again.

"Michael, your family is hilarious," Sharon said.

"Yes, we are," he said.

As soon as everyone had finished eating dinner and dessert, I excused myself from the table and walked up to the podium.

"Good evening everyone. I hope you all enjoyed your dinner. I'd like to take this time to thank Yvonne and my best friend, Jasmine. Please stand up, ladies. Thank you both for doing such a good, no, great job planning this Christmas party," I said.

I had to wait for all the applause to die down before continuing.

"I would also like to thank all my authors for taking time out to join us, and Michael Ramsey's family for traveling from Philly," I said. "I'm proud to announce that we at Rivers, Inc. will have three bestsellers in the next month. Yes, I'm claiming it!" I said, as everyone looked on stunned.

"I'd like to introduce you to the authors who will be on that list. Mr. David Hale, would you please stand up? As most of you know, David is one of my best editors, but what many of you don't know is he moonlights as C.E. Campbell, one of the best novelists I've had the pleasure to read. David, I want to be the first to say congratulations on your book, which will hit the stands in mid-January," I said, as everyone in the room got on their feet and clapped for him.

"Congratulations, C.E. Campbell," John said, and winked at a blushing David.

"Our next author on the list is Mr. Tyler Bray. Mr. Bray is our only horror writer, and if I do say so, his story is so real it will have you jumping out of your skin. Take my advice, and don't read him after dark," I said, as everyone laughed and he waved me off. "Mr. Bray's book will be released next week... just in time for Christmas.

"And last, but not least, is an author who has already been on the Times bestseller list…Mr. Michael Ramsey," I said, as everyone applauded. "Mr. Ramsey's third book, Determined, is ready to hit the shelves. So, we thought we'd give everyone a sneak peek. John, if you would please," I said, as John pulled the drape from off the easel, to everyone's applause. "Ladies and gentlemen, the cover of this book was designed by my good friend and a wonderful artist, Damon Jennings. Damon, would you please stand so everyone can see you?" Everyone was overwhelmed by the detail of his artwork. "I hope you brought plenty of business cards," I said to him, as everyone applauded and nodded their heads.

"Wow, big brother, that guy in the painting looks a lot like you," Debra said, and his parents agreed.

"That's because the artist has a good eye, and painted him to resemble me," Michael said. "I'll have to introduce you all to him."

"Mr. Ramsey's book will also be released next week, and each of you will receive a copy of both his and Mr. Bray's book," I said. "Thank you again for your attention. DJ Hollywood, it's your party, let the music play," I said, and walked back to my table, only to be stopped by Michael. He pulled me into his arms for a tight hug.

"I can't wait to get you alone tonight, and peel that dress off your body," he whispered in my ear. "Thanks for making this one of the most memorable nights in my life, baby."

"You're welcome, Michael," I said smiling, while looking him in his eyes.

"Congratulations, Michael," John said, as he walked up behind us. "I bet you'll be on the bestsellers list before January is out."

"From your lips to the reader's pocketbooks," Michael said, with a laugh.

"Can I steal Michael away from you for a minute?" Pam asked, as she walked up behind us.

"Sure you can," I said smiling. "I need to say hello to the board members. Come on, John," I said.

"Can I have a word with you outside, Michael, so we aren't interrupted?" Pam asked, and led the way, not noticing Debra watching them. "What exactly is going on with you and Michelle?" she asked, quite angrily once she got Michael outside the ballroom.

"Pam, I'm not going to discuss my relationship with Michelle with you," he said, looking directly at her.

"Oh, I see. So, you're having a relationship with her?"

"This is neither the time nor the place to go into this. But yes, Pam, I'm having a relationship with Michelle," he confirmed.

"Fuck that, Michael. This may not be the place, but it is the right time. How are you just going to tell me you're involved with my boss, and think that's going to go over well with me? What was I, your personal Atlanta whore, you sorry bastard," Pam said angrily.

"Lower your voice, Pam. Look, I didn't mean to hurt you, and I'm sorry if you think that," he said, grabbing her hand and pulling her further away from the door.

"Get your hands off me, Michael. I still can't believe you're fucking her. How could you do this to me?" she asked, as she attempted to slap him. Tears were flowing down her cheeks.

"Pam, things were good between us while they lasted. But you were trying to take it to a whole other level…one which I wasn't ready for," he said, trying to calm her down.

"I can't believe this," she said walking away, shaking her head. Pam took a walk outside to calm down, and then went to the bathroom to repair her make up. "I can't believe I'm crying over that bastard," she said to herself.

As Michael turned to walk back into the ballroom, he noticed his sister standing in the doorway. She had been standing there the whole time watching them.

"Is there a problem, Michael?" Debra asked, as he reached her side.

"There's nothing for you to worry about, sis," he said.

Hollywood was playing slow jams when Pam walked back into the ballroom, and she noticed David sitting alone at his table.

"Hi, baby. They're playing my song, and I haven't had a chance to dance with you all night," she said, as she walked up to him.

"Maxwell is a favorite of mine, and I've been waiting to hold you in my arms all night," David said, getting up to dance with her.

Meanwhile, across the room, I had been watching Michael talking to Debra. I excused myself from the board members and walked over.

"Hello, you two. You both look so serious over here," I said. "Are you enjoying the party, Debra?"

"Yes I am, very much. Thanks for inviting me. I'm going to get something to drink, would either of you like something?" she asked.

"No, thank you. I'm going to try and convince your brother to dance with me," I said smiling.

"Baby, you don't have to do any convincing. I'll take any excuse to have you in my arms," he said, smiling for the first time since I walked over.

"You two have fun," Debra said. Before she got a chance to walk away, Keith from the printing department grabbed her by the hand.

"Hello, gorgeous. Would you like to dance?" he asked. Keith was a very handsome young man in his twenties. Debra glanced over at me. I smiled and winked at her, as the two of them walked to the dance floor.

"Michael, are you okay baby" I asked.

"Just missing you," he answered, taking me into his arms.

The party was a huge success. Everyone commented on how much they enjoyed themselves. I was really glad that Michael's parents and sister were here to enjoy the party, and the unveiling of his new book cover. Yvonne and Jasmine really outdid themselves in planning the entire evening.

After a long, but fulfilling day, I retired to my hotel suite to settle in for what I knew would be wonderful night with Michael. He joined me after seeing that his family was taken care of.

Chapter 29

THE peaceful silence was interrupted by the sound of the ringing phone.

"Hello? Hello?" Michael answered, still half asleep.

"Who was it, baby?" I asked, as I turned and put my hand on his hardening manhood.

"They hung up the phone, whoever it was," he responded, kissing me on the forehead. "Are you ready to go another round?"

"I put your lights out once. Twice isn't out the question," I said smiling, while massaging him to full erection.

The phone rang once again.

"Hello? Hello?" he answered, and again there was no response. "Someone doesn't have anything better to do then to call and hang up the damn phone at eight o'clock on a Sunday morning. Hmm, keep it up, baby, and I'll start on repaying you for last night," he said, as he slowly began to massage my firm breasts.

Once again we were interrupted.

"Damn, would you stop playing on this phone and get a life!" Michael shouted into the phone.

"Hello, this is Robert, and I do have a life," a deep voice responded, with a chuckle. "Is everything alright over there?"

"Wow, Mr. River, I apologize. Someone's been calling and hanging up the phone," Michael responded humbly.

"Mary and I want to invite you two, your parents and sister over for brunch at our house. How does that sound?"

"You're inviting us to brunch? That sounds good to me," Michael said, as I reached for the phone.

"Good morning, Daddy. I heard you're cooking this morning," I said laughing.

"Yeah right, don't hold your breath," he responded. "We're about to check out, so we can go and get everything together."

"I'll give Jasmine a call and let her know too," I said.

"Been there, done that, baby. Jasmine and Alex are heading out with us to help," my dad said.

"Isn't that special? I'll get the limo to bring us all over after we check out," I said.

"We'll see you when you get to the house. Bye," he said.

"Bye, Daddy," I said, hanging up.

"That's nice of them to invite my family over for brunch. I like your parents, Michelle. They seemed so down to earth," Michael said.

"It looked like both of our parents had a good time last night. After all these years, I've never seen my daddy dance with another woman," I said smiling.

"They were cutting the rug, weren't they?" he said laughing. But his laughter quickly subsided as I reached up to kiss him.

I slowly kissed my way from his lips down to his chest, as he slowly ran his fingers through my hair. Gently, I nibbled and licked each nipple, and they instantly hardened. The pace became quicker as I kissed my way down his lightly hairy stomach, while massaging his manhood, which was now fully erect. It throbbed in my hand to the beat of his heart, as I kissed the head with my soft, wet lips. Slowly, I engulfed his firm dick, causing him to moan and writhe with pleasure.

"Do you like that, baby? Do you like how my hot rod feels in your mouth?" Michael asked. I nodded yes.

I licked the entire length of his missile, like it was an ice cream cone, causing him to call out my name.

"Oh yes, Michelle, suck it, baby! It's yours. Suck it, baby," he said.

He felt the wetness of my pussy as I gently grinded on his leg. Michael wanted to taste me, so we made the most of a sixty-nine position. Slowly I turned until I had straddled his face with my smooth shaven valley. My pearl, already hardened, got his immediate attention. He flicked his tongue across it eagerly, licking it up and down, and side to side. My hips were grinding in sync with his licking.

Suddenly, I screamed out, "I'm cumming!" A large gush of my sweet nectar splashed onto his face.

"Damn, baby," Michael, said, as he had never seen this much cum released before.

I got up and quickly straddled his waist, and lowered my soaking wet pussy down onto his glistening manhood. Inch by inch, he penetrated the depths of my well. I rode him like a jockey heading for a photo finish. He could feel my muscles tightening around his tool, and then he too was reaching the point of no return. I dismounted him when I realized he was about to cum, and went down on him, sucking furiously until he made one more firm upward thrust, before an explosion like no other took place.

Michael's body trembled and shook, and his juices erupted onto my face and chin as I slowly, methodically continued to suck him until the last drop had been released.

"What got into you this morning, baby?" he asked. "You were in some type of zone or something."

"You helped take me there, and I've come to realize a few things about myself in the process," I said, as the mood turned rather somber. "When I'm away from you, I think about you all the time. I really feel safe when I'm with you. Even when you leave a phone message, I find myself replaying it over and over again, just to hear your voice. I've never told you this before, but I was in love with only one other man in my lifetime, but it was never like this," I said, with tears in my eyes. "I'm in love with you, Michael."

The room got so quiet; you could hear a mouse piss on cotton. Michael was caught totally off guard. He pulled me close to him, wiped the tears from my eyes, and passionately kissed me. Again, the phone interrupted the mood.

"Hello," Michael said, answering the phone.

"Hello, this is the limousine service. We're just confirming your stretch Excursion for twelve o'clock this afternoon," the woman said.

"That will be fine, thank you," he said, glancing at the clock, which read ten forty-five. "That was the limousine service on the phone, baby. They'll be here to pick us up at noon."

"That's fine. We'll be ready. Would you like to join me in the shower?" I asked.

"I'm right behind you."

"That's what I was hoping for," I said smiling, as I headed for the bathroom.

Michael sat there admiring my nakedness, as I walked towards the bathroom. "I'll be right there. I'm going to call my family, and let them know about the limo," he said, with a raised voice.

"Okay," I responded.

He dialed Debra's room. "Good morning, Debra," he said, when she picked up the phone.

"Good morning, Mike. Your girl sure knows how to throw a party. I had a great time," she said.

"I know you did. I saw the look on your face when dude asked you to slow dance with him," he said laughing.

"Oh, you saw that?" she asked. "So, what are we doing today?" she asked, changing the subject.

"That's what I'm calling you for. We've been invited over to the Rivers' home for brunch. The limo will be waiting downstairs at noon to take us over there. Do me a favor…call Mom and Dad to let them know? And don't think I didn't notice you changing the subject, Sis," he said chuckling.

"Brunch sounds good. I'm famished. I'll let Mom and Dad know we've been invited to their house. I want to give you my opinion on something. Michelle's a keeper, bro. That's all I'm going to say. We'll see you downstairs at noon after we check out," she said.

"Okay. We'll meet you downstairs."

Michael was glad his family approved of Michelle…his sister especially. He walked into the bathroom and pulled the shower curtain back.

"Hey, baby, everyone's been told about the limo and brunch, so we're all set," he said, entering the shower and rubbing on my butt.

"Keep it up, and we'll be late checking out," I warned, but with a smile on my face.

We all met in the hotel lobby around noon, and the limo driver was already waiting for us. After he put our luggage in the back of the beautiful white stretch Excursion, we got inside for the trip over to my parents.

"Michelle, thank you so much for arranging for us to be here to join in the celebration," Purnell said. "I've enjoyed myself so much since arriving in Atlanta, and I have to admit you know how to throw a party."

"It was my pleasure. I wanted to make sure Michael's family was a part of this celebration. I know you three are so proud of him, and it just wouldn't have been complete if you all weren't here," I said.

"Michelle, that's very nice of you to say," Purnell said smiling, as he leaned in to give me a hug.

✳ ✳ ✳

"Hello, Pam. I've been calling you all morning, but the phone has been busy. Are you okay?" Sharon asked, as soon as Pam answered.

"No, I'm not doing okay. My head has been all fucked up ever since that conversation with Michael last night. I can't believe he admitted to being in a relationship with that bitch. That's just wrong on so many levels," she said sniffing.

"I know damn well you aren't over there crying over that man. He's not worth your tears, girlfriend."

"Sharon, you just don't understand. I'm so mad I could chew nails. I was good enough to fuck, but not good enough to be in a relationship with. How dare he get involved with that bitch...of all people? I could cut off his fucking balls," she said angrily. "No, I'm not crying over him...I could kill him."

"Pam, don't even waste your time on him. He's not worth it, and sooner or later, every dog has his day. Girl, he will regret he ever fucked you over, trust that," Sharon said.

"I tried calling him several times this morning, to cuss his ass out. But every time he answered the phone, I couldn't bring myself to say anything. I bet that bitch was in bed with him...probably sucking on his dick. But I know she's not as good as I am. I used to have that bastard's eyes rolling up in the back of his head," she said, smiling at the memory.

"Girl, please, her prim and proper ass isn't about to get down on her knees. Fuck that bitch...fuck both of them. Listen, why don't you get dressed, and let's go have brunch at the *Cheesecake Factory*...my treat," Sharon said.

"Okay, give me twenty minutes and I'll be ready. And Sharon...thanks for listening. I love you, girl."

"I love you too, and no thanks are necessary. I'll see you in a few minutes," she said, hanging up.

The limousine turned into a beautiful subdivision called Lakeside on Redwin.

"Your parents have a gorgeous house, Michelle. What part of town is this?" Mary asked.

"Thank you, Mom. We're actually in a suburb of Atlanta. It's called Fayetteville," I explained, as we pulled into the driveway.

When we walked inside, my dad greeted us at the door. "Hello family, let me take your jackets," he said smiling.

"Your home is just as beautiful inside as it is outside, Mr. Rivers," Debra said.

"Thank you. Michelle can take you on a tour if you'd like. I'm helping Mary and Jasmine set up everything, so we can get this brunch on the road," he said, as everyone laughed.

"Don't tell me they have you switching in the kitchen?" Purnell quipped.

"You know the deal Purnell…a man's work is never done." Purnell burst out laughing, as Christine playfully elbowed him.

"Why don't you show them around Michelle until we're ready?"

"Okay, Daddy. Follow me everyone," I said.

After the walking tour was complete, we all came back to the dining room, where the table was beautifully set, and the chafing dishes were steaming on the server. My mom really loved entertaining guests. Ever since my dad had served as the head of his Masonic Lodge, and was asked to cook for some of the meetings that he would host at their home, she's been more than willing to kick in with her vast skills. There were eggs, sausage, bacon, shrimp, grits, home fried potatoes, applesauce, toast, biscuits, coffee, tea, champagne, orange juice, and her renowned sweet potato pie.

"Who in the world is going to eat all of this food?" I asked.

"Oh, it won't go to waste…I promise you that," Alex said, rubbing his hands together.

After my dad rendered a prayer, and welcomed the Ramsey family, everyone commenced to enjoy the fantastic meal.

"I'd like to propose a toast to the Rivers family. Thank you, Mary and Robert, for accepting my family into your home, and for the wonderful meal. Michelle, I'd like to also thank you again for helping to make it possible for the three of us to come down to Atlanta," Purnell said, as he held up his glass of champagne.

"Baby, do you need me to help you clear the table?" my dad asked, after everyone had eaten their fill.

"No, we have everything under control. Besides, you know you want to go and turn the game on anyway. Go ahead and enjoy yourselves," she said, as the men went into the family room, and turned on the big screen television to the Falcons and 49ers game.

"There are some refreshments in the fridge next to the bar. Michael and I will be right back," my dad said.

That was Michael's cue to follow him to the library, so they could have a few words with one another.

Meanwhile, in the kitchen, the ladies were having their own conversation.

"Michelle, that was a great party your company threw last night," Christine said. "I haven't danced that much in years."

"And you looked good too, Mom," Debra said smiling.

"Thank you, Mom. I can't take credit for it though. That was all Jasmine and Yvonne's doing," I said.

"Don't act like you had no say in the matter, heffa," Jasmine said smiling, with her hands on her hips.

"Alright, I had a little something to do with it," I said laughing, as everyone joined in.

"So, Michelle, you're really feeling my brother, huh?" Debra asked.

"Yes, Debra, I'm feeling your brother...as you say," I confirmed, with a big grin on my face. "I haven't felt this good about anyone in a long time."

"I'm glad to hear that, because Mike seems to be feeling you also. People think my brother's a big player because of what he writes, but he's really a good guy," she said seriously.

"Listen, Debra, I feel where you're coming from, and trust me when I say I would never hurt Michael intentionally. I'm in love with your brother," I said, as everyone in the room gasped. "Yes, I said it. I, Michelle Rivers, am in love with Michael Ramsey. I'm proud to admit it," I said to the ladies.

"Michelle, are you sure about this? And how does he feel?" my mom asked.

"I'm sure, Mommy. But I can't speak for Michael," I said.

"Well, I can speak for my son. From what I've seen of him lately, he feels the same way. Knowing Michael as I do...he's like his father, and he probably won't say so in words, but actions," Christine said.

"I agree. It's funny how he can write all the words in books, but can't say them out loud," Debra said.

"He'd be a fool not to love you too," Jasmine said seriously.

* * *

Robert and Michael settled into the library and talked. It was bound to happen sooner or later. One of those, *what are your intentions with my daughter* conversations was about to take place.

"Michael, I just wanted to grab you for a few moments to talk with you about a some things. I want to congratulate you on your new book. I've read your other two, and you have some serious writing skills," Robert said.

"Thank you, Mr. Rivers. I really appreciate that," Michael said.

"Michelle's a strong young woman, and in spite of the recent threat she received, she's keeping her head up high. I can tell she's very fond of you, and so are we. We see how you two are with each other, and it's a wonderful sight to see. She talks to Mary and me all the time about you. Believe it or not, you're really helping her keep a sense of balance in her life. Do me a favor and take care of her. Please don't hurt her. I'm not trying to make you fear me or anything like that, but as her father, it's my job to protect her."

"Mr. Rivers, you don't have to worry about that. I'm very fond of Michelle. She also brings a lot of happiness into my life. I wouldn't trade one moment of being with her for anything in the world. I promise I will never hurt your daughter. I must say I appreciate what you're saying, because one day if I'm blessed to have a daughter, I know I'll say the exact same thing," Michael said.

Robert extended his hand to Michael and they shook hands. He reminded Michael so much of his father in a sense…that he was going to protect his family no matter what. When they walked back into the family room, Alex and Purnell stopped watching the game, and just smiled at Michael.

"So, Michael, I see you survived that infamous talk, huh?" Purnell laughed, slapping Alex a high five.

* * *

After we finished in the kitchen, we joined the men in the family room.

"What's all the noise for in here?" my mom asked.

"We're just watching the Falcons blow the 49ers away in this game," Alex said. "But they won't do so well when they get to play my Eagles," he added.

"Man, you better watch your mouth, talking about my Falcons. You're in Atlanta, baby." Jasmine laughed. "My man, Michael Vick, is going to run all over the Eagles."

"Baby, you better ask somebody. Don't worry y'all, she'll switch over to an Eagles fan…watch what I tell you," Alex said, laughing and giving Michael a pound.

Before long, it was six o'clock in the evening, and it was getting close to the time for the Ramsey's to be heading home.

"Well, everyone, we have to get ready to leave for the airport. Our flight leaves at eight. And if Hartsfield/Jackson is anything like Philly International, we'll need an hour and a half to get cleared through security," Purnell said.

"All of your bags are in my car already Mr. Ramsey, and I'm ready when you are," Alex said.

"Mary and Robert, thank you so much for inviting us to your home. You two will have to come up to Philly, so we can return the hospitality," Christine said, giving them both a hug. "Michelle, honey, thanks for everything. We'll see you when you get to Philly," she added.

"It was our pleasure, Christine. You're family, so you're always welcome here," my dad said.

"Nice meeting you, Jasmine," Debra said, hugging her. "I'll keep in touch with you."

"Do that, girlfriend," Jasmine said, smiling as Debra went out of the door.

"Mom, Dad, we're going to get ready to leave too," I said, as Jasmine and I started gathering our things.

"This was a great weekend, Michelle," Mom said.

"Yes it was, baby. You handled everything wonderfully," Dad said, while giving me a hug.

"Where's mine at?" Jasmine asked pouting.

"Girl, let me give you your hug, so you can stop whining," Dad said playfully.

"We'll see y'all later," I said, as Jasmine and I headed to my place.

* * *

After Michael and Alex drove his parents to the airport and said their so longs, they headed back to my place.

"Man, you pulled a fast one on me last night," Michael said, shaking his head.

"It wasn't me, brother. The ladies pulled one over on you. I had no idea what was going on. I was just as surprised as you. One thing is for sure… Michelle loves you, man. She pulled out all the stops, by making sure your family was here," Alex said smiling.

"I know she does. I feel the same way about her. Man, but you should've been a fly on the wall when Pam pulled me to the side. She almost went ballistic on me," Michael said.

"Really, what happened?"

"She saw me and Michelle hugging at the party, and she asked me what was going on between the two of us."

"What did you tell her?" he asked.

"First I told her it was really none of her business what was going on between us. But then I went on and told her we were in a relationship, and she tried to slap the shit out of me," Michael said.

"Oh shit, no she didn't?"

"Yes, she did, but I caught her before she hit me. Then she walked off. I think Debra saw and heard the whole thing."

"She better be glad she didn't make contact, because Deb would've been all over her," Alex said, shaking his head.

"I just don't want her to get herself in a jam, as far as her job goes. I know Michelle would cut her loose in a heartbeat if she knew what happened. But she's one hell of an editor, and I'd hate for her to lose her job over some bullshit."

"Michael, it's not bullshit. She obviously still has feelings for you. You better be careful. Women can be vicious when it comes to their feelings."

"Well, she had to find out sooner or later about Michelle and me. I hope we can at least still do business together."

"I think you need to cut her completely loose, man. As long as you still have contact with her, she'll still feel something for you. I'm telling you, cut her loose," Alex said, in a stern voice.

"You're right, brother. I just have to figure out how to do that without setting her off."

When they arrived at my house, Jasmine answered the door. There was a bottle of white zinfandel in an ice bucket, and some cheese and crackers on the table.

"Hello gentlemen. Welcome to Chez Michelle's. Would either of you care for some refreshments?" Jasmine said, turning to me and then cracking up.

"Yes, thank you. But first I'd like to taste your lips, please." Jasmine grabbed Alex and gave him a kiss. "Those weren't the lips I was talking about, but they'll suffice for now," he said, turning to give Michael a high five. We all burst out laughing.

"Did your family get to the airport on time?" I asked.

"Yes. They had plenty of time to deal with that busy ass airport. Debra said she'd call when they got home."

"I was so glad they could make it. Our parents got along well together, don't you think?" I asked.

"Yes, they seemed to enjoy each other's company. Can you pour me some wine, baby?" Michael asked me.

"I sure can but make yourself at home, it's not like this is your first time here," I said smiling, as I poured him a glass of wine.

"Oh, you don't have to tell me twice. Can I get another private tour?" he asked smiling.

"Oh, you'll get your grand tour after our company leaves," I said, as I sipped from my glass.

"Oh, please. You two need to cut that lovey dovey shit," Jasmine said.

"Heffa, I know you aren't talking. Tell Alex to get his hand off your thigh," I said, cracking up.

"You leave your hand right where it is, honey," Jasmine said, as she leaned over to kiss Alex.

* * *

Monday morning came quickly. Michael checked his cell phone messages, and saw that Debra had in fact called when they arrived home. Michael and I caught a one-fifteen flight to Philly. Luckily, he reminded me to bring a heavier coat to wear. We don't do snow in Atlanta, at least not as much as in Philly, and today just happened to be one of those days. It was cold and snow flurries were dusting the landscape when we arrived in Philly. It was truly beginning to look like Christmastime.

When we pulled up to Michael's house, it was around four o'clock in the afternoon. He put our bags in his bedroom, and then we relaxed for a few. We hadn't eaten yet, so that was next on the agenda.

"What do you have a taste for, baby?" Michael asked, while looking through his mail.

"I haven't had any Italian food in a while. Is there an *Olive Garden* or something like that nearby?" I asked.

"There's one not too far from here. Would you do me a favor, and give my parents a call? I want to let them know we made it here. Just press the letter A at the top, and it'll connect you," Michael said to me.

"Hello?" Debra said, answering the phone.

"Hey, Debra, this is Michelle," I said.

"Hey, Michelle," she said.

"I just called to let y'all know we made it safely. Michael got your message when you got home, but he was a little pre-occupied…with sleeping," I said laughing.

"Michelle, you're a mess," Debra said, laughing also.

"Well, we're getting ready to go out and get some dinner. And since Michael has to go back to work tomorrow, do you think you can take me to the mall? I'd like to pick up a few last minute gifts."

"Sure. You can go with me to meet my girlfriend, Sara, for lunch and then afterwards, we can go get our shopping on. I'll come pick you up around eleven o'clock, okay?"

"That sounds like a plan. I'll see you then. Bye."

"Oh, oh, it sounds like you ladies are about to do some serious shopping," Michael said, after I hung up the phone.

"Oh, shut up before I hit you up for some dollars," I said laughing.

"If you really need something, I…" Michael was saying, but stopped when he saw the look on my face. "Grab your coat, baby, let's go get some grub. Your man is getting hungry. Can't you hear my stomach growling over here?"

"Alright I'll be right back," I said laughing, as I went to the closet to get my coat.

I'm going to really enjoy having her here with me these next two weeks, Michael thought to himself.

Chapter 30

THE next day after Michael had left for work, I was cleaning up the kitchen, when his mother called to check on me. When I asked her to come do some shopping with Debra and I, she just laughed and said she had gotten all her shopping done weeks ago. She was going to spend the day baking while everyone was out the house.

Before I knew it, eleven o'clock had rolled around, and Debra was ringing the doorbell.

"Hey Debra, I see you're right on time," I said, opening the door and giving her a hug. "Give me two minutes to grab my coat."

"You look great, Michelle. I love that red sweater," she said, as I grabbed my coat from off the back of the sofa.

"Thanks, Sis. Red is my favorite color. I was told it brings out my skin tone," I said smiling, as we walked to her car.

"Whoever told you that was right, because it works perfectly for you. Now, let me warn you about my friend, Sara. You've probably talked to her on several occasions already…she's Michael's secretary," Debra said, laughing at the look on my face. "I know she can't wait to meet you, and she's as nosey as me when it comes to my brother."

"Oh, brother, I guess that means the two of you plan on double teaming me with questions, huh? I should've taken a valium before I left the house," I said jokingly.

"It won't be that bad. We won't even ask you how good he is in bed," she said, cracking up.

"Don't worry, I won't tell you that he curls my toes either," I replied, as she pulled up along side of City Hall.

"No, you didn't go there!" she said, cracking up again. "I really like you, Michelle."

"Thanks, Debra. I like you too. I believe we're going to be good friends," I said, reaching over to give her a quick hug.

We didn't have to wait long for Sara. She said she went to work early today, so she could take the rest of the day off and hang out with us. Sister girl said she didn't want to miss out on any of the good gossip.

We decided to grab something to eat at the mall before we began shopping. Although I had already bought small gifts for everyone prior to my trip, I bought some oddly shaped baking pans for Mom Ramsey and had some sent to my mother.

I bought Dad Ramsey a few jazz CD's for his collection, after Debra told me how much he loved jazz. They couldn't stop teasing me when I bought my baby an outfit...down to the silk boxers and socks.

"Do you really think he'll like this sweater?" I asked the girls for their advice.

"Michael will look drop dead gorgeous in that black cashmere sweater, and the slacks are cut just right. Don't you agree, Debra?" Sara said.

"I can't wait to see his face when he sees those silk boxers," she said giggling.

"See, that's why I plan to give them to him privately," I said, laughing so hard that tears ran down my cheeks.

I pulled a fast one over on Debra. I bought her a beautiful flowing red top, and a couple pair of jeans, along with this fabulous cape. I also bought a cape for Sara and myself. The green in Sara's cape was going to match her hazel eyes perfectly. I couldn't wait for them to open their gifts on Christmas day.

After we checked out the shoe store, and each bought a pair of boots, we decided to call it a day. I had Debra take me by the grocery store, so I could cook dinner for Michael and myself.

"Thank you ladies for a wonderful day, I've laughed more today than I have in a long time. We must do it again before I go back to Atlanta," I said, hugging them both as they were leaving the house.

"It was a pleasure meeting you, Michelle. Michael's a very lucky man," Sara said smiling.

"I'm equally as lucky Sara, but thank you," I said.

"I'll give you a call tomorrow, Michelle. It's been a blast. Bye," Debra said.

✳ ✳ ✳

"So Mike, how was the Christmas party in Atlanta?" Bob asked, as we stood outside my office.

"It was very nice. My publisher surprised me with the unveiling of a large replica of my new book cover. Then the best surprise of all was she had arranged for my parents and Debra to be there," Michael said.

"Awe, man, that's deep. You mean your woman actually pulled one over on you?" he said laughing. "Well, she's good. The cover was designed by the same artist that did the painting you showed me, right?"

"Yeah remind me to turn you on to his web page. You may see something that you like. But man, the women were there in full force. You would've had a field day. Everything was so festive…it was just beautiful. That's the only way I can describe it," Michael said.

"I'm glad everything turned out so nicely," Bob said.

"So, how's everything going with you and Carol?" Michael asked.

"Man, she's a dream. We get along well together. I'm surprised you never tried to connect with her," he said.

"We're just really good friends, my brother. We couldn't take it to that next level, being that I'm Kevin's big brother. I never really even thought of her in that way," he said. "How are you and my little brother getting along?"

"We're okay. He doesn't say a whole lot. I think he's still feeling me out, as most sons would, when it concerns their mother. I think it's only natural," he said.

"I agree it's instinctive. Listen, I'm about to give Carol a call now, to ask if I can come by to pick Kevin up tomorrow. I miss my little brother," Michael said.

"I'm getting ready to leave, so I'll talk to you later. I'd like to formally meet your publisher when you get a chance," Bob said laughing.

"You made your point. I'll get with you on that," Michael said, shaking his head.

Michael dialed Carol's number.

"Hello," Kevin said, answering the phone.

"Hey Kevin, How are you, little brother?" Michael said.

"Hey, Mike. Where have you been? I miss you," he said, excited to hear Michael's voice.

"I miss you too, Kevin. I went to see Ms. Michelle over the weekend. How are your classes going?"

"They're going real good. Ms. Chris is so nice. She said I'm going to make a good photographer when I grow up. You should see all the pictures I have."

"I'm glad you're enjoying the class and doing so well. Did you have fun at your Uncle's house?"

"I sure did. I met all my cousins, and my uncle took us all ice-skating and to the *New Jersey Aquarium*. My aunt made my favorite dinner -- macaroni and cheese, fried chicken and string beans."

"Man, Kevin, you're making me hungry," Michael said, as they both cracked up laughing. "Is your mom home?"

"No, she didn't get home yet. Wait a minute…here she comes. Mommy, Mike's on the phone for you!" he said, yelling to his mother. After a few minutes, she picked up the phone.

"Hello, Michael. How are you?" Carol said.

"Everything is fine. How are things with you?" he said.

"Things couldn't be better, and before you ask, Bob and I are doing fine too. I'm glad you're okay with us seeing each other," she said.

"Why wouldn't I be? You two look good together. As long as you're enjoying yourself, I'm okay with it. You asked that because of what we did, and because he's a friend of mine, didn't you?" Michael said.

"Yes, on both points," Carol said.

"Carol, I thought we agreed that what happened between us was just a casual thing, and we weren't going to dwell on it. If it's my blessing you're looking for, you got it. Bob's a great guy, and I couldn't have chosen anyone better for you and Kevin, if I had picked him myself," he said.

"Well, that's nice to know. You're a good man, Michael," Carol said.

"The reason I called is I'd like to come by and pick Kevin up tomorrow. Is that alright with you?"

"You know it is. What time are you coming by to pick him up?"

"I'll be over as soon as I get off from work, which will be around five o'clock. Plus my friend, Michelle, is here and I want you to meet her."

"That's the sister from Atlanta, right? I've been hearing a lot of nice things about her. Kevin still talks about her giving him that photography book. It'll be my pleasure to meet the love of your life. She must be very important to you, Mike. This is the second time she's been here in a few short months, isn't it?" she asked.

"I'm sorry, what did you say?" Michael asked, as his mind wandered for a moment.

"Michelle is your lady, right?" she asked again.

"Yes, she is," he said.

"She must be a special lady, because you seem to be at a loss for words when talking about her."

"She's special, Carol. At times, I just can't explain it."

"That's called love, Michael…plain and simple," she said.

"I know, Carol, I know. I just can't believe I finally found the woman I've been longing for. I never thought it would happen, but it has, and I need to recognize that fact. Thank you, for listening and being a great friend."

"You're welcome, Michael. I'll see you tomorrow. Bye," she said, as she hung up the phone.

After talking with Carol, Michael sat back and wondered to himself why he was having so much trouble expressing his feelings for Michelle to himself… let alone other people. Maybe it was the fact that he really loved her. He's never felt this serious about a woman. It seemed as though every woman he's ever had feelings for, actually fell in love with his writer's side, and not the real Michael Ramsey. Michelle was different, she didn't care that he was a writer. She was into him for him, not an illusion of Michael Ramsey, but the real Michael. That's what he loved about her.

When Michael got home from work, I was in the kitchen, finishing up preparing dinner.

"Hey, baby. How was your day?" I asked, as a wife would ask her husband after a long day.

"It wasn't too bad. I'm working on the plans for a new post office out by the airport," Michael responded, as we hugged and kissed each other. "How was your day with the girls?"

"I had a ball with Debra and Sara," I said smiling. "That Sara is something else. It's almost as if you have two sisters guarding your tail," I said.

"I know what you mean. Once, when we went out to a club, I was talking to this fine sister, and damn if they both didn't scare her off like mother hens," he said laughing.

"That's understandable. They both love their brother. Dinner's ready, go wash your hands," I said.

"Okay, Mommy," Michael playfully responded.

When he came back in the kitchen, I asked him, "Did you get a chance to talk to Kevin?"

"Yeah I'm going to pick him up tomorrow, take him to the arcade, and catch up on things with him. I want you to meet his mom also. I think you two will hit it off nicely," he said. "Something sure smells good in here. What are we having?" he asked, sniffing the aromas coming from the pots.

"Just some blackened salmon, linguine with clam sauce, steamed broccoli and garlic bread. Can you get the white wine from the refrigerator and open it, please?"

"Hmmmm, that sounds good. I'm starving," he said, opening the refrigerator.

* * *

The next day after work, Michael went by to pick Kevin up. Of course, Kevin had his trusty camera with him. Michael felt his enthusiasm for photography would lead to something great. They stopped by Kevin's favorite restaurant, *Friendly's,* to grab a bite to eat.

"So, are you all ready for Christmas?" Michael asked.

"Yes, I can't wait. My uncle gave me one hundred dollars for my bank. I want to use some of it to get Mommy something for Christmas," he said, while snapping a picture of Michael eating.

"What did you want to get her?"

"I want to get a necklace that says, *Number One Mom,* or something like that. I already made her a card. Do you think I have enough money?" he said.

"I would say so. I'll tell you what, after we finish eating, we can go to the jewelry store over there and see what they have," Michael said, pointing across the mall to the jewelry store.

After dessert, they went over to *Robbins Jewelry Store* to pick out a necklace for Kevin's mom.

"How can I help you, young man?" the saleswoman asked Kevin.

"Ms. Nancy Robbins, I'm looking for a gold necklace for my mom," he said, noticing her nametag.

"You're a very polite young man. I have a few that you can choose from. How do you like these?" she said, showing him five different necklaces.

"I like this one with the fancy writing. How much is it?" he asked.

"The necklace costs ninety dollars, and the charm costs twenty five dollars," she said.

Kevin stood there for a moment, adding the two numbers, and his look became sad.

"I don't have enough for the necklace and the charm. Can I see another necklace?" he asked, in a solemn tone.

"You really like this necklace and charm, don't you?" she asked. "Well today, the set is on sale for fifty dollars."

His face lit up, and he reached in his wallet for the money.

"Would you like me to gift wrap it for you?" she asked smiling.

"Yes, please. Thank you," he said, as he proudly paid her fifty dollars.

"After you're finish with him, can I get that charm bracelet, along with that book charm to go on it, please?" Michael said, pointing them out to her.

"I'll be right with you," she said, as she wrapped Kevin's package.

They both left the mall full of Christmas cheer. Kevin was so happy to have gotten his mom a gift with his own money. Seeing him so happy was something that Michael would cherish.

"Thank you for taking me to get Mom's Christmas gift, Mike," he said, as they got to his front door. Carol opened the door, and Kevin ran right past her and up the steps, so he could hide her gift.

"Stop running, boy, before you fall and hurt yourself!" she yelled up the stairs.

"We had dinner at *Friendly's* already, Carol. That boy's appetite is growing right along with him," Michael said, as they laughed. "You'll be at Mom's for brunch on Christmas, right?" he asked.

"Of course, you know Kevin and I will be there," she said.

"That's great. Then you'll get a chance to meet Michelle. I'll talk to you later. Kevin, I'll see you later," Michael said, as he came back downstairs to give Michael a hug.

Chapter 31

FINALLY, it was Christmas morning. Michael opened the bedroom drapes to let some sunshine in. The scenery was beautiful...it was a white Christmas. There wasn't a lot of snow, just a dusting, but enough to put you in the spirit if you weren't already. Michael thought *the best part of the morning was waking up next to Michelle. She was beautiful even when she was sleeping.*

Last night we were up until two o'clock in the morning, putting the Christmas tree up and all the decorations. His parents had called last night to see if we were doing the same thing they were...wrapping gifts and trimming the tree. His mom also said she expected us to come over this morning around eleven...to start passing out and opening gifts. Afterwards, we would all enjoy Christmas brunch.

"Good morning, Merry Christmas, baby," Michael said, kissing me on the cheek.

"Good morning. You're up early," I said.

"It's a habit. I still wake up early on Christmas morning like a kid. This is my favorite holiday, next to my birthday," he said, as I shook my head and smiled.

"I made some coffee. Would you like some?" he asked.

"That sounds good. Let me freshen up a bit, and I'll join you," I said.

Michael went downstairs to get everything together, while I freshened up. He put coffee, toasted bagels, cream cheese and strawberry preserves and some fruit on a serving tray, and brought it into the living room by the fireplace. The tree was sparkling with blinking lights, gold and silver garland, and plenty of ornaments. The R&B radio station was playing non-stop Christmas music. He couldn't wait to see my face when he told me I had to search on the tree for my gift.

When I came downstairs, my eyes lit up just like a child on Christmas morning.

"It looks so nice and cozy down here, Michael. You need to get a picture of this room, it's gorgeous," I said, as I came over to the couch and softly kissed him.

"You put your special signature on the room, Michelle. As far as taking a picture, I'm way ahead of you," he said, pointing to the camera that he had set up on the tripod. "Now you know I have to get a picture of you and me standing next to the tree. It's our first Christmas together. C'mon, let's stand over by the tree, and I'll get a nice picture of us." He hit the timer on the camera, and walked over to me, put his arms around me, and kissed me. The flash went off, signaling the picture was taken, but he couldn't let me go.

"Um, Michael, if you don't stop, we'll miss brunch," I said smiling. "I'll start pouring the coffee, while you open your gift," I said, handing him a small package from under the tree.

Michael slowly opened the gift, like he was trying not to tear the paper, which he wasn't.

"Michael, you're slow as molasses. What are you doing?" I said, as I began to eat.

"It's such a nice wrap job, I don't want to mess it up," he responded. I looked at him, shaking my head. "I like to put them back in the wrapping paper after I see what's inside," he said.

"Well, you go right ahead then, honey."

When he finally got the gift opened, he began laughing. "Well alright now," he said, smiling and winking at me. "These are nice, Michelle," he said, holding up a pair of black silk boxers. "They feel so good. I can't wait to try these on.'

"You really like them?" I asked.

"Oh yeah I'll give you a lap dance later on tonight, and then you can tell me how I look…wiggling around you in them." We both fell out laughing. "Now I have something for you, but you have to find it."

"Give me a hint where it is. I'll find it in no time," I said, looking around the room.

"Okay, I'll give you a hint. It's somewhere on the tree," he said smiling.

"It's on this tree right here?" I asked, pointing to the not so tiny tree.

"Yes, that one right there," he said laughing, as I began my search.

Of course, he told me when I was getting warm. He didn't want me to spend the rest of the morning searching. He took a few pictures of me in my quest, but before long I found it.

"Here it is right here," I said, as I pulled the silver ornament off the tree.

"How in the world did you find it so fast?"

"I'm just good like that," I said, with a smile as I opened the ornament. "This is beautiful, Michael," I said, as I pulled the bracelet from its resting place.

A big smile came across my face as I asked him to put it on for me. I leaned over and kissed him, licking some of the strawberry off his lips. "Hmm, your lips taste so good."

"We better finish eating and get ready to get out of here, because I can surely take your fine ass right now" he said, as we laughed and headed for the shower.

We already had all the gifts bagged up, and sitting by the door.

"Come on, Michael, I don't want to be late for my first Christmas over at your parents' house," I said, as I sat waiting patiently.

"You didn't say that an hour ago when we were in the shower, now did you?" Michael said, with a grin on his face.

"Well, that's another to be continued story," I said, as we headed to the car.

When we arrived at his parent's house, Michael had to make two trips to the car to retrieve all the presents we had bought.

They all seemed too happy to see me when we arrived. By the way his mom and Debra greeted me you would think they hadn't just seen me a few days ago. They whisked me off to the kitchen, leaving Michael's dad and him staring at each other.

"Where's the love for your only son and your only brother?" Michael asked them.

"Forget it, son, I'll help you put the gifts under the tree. We're just men folk…used for money and our brute strength," his dad said laughing.

As soon as they had got everything placed under the tree, Carol, Bob and Kevin arrived with their gifts, and the women came in from the kitchen with trays of hot chocolate.

"Wow, look at all those presents!" Kevin exclaimed, with wide eyes. "Can we open them now?"

"Kevin, at least say hello first," Carol said smiling.

"I'm sorry, hello everybody," he said, as everyone laughed, because he still hadn't taken his eyes off the Christmas tree.

"Kevin, would you like some hot chocolate?" Michael's mom asked, as she winked at Carol.

"No, Grandma, I'm too excited and I might spill it on the carpet," he replied, which started us laughing again.

"Okay, Kevin, you can go ahead and find your presents now," Michael's mom said smiling. "Michael, he reminds me of you when you were that age on Christmas morning."

"Shoot, I want to open my presents now also," Michael said smiling.

"Hello, you must be Michelle, I'm Carol, Kevin's mother," Carol said to me.

"I'm Bob, one of Mike's best friends, and neighbor from across the street. It's my pleasure to finally meet you," Bob said grinning. "I can see why Mike has kept you all to himself," he said, as Carol elbowed him and Mike glanced at him.

"I'm sorry, I was so busy looking at Kevin and the gifts, I forgot my manners," Michael said, as he made his way over to me.

"It's a pleasure finally meeting the two of you," I said smiling. "Thanks for the compliment, Bob."

"Kevin, why don't you open my gift first, instead of just sitting there staring at them?" I said. "It's the one wrapped in silver."

Everyone watched as he tore into the paper, and started screaming when he saw the digital camera inside.

"Oh boy, it's a digital camera like Ms. Chris has. Thank you, Ms. Michelle," he said, running over and hugging me, before running back to look at it again.

"Kevin, would you pass everyone else their gifts from under the tree, and then open the rest of yours?" Michael's dad said.

"Okay, I can do that. This one is heavy, and it's for Grandma from Ms. Michelle. I bet it's a good one too," he said, bringing it over.

"Mom, this one is for you from me," Kevin said grinning. "I hope you like it."

"I know I will Kevin, since it's from you," she said, smiling proudly.

"Hurry up and open it," he said anxiously.

"Oh, this is so… it's beautiful, Kevin," she said, hugging him. "I'm going to put it on now," Carol said, lifting the necklace with the charm on it out of the box, with tears in her eyes.

"Why do women always cry Mike, dang?" Kevin said, going back to the tree for more gifts.

"I can't believe y'all started opening gifts without me," Sara said, as she walked in with her gifts. "Merry Christmas family."

"You're late as usual, Sara. Merry Christmas to you also," Debra said, hugging her.

"Michelle, I love these baking dishes. I can't wait to bake some cakes in them," Michael's mom said, as I looked on smiling.

"Will you check out my CD's?" his dad said, all excited. "Michelle, how did you know Coltrane was one of my favorites? And I have Dorothy Norwood too! Thank you so much."

"Debra told me Dad, and you're very welcome," I answered smiling.

"No you didn't!" Debra exclaimed. "I can't believe you, Michelle. I thought you were buying this stuff for yourself. Thank you, thank you, thank you! I loved these jeans when I saw them in the store, and this cape is beautiful. This is so cool!"

"I got one also. Thank you, Michelle. Green is my favorite color," Sara said smiling.

"You're both welcome. Sara, I thought the green would go great with your hazel eyes. And Debra, I saw how you looked at those jeans and then put them back, saying you would come back after Christmas to get them. So I was happy when Sara distracted you long enough so that I could buy them," I explained smiling.

Meanwhile, Kevin was under the tree, opening the rest of his presents, grinning from ear to ear until he got to his video games, and then he started screaming again.

"Look at all these video games. Thank you Mike and Grandpa, Can I go play them now?" he asked.

"Only for a little while Kevin we're going to sit down and eat soon," Grandma said, as he shouted thank you and ran into the den, where the system was set up for him.

"Thank you all for making his Christmas special," Carol said.

"No thanks needed, Carol…only the best for my little brother. Why don't you open my gift? You too, Bob," Michael, said.

"Michael, this is beautiful. I've always wanted a charm bracelet," Carol said, when she opened it. She laughed when she saw the book charm hanging from it.

"Thanks for the gift card, Mike. I know just what I'm going to buy with it," Bob said.

"I remembered you said you were going to finish your basement, and thought a Home Depot card would be useful," Michael said to Bob.

"You thought right, man. Thanks again," he said.

"Alright everyone, let's get ready to eat. I know everyone must be hungry by now," Michael's mom said.

Another tradition at the Ramsey household was that everyone got a chance to offer up a few words after the blessing of the table. When it was Carol's turn, her words left a mark on all of our hearts.

"I would just like to say there are many times that I wish my parents were still alive to feel the love that radiates from this family. It's true they continue to live on through us. If they had lived long enough, they would see how blessed Kevin is to have a big brother like Michael. This family has taken Kevin and me into their hearts, and we appreciate you all for doing so. May God bless the Ramsey family...our family"

* * *

The week went by too quickly. Michael felt having me in Philly with him was a wonderful experience. It actually gave him a taste of what it would be like to have a wife. I had been very attentive to his needs, and in the short period of time that I had been here, I had left my mark on his house and the family... they all loved me.

The beginning of the New Year was only a few hours away. We decided to have a late candle light dinner by the fireplace, with the Christmas tree as the only luminary force.

"Those mussels were good, baby. I never knew you liked them," Michael said, wiping his mouth with a napkin.

"I'm glad you enjoyed it. I'm a seafood lover in general. I figured something light would be good for tonight. I know your mom is going to hit us with the black-eyed peas, greens and cornbread tomorrow." We both laughed.

"Mom always does the traditional meal on New Year's day," he said.

Michael had a bottle of Asti Spumante chilling in the living room for our New Year's toast. I had prepared some cheese, crackers and grapes to munch on while we watched the ball drop on television.

As we lay on a soft quilted blanket that Michael had spread in front of the fireplace, we talked about my company, and how scared I was when I first took over. I mentioned Yvonne, and how she had been a steady force for me throughout the months since my uncle had passed away, and how she helped to keep my confidence level up. Then there was John. He, at times, reminded me of my father. It was apparent that both men were cut from the same cloth. John was basically teaching me the publishing business, and I couldn't have asked for a better advisor.

"There's one minute left before the New Year," Michael said, as he opened the Asti and poured us each a glass of bubbly. "Here we go, the ball is dropping ten, nine, eight, seven, six, five, four, three, two, one...HAPPY NEW YEAR!!!" we both said, in unison. Then we shared a long, breathtaking kiss.

"Michael, these past two weeks have been some of the happiest times of my life. Meeting your family, spending the holiday with them, and shopping with the girls, have been really special. Most of all, sharing some of your space has been truly wonderful. I have one more Christmas gift to give you," I said, as I began to recite:

All I want is to love you for the rest of my life.
To share our hopes, dreams and the little things
That makes us laugh, and the not-so-little things
That we can't help worrying about, that's what I want.
All I want is to give you my love...

As a place you can always come to for understanding
Or the simple comfort that silence brings
When words left unspoken can still be understood.
All I want is to spend time with you...

To watch our life unfold before our eyes
Our dreams, one by one, come true.
All I want is to love you forever.

Michael sat there speechless. He was in a daze, not only by the delivery of what I had just said, but by the words and the thought behind them. It was beautiful. He leaned in and kissed me softly.

"Michelle, that's the most beautiful present I've ever received. I don't know what to say," he said, still reeling from the moment.

"Don't say anything, just make love to me," I said, as we disappeared into an abyss of pure pleasure.

On New Year's Day, we traveled back over to Michael's parents' house. All of the men gathered in the family room to watch the bowl games on television, while the ladies gathered to talk. One thing was certain...we all were going to get to taste some of those black-eyed peas. A lot of people say its good luck to have them on the first day of the year.

New Year's Day in Atlanta, found Pam and Sharon eating out at the *Atlanta*

Grill, since neither of them wanted to cook for themselves, and they decided to spend it together instead of with family.

"My mom makes better black-eyed peas, but these are decent," Sharon said.

"I have to agree. Their ribs are delicious, and this steak just melts in your mouth," Pam replied. "Are you going in to work tomorrow, since you're going to South Carolina on Tuesday?"

"I'm going in for a few hours, to tie up some loose ends after I pick up the rental car. What about you? When does the bitch get back from vacation?" Sharon asked.

"Yes, I'll be at work tomorrow, and she's due back tomorrow also. Our editorial department has a meeting scheduled with her that afternoon," Pam said.

"If I was you, I'd schedule a meeting with that bitch, and compare notes on Michael Ramsey," she said laughing.

"Girl, you need to stop it. I would if I didn't need this job. But one day we just may have to have that conversation," Pam said, cracking up.

"I'd love to be in on that meeting. Let's drink to her getting knocked off her pedestal soon," Sharon said, as they raised their glasses in a toast.

* * *

"Well folks, we need to head home. I have to get Michelle to the airport by six-thirty tomorrow morning," Michael said.

"I'll get your coats for you," Debra said.

"Mom, Dad, Debra, it's been really nice spending this time with you. Thank you for showing me a great time in Philly. Believe me, I'll be back soon," I said, giving them all hugs. "Debra, I had a lot of fun hanging out with you and Sara. You are two crazy ladies. I'm going to try to make it out to your graduation in May. Keep in touch with me," I said, as she handed me my coat.

"I'm looking forward to seeing you out there as well. My brother picked a winner," Debra said.

"Michelle, it was a pleasure to have you here with us. Have a safe trip back home, and give your parents our love," Michael's mom said. "Oh, I almost forgot. Do me a favor and give this gift to your mother and father. It's just a little something for their house," she said, as she reached under the tree.

"Thank you, Mom. Everyone, take care of yourselves and I'll see you soon," I said, as we headed back to Michael's house.

Chapter 32

MONDAY morning was here before we knew it, and it was time to get back into our daily routines. I had an eight-fifteen flight back to Atlanta, and I wanted to get to work by eleven. Michael got me to the airport by six-thirty…that was more than enough time for me to get something to eat before my plane was scheduled to take off.

"Michelle, thank you so much for surprising me the way you did at your Christmas party, and for coming to spend some time with me. You left such a wonderful impression with my parents and little sister. But most of all, you've created a space in my heart that no one will ever be able to occupy. Thank you for just being you," he said, as we hugged and kissed.

"I better get in this airport before I change my flight plans," I said smiling.

"Have a good flight, and call me as soon as you get settled," he said.

"I will, baby. I'll talk to you soon," I said, as we once again kissed.

The flight back to Atlanta was good. After a brief stop home to drop off my luggage and packages, I stopped by the post office to pick up the mail they were holding for me. I also called my parents to let them know I had made it back safely. Afterwards, I gave Jasmine a call.

"Hello, Jasmine. I'm back," I said, as she answered the phone.

"It's about time you made it back, heffa. I've missed you so much. I can't wait to tell you all about my holiday, and the reaction I got from Alex to that gown you bought me for Christmas. That is if you can call it that from the lack of material," she said laughing.

"Awe, it wasn't that skimpy, was it? We'll have to play catch up later tonight. I had a wonderful time in Philly, and I have a lot to tell you about. Listen, I just pulled up to the office, so we'll talk later," I said.

"Sounds like a plan. Give me a call when you get settled tonight. Have a wonderful day," she said.

"Bye Jasmine. You do likewise," I said, hanging up.

I hurried into the building, waving at the security guard in the garage, and greeting Curtis and his partner, Derek, at the front desk. It felt good to be back at Rivers, Inc. I couldn't wait to get an update on what had been going on while I was away.

"Good morning Yvonne, Happy New Year. How was your holiday?" I said, dropping down into the chair next to her desk.

"Hello Michelle, Happy New Year to you and welcome back. You look wonderful and well rested," she answered. "My holiday was lovely. I spent time with the family, and did a lot of shopping and baking. How was yours?"

"Mine was wonderful. I got a lot of rest, and even found some time to write," I said grinning.

"So, how is Mr. Ramsey?" she asked smiling.

"You don't miss much, do you, Yvonne?" I asked laughing. "Mr. Ramsey is amazing, and I miss him already. Now bring me up to date on what's been going on around here," I said, changing the subject.

"I was just leaving to pick up the reports from Gayle when you walked in," she said "Would you like me to bring you some coffee or herbal tea on my way back?"

"I'd love some of your coffee. Thank you," I said, heading into my office.

"I'll be back in a few minutes," she said.

I put in a call to Michael, to let him know I had arrived safely and made it into the office. I was missing him already, even though it had only been a few hours since I was with him.

After that, I barely had time to catch my breath before I had back-to-back meetings with John, and the rest of the editorial staff. I worked straight through lunch, stopping only to eat a quick salad. According to the reports, both of our new releases did pretty well during the Christmas sales week. David's book was ready and due to be released next week.

I made a note on my calendar to send him a card and a balloon bouquet… wishing him well with his book. Before I knew it, the day was over and it was time to go home.

"Michelle, I'm about to head out. Is there anything else you need me to do before I leave?" Yvonne asked, from the doorway.

"No, I think we've covered enough for one day, and anything else can wait. If you give me two minutes, I'll walk out with you," I said.

On the way down to the garage, we talked some more about our holidays, and then said our goodbyes as we each reached our cars. For it to be only six-thirty in the evening, it was pretty dark outside, so I decided to put off grocery shopping until the next day. Instead, I picked up dinner at the *Silver Dragon*

Chinese Restaurant in College Park. I called my order in, so I wouldn't be out too long in the darkness. The other businesses on the strip where the restaurant was located were closed. But you could always depend on Mr. Lee's restaurant being open.

"Good evening, Ms. Michelle. Your order will be out in a minute. How was your holiday?" Mrs. Lee asked.

"My holiday was wonderful, Mrs. Lee, thanks for asking. I hope you weren't so busy that you couldn't enjoy yours," I said smiling.

"We were very busy in the restaurant…just as we like it," she answered smiling. "Here's your order now. Please come again soon."

"Thank you, Mrs. Lee. Tell Mr. Lee I said hello."

Michelle didn't notice there was a car parked diagonally across the street from where her car was parked. She walked towards her car, placing her bag on the roof. When she reached down to open the driver's door, she heard the screeching of tires and bright lights approaching her. She dropped her keys and ran, trying to reach the safety of the curb. The car swerved towards her, the front barely missing her, but the back of the swerving vehicle clipped her legs and knocked her body into one of the parked cars. She hit the ground hard, with her pocketbook losing its contents, which were strewn all about. Car alarms were blazing, with their lights blinking wildly. Mr. and Mrs. Lee came running out of the restaurant, to see what the commotion was all about.

"Ms. Michelle, Ms. Michelle! Oh my goodness. Call ambulance, hurry" Mr. Lee ordered his wife. "Ms. Michelle, can you hear me?" I never responded. A couple that had just turned the corner, ran over to see if they could help.

"Did anyone see the car?" Mr. Lee asked.

"We saw a car speeding down the street, but we couldn't see the license plate because the lights were turned off. It was just moving too fast," the couple responded.

The ambulance and the police pulled up at about the same time. The police secured the area, and the paramedics checked my vital signs, and they were stable. They placed an oxygen mask on my face, and then the paramedics secured my neck with a brace. My left arm looked like it was broken or dislocated, so they put it in a splint. They slowly put me onto the stretcher, and placed me in the ambulance for the trip to Atlanta Medical.

The police had gathered all of my belongings that were scattered about, and found my cell phone and wallet. The officer checked to see if I had any emergency code numbers programmed in her phone, which I did. One of the officers checked the number, and the name Robert Rivers came up. He checked for ID in the wallet, and saw the name Michelle Rivers.

"Well, I'll be damned," the officer, a lieutenant named Smith, said. He turned to one of the other squads and said, "I know this woman's family. Can you question these people for me, and I'll call and inform them of the accident?"

"Yes sir," one of the officers responded.

Lieutenant Smith placed a call to Robert Rivers.

"Hello," Robert answered.

"Hello, may I speak to Bobby Rivers, please?" he said, while in route to the Rivers home.

"This is he. And you are?" Robert asked.

"This is Brother Jasper Smith," Lieutenant Smith said.

"Hey Officer Smitty, How are you, my brother?"

"Not doing well, my brother. Your daughter, Michelle, was involved in a hit and run about thirty minutes ago."

"What!" Robert shouted into the phone. "How is she, where is she?" he asked frantically.

"She's with the paramedics, on her way to Atlanta Medical."

"Mary, get your coat!" he shouted to his wife, his voice cracking.

"Bobby, I'm two blocks away from you. I'll escort you to the hospital. Everything is going to be fine."

"Thank you, Smitty."

"Mary, Michelle's been hurt in an accident. We need to get to Atlanta Medical right away."

"Oh my God, no" Mary cried out.

"We've got to keep it together, baby. Let's get ready to go."

Lieutenant Smith was waiting outside to escort them to the hospital. He turned on his siren to help clear the traffic as they sped towards the hospital.

As they were making their way to the hospital, Robert put in a call to Jasmine.

"Hello, Jasmine. This is Dad Rivers," he said, when she answered the phone.

"Hi Dad, Where are you?" she asked. "I hear all those sirens in the background."

"We're on our way to Atlanta Medical. Michelle was involved in a hit and run accident."

"Oh no!" she shouted. "Is she okay? Never mind, I'll meet you there," Jasmine said, quickly hanging up the phone. She then called Alex.

"Alex, Alex," Jasmine said, crying into the phone.

"Hey, baby, what's wrong, why are you crying?" he asked.

"Michelle was in an accident. They took her to the hospital. Can you come and get me?"

"Okay, baby, I'll be right there. Everything is going to be alright," he said.

"Hurry, baby, hurry," Jasmine said.

After Alex picked Jasmine up, they hurried to the hospital. Alex had the difficult task of calling Mike to let him know the situation. He called while they were in route to the hospital.

"Hey Sara. Can I speak to Michael?" Alex said, when she answered the phone.

"Hold on for a minute," she said.

"Hello, Michael," Alex said, when he got on the line.

"What's going on, brother?" Michael asked.

"I have some bad news for you, man. Michelle was in a hit and run accident, and she's in the hospital," Alex said, with Jasmine in the background crying. "Mike, are you there?"

"What the fuck happened, Alex?" he asked, after the news set in. "Is she alright? Damn it, is she hurt?"

"I don't know yet. Her parents, Jasmine and I are headed down there now to find out."

"Oh God, please don't let her be hurt badly," Michael said. "What hospital was she taken to?" he asked, his voice becoming raspier.

"It's going to be alright, Jas," Alex said, trying to calm Jasmine down. "They took her to Atlanta Medical, we're almost there now," he said to Michael.

"I'm on my way to the airport."

"Okay, Mike, I'll see you when you get here." He turned to Jasmine and said, "He's coming down, baby. Everything is going to be alright," he said to her.

* * *

Back at the scene of the accident, the officers were questioning the Lees and the other couple.

"So, you said after you heard the screeching tires and the car lights, you ran to see what the noise was, am I correct?" one of the officers asked the Lees.

"Yes, I heard the screeching, and car lights and alarms started going off. I knew something had happened because I heard a thump too. When I got outside, Ms. Michelle was lying on ground. Then I went back in and called 911," Mrs. Lee told the officer.

The other officer talked to the couple. "Can you describe to me what happened?" the officer asked.

"My girlfriend and I had just come out the ice cream store, when we heard these tires screeching and car alarms going off. When we got near the corner, a car zoomed by us very fast, without any lights on. When we turned the corner, we saw a couple of people leaning over someone on the ground," the young man said.

"Did you get to see the license plate?" the officer asked.

"No, it was too dark, and the car didn't have any lights on. I couldn't even see the color of the car…it was moving so fast," the young woman said.

"Thank you. Can I have your numbers in case we have some more questions later?" the officer asked. The couple gave him their information.

* * *

When the Rivers' arrived at the emergency room with Smitty, a physician was already seeing Michelle. Soon after, Jasmine and Alex came rushing in.

"How is she, Mom? Is everything okay?" Jasmine asked, as she hugged Mary.

"The officer went in the back to see if the doctor can come out and tell us what's going on. Robert is at the registration desk…giving them Michelle's information. We'll just have to wait for the doctor to come out," Mom said, still wiping back tears.

"Hey, Smitty, thanks for helping us get down here so quickly," Robert said.

"That's what I'm here for. You know I'd do anything for you. The doctor said she would be out in a moment. I'm going to head back to the station to get the report. If there's any info on this, I'll give you a call. I'll be praying for you," he said, as he shook Robert's hand and hugged Mary.

Soon after, the doctor came to the waiting room to speak with the family.

"Hello, my name is Dr. Renee Joseph. Are you Ms. Rivers' family?" she asked, as she sat next to us in the waiting room.

"Yes we are. I'm her father, Robert Rivers, and this is her mother, Mary. How is she doing?"

"Ms. Rivers isn't in any danger. The x-rays showed she has fractured ribs. She also suffered some head trauma, but the CAT scan showed up negative for any bleeding. She's still unconscious and heavily sedated, but all of her vital signs are stable. We placed her on oxygen and will be taking her upstairs to the ICU, mainly for observation."

"Thank God it's not any worse," Mary said.

"Yes, I agree it could've been a lot worse. Listen, she'll be fine. We just have to keep an eye on her level of consciousness," Dr. Joseph said.

"When can we see her?" Jasmine asked.

"Once the nurses get her settled in her bed, you can see her. I'm going up there now to write some orders on her chart. I'll go up with you and show you to the family room."

"Thank you, Dr. Joseph," Robert said, shaking her hand.

"Mr. Rivers, Michael's on his way down to here. I called him when I heard about what happened," Alex said.

"He's a good man. I figured he'd want to be here once he found out," Robert said.

After about an hour, a nurse came out to the waiting room to speak to the family.

"Hello, my name is Rose, and I'll be taking care of your daughter tonight. You can come in and see her now," she said.

When they walked into Michelle's room and saw the intravenous bag, the heart monitor, with its occasional dinging, the oxygen running into her nose, and her body motionless and oblivious to the fact they were even in the room, Mary and Jasmine burst into tears. Robert and Alex were there, thank goodness, to help comfort them.

"Why would anyone want to hurt my baby?" Mary asked, while rubbing Michelle's hand. "Robert, find out who did this to my baby. Do you hear me? Find out," Mary said, as she, Jasmine and Alex went back to the waiting room.

"Excuse me Rose, my daughter's fiancée is flying in from Philadelphia tonight. There will be no problem for him to come up and be with her, will it?" Robert asked.

"No, that will be fine," she responded.

"I'm going to go back to the waiting room. If there is any change in her condition, could you please let us know?" he said.

"I sure will, Mr. Rivers. What's her fiancée's name, so that I can let security know?" she asked.

"His name is Michael Ramsey."

"He wouldn't happen to be Michael Ramsey, the writer?" she said, as her eyes lit up.

"Yes, he's the writer. You've heard of him before?"

"Yes, I have. I've read a couple of his books, and I thought the name Michelle Rivers was familiar also. She owns Rivers, Inc., right? I read an article in the newspaper about her. This is truly an honor to be taking care of her. She's going to be fine. We'll take good care of her."

"Thank you for being so kind, Rose. Let me go check on the family," he said, as he walked out of the unit.

* * *

"Hello. I'm here to visit Michelle Rivers," Michael said, as he approached the security desk.

"I'll check her room number, sir. Can I have your name, please?" the guard asked.

"My name is Michael Ramsey."

"They're expecting you. Take this elevator to the fourth floor and turn right. Once you walk a few feet, you'll see the sign that says waiting area. The unit is directly across."

"Thank you very much," he said, as he quickly boarded the elevator.

While walking towards the waiting room, Michael wondered what he would see when he saw Michelle. He had to get himself prepared, because it wouldn't be the same smiling face that he last saw before she went inside the airport in Philadelphia. He couldn't believe someone would do something like this, and not stop to try to help her.

It was twelve-thirty in the morning. When Michael walked into the waiting room, Robert was pacing back and forth, talking on his cell phone. Mom and Jasmine were sitting and holding hands, sharing a box of tissues, and Alex was sleeping.

"Hello everyone, how is she doing?" Michael asked, in a somber voice.

"Thank God you're here, Michael," Jasmine said, as she stood to hug him.

"Mom, Dad, how are you two holding up?" he asked.

"We're okay Michael. Glad you made it, son," Robert said. "How are you?"

"I'm anxious to see Michelle. All sorts of thoughts have been running through my mind. Does anyone know what happened yet?" he asked.

"Not yet, but I'm working on it now. I just got off the phone with John… to let him know what happened," Robert said.

Alex stood and shook Michael's hand before he went in to see Michelle. Robert walked in with him.

"Hello, Mr. Ramsey," Rose said, extending her hand. "I'm Michelle's nurse. If you need anything or have any questions, just let me know."

"Thank you," Michael said.

When he first looked at Michelle, and saw all the monitors and lines that she was attached to, he thought to himself, *why did this have to happen to her? If it's the last thing that I do…I'm going to find out who did this to her and make them pay.*

He leaned in and kissed me on the cheek and said, "Baby, its Michael. I'm here for you. I'm going to be the first person you see when you awaken from your slumber."

He began reading a poem from the book that he wrote in when he was deep in thought. Tears began flowing down his face.

He gently laid his head down on the bed, and said, "Michelle, I know that sometimes I don't express to you in words how I truly feel about you. This may not even be the time or the place. But I just want you to know that I love you. I love you more than life itself. As I lay here beside you, gazing at your sleeping face, my mind starts to wonder to a far away place. I think back to the time when we first met. The sparkle that was in your eyes that day, I will never forget. I'm so blessed to have captured your heart. I will do everything in my power to keep you satisfied…mind, body and soul."

Michael didn't notice that Robert had left the room while he was talking. He was oblivious to the fact that a smile had come across her lips. He leaned back in the chair and began to write the first thoughts that came out of his head:

You are like the sun on a gorgeous summer day
You bring life into my total being.
My heart melts at the very mention of your name.
Are you the love that I have longed for?
I've had this fantasy for so long
And now it is becoming reality.
How did you know that I needed you?

How did you know that I craved you?
You have such an irresistible glow about you.
I can't tell you how immersed
The thought of you makes me.
Since I have found you, I request no other.
You are the steadying force that I need,
and the foundation that I yearn for.
Sweetness, if only you could see what I see
When I gaze into your dreamy eyes.
I see your soul,
The soul of a great woman,
A loving and sharing woman
with a heart that extends beyond the cosmos.
A woman who gives so much of herself
In everything that she does,
And not once ever asks for anything in return.
Are you the love that I've
Been waiting my whole life for?
Are you the quintessence of my being?
Are you my soul mate?

When he finished writing, he moved his chair closer to the bed, and laid the book near me, and laid his head near mine and fell asleep.

I woke up and looked all around in confusion for a minute, before I realized where I was. I was a little afraid, until I looked down and noticed Michael sleeping beside me. Reaching down, I picked up the book and read what he had written and smiled. I then picked up the pen, and although it was difficult to write, I penned:

Like the wind, you blew into my life, like a gentle breeze.
My heart skips a beat at the mention of your name.
I dreamed of eternity and your face appeared...
I am your Nubian Queen
And you are my Nubian King!
The fantasy you had for so very long
Has become the reality we live.
You are all I need,

You are all I want,
You are all I desire,
You are everything I have craved.
Your every word entrances me.
Since I've found you, nothing or no one can compare…
Baby, If only you could see what I see
When you are looking into my eyes…
I see our souls entwined.
I see a strong man,
Who tenderly loves me?
Who shares his past hurts and triumphs with me?
A man rich in family,
A man who puts everyone else's needs first,
A man who gives everything
And expects nothing in return
You asked whether I'm the woman
You've waited your whole life for…
My answer is simply, yes!
You are the man I want to spend
My lifetime with
The man who completes me,
The man who challenges me to be better…
Yes, I am your soul mate!

After reading it over one more time, I caressed the back of his head and fell back to sleep. Neither one of us woke when the nurse came in to check on her patient. She smiled at the sight before her, turned and left the room.

www.ingramcontent.com/pod-product-compliance
Lightning Source LLC
Chambersburg PA
CBHW072309020726
47501CB00002B/458